THE
CLINIC

An absolutely addictive psychological thriller

SALLY-ANNE MARTYN

Joffe Books, London
www.joffebooks.com

First published in Great Britain in 2022

Cover art by The Brewster Project

ISBN: 978-1-80405-569-4

For 'My Dear Old Pal', otherwise known as Dad.

PROLOGUE

NHS Pine End Asylum
Hospital for Mental and Nervous Disorders — 1975
Crowthorpe, North Yorkshire

The rain battered the iron gates as the headlights of a rusting Morris Marina passed through, shining yellow light onto the gravel drive leading up to the asylum. Its tired windscreen wipers swooshed back and forth — the crumbling rubber blades no match for the torrent of water that fell. They drove down the track, disappearing beneath the shadows of ancient trees that loomed over the car like withered old hags. Their crooked branches swayed back and forth in the wind, which rattled against the car windows and whistled through the dense woods that surrounded them.

The car came to a grinding halt outside the main entrance, catching the small stones tight beneath its tyres. A woman exited the driver's door clutching a bundle of folders and files. She pushed her rain-splattered glasses back up her nose as her handbag slid down her shoulder. Floury fingerprints trailed down the front of her flared jeans, evidence of a quick exit from making a family dinner.

The wind snatched a piece of paper, which broke free from a folder and whipped onto the ground, rain smudging the blue ink scribbles. She cursed as she bent down and grabbed it, shoving the crumpled form back into a manila file. Turning back to the car she gestured impatiently towards a small dark figure on the back seat. The back door of the car opened, and Jenny, a scrawny young teen, stepped tentatively onto the gravel as if it might give way and swallow her up. Her small Doc Marten boots crunched down on the stones as she made her way to the large granite entrance to the hospital, squinting as the rain battered her face and the wind blew her ebony hair into her eyes.

She paused by the stone archway and looked up to the giant clock tower high above the doors, her eyes wide and blinking as if she were in a dream. Eleven p.m. — her friends would still be at the park drinking cider from plastic bottles and smoking tab ends, rescued from ashtrays and the littered streets. Something caught her eye in a window below the clock tower. A young woman with her hand against the thick glass was staring down at her. Her complexion was pale and ghostlike, her features partly obscured by the iron bars fixed to the window. A fat drop of rain hit Jenny's eyeball and her attention was drawn back to her harassed guardian, who was disappearing into the hospital reception. She followed quickly behind.

Jenny stood in the middle of the space looking up to a string of balding tinsel tacked unevenly to the desk, then to a chiselled marble face that glared disapprovingly ahead.

'That's Matron Dawson,' the woman said, following the young girl's gaze up to the marble bust. 'You'd better behave yourself; she won't take any messing.'

Jenny nodded slowly, wiping water away from her eyes with a rain-soaked cardigan sleeve, black eyeliner dragging down her cheek. The woman turned back to the desk, giving the receptionist the relevant information needed to admit the girl, who seemed to shrink, like Alice in Wonderland, in the vast space. Her dark bobbed hair fell lank against her pale face. Her thin fingers clutched a supermarket carrier bag that contained essentials, snatched in a hurry — underwear, pyjamas and her childhood teddy with patchy fur that she had plucked as a toddler.

She pressed her pale palms tight to her ears as a siren pierced through the air and a burst of profanities echoed along the corridor. Her eyes darted towards the noise, her eyes blinking rapidly as a bare-chested man, covered in tattoos that curled to the top of his neck, ran towards her. He brandished a pool cue, swinging it in the air and shattering a strip light, causing splinters of glass to fall to the floor. The tattooed man's head twisted up towards the broken light and he cackled with a delirious fever.

Heavy boots echoed around the room as giants of men appeared from all directions. Dressed in bright white uniforms they attempted to wrestle the deranged man to the floor.

'Fuck youuuuuu,' the man screamed, as he dived headfirst towards the ground.

Jenny lowered her hands and wandered closer, transfixed by his ink-covered body, which squirmed like an eel beneath the seven men, who pinned his writhing limbs down with their weight, pushing him onto the broken glass.

'Leave here while you've still got the chance,' the man shouted, 'otherwise you'll never escape.'

She watched as his dirty jeans were lowered to expose a milky-white buttock and a needle was lifted high, before being inserted deep into the muscle. The wild man's eyes caught hers and he gave her a brief brown-toothed grin, before his eyes rolled back in his head and his body slumped to the floor.

She turned back to the reception. Her guardian spoke in hushed tones to the receptionist, who looked to Jenny with an expression of resigned knowing. As the woman began to walk towards her, the teen clutched her carrier bag and picked up her feet, running back to the main entrance as fast as she could. The guardian reached out to stop her, but Jenny pushed her back into the wall, causing the woman to cry out in pain. When Jenny reached the heavy oak door, she pulled at the iron handle, but it was locked tight. With pale fists she beat at the solid wood, tears streaming down her hot red cheeks as she screamed to be freed.

A door to her left swung open and an arm reached out to her, grabbing the back of her denim jacket and hoisting her in the air like a hunter handling a limp rabbit. The arm turned her back in the direction of the asylum's belly, letting her feet drop to the floor, and marched her back down the corridor.

The trembling girl looked up to the ceiling as she was pushed along, blinking at the fluorescent strip lights. She reached her hand into the carrier bag and clutched the soft fur of the teddy bear. As ragged moths danced in and out of the light above her, she was moved further into the darkness.

CHAPTER 1

The Beautiful You Clinic, formerly Pine End Asylum
December 2002

The lift rattled upwards, creaking to a halt when it reached the ground floor. Dr Rebecca Cavendish stood in the silence for a moment, rolling her swanlike neck slowly from side to side, faint creaks and crackles audible as the knots unfurled and her muscles relaxed. She brushed the fabric of her tailored suit, speckles of plaster dust falling down and landing on her patent Manolo Blahniks. She tutted, and taking a white handkerchief from her breast pocket, wet it with her pale pink tongue and polished the toe of her shoe until it shone again.

Dr Cavendish's first peek at the world had been from the bed of a Silver Cross pram, looking up to the face of a uniformed nanny. Forty-five years later, style and luxury were the values upon which she firmly hung her Philip Treacy hat.

She pulled the iron scissor gate open and pushed at the swing door in front of her, stepping into the dreary, graffiti-daubed corridor. The corridor was the gateway between the old asylum and the new clinic, and no matter how many times she stood in this small un-refurbished area, she couldn't get used to the acrid smell of urine. It was impervious to bleach — human waste that had gathered over years of dereliction had penetrated the walls and floor like oil into cloth. The doctor lifted her pale wrist to her nose, inhaling rich amber perfume. The scent revived her, like smelling salts to the swooning Victorian lady.

Turning the large metal key, she unlocked the door opposite the lift and stepped through into the clinic, leaving the last bitter traces of human waste behind her. Winter sunlight found its way through the granite clouds and shone through the small squares of glass in the large windows, grids of orange light on bright white walls and varnished tile flooring. She basked in the warmth of the December sun for a moment, a satisfied smile creeping across her glossed lips, enjoying the tranquillity of the Beautiful You Clinic. *Her* clinic.

Vases of billowing giant lilies infused the air with their potent scent, masking the smell of a recently applied coat of white paint. There had been complaints from previous clients about a strange smell permeating the walls and possessing the air. She had assured them it was completely normal in a building this old and, like the creaking floors and occasional dip in electricity, all part of the character. Yet, to avoid further criticism, she had called the decorators in and scrapped the feedback forms.

The Beautiful You Clinic was housed on the expansive ground floor of the old Pine End Asylum, a Victorian red-bricked behemoth that loomed high on a pine-covered hill outside the crumbling northern town of Crowthorpe. Once alive with a thriving population of asylum workers that scuttled around the town and crawled up and down the hill like ants, it was now known for its disproportionate number of dilapidated shop fronts and a longer-than-average queue outside the post office on a Thursday morning. The asylum had been built first and the town an afterthought, created to keep the hospital alive with staff, and when the heart stopped beating, the rest of the body was left to decay and die.

Dr Cavendish had decided to clear out and mothball the first floor of the building, until she was ready to expand the empire further. The council had granted her the lease of the building for three years, and she had two years left to prove her worth and secure it indefinitely. Her inheritance would be enough to purchase it outright when they let her, and then her future and that of the building would be secured.

The layout of the ground floor had a symmetry that Dr Cavendish had enjoyed from the first moment she had set foot in the building. Originally designed to separate the sexes during its days as the asylum, each end had a small number of bedrooms, day rooms and bathrooms. Joining the two halves in the centre was an industrial-sized kitchen, dining room, library and the galleried day room. The clinic was entered via an imposing stone arch at the centre of the building, welcoming clients into a large, ornately tiled reception area.

Dr Cavendish walked down the corridor like Cleopatra entering Rome. Slow, dramatic steps, head held high and glossy hair pulled back tight into a smooth chestnut bun. The anticipation of new arrivals always created a buzz of excitement inside the doctor. There was no need for adoring crowds to line Dr Cavendish's way; her success was enough.

As she walked, fractures of her elegant figure flashed across the ornate mirrors that covered the walls between doorways and windows. Rescued from the old hospital, Victorian and Art Deco antiques, each had been brought back to life by a local furniture restorer. They provided light, decoration and a daily reminder of why a client was here. For the first few days she watched as the clients avoided them, but as time went on, she celebrated as they appeared to lose their fear and revel in the results of her programme. Accountability was key to success — unless they faced the size of the problem in front of them, how could she truly help?

The tiled flooring had been in place since the asylum's opening in 1899. The advice had been to rip it up and start again with clean white tiles befitting the clinic she wished to create, but Dr Cavendish had refused point blank. Each scratch and scuff was evidence of a footstep or wheel that had travelled through the doors of the building. A gouged-out history of the madness that had come before that she felt was an important part of the building to keep. Instead, she had the decorators varnish the floor so heavily that the etched ghosts of the past were sealed permanently in place.

In the reflection of a large antique mirror, she caught sight of something on her shoulder. She moved closer to inspect herself, flicking away the tiny specks of plaster caught in her cotton tweed jacket. As she was about to move away, she noticed something moving outside, beyond the window.

A dark figure disappeared into the woods, through trees that provided a gnarled wooden army, buffering the clinic from the outside world. Across the path, two of her security guards were playing cards on the metal steps of their Portakabin, completely oblivious to the intruder. The muscle beneath her eye twitched and her lips clamped tightly together as she raised her fist, rapping her knuckles so hard on the thick glass it rattled within the antique frame.

The two security guards looked up to the building, scanning the windows. When they saw her staring back at them, they hastily gathered the cards up and pushed them back into the box, scattering a few on the ground. One of the guards scooped them up from the dirt and put them in his trouser pocket. Both stood straight and began to patrol the outside of the building as if there had been no break at all in their duties. Dr Cavendish looked up to the sky and watched as a charcoal cloud crept over the sun, the light gradually fading and greying as the sun disappeared behind the gloomy curtain of rain.

Dr Cavendish continued towards reception, her mind racing. One of the things she hadn't expected to be so difficult was getting the security guards to do their jobs properly. She had, however, been more successful with the others. There were her two assistants, Kim and Tina, who helped with classes and general client care. Anya, her cook and housekeeper, and Robert, head of physical activities and the doctor's right-hand man. The doctor had known Robert for years and they shared common interests. He helped her with applications and overseeing the staff when she couldn't be present. She trusted him to take on the more difficult tasks that running a clinic entailed, leaving her to do the work she most enjoyed.

The staff that worked within the clinic seemed to manage their work to her standards, but the security guards were a constant test of her patience. An ex-asylum was a magnet for all kinds of undesirables, from devil-worshipping ghost hunters to squatters looking for somewhere to shoot up. She needed reliable protection for herself and her clients if she was to continue to make a success of the business and ensure that she was granted permanent ownership.

Dr Cavendish walked past the galleried day room, now named the Relaxation Room. A three-piece suite and various high-backed armchairs had been recommissioned from the old hospital and covered in fresh, chintzy floral fabric. A low wooden coffee table, sanded down to erase the biro profanities, sat in the middle, laden with large books on gardening, nature, healthy food and beauty. A large bookshelf to the side was stuffed with scuff-edged books, yellowing Jilly Cooper and Stephen King tomes. Well-thumbed paper distractions and escapes from the lives the ex-patients had endured in the asylum.

She had recovered the books from the old library but had decided to burn the magazines she had found, some of which dated back more than fifty years. Pages stuck together with coffee, spilled by shaking hands. Cigarette ash smudged across travel articles on St Tropez and the Algarve, places so cruelly out of reach for the reader, they served to taunt as much as entertain.

The hospital had closed its doors five years previously, and the exit of its residents had been so sudden and unceremonious, it was as if they had just nipped out to the supermarket for a loaf of bread and twenty Embassy Reds. Beds were still made, teabags still stewing in tall metal teapots waiting to be poured, and medication laid out waiting to be administered. When the council began taking proposals from interested parties, they had leaned in favour of those who wanted to keep the historic building as it was. This frustrated developers who were eager to tear it down and replace it with shiny new identikit houses. Dr Cavendish, however, saw the beauty in its history. She took great pleasure in preserving whatever she could and celebrating its past.

Not everyone had been happy when she had been chosen to take on the lease, not least those grubby developers, who had been salivating at the trough of profit that the land might bring. Their mechanical diggers had no respect for the ancient woodland, and as for the building itself, to them it was just misery-soaked dust and stone to be knocked down and rebuilt better. In the end, it was felt that a beauty clinic would bring a touch of luxury and cachet to a dying town that had relied heavily on the employment of the former asylum. There seemed little point creating more houses when there were no tenants to fill them.

After years of illegal raves, and troubled teenagers summoning the dead in the old morgue, there was a push for the clinic to open and Dr Cavendish had duly been awarded the lease. The wide-eyed ravers and ghost hunters had persisted for a few months, breaking windows and painting strange symbols onto the floors of the derelict rooms, but they had soon realised they were no match for a woman with ambitions as strong as the doctor's. The developers, though, were a tougher breed. They would never have the courage to battle her face to face, but she could feel their animosity and presence hanging in the air like an ancient curse.

Her predecessor, the former guardian of the building, Matron Dawson, had been unable to halt the closure of the asylum. Dr Cavendish was determined that her tenure would be far more successful, and that she would keep the building away from the hands of developers, something Matron would have been extremely pleased about. Picking up a discarded newspaper, Dr Cavendish now walked on through to reception, her broad steps faltering when she saw the unexpected visitor.

'Hello there.'

The portly man gathered his pen and clipboard in one hand and held out the other to greet Dr Cavendish. After a moment's pause, the doctor met his hand with hers, repulsed by the rough calluses on his palms that scraped against her soft skin. She noted his Bart Simpson comedy tie, no doubt an early Secret Santa gift.

'Good afternoon. I wasn't expecting any visitors.'

'You nearly didn't have one. It's the back of beyond here, isn't it? I hope your guests have got good maps. I reckon I should have bought a Sherpa with me.'

'I find retreats are more effective when clients are cut off from the stresses of everyday life. The more remote the better — that's why Pine End was so perfect for the clinic.'

'Aye, well, I suppose they had to do something with the place after everything that went on, though I'd have knocked the bugger to the ground if it were up to me.' He shuddered, grimacing at the doctor.

Dr Cavendish bristled but pasted a smile onto her face. 'I'm sorry, how can I help you?'

'Ah, yes, sorry for the lack of notice, only we've had a report that I need to follow up on. I was passing, so I . . .' He looked up to her face, appearing transfixed by the willowy woman stood in front of him. 'I have to say, I was expecting someone more, well, plain, being a doctor and all. What a nice surprise.'

His eyes travelled up from her slim ankles, his tongue darting across his lips as he scanned her like a prized object. She coughed sharply, his admiration a predictable bore to her. 'A report?'

'Sorry, sorry,' he flustered, tearing his eyes away from her face. 'Is there a Mr Cavendish? Perhaps he should be here also.'

'There is no Mr Cavendish, it's my clinic, Mr . . .'

'Mr Greaves. I'm from the council.' He handed her a card. She scanned the details before looking up and giving him a wide smile.

'Can I get you a cup of tea?'

'If it's proper builder's tea, yes please. But not if it's that hippy flowery stuff the wife drinks. Gives me gyp.' He held his pudgy fingers to his belly.

'We have all kinds of tea, Frank,' she smiled.

'How did you know my—'

'The card.' She patted the pocket into which she had slid the card.

'Ah, of course, and what may I call you?' he said.

'Dr Cavendish.'

'Right, well, thank you for the offer, Dr Cavendish. A good old builder's tea would be great, if it's no trouble.'

'Not at all. Let's go into my office, shall we?'

He began to protest but she had already lifted the receiver from the telephone that sat on the wooden reception desk. Beside it stood a small silver Christmas tree, decorated with metallic baubles that swung gently in the chilled air that crept in under the main door.

'Tina, please bring two teas to my office.' She covered the receiver with her hand and mouthed, *Sugar?* Frank nodded. She put her mouth back to phone. 'Yes please, Tina. Thank you.'

She replaced the receiver and walked over to him. Standing closer to him she could smell his cheap cologne, heavily slapped on his bristled cheeks to mask that lunchtime beer, she guessed. She placed a hand on his arm, her skin prickling as it touched the cheap polyester material of his suit.

'Just through here, and you can tell me all about this report.'

* * *

Frank perched on the edge of the chaise longue that spanned the bay window in Dr Cavendish's office. His large belly protruded over his thighs, the buttonholes of his shirt pulling at their respective buttons, exposing his pale hairy stomach in the gaps. He raised his voice slightly, an attempt to be heard over the rain that battered at the window behind him.

'We had a strange call this morning, from a —' he bent down to his briefcase and shuffled through the papers, pulling out his clipboard — 'Jeff Conner?'

Dr Cavendish shook her head slowly, tapping her nails on the desk she leaned against.

He continued, 'A decorator, I believe. Says he was working here for a few days last week?'

'Of course,' she said, shaking her head and smiling. 'Apologies, Frank. So much to do at the moment, my mind is all over the place.'

'I completely understand, Dr Cavendish, you don't need to apologise. Only . . . this Jeff says he saw a young Asian woman in distress, here in your reception. Says he saw her bleeding heavily from her forehead.' He pointed to his head. 'Was in quite a bad way by all accounts, crying out for help, and it says here, "She looked like something from a horror film."' He looked up from his notes to the doctor, his eyes wide.

'Oh heavens, how dramatic,' she smiled. 'That would be Pippa.'

'Pippa?' Frank said, his forehead wrinkling.

'As I'm sure you know from the calls I've made to the council, this otherwise beautiful haven has been plagued for years by undesirables. Before I took over you could barely cross the car park without tripping over a discarded needle or empty beer can. I've managed to eliminate most, it's true, but some are former patients and they still feel this is their place to come and shoot up, or get completely blotto. I'm afraid Pippa is one of the ex . . . if you'll excuse the phrase, Frank . . .'

He smiled at the comfortable familiarity she was showing him.

'. . . *lunatics* that used to be treated here. Please, God, don't write that word down!'

Frank tapped his nose, gesturing his complicity in her turn of phrase.

'She simply refuses to believe the hospital has really gone, and that there are no more drugs to be had. It's very sad, but that's addiction for you, Frank. Regrettably, I'm just not set up to help her or others like her.'

'I see, a druggie,' he said, scribbling onto his paper. 'And the cut? Why didn't you call an ambulance? This *Jeff* fella says you refused to call one, saying you'd deal with it yourself?'

Dr Cavendish was pleased to hear the way he spat the name Jeff out, as if it was only allegedly his name.

'I'm happy to say that Jeff was mistaken. She's covered in bruises from constant falls; she's out of it most of the time. They look pretty severe to the untrained eye, but there were no open wounds and no need for an ambulance. I gave her a cup of tea and a biscuit and sent her on her way. I'm afraid she's not the only one, Frank. That's why I have to have all this security. I have spoken to Councillor Patton on several occasions, but it seems I'm solely responsible for keeping the place safe. There were over a thousand patients at one time, so you can see that that might sometimes be a difficult task.'

As if on cue, a guard walked by the window and nodded sagely to Dr Cavendish and Frank as he continued his patrol.

Mr Greaves thought for a moment, scratching his unshaven chin with his fingertips. 'He did seem very sure, Dr Cavendish. About the blood, I mean.'

There was a knock at the door, and Tina pushed in a white trolley laden with a tea service, and a plate piled high with sugar-dusted biscuits. The doctor watched as Frank's eyes followed Tina's lithe body from the door to the table, before being forced to look up to her face when she held up the sugar bowl.

'Two, please.' He watched her drop two cubes into the teacup, the gentle clink of metal against porcelain as she stirred the sugar into the hot tea.

'Biscuit?' Tina held the plate in front of his face.

'Don't mind if I do.'

He picked a sugary biscuit from the top of the pyramid and bit into it, buttery crumbs falling to his lap. Tina poured a cup for Dr Cavendish and left the room. Frank didn't notice her exit, now more engrossed in the sweet treat he held in his chubby fingers.

'I don't expect you offer these to your slimmers?' he said, more crumbs falling from his mouth to the floor, as a faint rumble and crack of thunder bellowed in the distance.

Dr Cavendish smiled before rising from her desk and sitting down on the chaise longue next to him, her leg touching his. She reached down and removed a crumb from his knee.

'It's an unfortunate fact, Frank, that when people come across psychiatric patients, they often make assumptions about their behaviour and appearance that just aren't based on reality. Too many scary films, I think.' She plucked at another crumb on his thigh, her nails catching the material on his polyester suit. He flinched and pulled at his collar as his cheeks reddened.

'I don't blame Jeff for worrying. In fact, I'm glad he was showing concern — if only more people cared for the old patients of Pine End — but she left satisfied with what I could offer, even though it wasn't much. I got her a taxi back down to the town and that was that.' Dr Cavendish lowered her head and sighed, pushing at a hint of a tear in her eye with the edge of her finger.

She remained still as Frank put his callused hand on her arm.

'You did all you could, Dr Cavendish. I'm sorry for bothering you, but we have to check, you understand, what with the history of this place and everything that happened before you arrived.'

Dr Cavendish sniffed delicately and raised her handkerchief to her cheek. 'It's not easy to see these people who are clearly suffering and not be able to do more for them. I sometimes wonder if I should have carried on with more worthy work as a doctor, rather than mere aesthetics.'

'No, no, no, not at all; I'm sure you provide a much-needed service, Doctor. I'm sorry if I've upset you.'

'Thank you, Frank.' She wiped the invisible tear away and stood. 'You are only doing your job, and I, for one, appreciate that.'

He smiled, his facial expression one of relief.

'Righto, well, I think we're all done here. Thank you for the tea and biscuits.'

'My pleasure. Any time,' she lied, holding her hand towards the door. He walked by her and back into the reception area.

As he passed the reception desk he paused, pointing a finger at the marble bust that sat there. He walked over to it, studying the face. A flash of lightning flooded in through the windows, illuminating its sharp stone features.

'Is that her? The infamous matron of the old asylum?'

Dr Cavendish raised her eyebrows, expressing surprise at him recognising the former guardian of the building. 'Yes. I never met her, but I believe she was quite the force of nature. It seemed right to keep it there, in her memory.'

Frank raised his eyebrows. 'You wouldn't want to go home to her a pound short in your wages, would you?' he chuckled. 'Gives me the willies that being there, knowing what happened to her and all.'

'Is there anything else I can help you with?' Dr Cavendish said, looking up at the clock on the wall.

'No, I've kept you long enough as it is. I'll be off now.' He picked up a brochure from the desk, studying it. 'How much for a week here?'

'I'm afraid it's women only, Mr Greaves.'

'Not me, for the wife. Let herself go the minute the ring was on her finger. I'll tell you what, if she'd come home looking half as good as you, I'd pay twice the price.' He put the brochure in his coat pocket. 'Cheerio, then. Sorry to bother you.'

He held out his hand, and as she met it the sleeve of her jacket rose just above her wrist. Frank's eyes fixed on the exposed skin, white scarring that dented and criss-crossed her otherwise smooth forearm. When she followed his gaze, she dropped his hand and pulled down her jacket sleeve.

Lightning gathered above the clinic, its bellowing boom of thunder followed each explosion of light. Frank looked uneasily from her to the tempestuous skies outside, before holding his clipboard above his head, pulling the door open and making a dash for it.

'Goodbye, Frank. It was lovely to meet you,' she called out, her words muffled and lost in the rain.

Dr Cavendish watched as Frank lumbered across the gravel drive, the papers on his clipboard now sodden. There was a grinding sound as the engine of his old Vauxhall chugged to life and sped off, plumes of smoke rising in the wet grey air. She looked down to the porchway and noticed in the crack of lightning that the large red stain she had scrubbed at so diligently earlier had not fully disappeared. With two hands she dragged a large planter across the stone, covering the spot, before going back to the office to make further preparations for her new arrivals the next day.

CHAPTER 2

Jenny tipped the contents of the shoebox onto the bed, something she did whenever she wanted to try and make sense of the past forty-two years of her life. The photographs and articles were like jigsaw-puzzle pieces that never seemed to fit together, no matter how much she moved them around and arranged them. Her room was on the first floor of a shared house. There were six tenants in all, and of those she knew no names, just the familiarity of the different beats of shoes and blurs of hands disappearing out of the front door.

Her bobbed ebony hair and kohl-lined eyes were stark against an oversized emerald-green cardigan, which she pulled around her body like a security blanket. Her legs knotted over each other like an advanced yogi. She had the poise and flexibility of a ballerina despite never making a scrap of effort in the name of exercise. Her narrow shoulders were hunched over, her hair tucked behind her pierced ears, revealing a row of sparkling studs glittering in the light of the bare bulb hanging from the ceiling. A small portable heater in the room glowed orange, the wire stretching as far as it could reach to her bed. She padded a hand around until it fell on the small metal tin, which she pulled towards her body.

Every room in the house had been drenched in magnolia paint, the process repeated every three years to cover the damp patches and scuffs on the walls. Jenny had decorated her room with her artwork and photographs, but as the communal areas became ever more uninhabitable, the tenants retreated to their own private corners of the 1960s semi.

Without taking her eyes off the box's contents, Jenny opened the tin and took out the pouch of tobacco and packet of Rizlas. She expertly sprinkled the tiny brown shreds of moist tobacco onto the thin paper, and between her thumbs and fingers, rolled it into a scrawny cigarette. Taking a lighter from the oversized tin, she flicked the tiny metal wheel, lit the roll-up, and stuck it between her plum-coloured lips. She drew in the nicotine.

Smoking was a habit her therapist occasionally berated her for during their sessions — she had given up so much, why not this too? But as far as Jenny was concerned, of all the bad habits she had accumulated during her forty-odd years on earth, nicotine was by far the least toxic.

Outside her room she heard another tenant cross the landing and the door to the shared bathroom open and close, the small bolt clicking into place. She looked down at her watch: she had missed her allocated shower time. Her pale skin still tingled from the cold walk home from town, a wasted walk, as when she had reached the old Methodist church she had shied away, hiding in the shadows as the other men and women entered the dusty hall with its fold-up chairs and stale coffee stewing in a metal urn.

She picked up a large gold coin from the bed and read the words that curved around the edge: *To thine own self be true.* In the centre was the Roman numeral representing the number two for the years she had now been sober. Jenny was prepared to turn over her problem to a higher power — they couldn't possibly make more of a mess of things than she had — but asking her to remove *her* shortcomings felt far too much like absolving everybody else of theirs.

She drew on the cigarette again, removing a tiny shred of tobacco from her mouth with her thumb and forefinger. As the electric shower whirred to life on the other side of the wall, Jenny thought about how intimately she lived with these strangers. Just the other side of the wall there was a naked man soaping himself. She shuddered — it was the kind of life she'd had experience of in the asylum, but at least back then she knew what the strangers looked like. She reached over and pressed play on the CD player, Tori Amos drowning out the sound of water hitting the plastic shower tray.

It was no surprise that tenants in these houses rarely met; the communal areas were hardly enticing. A drab lounge with a sticky shagpile carpet and fag-burnt three-piece suite, where you sat in fear of another lost soul joining you in an awkward silence for the duration of *EastEnders* or *The Bill*. The kitchen wasn't much better. Navigating a tenant's forgotten sour milk and a cooker that looked like molten lava had dried into the grill pan, it was hardly the ideal place to make light chat and form new friendships. Or maybe that was the point of living here. The people that lived in these kinds of houses didn't want to socialise — at least, Jenny didn't.

There was a sharp knock on the door, causing Jenny to jolt, ash falling down onto the bed. She batted at a tiny red spark until it dulled to black, leaving a tiny hole in the duvet cover.

'Shit!'

She crushed what was left of the roll-up onto a saucer by the bed, grey smudges of ash staining her fingers, which she rubbed together as she crept to her bedroom door.

'Who is it?'

'It's me, Bob.'

Jenny unlocked the door for her landlord and pulled it open as far as the safety chain would allow. When it snapped tight, Bob eyed the chain disapprovingly, before looking back up to Jenny.

'For fuck's sake, Bob, it's a bit late, isn't it? Haven't you got better things to do, like getting drunk with your cronies?'

'And a good evening to you too,' he sniped.

She closed the door and unhooked the chain, before letting Bob in.

He turned off the music before moving over to the wall by the side of her bed, studying the latest seascape paintings she had created, as if he were perusing an exhibition at the National Gallery.

'Nosey bugger.'

She joined him by the bed, scooping up the shoebox contents and putting them back into the box, placing it on the table by the window.

'Not half bad, these paintings. You should have gone to art school, you know.'

'I was otherwise occupied at the time, wasn't I?' she said, reaching for her roll-up tin again.

Bob grunted and sat himself down on a metal chair by the table, relaxing back with his knees apart. He took a tarnished silver hip flask from his inner coat pocket and unscrewed the miniature lid. Jenny watched as he slurped greedily at the opening like a bottle-fed lamb, before screwing the lid back on and squirrelling it away again. Jenny stayed on the other side of the room, using the top of a small bookcase to rest her tin down while she produced yet another roll-up.

'Aren't they what old men smoke?' Bob said.

'Old men and poor women.'

'Don't you start with the "poor woman" bollocks. I've been more than fair to you and you know it.'

Bob took out a large white handkerchief from his coat pocket and blew his nose.

'It's brass monkeys in here,' he said, placing the hanky back in his pocket.

'I'll put in a complaint to the landlord, then, shall I?'

'Very funny. I provided you with a heater, didn't I?'

Jenny pointed down to the three-bar heater. 'Wouldn't heat a hamster cage properly, that thing.'

Bob's eyes burned into her as she nervously dragged on the cigarette. The shower next door turned off, followed by the muffled sounds of teeth being brushed and an aerosol can hissing. She owed three weeks' rent now, but the caricature business was slowing down. Soon she'd be relying only on selling her small paintings at Christmas fairs, and the first one wasn't until two weeks away. Bob reached his hand into the cardboard box and took out a newspaper clipping.

'Don't—'

'You know this place better than anyone I know,' he said, jabbing at the paper.

Jenny nibbled at her fingernails, watching Bob scan the words.

'So?'

'So, that's why I'm here and not getting pissed with my cronies, as you so kindly put it.'

'What do you mean?' she laughed nervously. 'Why are you interested in Pine End?'

He leaned forward on the chair and clasped his hands together, the whites of his eyes looking yellowish and sickly. She worried about that sometimes, that he would get ill and die and she'd be out on the streets again. He gestured to the endless seascapes she had painted that were tacked to the wall.

'You want to get out of this place, don't you? Dreams of moving to the seaside?'

'Whitby,' Jenny said, the place always at the front of her mind.

'Well, it's your lucky day, then, because I've come up against a bit of a brick wall — excuse the pun — in my property development empire and there's something I need your help with.' He narrowed his eyes, fixing them on hers. 'And with the current state of your financial affairs, I don't think you can afford to refuse.'

CHAPTER 3

Dr Cavendish studied the photographs neatly placed across her desk. Images of the six women who would arrive tomorrow in the hope of transforming their looks and lives for good. Two friends eating ice creams in candy-striped deck chairs; a brassy-looking woman on a hen night, the signs of aging already apparent despite her relative youth; a catwalk photo from Paris; a lone older woman, loose-skinned and gaunt-faced; and a young woman looking away from the camera as she drank a fizzy drink outside a caravan. These were her chosen few.

If they were prepared to do as they were told and follow her plan, she knew that all their hopes and dreams were possible. They would leave in a few weeks' time and spread the word of her good work, and yet more would come. She unlocked her drawer and took out a scrapbook and opened it on a blank page. Taking a stick of glue, she dabbed the edges of the photographs and lay them onto the rough paper, smoothing over the sticky edges to secure them in place.

When she had finished, she turned back through the pages, searching and tearing out several of the photographs from the book. She dropped them onto the desk, her face remaining impassive as she shuffled through the images of her failed clients, each unable to reach their targets or lose the years their lifestyles or genes had burdened them with. Then she took out a pair of large sewing scissors and sliced through the images with swift, sharp snips until the women were nothing more than unidentifiable slithers of paper. When she had dismembered each image, she swept them into a bin under her desk and sat back in her chair. Resting her hand on the refreshed folder, she took slow steady breaths, and gazed out to the dimly lit car park, humming gently.

Hush, little baby, don't you cry . . .

CHAPTER 4

Welcome to our 14.20 Northrail service to Crowthorpe. We will be calling at Sheffield, Barnsley, Wakefield, Leeds, York, Bettleborough and Crowthorpe, arriving at our final destination of Crowthorpe at approximately 16.38. The buffet car is located in carriage C and is serving hot and cold drinks and a selection of crisps and sweets. Northrail would like to extend a very special welcome to those of you joining us today in first class. We will shortly be commencing our waitress service for you, serving a delicious hot meal, with complimentary wine and coffee.'

The seats either side of the narrow aisle dug into Amy's hips as she wrestled with her bulging suitcase, its plastic shell straining against the fabric of the zip. She leaned her body back on the chair, and using her foot, forced her case further into the small space in the luggage compartment at the end of the carriage.

'Excuse me,' a voice clipped.

Amy looked up to see a woman trying to find a way around her, her eyes rolling as she tapped on a headrest with her fingernails, scarlet and glossy under the carriage lights. The familiar checked lining of her Burberry coat and flash of diamonds from her watch caused Amy to dither, intimidation burning at her cheeks and causing further flustering.

'Sorry, I'm just trying to—'

'Can I get by?'

With one last shove, Amy managed to jam her case so tightly in that it could no longer move either in or out, but still it protruded into the aisle by a foot. She straightened up and edged back into the toilet area to make way for the woman, whose scent smelled of almond and oranges. The woman clicked her tongue against the roof of her mouth as she was forced to manoeuvre around Amy's luggage, her smart black roll-along slapping against Amy's case as it wheeled past.

The lock on the toilet behind Amy snapped and the door swung open, hitting her on the arm as the sweetly perfumed air was replaced by a heady cocktail of disinfectant and urine. A young football fan shuffled past, still zipping up his flies as he pushed past her as if she were invisible, not pausing to excuse himself. Amy turned and caught her reflection in the toilet mirror. Alarmed, she moved towards it.

Her cheeks and chest had flushed bright red, and any traces of make-up that she had applied that morning had now been sweated away, leaving her skin looking pale and puffy. The hair that had fallen out of the loose ponytail was now stuck to her clammy face. She peeled the strands of hair from her skin and tucked them behind her ears. Pulling out a rough paper towel from the dispenser, she held it under the trickle of cold tap water and dabbed her cheeks and forehead as she tried not to breathe in the stale pee of a thousand passengers. The cool paper felt like balm against her skin.

She had only just caught the train, running stop-start all the way from the bus stop. Her suitcase had only just survived the numerous potholes and kerbs it had been dragged across and her ankles were splattered with mud from the roadside puddles.

Amy wore black leggings that were translucent over the tops of her legs where the material had been stretched and worn beyond the manufacturer's promise. A shapeless floral dress hung just below her thighs, ensuring her bottom was covered, and if that didn't do the trick, then the baggy cardigan that hung lower still would do. Her mum seemed saddened that she felt the need to camouflage her body, and her friends constantly told her she was beautiful. But she just couldn't see it herself. Amy knew what she saw in the mirror, and no amount of well-meaning pep talks or reassurance could persuade her that her body was normal.

Though she could never be described as obese, it didn't matter to Amy — each pound above the weight the magazines said she should be was a pound of failure. Right now it was forty-two excess pounds, according to her favourite magazine, *Body Gorgeous*. If she was famous the newspapers would allude to her *curves* or her *voluptuous* body. In her mind, she was just fat, and every female television and film star picked to play the romantic lead seemed to confirm this. If ever she dared mouth her disappointment at herself she would be showered with reassuring platitudes. None of it helped; the only thing that was going to help her was to shed the weight at the Beautiful You Clinic and return home fixed.

Staring into the mirror, she pulled her face back into her neck, watching as a double chin appeared and bulged, then released it and stretched her neck out as far as she could. There was a small knock on the toilet door, and Amy spun round, horrified she had been caught in such an act of self-deprecation.

A mother stood behind a little girl who was bobbing up and down, spaghetti legs crossed and hands holding onto her crotch. The mother gave an apologetic smile to Amy.

'Sorry, I'm finished,' Amy said, pushing the wet paper towel into the vicious mouth of a metal bin and turning to leave.

The little girl pushed past her and was already lifting her skirt as Amy stepped back into the carriage, the toilet door locking behind her.

Making her way down the aisle Amy navigated the narrow walkway and stray elbows, looking for somewhere to sit. Passengers tutted as she knocked into their lanky legs. She scanned the carriage, while the eyes of others, eager to keep all the space to themselves, darted and flickered in her direction and away again. Some pretended to be asleep, legs lazily sprawled across two places. Bags were surreptitiously pushed onto empty seats, non-existent companions due back at any moment.

'Excuse me, is anybody sitting there?'

A businessman who had not seen her coming and so was not able to defend his extra seat was caught off guard. He looked up from his Filofax, his face dropping as he realised he would have to surrender the seat his briefcase was currently inhabiting. Begrudgingly he took the case off the seat and placed it by his feet. He gathered up the files and paperwork that had spilled across the table and shuffled them into a neat pile in front of him. When Amy sat down, her thigh touched his and he jerked his leg away, taking a sharp indignant breath before drawing the armrest firmly down between them, catching her flesh tight.

'Sorry,' Amy apologised, even though she was the one hurt.

A gaunt-faced young mum on the other side of the table was busy trying to placate her toddler, who was screaming blue murder. The mum put down a box of crayons in front of him, which he duly threw into the air, red, yellow and blue sticks of wax rolling away down the aisle.

'Needs a good hiding, he does,' an elderly man across the aisle said to a stranger sitting opposite. 'I've been listening to that racket since we left Derby.'

The toddler's mother heard him, and her frustration turned to venom as she leaned forward and turned on him.

'Fuck off, you miserable old git.'

The old man pursed his lips and sat back, his arms folded in righteous indignation, looking to his fellow traveller for support. The man opposite lifted his newspaper higher and disappeared into the sports pages.

Amy pulled her handbag up from the floor, trying to lift it without disturbing her fractious neighbour. She placed the heavy cloth bag on the table and unzipped it, reaching a hand in and fumbling around until her fingers brushed the brochure for the Beautiful You Clinic. She put the brochure on her lap, leaning it against the table as she sought out the packet of crisps she had bought at the station.

Popping a cheese puff in her mouth, she wiped away the dusty orange crumbs from the shiny pages and began to read.

> *Bev was caught up in a cycle of eating and drinking to cover up her misery of gaining weight, losing it on fad diets and then regaining it all. Overweight, lonely, and with skin like parched leather, she finally plucked up the courage to make a change and booked her place at the Beautiful You Clinic. Just one month later, two stones lighter and with the skin of a teenager, Bev is finally able to wear those size-ten jeans and visit her local disco-theque, where she hopes to pick up the toy boy of her dreams!*

Beneath the blurb there was a photograph of Bev, her bottom pointing at the camera, head turned back looking over her shoulder seductively. Amy read on.

> *Debbie thought that love had passed her by for ever. How could she find the man of her dreams while trapped in the body of her nightmares? Just two months after her stay at the Beautiful You Clinic, Debbie is pleased to report that she has not only found a new lease of life, but her soulmate too. The only excess weight she carries now is the two-carat diamond engagement ring her fiancé put on her finger!*

Amy looked at Debbie and the man of her dreams and couldn't help but think that Debbie's dreams were a little limited.

> *With the latest beauty and diet science from around the world, we will have you looking your best!*

She dreaded to think how much this present had cost her mum and stepdad — an entire month's stay at the Beautiful

You Clinic, one hundred percent non-refundable. They had forfeited their summer holiday to Bridlington and gone to great lengths to organise her extended holiday from her job, thanks to her stepdad still having connections at the biscuit factory where she worked.

Amy ate the last cheese puff and scanned the rest of the brochure for hints at what the magic regime would be that promised to transform her life, but just found details of how to get there and a list of things to bring. There was also a smaller list of things to leave at home, including food and beverages of any description and mobile phones. There was a number for families to call in an emergency, but other than that she would be cut off for a month in order to concentrate on 'the new beautiful you!'

'You going there?' the young mother asked.

'Sorry?'

She pointed at the brochure. Amy looked down and flushed, pushing it back into her handbag.

'Yes, just for a few weeks. Have you heard of it?'

The woman stroked her child's matted hair, smoothing it over his hot forehead.

'Everybody in Crowthorpe knows that place, and we know to keep as far away from it as we can.' She looked back out of the window, holding her child a little tighter.

The men across the aisle shook their heads gravely at her and turned away again. Amy sat back in her seat, a shudder of unease passing over her.

* * *

When they reached York station, the businessman tapped her arm.

'Excuse me.'

He was already looming over her, his papers and pens back inside his leather briefcase. Amy pulled herself out of her seat and stood up, knocking into the men standing opposite, who were also York-bound. Passengers scuttled and weaved down the aisle and off the train onto the busy platform.

When she sat back in her seat, Amy looked up to see that the train was almost empty. Down the carriage an elderly woman stared anxiously out of the window, her fingers opening and closing the metal clasp on her handbag. Next to her a stocky young man dressed in a childlike anorak read a comic, his face twitching and grinning along with the superhero story.

The further they travelled away from the city of Vikings, the greyer the skies became. It was as if someone were gently turning down a dimmer switch in the sky. The urban landscape gradually dissolved into suburbia — terraced houses with sagging washing lines and faded toys left out in the garden, and beyond that, the retail parks.

Soon they left all signs of human life, as the train pushed into the thick woolly mists of the Yorkshire moors. Thick tufts of dormant heather and yellowing grasses cowed under the rain. The only visible sign of life was a lone bird, its blue-black wings and body bobbing against the wind and rain until the train sped away past it, moving further north.

When the train slowed towards its last stop, the toddler opposite loosened his grip on his mum's top and began to wail again. His mum sat him on the seat next to her and gathered up the belongings that hadn't been thrown to the floor. She placed them in a large holdall, which she flung on her shoulder before gathering up the wailing child again, who squirmed from side to side, wrestling to be freed. Amy stood in the aisle, zipping up her handbag. She could feel the tension of the mum and child behind her, the heat of tears and the end of a tether being reached willing her off the train. Amy put her handbag over her shoulder and headed towards the door. As she did so, the headline of a coffee-stained *Crowthorpe Post* strewn across a table caught her eye.

Another woman missing.

Amy hurried out of the station, the heavy glass door swinging into her behind and launching her into the gloomy high street. She took a crumpled piece of paper from her coat pocket and read the scribbled directions she had been given by the clinic. She spotted the white minibus parked in an empty taxi rank on the opposite side of the road. The driver was leaned against a fence post reading a paper and smoking. As she crossed the road a car screeched to a halt, inches from her body. She held her hands over her head as if she was about to be hit.

'Watch out, Bertha!' a bleach-haired boy shouted from the passenger window of the small car, an eyebrow piercing glinting in the light, his words only just audible over the boom box that thudded from the back seat.

Red-faced, Amy continued to cross, looking both ways repeatedly as the car sped off into the distance. By the time she reached the minibus driver, she was panting under the heat of her woollen cardigan and humiliation. The driver looked up from his *Racing Post*, and seeing her, threw his half-smoked cigarette into the litter-strewn scrubland by the road. He had a name badge on the pocket of his plaid cowboy-style shirt. *Glen*.

'The Beautiful You Clinic?' He held out his hand.

Amy took his hand and shook it up and down, but it stayed stubbornly still. He turned his palm over, freeing it from hers.

'I wasn't shaking your hand, duck, I was offering to take your luggage.' He looked down to her hand and then behind her. Travelling light, are we?'

Amy spun around, looking to the floor and then back to the station, just in time to see the train, and her suitcase, disappear down the track.

CHAPTER 5

Jenny marched along the road to the beat of the Smiths' 'This Charming Man', playing on her Walkman. The dark circles under her eyes were barely covered by the thin veil of foundation she had managed to squeeze from an ancient tube, found in a box of oddments under her bed. Sleep had finally arrived in the early hours, but its visit had been brief and fitful as Bob's offer had played over and over in her mind. It could be the answer to her dreams, if only it didn't involve plunging her back into her worst nightmare.

Like the photographs on the wall in her room, there was little evidence anywhere of any time having passed between being fifteen years old and now. She still looked girlish in her red mac, black denim miniskirt and the Doc Martens she had always worn. AA had taught her that once she had started using alcohol to medicate, time had effectively stood still and so she was stuck with the coping mechanisms of a teen, which was effectively to defend herself by any means. Two years sober and she was beginning to face up to things without the support that booze offered.

Part of her had felt a strange pride that Bob had trusted her to carry out his task: to break into the asylum and take photographs of any building hazards she could find, enough to scare health-and-safety inspectors; to riffle through paperwork, anything to find out why the doctor got the contract and not Bob. His ego couldn't take being so unceremoniously dismissed as the next owner of Pine End. Few people knew the hospital like Jenny did — the maze of corridors and rooms, some renovated and some remaining in gloomy gothic darkness.

Most patients had scarpered from Crowthorpe as soon as they left Pine End, the constant double-takes and sniggers from locals too much to bear. Jenny was too obstinate — and more pertinently too poor — to move away. When the asylum had closed, Bob had seen an opportunity to create a cheap halfway house for ex-patients. He had welcomed her with open arms to stay until she was back on her feet. Almost five years later and she was the only ex-patient left in the house. She had never felt ready to move before, but now the possibility of escaping the town burned within her.

The money Bob had offered would bring her rent up to date and give her enough money for a train ticket to Whitby, a deposit on a flat and more. His generosity revealed his desperation and, in a small way, an affection for the young woman he often treated kindly despite himself. He had given her two days to think about it, and at that point, next week's rent would be due, so if she didn't have a better plan, she would have to find somewhere else to live. No matter how fond he was of her, she knew he wouldn't let her live there rent-free indefinitely.

Bile rose in Jenny's throat as her parents' house came into view. Flashes of her last brief and shambolic meeting with her mother began to snap through her mind in rapid projection. Since that day she had almost been evicted twice, gone without food for three days and endured a gaping hole in her boot throughout winter, yet still she hadn't come back here with a begging bowl; her pride and fear wouldn't allow it. If anything were to illustrate the depths of her fear of going back into Pine End for Bob, it was that this was the better option.

Jenny's hand trembled as she opened the low metal gate, closing it gently behind her. As she faced the house, her hand instinctively reached to the metal tin in her pocket, letting go of it when she realised there was no time to smoke between where she stood and the front door. She stepped from one lightly coloured paving stone to the next, avoiding the concrete-filled cracks in between. That had always been her little game; she was pretty good at it, but it had never stopped the bad luck coming.

She pressed the doorbell and the Westminster chime rang out. Through the frosted pane she could see a dark blurred shape appear from the kitchen, getting larger as it approached the door. There was no lock to be unlocked or chain to pull across; instead, the handle turned and the door opened wide.

Apprehension turned to confusion as Jenny scanned the woman standing in front of her, like an item of shopping in a carrier bag that she hadn't remembered buying. She had expected a little girl, but now before her stood a teenager. Thick golden hair was piled loosely on top of the girl's head and her bright blue eyes sparkled. She wore baggy combat trousers, an oversized hoodie and silver hooped earrings. Her eyes were familiar in shape — her mother's. Her high cheekbones, her father's.

There was a sudden recognition.

'You must be Clara. We haven't really met — well, not . . .' Jenny trailed off.

'Jenny.'

'You remember me?'

Clara smiled, eyebrows raised. 'You'd be pretty hard to forget.'

Jenny felt her stomach clench as the humiliation rippled through her insides.

'Right.'

'Come in.'

Jenny was taken aback by Clara's familiarity and the ease with which she welcomed her. Her younger sister held the door for her, and Jenny passed by, inhaling Clara's coco-nut-and-vanilla perfume. Clara closed the front door and led Jenny into the living room.

'Mum's just popped out to the shops. She'll be back soon. It was her you wanted to see?'

Jenny nodded, gazing around the homely living room that for her had been anything but. A white fireplace sur-round with a brass guard, behind which a faux coal fire could provide instant heat with the flick of a switch. The piano by the bay window, the music book held open by small metal clips. The pain of what could have been burned inside, but the tears threatening to escape her eyes were rubbed away before Clara could see.

'Do you play?' Clara asked.

Jenny shook her head, a grimace appearing on her face before she could stop it.

'I bet she tried to make you though, right? I was having lessons practically before I could speak.'

'Did you learn?' Jenny asked.

Clara paused, as if sensing the chip of pain that had left Jenny's mouth.

'A bit. I can only do the basics, really. I play a mean "Chopsticks".'

Jenny looked down to Clara's slender fingers, perfect for the piano, and felt a pang of jealousy. She was the chance their parents had of a better daughter to replace her, and she fought the pain of knowing that they might have succeeded.

'What do you do? For work, I mean,' Clara asked.

'I'm an artist — well, kind of. I do silly caricatures in the park, a few art fairs. It's not much.'

'Mum and Dad never told me that.'

'I don't suppose they told you much about me.'

Jenny looked around the walls: family photographs of holidays, school plays, award ceremonies, council functions. Her eyes scanned each image until she was sure, every last sun-shining, gift-giving smiling photograph. She wasn't in any of them — she had been completely erased from the family.

'A little bit,' Clara said.

'Pardon?'

'They told me a little bit. You know, that you weren't well and needed special help. I suppose they didn't want to, I don't know, invade your privacy by telling me everything. I was little when you were there; they probably didn't want to scare me.'

Jenny held back the bitter laugh, biting her lip until it hurt.

'She should have told you, though — about Dad's funeral, I mean. It wasn't fair; he was your dad too.'

Clara gestured to the sofa, but Jenny shook her head. The need to be ready and close to an exit was always on her mind. She didn't want to sink into the marshmallow-white sofa; she wanted to see her mother, get it over with and then have a cigarette. In the corner of the room a budgerigar scratched its claws across the sandpaper floor of its silver cage.

'I could tell Dad wanted to talk about you, though. Especially when he'd had too much red wine and she was out of the room. He really missed you. I think he felt—'

'Do you know when she'll be back? Only I've got—'

'It was him that told me about your baby. Well, he started to and then she, I mean Mum, came back in the room. I'm really sorry; that must have been a horrible thing to go through.'

Jenny felt her heart race. She reached for the blue heart on her necklace, bought in the antique shop for a tenner. Her fingers rubbed at the cool stone as if she were trying to summon strength from it.

'I can't imagine what it must have—'

'I should go. I don't know why I came, really. It was nice to see you again, sober this time.' She smiled as she headed towards the door. 'Don't worry about telling her I've been. This was a mistake.'

As Jenny reached out to the door handle it turned from the other side and opened. Her mother's eyes widened as she looked across to Clara and then back to Jenny.

'What are you doing here?' her mother demanded.

'I'm just leaving.'

'Mum, Jenny just came to—'

'Clara, go to the kitchen now.'

'But Mum—'

'Now!' she shouted.

The look on Clara's face told Jenny that their mother rarely shouted at the younger of her children. How lucky she was, golden in every way. Clara huffed to herself and marched out of the door. Her mother winced as she slammed it behind her, the small chandelier above their heads rattling.

Her mother wore a heavy red wool coat, her light brown hair now lighter and flecked with silver, resting on its faux fur collar. Beneath the coat Jenny noticed her chest rising and falling, rapidly taking in air thick with the scent of plug-in air fresheners and pent-up anger.

'What do you want, Jenny?'

She had not expected a fatted calf, but still. 'I'm fine thanks, Mum, doing really well. You?'

'Don't be facetious.'

Her mother spoke as if trying to spit out a bitter pill. Jenny dug her thumb into her forefinger, the short nail denting her skin.

'I'm sorry about Dad's funeral. I . . .' She was what? Drunk, angry, grieving, all of the above? Looking for reasons didn't change the outcome. 'I should never have come in that state. I'm sorry.'

'I was right not to tell you though, wasn't I? You couldn't even behave yourself long enough for us to bury him.' Her mum's cheeks reddened, her eyes glassy.

'I would never have got like that if I'd had a chance to say goodbye properly.' Jenny tried to keep her voice even and soft.

'I knew I couldn't trust you. Every report we ever had from Matron told us that you were never going to be functional again.'

'Jesus Christ, I wasn't a faulty toaster, Mum, I was your daughter. I *am* your daughter.'

Her mother sucked in a breath, eyes narrowing and looking from Jenny's boots back up to her face.

'Why are you here, Jenny?'

'I'm behind on my rent, I need—'

Her mum shook her head, a spiked laugh escaping her mouth. 'I thought as much. Where does your money go if not the rent? Drink? Drugs?'

Jenny began to feel the rage inside her spark to life, as if a switch had been turned on. She tried to place herself back in the chair in the therapist's office.

Stay calm. Breathe.

Her mum had started. 'It took months to get over that day. As if burying my husband wasn't hard enough, I had to deal with the humiliation of you turning up at his graveside screaming like a banshee.'

'I was in a bad way, I—'

'And what else was it?' She was on a roll, her cheeks raging and body trembling as if the words were being ejected, not spoken. 'Ah, yes. *A terrible mother*, you shouted — no, screamed. *Wicked*, I think was another word you used. Now, was that before or after you began to pull apart the wreath on his coffin when it was *in* the ground?'

Jenny flinched. She thought she might throw up again right there in the living room, the shame prickling her skin.

'The only positive thing to come out of your outburst was that once you had finished there wasn't a single person present that didn't understand why you had been sent to the asylum in the first place.'

Jenny had only heard about her dad's death from a guy at the pub that she gave blow jobs to in return for beer money and cigarettes. He had broken the news to her as he zipped up his trousers. Then she called the sole funeral director in the town and he had confirmed it, along with a date and time for the funeral.

The full events of the day were relayed to her by friends of the family and the police report. Her display of drunken anger and grief was so spectacular that she had been arrested and spent the night in a police cell. When she awoke the next day, she was sore and stiff from the concrete bed and draughty cell, and so empty inside she thought she might die. Her first thought was to go home to the bottle of cheap wine in the fridge; the second, and the one that likely saved her, was to open the *Yellow Pages* and find a local AA meeting. That day she had reached her bottom and she had a choice: find a way back or give up completely.

'You can't just waltz in here like this and expect all to be forgiven just like that; it's not how life works, Jenny.'

'You know what I lost. He—'

Her mum sounded exasperated as she cut her off. 'You can't keep going on about that, you have to move on with your life.'

'He was my baby!'

Her mother stopped what she was about to say and waited.

'I just needed your help. I was alone, in that . . . that prison.'

'You were out of control, Jenny, and beyond anything me or your dad could help you with. We sent you there for your own good. It wasn't a prison, it was a very good hospital. It's not our fault you made it even worse for yourself while you were there.'

'I shouldn't have been dumped there. You have no idea what it was like because you never came to see me. I was injected, sedated, shocked and vilified, and for what? Because I drank in the park? Stole the odd pick 'n' mix from Woolworths?'

'We were good parents. I *am* a good parent,' she flicked her head towards the kitchen. 'It just took having a good daughter to have the chance to prove it.'

Jenny spoke quietly, her voice shaking as small tears ran down her cheeks. 'You're not a good parent. A good parent stays by a child no matter what. You gave up, you failed.'

Her mum opened the lounge door and stepped to the side.

'Get out. You should never have been able to leave that place!'

Jenny hugged her coat around her body and ran from the room. As she entered the hall, she turned to the kitchen to see Clara's face peering back. Clara flashed a small, sad smile at her. Jenny left the house, slamming the door behind her so hard that the glass in the idyllic family photos that lined the hall rattled against the force of the blow.

CHAPTER 6

Dr Cavendish straightened the pile of papers on her desk, tapping the edges with the palms of her hands until all the paperwork regarding her new women lined up perfectly. Just so.

There was only so much you could garner from the application form and single photograph she required of anybody that applied for the beauty transformation programme. On rare occasions she would call an applicant if she wasn't sure they were the right fit, but mostly she went by her much-trusted gut instinct. She could only hope that this time it hadn't let her down as it had done previously.

On the desk before her, a crystal glass of water sparkled, beside it an array of colourful pills. Taking the tablets delicately between thumb and forefinger, she swallowed each one down with ease, taking only the barest of sips from the glass. When she had swallowed the last pill, she unlocked the drawer beneath the grand wooden desk and she took out a battered folder, fat with paperwork. When she had first sought to take over the building, she had been pleased, but not wholly surprised, to find that there were still patient records in the crumbling asylum. Administrative order, she had found, was not the council's strong suit.

Some professionals found a round of golf or a jigsaw puzzle a relaxing distraction, but the doctor found escaping into the lives of the previous patients not only relaxing, but fascinating and educational. Their lives unfolding before her eyes, the feel of the clinic's past within reach of her imagination, was another way to bring the architecture of the Beautiful You Clinic to life.

The dog-eared folder landed on the desk with a dull thud, its overstuffed contents hanging beyond its manila skin and straining against the frayed treasury tags.

Dr Cavendish opened the file and let the words wash over her.

CHAPTER 7

ADMISSION REPORT
Patient: Jenny Patton

Patient was bought into the adolescent unit at 10 p.m. last night by Crowthorpe social services after a call from her parents, concerned at her 'mental state'. Patient was found in the park with several friends, reported to be intoxicated with alcohol and using marijuana. She was in an agitated state, and threatened police with violence, but at fifteen years old and a very slight girl, police were not concerned and no action was taken by them. She was eventually able to be calmed down and agreed to come to Pine End Asylum, accompanied by a social worker (Mrs D Hawker).

Admitted to Anderton Ward on arrival. Although appearing sober on admission, blood tests taken showed high levels of alcohol and traces of cannabis. Appeared lucid this morning, very quiet, but it was decided to leave her to sleep it off on the ward and reassess later today. It is my initial opinion that this is more a case of rebellion and teenage angst. The patient may possibly be discharged later today and returned to the family home.

She is with Matron Dawson, who will oversee her care until such time as she can leave.

Signed: Dr Kahn — Clinical Psychologist
Date: 21 November 1975

CHAPTER 8

Amy left the address of the clinic with the glum-faced station manager, who offered little hope of her suitcase's return. A vague promise to send on her suitcase if and when it was returned to the station was the best she could hope for as she walked back to the minibus in the driving rain.

The engine was already running as Glen ushered her on board.

'Hello, slow coach!' a woman with short spiky hair called out as Amy clambered up the last step, water dripping from her hair.

Amy stumbled, surprised to find anyone else on the bus. She had been so distracted by the loss of her case she had not had time to worry about meeting the other women for the first time. No matter how old she got, the first day of anything always felt like the first day of school, as though watching through an impenetrable window all the popular people getting along like a house on fire.

'Sorry, everyone. Hi,' she said to the spiky-haired woman, repeating it quietly like a blessing to each of the other five women on the bus.

'Right, ladies, are we all ready to go?' Glen gave a crook-ed-toothed smile into the rear-view mirror. The engine rumbled to life, giant windscreen wipers clearing the rain away.

Amy took her seat near the back and placed her handbag next to her.

Glen pushed a cassette tape into the stereo and a twangy female voice sang out about her broken heart at the hands of cowboys. The minibus swerved sharply out of the taxi rank and onto the main road, as the women held tight to the seat in front.

'Enjoyed your last supper, I hope?' he called over his shoulder. 'I've heard it's all thin air and dust up there on the hill.'

'I had a lovely Chinese last night — spring rolls, fried rice, crispy duck.' A woman with copper curls leaned forward to confess her sins to Amy. She held her hand out and Amy took it.

'I'm Gaynor.'

'Amy.'

Gaynor had sparkling green eyes like a cat and wore red lipstick on her full smiling lips.

'Terrifying, innit?' Gaynor said like an excited teenager.

She looked to be in her early forties, with laughter lines when she smiled and caramel freckles — she smelled like fresh flowers.

Amy smiled, happy to have found a comrade so early in the journey. You just needed one friend at times like this. Strength in numbers, even if it was just two.

The minibus pulled up to a kerb, the engine still running. The women peered out of the window.

'Are we here already?' a dour-looking woman in her sixties asked.

'This, ladies, is where you come when you've had your fill of cabbage soup and face packs. My other little business, the one and only Lazy Spoon Diner.'

Amy rubbed the condensation from the window and peered through the smeared glass to the café beyond. There was a large window with a greying net curtain that drooped across the bottom half. The Lazy Spoon Diner had been clumsily painted over the previous signage, ghosts of letters still visible through the white background.

'Burgers, hot dogs and fries, just like the good ol' U-S-of-A,' Glen said, his Yorkshire twang pushing through his attempt at a Texan accent.

Amy's stomach rumbled.

'Drive on before I'm tempted to get off the bus!' said the spiky-haired woman, waving at an elderly waitress inside the café. The waitress was wearing a lopsided cowboy hat and stared blankly back as if she didn't know where she was.

'Oily foods and salt play havoc with your skin,' said the glum-looking woman to no one in particular.

As Glen hit the indicator and pulled away, Amy noticed a woman marching up the street, her bright red mac stark against her black glossy bob. Amy thought she looked like a character from an arty French film as she puffed on a thin cigarette and blew smoke defiantly in the air. Glen beeped the horn and waved at her — the woman turned and raised her middle finger at him, before disappearing down a different road.

'Friendly round here, then?' Gaynor cackled down the bus.

Glen sighed. 'Welcome to the madhouse, ladies — and there goes one of the ex-patients.'

'What was that?' Gaynor leaned forward towards the driver.

The minibus turned away from the high street and down a bypass signposted towards an industrial estate.

'Well, you know about the history of the Beautiful You Clinic, don't you?' he said, turning down the stereo.

The six women on the bus all shook their heads in unison, hanging on the driver's every word. Glen took a dramatic intake of breath and peeked darkly into the rear-view mirror before turning his attention back to the road and beginning his tale.

'Well, it was the county's loony bin, weren't it? All the nutters from miles around were sent here to Crowthorpe, to the big house on the hill. Built in Victorian times, it was. Beautiful building on the outside, of course, but from what I've heard it's a different story inside those red-brick walls.'

He let out a loud and long puff of breath, shaking his head. The woman sat next to the spiky-haired woman looked at her companion, eyes wide and accusing.

'I didn't know anything about this,' the spiky-haired woman said defensively, as Glen continued.

'Decades ago, you couldn't move in the town for the nursing staff buzzing to and from there, not to mention the occasional escaped patient running riot in the park. My café did a roaring trade back then; between the day and the night shifts I was run off me feet. Then the government saw fit to bring in that care-in-the-community malarkey, didn't they? Well, that was that: the beginning of the end for Pine End Asylum.'

They drove past a derelict industrial park littered with broken windows, weeds crawling up the grey rendered walls. The falling rain pooled in dips in the tarmac car park, a burnt-out car and an upended trolley the only signs that life had once existed there.

'A . . . an asylum?' Amy gasped, leaning forward and placing her palms on the worn velvet seat in front.

'Well, that's not what they call them now,' Glen continued. 'Not politically correct, is it? It became a *hospital*, but a name doesn't change what something is inside, does it? The stories that came out of that place, oof! They'd give you nightmares for the rest of your life.'

Amy turned wide-eyed to Gaynor. 'Did you know about this?'

'No,' she giggled excitedly, 'but I like the sound of it. I love ghosts and things like that, don't you?'

Amy shook her head and turned back to the driver.

'They reckon there've been at least seven murders and umpteen suicides in the place, and that's just the ones they've documented. They had that TV crew there a few years back — what are they called? The one with the curly-haired lass?'

'*Ghostly Happenings*?' the spiky-haired woman offered.

'That's the one. Jeepers, you should have seen the things they filmed at night, especially in the graveyard.'

The dour-looking woman turned away from the window, twisting a set of rosary beads around her bony fingers. 'Graveyard?'

'The patients' graveyard in the grounds — had to have somewhere to bury the dead, didn't they? Poor buggers, most didn't have a single family member bother to attend as they were lowered into the ground. I said to my wife, I said, when I die—'

'Stop it!' a voice cried from the back of the bus. 'Please, stop. You're scaring me.'

Everyone turned to the young girl sat at the back of the bus. Glen sighed and returned his attention to the road, turning up the warbling country song. Amy gave the girl a sympathetic and grateful smile.

'I'm Amy.'

'Jasmine,' the girl said, her cheeks flushed. 'I didn't mean to shout, I just . . .'

'I didn't know about the place either, but I expect it's completely different there now.'

The spiky-haired woman turned in her seat to face everyone behind her.

'I'm Caroline, and this is Vicky — we're from Newcastle.'

Vicky turned and waved. Caroline spoke again, 'Where are you all from?'

'Watford,' said Gaynor. 'I've never been this far north. I think I'm going to get a nosebleed!' She grinned.

'I'm from Derbyshire,' said Amy. 'A small village — you won't have heard of it — near Sheffield.'

'That's Yorkshire, isn't it?' said the dour-faced woman, the rosary beads now completely bound around her hand.

Amy felt flustered. 'Yes, Sheffield is, but I'm on the outskirts . . . I . . .' She always wished she'd just said Sheffield.

'What about you? Where are you from?' Vicky said, trying to draw the woman into conversation.

'Liverpool.'

'What's your name?' Vicky coaxed.

'Audrey. Audrey Dutton.'

And that was as much as anybody was going to learn about Audrey on that journey. She turned back to the window, staring out into the darkness. Caroline, who now knelt up on her seat facing the others, turned her attention on Jasmine, who was sitting at the very back of the minibus.

'Do you work at the clinic, Jasmine?'

The girl shook her head. 'No, I'm going to lose some weight.'

Amy looked down at her slim body — she looked like one of the women on her 'Goals for 2002' vision board.

'You can't be going to lose weight!' Vicky exclaimed. 'There's hardly anything of you!'

Audrey turned to look, and on seeing the thin girl, shook her head disapprovingly.

'I'm fat in the modelling world,' she replied, their eyes surveying her body. 'Too fat for couture.'

There were no rolls of flab hanging over the top of her stretch leggings, and delicate shoulders revealed by a slouchy wide-necked sweater suggested a ballet dancer rather than a fat-farm resident.

'I'd do anything for your figure.' The sycophantic words left Amy's mouth sounding just as pathetic as they had in her head. Too late to take them back.

'Nothing wrong with your figure, love, and you've got a very pretty face,' said Caroline, pointing at Amy. 'Hasn't she, Vicky? Very bonny.'

Vicky turned. 'Oh aye, very pretty.'

'I'd kill for your smooth skin,' said Caroline. 'That's the main reason I'm going — see if the doctor can't take a few years off this mug.'

Caroline pulled her cheeks back with her fingers, her teeth exposed and eyes stretched. 'I reckon I could easily pass for eighteen with a few miracle creams, don't you?'

They all laughed at her comical face — even Audrey managed a small smile. The first crack of the ice broken within the group.

* * *

The juddering of the wheels across stones and displaced earth woke Amy up, and she peered out to the moonlit woods. It was hard to believe that this had once been the approach to a thriving hospital, alive with staff and patients. It seemed so far away from everything. Amy recalled what the driver had said about the graveyard and shuddered, her imagination creating images of skeletons rising from the earth and click-clacking into the clinic at night, bony knuckles knocking on her door.

With her coat sleeve she wiped the sleepy drool from her chin, looking around to make sure nobody else had seen it. The minibus was in half-darkness, the other women all asleep. Caroline and Vicky were using each other as head rests, Audrey's head was knocking gently against the window and Jasmine's was perfectly upright, resting on a neck pillow. Amy turned to see Gaynor behind her, her head back and mouth open, snoring.

The rain had paused, but still the half-moon provided light across the forest, silver slithers of light shining on bark. Another song about faithless cowboys warbled faintly out of the cassette player as the minibus disappeared further into the dense woodland.

One by one the women yawned and stretched themselves awake, groaning with tiredness and disorientation as the bus travelled its final mile.

'I'm starving. I wonder if we'll get anything to eat tonight?' Vicky said.

'I doubt it. If you have any secret stash with you, I reckon you should eat it now,' said Gaynor, winking conspiratorially.

'I've heard we're going to be starved,' Audrey said, staring gloomily out of the window again. 'The doctor is supposed to be very strict.'

'It'll be extreme,' said Caroline. 'They always are, these things, but what matters is the results. I don't care what she does to me as long as I'm looking young and hot by the end of it.' She grabbed Vicky's arm and the women shuddered with excitement.

'It'd better work for the price we're paying,' said Vicky.

'Yeah, but think about all those diets clubs we've joined, a fiver a week for years. The magazines we've bought and those shakes and powders. If this does the trick in four weeks, it's a bargain,' Gaynor reasoned, Vicky nodding back.

Amy's head snapped back as she spotted something moving through the woods, a flash of darkness running through the trees.

'Did you see that?' she hissed to Gaynor.

'What?' Caroline leaned over Amy, her chest skimming her face. 'Probably a fox or something. It's all that talk about murders and crazy people that's got your mind working overtime.'

'It's been a long day,' said Gaynor, smiling kindly at Amy.

Amy looked back to the forest, watching as the shadow of branches swayed back and forth. She wished she hadn't said anything; she didn't want the other women to think she was an idiot. She didn't want them to think anything of her. Right now, she just wanted to go home to her own bed.

'Now, you're all about to go round the bend,' Glen piped up.

'Enough of that, you'll spook the young lass again,' Vicky said, her hand resting gently on Glen's shoulder.

'No, it's a saying. *Round the bend*, it comes from the fact that loon— I mean, these hospitals were always built just out of view from the road, away from prying eyes. Round the bend, see?'

'A regular Magnus Magnusson,' Audrey sniped.

Amy looked across at the drawn-looking woman, hoping that she wasn't going to be partnered up with Audrey in any way while she was here. The idea of playing 'getting to know you' games with a woman that seemed only to speak in grunts filled her with dread.

As the bus entered the black iron gates and moved into the grounds, Glen ejected the cassette tape.

'Welcome to the Beautiful You Clinic, ladies!'

They all strained their necks looking ahead through the avenue of trees, whose tall, spindly branches twisted and arched over the drive like bony fingers woven together at the tips. When the imposing building finally came into view, with the darkness wrapped round it like a heavy black cape, the women fell silent. There was no more idle chatter, just the sound of needling rain hitting the minibus windows as the skies opened again.

CHAPTER 9

Jenny took a sip of tepid coffee and winced. Reaching across the table, she picked up the coffee tin and shook it, the sound of a few scant granules rattling around the metal container ending any hopes of a fresh cup. She gulped down the last grainy dregs and pushed the mug away in disgust.

An anglepoise desk lamp lit the table in front of her as she took a pile of nine A4-sized papers and began sliding them together, three rows of three in landscape. Tearing strips of Sellotape with her teeth she secured the pieces, creating a large canvas. She turned it over and regarded the blank sheet before her. Taking the squat charcoal stick in her hand, she gripped it tightly as she fretted over where, and how, to begin.

Jenny began to dig deep into the cave of her memory, but like pulling rusty metal from a wound, there was a risk that the extraction could do more damage than the injury itself. Her eyes flickered up to the window and the curtain of rain beyond. Her bedroom was reflected back to her. Everything she owned was within these four damp walls — no need for an attic or a spare bedroom. From the age of fifteen she had had no choice but to travel light, though she had progressed from black bin bags to three or four plastic boxes. It had forced her to choose the things that really mattered and let go of those that weighed her down, physically and mentally.

The best of her artwork leaned against a wall in the corner of the room, rolled up and held by a rubber band. Charcoals, watercolours, pencil and oils bundled together, waiting for the day when she would have enough wall space to display them all. A pot filled with paintbrushes and an old wooden oil palette sat on the shelf above her bed below a display of dramatic seascapes, painted on postcard-sized paper.

Photographs Blu-tacked to the wall provided a pictorial mosaic of her early life: a yellowing picture of her as a pink-cheeked toddler, face up from a stripy canvas pushchair, lips stained orange from an ice-pop clutched in her chubby hand. Teen pictures of school outings and discos, arms draped over shoulders and cocky smiles beaming, not yet aware of the pain of love, mortgages and taxes. Almost each year of her life was documented until she was fifteen. It was as if her life had ended right there at the final photograph, on a coach trip to London to see *Godspell* with the Methodist youth club.

She fiddled with the oval silver locket that hung around her neck, opening and closing the clasp with one hand. It had been left to her by an optimistic great-grandmother, presumably foreseeing a blue-eyed, fair-haired descendent worthy of such a gift. Jenny suspected she would have been rotating gracefully in her grave when it had been unceremoniously handed to her, pushed across the Formica table by her downcast father during hospital visiting hours, along with a pouch of Golden Virginia and a tube of toothpaste. The tiny blue stone heart that clinked against the silver was a later addition — she wished she had asked for a lock of his hair, but grief had rendered her mute.

Jenny began sketching furiously, scratching and rubbing at the paper, joining lines to form rectangles and curves to form arches. She blended with eager fingers until parts joined together to form something recognisable that fired at her insides. Her fingers gripped the nub of charcoal so tightly that the whites of her knuckles appeared through her skin.

She was worried that if she stopped, then she would forget and miss something, and she needed everything to be in place and clear, nothing vague. A memory captured. As the image appeared before her, like a dark figure emerging from the mist, she felt a spark of adrenaline so powerful, it momentarily suffocated the fear inside her trembling body.

When she had finished, she took the giant piece of paper over to her bed and wrestled it against the wall, using small dots of Blu-tack to fix it in place as she tried not to smudge the black powdery surface. As she reached up to secure the final corner there was a knock on her door and she let go, letting the loose paper curl down on itself.

Jenny took the chain off and opened it, fully expecting to see Bob on the other side, anxious for her decision. When she saw the strange face peering back at her, she balked, her fingers reaching for the door handle.

'Hi, I'm Tom, your new neighbour — well, neighbour might be a bit grand.' The words tumbled from his mouth like marbles from a velvet pouch. 'I mean, not neighbour really. I'm in the room next to yours. I just moved in and—'

Jenny was about to shut the door again and reinstate the safety lock, but the stranger's foot was against the door, holding it open. When he realised he quickly stepped away.

'What do you want?' Her eyes narrowed.

'I'm out of tobacco, any chance you could lend me some? I haven't had time to find out where the local shop is and—'

She sighed. 'All right, spare me the life story.'

She turned back to the table and Tom put his foot back out, holding the door ajar again. Jenny took a used envelope out of a drawer and opened it, putting some of her tobacco inside.

'Nice artwork. You do this?'

She spun around; she hadn't heard the door close. He was standing by her bed, his eyes scanning her drawings and paintings.

'Yes, it's mine.' Her reply was clipped, no invitation for further discussion. 'Here, that should keep you going until the morning.' She held out the tobacco at arm's length, wishing him away.

He took the envelope from her. 'Any chance of a couple of papers?'

She huffed, unable to hide her irritation. 'You don't ask for much, do you?'

His eyes widened as if amused by her shortness. 'I'll pay you back when I get to the shop.'

Jenny reached over to the window to retrieve the tobacco tin, and opened it to find the Rizla packet empty.

'Hold on.' She turned her back on him, walking over to the tiny makeshift kitchen area.

Opening a drawer, she took out a fresh packet of Rizlas; it was then she saw his reflection in the kettle, his hand holding a photograph that he had taken from the shoe box on the table. She turned and ran towards him, grabbing her art knife as she lunged in his direction, bringing the knife down between the fingers of the hand that rested on the table.

'You're a fucking lunatic!' he screamed, dropping the photograph as she yanked the Stanley knife out of the wood. 'You could have taken my finger off with that.'

He cupped his hand to his chest as if she had really cut his skin.

'Keep your hands off my stuff,' she hissed.

'I should have listened when they said you were mad. I thought I'd give you a chance, but you're loop the fucking loop.' He backed off towards the door as he spoke, his eyes blinking.

Jenny picked the envelope and papers up and held them out to him. He snatched them without thanks and rushed from the room. Jenny slammed the door behind him and snapped the safety lock back on, resting her forehead against the door as relief at his departure settled into her body.

She walked back over to the table and crouched to the floor, picking up the photograph that had fallen from her neighbour's shocked hand. A small, slightly faded picture of a tiny newborn baby with a shock of soft pale hair. Swaddled tightly in a white blanket, his eyes were closed and lips perfectly pink, like a china doll's. Jenny drew her finger gently over the image, her thoughts silenced for a moment.

Jenny sat down at the table and thumbed through the box, taking out a bunch of newspaper cuttings which she spread across the smooth wooden surface, carefully unfolding them and brushing them straight.

'Last night of the madhouse!'
'End of a bloody era!'
'Care-in-the-community chaos!'

Article after article wringing dry every last drop of sensational detail from the old asylum. Had it just lumbered along until the council had replanted the patients safely into the community as promised, it would barely have made page ten. That it closed under such spectacular and macabre conditions with the untimely death of its matron only added to the salacious headlines.

She walked back to the wall and pushed the fallen corner of her charcoal drawing back up, fixing it securely. Standing back, she regarded her work in its full gothic glory, a faithful portrait of Pine End Asylum, its looming clock tower imposing against the charcoal-smudged skies. She punched numbers into her Nokia mobile and put the phone to her ear.

'Hello, Bob? It's Jenny. I'll do it.'

CHAPTER 10

The welcome drinks were waiting in reception. Everything ready for the new arrivals, eager for the opportunity to transform their looks and change their lives. Dr Rebecca Cavendish sat in the darkness, looking out of her office window into the stormy night, waiting. The desk before her had been handed down from her father. She ran her fingers along the smooth walnut edges, the burl of the wood twisting and curling beneath her delicate hand. The green leather inlay on the top still bore the evidence of her father's labour — occasional dots from his Parker pen and a small tear that had been clumsily glued down, the scar of damage remaining.

If he were alive now, she knew he would be proud of her achievements at the clinic. It had taken her time to find her purpose in life, but she had never lost faith that one day she would get there, and now, here she was. Framed certificates lined the wall behind her, evidence of hard work and the rewards that it brings. Her father had reached the peaks of power in his own field of science and pharmaceuticals, introducing revolutionary drugs to the market. With hard work he had provided his wife and daughter with everything they needed, her mother enjoying a life of entertaining dignitaries from around the world.

Each weekend the long table in the dining hall was a banquet of drool-inducing, calorie-rich foods. Roast duck with blackberry sauce, filet mignon and fried potatoes, blue cheese with poached pears and gluey hot camembert with baked bread. The guests would snuffle the savouries up, before sinking their teeth into powdery sugar meringues and sherry-drenched chocolate gateau.

They came and went, a rota of greedy faces. They were like wild birds waiting in the trees for the fat balls and seed holders to be refilled, before swooping down and emptying them once more. Rebecca would watch as a child, standing in the hall in her tailor-made satin pyjamas, peeking through the door to admire the rich silk dresses and sparkling gems that rested on alabaster necks and lithe bodies. Then she would gaze admiringly at her mother.

In Rebecca's early memories, her mother was the epitome of 1950s Hollywood. Jet-black curls and bright blue eyes that sparkled like crystals. Her generous chest and slim waist were the envy of all the women that visited. There were a succession of compliments from each guest she greeted — for her porcelain complexion, Elizabeth Taylor curls and perfectly manicured nails. Her mother was the kind of woman that all little girls dreamed of becoming, and her daughter was no exception. Her mother was perfection.

A soft glow of headlights curled around the bend, creeping across the drive and throwing a flash of light across the office. Dr Cavendish stood up from her desk and walked towards the large window, standing far enough back in the darkness that she couldn't be seen. Her eyes followed the minibus until it came to a gravel-crunching stop at the front entrance. When the engine was turned off there was a low buzz of chatter just audible beneath the hiss of rain as the women gathered their handbags and began to disembark.

Her two clinic assistants descended the stone steps to greet the guests holding giant golf umbrellas, and ushered the women under the shelter. The assistants wore identical, body-skimming navy dresses, their hair pulled back tightly into buns with identical painted doll faces. They were the bridesmaids to the doctor's bride, the backing singers to her lead vocals: complementing but never upstaging her. Dr Cavendish looked on approvingly as they gently corralled the women into the clinic one by one.

She recognised the dour woman as Audrey, and watched her flinch as she tried to pick up her case, the taxi driver taking it from her and bringing it to the step. Caroline and Vicky were easily identifiable, and she felt a pang of admiration as the practically perfect Jasmine came into view, as slender as her picture. It would take no time to get her looking better, smooth out her skin, add more tone in her arms — she was not quite perfect. Gaynor bubbled among the women, pointing and cackling at something the driver had said. Dr Cavendish winced a little as the red-headed woman that had just made her cut of applicants howled with laughter before following the others towards the entrance and out of the rain. That was five women, where was . . . ?

Amy appeared from behind the minibus and Dr Cavendish exhaled again; it was not unheard of for a client to change their mind before the programme began. For some, the non-returnable fee was little more than a dent in a monthly allowance. Amy was just as Dr Cavendish had expected as she shuffled across the car park, like a rabbit caught in headlights. She felt a rush of excitement as she imagined the changes she would make to this young woman. She would bring the biggest challenge, but ultimately the highest satisfaction, to the doctor.

A figure moved out of the darkness behind Dr Cavendish and stood by her shoulder looking out to the car park.

'Is that her?' He took a sip of whisky from a thick-bottomed glass.

Dr Cavendish nodded, recoiling at the peaty odour of the drink and irritated by his presence.

'Very nice,' he said, licking a drop of single malt from the corner of his mouth. 'Your choices are impeccable as always.'

Dr Cavendish let his words dissolve away, her eyes fixed firmly on the woman who looked like she might turn and run at any moment.

CHAPTER 11

Amy looked up at the clock tower and across to the scrunch-faced gargoyles crouched on the ledges, which looked like they might pounce on her at any moment. The rain poured down the dark red bricks, overflowing in the gutters and spilling to the ground as thunder rumbled from beyond the surrounding trees. All Amy needed to see now was a black-cloaked figure crawl down the side of the wall and she would be begging Glen to take her back to the station.

Something jumped into the overgrown grass behind her and she spun round just in time to see a cat's tortoiseshell tail disappear into the darkness, giving her a momentary feeling of joy. When she turned back, a smartly dressed woman was standing in front of her, an umbrella held over both their heads. Amy gasped and held her hand to her chest.

'Come on in, Amy,' the woman urged, putting her hand on Amy's sodden shoulder. 'I'm Dr Cavendish. Welcome to the Beautiful You Clinic.'

There had been no photograph of the doctor in the brochure and Amy had somehow expected a bespectacled, stern woman, not the glamorous, smiling face that stood before her.

She raised her voice against the rain, 'Sorry, I was just looking at the . . . It's so big, the building, I wasn't expecting—'

'Come on inside; we don't want you getting sick before we've even started, do we?'

Dr Cavendish led Amy in by her hand as if she were a little girl and brought her into the foyer to the gathered group. Amy was about to step onto the mosaic-tiled floor when the doctor held out her arm to stop her.

'Leave your shoes here, we have slippers for you.'

Dr Cavendish clicked her fingers and one of her assistants turned instantly.

'Kim, could you bring some slippers, please — size . . .' She looked to Amy.

'Five, please,' Amy said.

Kim nodded and disappeared behind the reception desk, reappearing with a pair of flannel slippers with the Beautiful You Clinic embroidered on the front.

'Here you go,' Kim said kindly, placing them on the floor by Amy's feet.

Dr Cavendish and Kim looked down at Amy's feet as they squirmed out of the sodden ballet pumps, the ridges of her toenails filled with dirt from the wet pavements.

'Don't worry, you can wash them when you get to your room,' Dr Cavendish reassured her.

Amy pushed her damp feet into the warm slippers and bent down to pick up her shoes.

'No need,' Dr Cavendish said, gesturing to Kim.

Kim picked up the pumps by the very edges of the leather and dropped them in a thin plastic bag she had taken out of her pocket.

'Right, looks like we're all here now.'

Dr Cavendish guided Amy to where the others stood in the vast reception. Vicky and Caroline were admiring the mosaic-tiled floor, Jasmine was yawning and stretching in the corner and Audrey sat glum-faced reading through a pamphlet she had found on the reception desk.

'Posh, innit?' said Gaynor, grabbing Amy by the arm. 'I wonder what's up there?'

Amy peered around the corner to a dark wooden staircase that was closed off with a single piece of scarlet rope. Amy shrugged, her senses overwhelmed by everything around her.

'I bet the bedrooms are plush,' Gaynor said.

'Ladies!' Dr Cavendish clapped her hands together. Caroline began to tell Vicky about the last spa she had been at. Dr Cavendish clapped harder. 'Ladies, if I could have your attention.'

Caroline looked up red-faced as Dr Cavendish continued to speak.

'I want to take this opportunity to welcome you all to our wonderful clinic. For the next few weeks, our home—' she gestured to her two assistants that stood either side — 'is your home. Incredible things will happen here if you are prepared to put the work in.'

'We're ready, ain't we!' said Gaynor, to a ripple of approving laughter.

'*Aren't* we,' corrected the doctor.

'Eh?' said Gaynor.

'Pardon,' corrected the doctor.

'Pardon?' said Gaynor.

'That's better,' said Dr Cavendish, smiling approvingly at Gaynor, who in turn looked like she had just been asked to explain the theory of relativity. 'I'll just introduce you briefly to our team, faces you will come to know very well over the next few weeks. You've already met Tina and Kim, my wonderful assistants. Tina has been with me since the beginning of the clinic, an expert beautician and hairstylist, and the lovely Kim has just recently joined us fresh from a cruise ship in the Mediterranean where she ran all the fitness activities for the holidaymakers on board.'

Gaynor leaned over and whispered in Amy's ear, 'Fancy giving up a cruise ship in the Med to come and work in this place.'

'Anya is our housekeeper and head cook. I'm afraid she's busy at the moment, but you'll meet her in the morning.

And—' the doctor turned as a door to her left began to open — 'here is Robert.'

Caroline nudged Vicky, who had been picking her nail varnish. Vicky looked up, wide-eyed, when the broad man entered the reception and stood beside Dr Cavendish.

'Now we're talking,' Gaynor said to herself.

Robert looked to be in his late forties, a rugged-looking man with dark blond hair dragged back into a stubby ponytail. His eyes were pale blue like starling's eggs and his skin swarthy as if he'd spent long summers toiling outside somewhere other than the north of England, the ghosts of pockmarks still evident on his rough cheeks. His suit hung awkwardly, as if he had been dressed for church by his mother. Amy shuddered when she saw the wiry hairs on his sockless feet, poking above his tan loafers.

Dr Cavendish continued without making eye contact with him.

'Robert will be leading your fitness programme, assisted by Kim and Tina. And I should warn you now, he is a tough taskmaster.'

Amy noticed Tina furtively looking across at Robert, her cheeks slightly flushed. Kim kept her eyes forward, the occasional encouraging smile directed at the gathered women in front of her. Robert stared straight ahead.

'The clinic is conveniently located on the ground floor. I kindly ask that you don't wander to the first floor—' she gestured to the red rope — 'which is still being refurbished and is also home to some of our staff. Please remain within the rooms designated to your stay — that is, your bedrooms, the bathrooms, the dining room and the relaxation area. If there's an emergency during the night, Kim and Tina reside in the room next to my office.'

The women nodded, each trying to keep up with the geography of the building.

'I just need you all to sign some consent forms and then Tina and Kim will take you to your bedrooms.'

As they filed out of the foyer behind the doctor and her team, Amy paused at the reception desk, hesitating to pass the marble bust that stared out in front. As she walked by she averted her eyes, in fear that if she didn't, it might turn her to stone too.

* * *

The relaxation room was a huge galleried space in the centre of the building. They were all huddled on the sofas and chairs, studying the paperwork they had been handed by Kim and Tina, who now stood back, watching the women through electric-blue curled eyelashes.

Amy blinked at the paperwork, fighting to keep her eyes open. Sleep-deprived and hungry, the words began to dance around the page. She chased them, trying to make sense of the form. Gaynor nudged her in the side.

'Look at you, reading the small print. I just signed mine. The sooner you do, the sooner you can go to bed.'

Amy looked back down to the form.

1a. I agree to adhere to the clinic programme as set out in the following pages until I reach all goals set out for me, as agreed at application stage.

She had no idea what goals had been agreed between her parents and the doctor, but she hoped they were realistic. It was four weeks until Christmas, and the thought of being away from home then made her stomach lurch. Besides, she hoped, surely the factory couldn't have agreed more than a month's leave?

1b. Dr Cavendish is an expert in the field of body aesthetic transformation, and I will follow her methods and the advice provided. At times this may appear contrary to what I believe to be true, but I will trust in her guidance and do as instructed at all times.

Her eyelids began to get heavier by the second.

'How are we doing, ladies?'

Caroline and Vicky sat up straight when Dr Cavendish re-entered the hall, Gaynor giggled nervously and Audrey looked up po-faced. Jasmine was busy scratching her biro across the pages.

'Excuse me, Doctor, but the final clause, I mean . . . sounds a bit much to me,' Audrey said.

Dr Cavendish smiled and turned to Tina and Kim. Tina smiled back at her before the doctor turned to face the guests again.

'I promise you, Audrey, that if you follow my plan, all goals will be reached. That clause is really just my promise to you that you can stay as long as is needed for you to be successful. We know you are here because nothing else has worked for you. You all feel let down by your faces and bodies and we want to change that. We want to be the difference.'

Audrey grunted and signed her form, holding it out for Dr Cavendish to collect.

Amy turned the pages, scrolling through each clause until she reached the final one that Audrey was referring to.

23c. By signing this contract, I agree to remain at the clinic until such time as I have reached my goals as previously set out in my application. I may not at any time leave the building or its grounds without the express permission of Dr Rebecca Cavendish. I sign here to hand over the care of my body to her until such time as I have succeeded.

Dr Cavendish stood over Amy, the pen hovering above the dotted line. Amy felt the eyes of all the other women begging her to get it over with so they could all go to bed. The sweet scent of amber perfume floated in the air as the doctor crouched down to Amy, smiling gently. Amy pushed the pen to the paper and signed her name.

'You won't recognise yourself by the time you leave, Amy. It will be the best thing you've ever done, I promise.' She patted Amy's knee with her beautifully manicured hands.

Now she had the last of the consent forms, the doctor rose and addressed the six women.

'I can assure you that by hook or by crook we will have you all looking like Hollywood film stars in no time at all. Whatever your targets were before you came here, whether it's weight loss or more tone or better skin, we will reach and surpass them.'

Caroline and Vicky looked up at her as if they were Moses on Mount Sinai, their eyes glazed and adoring.

'We will officially start tomorrow morning with a weigh-in and measure and then a brief talk during breakfast.' She smiled reassuringly at the women. 'You will all do well, I can feel it in my bones. Now, has anybody tried to sneak in anything they shouldn't?'

The women shook their heads, Caroline laughing at such a suggestion. Amy noticed Gaynor looking sheepish as the doctor's assistants laid all the cases on the floor and began to open them, searching through the contents one by one.

* * *

All eyes were on the box of teabags that Dr Cavendish held aloft.

'I can't live without a proper cup of tea,' Audrey moaned.

'The rules were very clear, Audrey: no food or drink. The programme is very strict, and the slightest thing can drive you off track. Have you any idea how harmful tannins are to your complexion?'

Kim held out a black bin bag and Dr Cavendish dropped the box, which fell with a swish into the plastic, joining the mobile phone that Vicky had forgotten to leave at home.

'I can't be too clear about this — you must all do as you are told if we are to succeed. Am I clear?'

Audrey grunted, staring down at the bulge at the bottom of the bin bag.

'Yes, Dr Cavendish,' the women's tired voices called out.

Dr Cavendish counted the cases, pausing and recounting. 'Are we missing someone?'

Amy felt her heart beating in her chest and her face burning as she raised her hand.

'I left my case on the train, but they're sending it back as soon as it's found, so it should only be a few days. I'll be fine until then.' She placed her hand back down over her handbag, remembering the half-full packet of eclairs she had forgotten to dispose of before getting on the minibus.

The doctor's face was blank for a moment, as if processing the information, then a hint of an excited smile appeared.

'Not a problem at all; we have plenty of spare clothes here. I'll have something brought to your room later.'

Amy exhaled and smiled, relieved to have got her ineptness out in the open.

'Ladies, we have a mantra here, and if you follow it you will succeed.' The doctor signalled to Tina and Kim, who joined her in saying, 'Discipline and diet determine your destiny!'

The rallying call fell on tired ears. The doctor smiled resolutely before beginning to usher the women away.

'I'm sure you're exhausted and need a good night's sleep. Follow the girls and they will show you to your rooms. You'll find one of my signature relaxation pills on your bedside table. I ask that you take these each night in order that you sleep properly while you're here. While you're asleep your body is doing important work healing itself, and it's important we all get the optimum rest.' She waited until they had all nodded in agreement before continuing. 'I will see you all in the dining room in the morning. Sleep well, ladies. I look forward to beginning your new life with you tomorrow.'

Amy trudged behind the others, her slippers dragging lazily across the shiny floor. When she reached the centre of the room, she glanced up to a figure on the small galleried landing high up on the far wall. Robert was sitting in a shabby high-backed chair looking down on the women as they left the room. When his eyes rested on Amy, he smiled. She scuttled away, trying to shake the prickles of unease his crooked grin had caused.

CHAPTER 12

The pungent fumes of fresh paint took Amy's breath away and made her eyes water. She thought the clinic had been open for almost a year now, so was surprised to find her room newly decorated. Though it was spotlessly clean and bright, the plushness Gaynor had hoped for was lacking. The walls were the colour of pallid pink medicine; there was a single metal-framed bed that had been painted white, covered with crisp white sheets and a scratchy woollen blanket that were tucked tightly beneath the mattress. There was a small bedside table, and just a short row of brass hooks on the back of the door to hang clothes on. On the wall was a framed series of images featuring famous beautiful women: Marilyn, Naomi, Cindy, Kylie and Lady Diana, the wedding years. Amy tried to avoid the eyes of the women, which followed her round the room. She peered beyond a thin wooden door, where there was a white-tiled room with just enough space for the toilet, slim shower and half-sized sink.

As she put her handbag on the bed, Amy noticed a small plastic cup next to a glass of water. A handwritten note by the side of the glass directed:

> *Welcome to the Beautiful You Clinic, Amy. Please take this tablet for the ultimate beauty sleep. We can't wait to see your success on the programme!*

Amy picked up the plastic cup and peered at the small powder-filled capsule in the bottom. She rattled the cup as if this might reveal more of the tablet, before drawing it up to her lips and placing the pill on the back of her tongue. She gulped down the water, feeling the tablet catch on the side of her throat as it tumbled towards her stomach.

A small draught blew through the sash window before her, and expecting it to be open slightly, she went to close it. She pushed down with the palms of her hands, but the frame was as far down as it would go. There were no obvious gaps, just a soft breath of cold air blowing through as if the glass were made of fine net. The rooms were all on the ground floor, and from the window she looked out onto the back of the clinic, where dull street lamps provided scant orange light. Straight across the pathway that ran around the clinic, there was a shelter of some kind with long cracks in the thick Perspex panels, which were misted with age, spray-painted monikers unreadable in the gloom. Beyond the shelter was the woods. In daylight she imagined they would be mystical and pretty, but now she had a childish thought that the dark army of trees might lunge forward and pull her into their wooden underbelly. She yanked the curtains together, holding them there for a moment as a feeling of tired wooziness washed over her.

The radiator beneath the window was ice-cold and the nozzle to turn up the heat was missing. Her clothes were now dry, so she pulled back the bedding and crawled into bed fully dressed. She reached down to her handbag, took out the clinic brochure and put the thin pillow against the hard metal headboard, resting her head back. She read idly until a bell rang out from somewhere down the hall and the lights snapped off.

She sat blinking in the pitch black, her eyes trying to adjust to the sudden darkness. At home she had a small battery-operated nightlight in the shape of a kitten — she wished she had brought it now. The minibus driver's stories of the old asylum were coming back to her. Hanging bodies creaking at the end of ropes and tormented souls roaming the corridors.

Amy tried to make out familiar shapes and shadows in the room, but it was a solid black fog and she couldn't see anything beyond the end of her nose. She closed her eyes and pulled the covers up to her chin, tossing and turning as her body adjusted to the unfamiliar and uncomfortable bed. Somewhere in the distance the faint sound of music caught her attention and she let the gentle melody lull her off to sleep.

CHAPTER 13

'All I'm saying is, you didn't need to stab the poor bloke.' Bob put the cigar back in his mouth, puckered his lips around it and released them, thick white smoke pluming into the air.

Jenny reached across him to open a window. 'I missed, didn't I?'

'Hardly the point, Jenny.'

Bob had wasted no time in sealing the deal with Jenny, appearing just a couple of hours after her call. He dug his hand deep into his coat pocket, took out a box and slid it across the table. She caught it in her hand like a cowboy halting a glass of whisky on the saloon bar. Jenny opened the box and took out a digital camera.

'Nice, I could do with one of these for my artwork.'

She jabbed at the buttons and spun the tiny dials.

'Well, if you do a decent job you can keep it. I've got a whole box of those at home I'm trying to flog.'

Jenny took a cable out of the box and connected it to the camera, plugging the other end into a socket by the skirting board. A tiny red light flashed as it began to charge.

'Listen: I need you to keep . . . well . . . keep your head when you do this.' Bob fixed his eyes on Jenny.

She looked up from the floor where she was still crouched, holding the camera and eager to keep playing with it.

'There's a lot of security up there. I don't want you getting into trouble with them. If you alert them and it comes back to me, it'll put the kibosh on me ever developing that site, or any other in this godforsaken town, for that matter.'

'It'll be fine, don't panic.'

Bob walked over to her drawing of Pine End, his head in a cloud of cigar smoke.

'Gives me the creeps, that place. The sooner the council agree to bulldoze it to the ground the better, I reckon.'

'You speaking for the good of the town, or your pocket?'

'You won't do too badly out of it, provided you get me what I need. I bet it's a long time since you've had three grand to your name.'

Jenny had never had anywhere near that amount of money at once; she had gone from titbits of pocket money to benefits with very little in between. Bob took a fat envelope from the inside of his sheepskin coat and threw it down on the bed.

'Here's a bit to be going on with. You'll need to buy some bits, a torch and whatnot. You'll get the rest when I've got enough mud to stick on that Doctor. I'll drop by again next week — hopefully you'll have something for me by then.'

Jenny looked at the open envelope on the bed, ten-pound notes bursting out. Bob continued his instructions as he headed to her door.

'In the meantime, leave my other tenants alone. If they do a midnight flit in terror, it'll be you I'll be chasing for lost rent,' he warned, pointing at her. 'Got it?'

As he turned to leave Jenny screwed her face up and stuck out her tongue, closing the door behind him and sliding the safety chain back on.

She threw herself onto her bed and grabbed the envelope. Two hundred pounds was the most cash she had ever seen in one go. She turned over and lay back on the bed listening as Tom's portable telly came to life in the next room.

They had met again in the communal kitchen earlier as she was making beans on toast. When he had seen her holding the long serrated knife, ready to cut the bread, he had turned on his heel and scuttled up to his room, his door slamming shut before the knife had even hit the bread board.

Her eyes travelled along the picture of Pine End. Part of her fizzed alive at the thought of being so close again, but another part wanted to retreat into a ball and scream for her to stay away. Pine End had taken so much of her for so long, grabbing at her insides and warping her sense of self until she was unrecognisable from the child that had entered there. She had managed to leave just in time to keep a shred of sanity; she could only hope that when she went back inside, it wouldn't steal that too.

WEEK ONE

CHAPTER 14

A bell rang furiously, jolting Amy awake from a night of disjointed and disturbed dreams. She listened carefully to the faint rustling of bedclothes in the next room. Gaynor was waking. Relief swept over Amy, remembering she had already made a friend, someone to navigate the first few days with, until she found her feet.

It was already light outside as she squinted down at her watch, the sun trying to break through the heavy curtains.

11 a.m.

Amy jumped out of bed with a start. She felt disorientated, scrambling from side to side, not knowing whether to brush her teeth first or get dressed. Blood plummeted down to her feet and she swayed a little, having to steady herself against the bed frame. It was the best night's sleep she could remember having — she felt fully rested. She went over to the window and opened the curtains. The pale grey clouds allowed just enough of the sun through so that she could see the bottle-green trees ahead, an opening between them forming a pathway where the forest floor seemed to clear.

The bell reverberated with a final clang, fading into an imperceptible hum before disappearing altogether. Amy turned back to the room and her eyes were instantly drawn to the unfamiliar. She walked slowly over to the hooks on the back of the door, where a tent-like flowered dress now hung. It had long sleeves gathered at the cuffs, a Peter Pan collar and large pockets. Was that the only outfit that Dr Cavendish had been able to find for her? Amy looked down to her own clothes, which she had worn all day yesterday *and* slept in. Beggars could not be choosers.

Then another thought occurred to her. The dress hadn't been on the door when she had gone to sleep last night, so someone had brought it into her room while she slept. A shiver travelled up her spine as she made her way to the bathroom, stopping and cursing herself when she remembered her toothbrush and toothpaste were also in the lost suitcase.

* * *

'Christ, is this it?' Gaynor stared down at the small glass of tomato juice and the paper-thin slice of apple wedged onto the rim. Beside the glass was a small white plate with a variety of candy-coloured pills.

A laminated sign on the wall demanded that no food or drink was to be consumed until Dr Cavendish had given them permission to do so. Amy tried not to look at the slice of apple; she had never been so excited about eating fruit in her entire life. It was almost twenty-four hours since food had last passed her lips. Her stomach wasn't just growling for the next meal, it was roaring. When they heard heels clipping against the tiled floor, the women all sat up straight in their chairs like schoolgirls awaiting the headmistress. Dr Cavendish entered the room, smiling brightly and waving her hands in the air.

'Morning, ladies, I trust we all slept well?'

'Like a baby,' said Caroline.

'Excellent, that's what I like to hear.'

Caroline turned to Vicky and smiled, happy to have pleased the doctor.

Dr Cavendish was wearing another beautifully tailored suit, her hair still pulled back into a sleek bun. Amy noticed her nails, long and pointed, painted blush pink. Perfect. They must be false, she thought, looking down to her own stubby nails. She was sure she had seen somewhere that nail care was on the programme, along with make-up application and proper teeth cleaning — nothing was going to be left uncovered.

Audrey freed the slice of apple from her glass and put it up to her lips.

'Not yet, Audrey,' Dr Cavendish demanded firmly. 'First we must be brave and face our worst fears.'

Audrey dropped the slither of apple onto her plate and watched with the other women as Dr Cavendish held a set of scales aloft and a tape measure that skilfully unravelled itself from its coil and spun toward the floor. There was a collective groan.

'Like the mirrors that adorn this beautiful building, you should see this as your friend, not your enemy, ladies. Only by seeing the changes for yourself can you measure your success.'

'I imagine nobody is going to volunteer, so I'm going to call you up, one by one.'

Dr Cavendish put the scales on a raised plinth in front of a large bay window.

'Can't we do it in private?' Jasmine pleaded.

'Accountability is key, Jasmine. You will find that once everyone else knows your goals, you will work much harder to achieve them.'

Amy looked over to Jasmine, who was leaning back, her long legs stretched out in front of her.

'I'll go first,' Amy suddenly blurted out — the waiting would be worse.

'Excellent, Amy, well done. Up you come.'

Amy pushed her chair back and stood up, the ankle-length floral dress billowing out as air caught underneath it.

'Blimey, I didn't know it was a black-tie breakfast,' Caroline chirped.

Amy gave her a look by way of an apology on behalf of the dress. Dr Cavendish looked down at the garment and for a second stared blankly at it as if she were lost somewhere.

'Shall I get on?' Amy asked.

Dr Cavendish snapped back to the present moment, her eyes regaining focus. 'Sorry? Oh yes, of course.'

Amy took her slippers off and stepped tentatively onto the scales, keeping her eyes on the window outside as the needle whirred back and forth beneath her feet. Outside she watched the long grass flatten and rise in the wind.

'I don't want to know what I weigh,' she whispered to the doctor, still looking away from the scales.

'Thirteen stones on the dot, Amy!' the doctor announced to the room. 'Now, how tall are you — do we have that information here?' Dr Cavendish scanned the sheet of paper in front of her. 'Ah yes, five feet, three inches.' She shook her head and clicked her tongue against the back of her front teeth disapprovingly.

Amy gulped back embarrassment, her weight suddenly a shared fact among virtual strangers. Audrey raised her eyebrows as Amy walked by with her head bowed. Gaynor smiled sympathetically and patted Amy's arm.

'Good for you going first, Amy.'

She had set the bar low and could feel the relief in the room from the other women, who she was sure couldn't help but feel better about themselves now. They could now approach the scales and the doctor's pen and paper with renewed confidence that their results wouldn't be as bad as hers.

'Who will be next?' There was silence. 'No apple slices until all are weighed, I'm afraid. That is our reward.'

Amy looked down to the oxidising apple, willing the minutes away.

* * *

Anya had not been formally introduced, other than a brief mention the evening before, and she just appeared spectre-like in the dining room when they had finished their meagre breakfast. She cleared the empty glasses without saying a word. Her towering presence caused surprise and unease in equal measure. Caroline nudged Vicky and looked at her as if the strange face was the newcomer and not them. Jasmine's eyes widened as Anya's shovel-like hands stacked the glasses on top of each other, spatters of stray tomato juice catching her white overall.

She was over six feet tall and looked like she had the strength for Olympic-standard shotput. Amy leaned back as she reached in front of her, crushing the paper napkin in her fist and shoving it into the glass, the final dregs of juice seeping into the paper. Amy peered up to Anya's face — it was pale and pudgy, a lack of sunshine evident. She was probably only in her early thirties, but it looked like life had stolen some of her youth.

With glasses stacked high and tables all cleared, Anya left the room as silently as she had entered, leaving the women quietly watching, for a moment forgetting the trauma of the scales.

'What time is lunch, Dr Cavendish?' asked Audrey.

Dr Cavendish smiled. 'Now, Audrey, don't be so obsessed with food — this is the problem. We have barely finished one meal before we are thinking about the next. Sometimes even the one after that.'

'I agree, Dr Cavendish; we've forgotten what hungry feels like,' Caroline piped up.

Vicky nodded in agreement, both women looking admiringly up at the doctor as Audrey scowled at them both.

'Exactly, Caroline. We need to get back in touch with our bodies and learn to distinguish between want and need.'

'I want and need more food,' said Audrey, glumly.

'We will all meet in the relaxation room in ten minutes and we will get to know each other a little better. Please be on time, ladies, and remember — discipline and diet determine your . . . ?' She put her hand to her ear and waited.

'Destiny!' they chorused, before leaving the dining room one by one.

* * *

Amy couldn't hold on any longer: a diet of water and juice with little to soak it all up was having a detrimental effect on her bladder. She passed the kitchen on the way to the toilets, peering through the partially opened door. Anya was washing the glasses with a dishcloth, staring out of the window, deep in thought. A small radio played a kind of folk music, interrupted by an Eastern European voice, in a language Amy didn't recognise. When Anya saw Amy, she dropped the dishcloth into the sink, walked over to the door and slammed it shut. The notice stuck to the door read:

NO ENTRY — Don't knock.

* * *

Amy sat down on the toilet, listening as a daddy longlegs bashed itself drunkenly against the frosted glass behind her head. She pulled at the flesh on her inner thigh, inspecting the raw, chafed skin, a consequence of her thighs rubbing together as she walked. The thick cream she applied each night was in her suitcase and shame prevented her from asking the doctor for a replacement. The lip balm in her handbag would have to do until the suitcase was returned. The chafing felt like the salt in an already burning wound. Was it not enough that she felt so bad about herself without her own body turning on her? She decided that in a week she would lose enough weight to ease the sore skin — that would be her first reward.

She turned sharply when heavy boots and the blurred shadow of a guard passed the window. It was strange that the clinic had security guards, especially as, somehow, it didn't make her feel any safer.

She was about to flush the chain when she heard music again, the same music she had heard right before she fell to sleep last night. Opening the cubicle door, she stood still, waiting for her ears to attune to the musical notes again. It was coming from a grate in the wall. Amy knelt down on the cold tiled floor and put her ear to the vent, listening to the strange discord of sweet music that echoed from somewhere deep within the clinic.

CHAPTER 15

Hot egg yolk oozed out of the soft bun as Jenny took a ravenous bite, the bright liquid dripping onto the plate in front of her. Jenny had decided to forgo the miniature box of stale cornflakes in her room and treat herself to breakfast at the Lazy Spoon Diner. She was in town to buy supplies for later that night. A torch at the hardware shop a few doors down, and new gloves, she thought, the kind that you could sweep away broken glass with without severing an artery. Next to her plate was a steaming mug of strong coffee; she took tiny urgent sips, burning her tongue, too impatient to wait for it to cool.

She tried to push thoughts of the night ahead out of her mind — it interfered with the enjoyment of the food in front of her. Thoughts of Pine End always sent her heart racing and her stomach turning. She had paid five pounds for this breakfast; it wasn't going to go to waste.

'Refill?'

Jenny looked up at the waitress who was holding out a pot of coffee in her bony hands, the dark liquid rippling from her softly trembling grip. She wore a pink American diner-style uniform, which sagged on her frail frame. Heavy smoking and the oil-filled air of the café had left her with deeply creased skin, causing her red lipstick to run into the lines around her thin mouth. The décor was down to Glen, the taxi-driver-cum-restaurateur extraordinaire. Several years ago he had spent a summer driving a Cadillac down Route 66, and on his return he had stripped down the faded pictures of full English breakfasts and tea and toast and replaced them with rusty old American licence plates and photographs of Doris Day and John Wayne. On the tables, bottles of rancid American mustard gathered dust, rejected in favour of HP sauce when the few customers he had left threatened to boycott him. When trade slowed down in the years following the asylum's closure, he started a sideline driving the minibus taxi, often dropping unsuspecting visitors at the café en route.

Jenny pushed her mug forward and watched as the coffee dribbled from the pot. Before she could thank her, the waitress had wandered off complaining to herself about bunions and tired feet.

The streets outside were deserted; a crisp packet curled and spun down the pavement and disappointed pigeons cooed to each other, no doubt planning a move to somewhere richer in scraps.

Jenny ran her finger around her plate, gathering up the last of the yolk and licking it from her cold skin. When she looked up to the window, she bit down on her fingertip and cried out as a girl stared straight back at her, waving enthusiastically. It took a moment for Jenny to register who it was, but by the time Clara had run around to the door and into the diner and then plonked herself opposite Jenny, she was in no doubt. Clara took off her pink padded coat and squashed it into a tote bag covered with bright shiny badges: a rainbow, a unicorn and other seemingly childish emblems. Jenny looked about her, checking if anyone had seen Clara approach her.

'I thought it was you!' Clara said.

Jenny said nothing and looked down into her coffee cup, pressing her palm against the hot surface until it stung.

'It was so nice to see you the other day. I'm just sorry that Mum—'

'It's fine,' Jenny interjected. She wasn't in the mood for a reprisal.

The thought of her mother so early in the day sent her shaking hand straight to her tobacco tin. She took out all she needed and spread it out in front of her.

'What can I get you?' The waitress had appeared from nowhere, standing like a small hawk over Clara, her small pad and pen ready.

'Oh, I haven't been here before — what do you recommend?' she said brightly.

Jenny smiled, looking up at the crabby waitress, who remained silent.

'The fried egg in a roll is nice,' Jenny offered.

'Isn't it supposed to be American? Do you do pancakes?' She looked up at the waitress, who gave a curt nod. 'Great, I'll have pancakes and a cup of tea, please.'

The waitress disappeared through a plastic curtain and into the kitchen at the back of the diner as Clara turned and called out, 'Do you have maple syrup?'

Jenny smiled in the direction of the counter, as Clara studied the assorted American licence plates nailed to the walls.

'Why do you stay here?' Jenny asked.

'I didn't feel I could just leave, not after Dad died. Mum would be too upset. I . . . sorry, is it weird me talking about this?'

'It's fine. I asked, didn't I?' Jenny lit her roll-up. 'So, what do you do now?'

'I'm at the college in Bettleborough. I'm doing a course in creative writing. I'd like to go to York Uni after and do journalism.'

'You'll definitely have to move, then. There's sod all to report on around here.'

Jenny pulled a novelty ashtray towards her coffee mug, letting the ash scatter over a badly rendered image of Elvis Presley etched into the glass.

'Where do you sell your art?' Clara asked.

The waitress plonked a plate of emaciated English pancakes and a small plastic container of Robertson's strawberry jam down on the table in front of Clara, followed by a mug with tea stains dripping down the sides. Clara opened her mouth to speak to her but then seemed to think better of it.

Jenny puffed on her cigarette and sat back, holding her coffee in the other hand. She watched her sister gently cutting the pancake up, spreading the jam evenly on each piece.

'I'm not really a proper artist yet. I draw cartoons for coins and occasionally sell the odd oil painting at second-rate art fairs.'

'Sounds like a proper artist to me,' said Clara, stuffing pancake into her mouth.

'I suppose, of sorts. Listen, it's nice to see you, but . . .' Jenny made a move to get her things together.

'Don't go, not just yet. I want to chat. I'd like to get to know you better so we can be like proper sisters.'

Jenny exhaled a cloud of smoke towards the window. 'Proper sisters?' she said, unzipping her purse and reaching in for some money.

'Let me get this,' Clara offered.

'It's fine. I'm not a down-and-out, despite what Mum might have told you.'

'Sorry, I didn't mean to—'

'It's fine, I'm kidding. Kind of.'

'Oh, good. Only there's something I want to ask you,' Clara said, looking expectantly at her sister.

'What?'

'I wondered . . . I mean, as part of my coursework I have to write an article of historical interest and . . .' Clara shifted in her seat.

'And?'

'Well, I want to write an article about the old asylum and I . . .'

Jenny shook her head in disbelief. 'No. No way. Some things are best left in the past, Clara, trust me. You don't want a place like that in your head.'

'But—' Clara pleaded.

'I said no.'

Jenny put a fiver on the table, her purse in her bag, and pushed her chair back, the wooden legs dragging on the grey lino.

'Do yourself a favour and write about something else. Old Mother Shipton, Whitby ghosts, how about our dark family history? God knows I've given you enough material there over the years for endless articles.'

Jenny walked away, not wanting to see the disappointment in Clara's face. It was too late to try and form any kind of sisterly bond with her now, but she didn't want to hurt her. It wasn't her fault either that their parents were who they were. She pushed open the heavy café door and a gust of wind blew in, sending the laminated menus scattering across tables and onto the floor. She turned to her sister.

'See you around, Clara.' She let the heavy door swing shut behind her.

CHAPTER 16

Audrey paused mid-sentence, and the room fell quiet. They turned to watch as Amy edged into the relaxation room, trying to remain inconspicuous in her billowing silk dress.

'Sorry, I got distracted, I—'

'Discipline, Amy,' Dr Cavendish interrupted, tapping at her watch.

Amy mouthed an apology and sat down in a high-backed armchair that formed part of a circle where the other women were waiting. Gaynor was slumped back, her eyes studying the cornicing above, as the other women listened intently to Audrey as she continued to speak. 'He said I've forgotten how to enjoy life.' Audrey twisted in her chair, wincing slightly.

The other women studied Audrey, who indeed looked like every last speck of enjoyment had been sucked out of her.

Gaynor looked down from the ceiling. 'Bastard,' she spat.

'He said I've given up and let myself go. Yet he seems younger than ever — parachuting, rock-climbing. Out until all hours with his friends. We're both sixty but he seems so much younger than me.'

'He's right though, isn't he?' Dr Cavendish stated.

'Pardon?' Audrey blew her nose into a cotton hankie.

Dr Cavendish pointed at Audrey's clothes. 'I assume you didn't wear sweat pants and baggy cardigans when you were first dating?'

Audrey looked down to her outfit, tugging at the loose-fitting cardigan. 'Well, no, but I hadn't had kids then, had I?' she said, her tone defensive.

'How old are your children, Audrey?' the doctor asked.

Audrey paused for a moment, staring at the doctor. 'Forty and forty-two.'

Dr Cavendish smiled. 'Then I assume you don't need to worry about spilling apricot puree down your clothes anymore? And baby fat shouldn't still be an issue?'

Caroline and Vicky exchanged wide-eyed looks.

'It shouldn't matter how she looks — he promised to love and cherish her no matter what,' Gaynor protested, an edge of shared experience spiking her voice.

'That's all very well when the colours are beaming through the stained-glass windows and the scent of roses fills the air, Gaynor, but when the reception is over, you still need to keep your wits about you if you want to keep the spark. Like it or not, that's just how it works. When you buy a new car, you accept a little scratch or two as the years go by, but if the engine blows out, it's reasonable to think about exchanging it for a new one.' Dr Cavendish looked around the room. 'Ladies, when we talk about transforming through discipline, it is not just about food. A woman is judged by the way she speaks, the glow of her skin, her age and, yes, the clothes she wears. Dress for the job you want and, I would add, the husband you desire.'

'Jesus Christ,' Gaynor said with a gasp of laughter, 'what year is it again, 1950?'

Dr Cavendish turned her laser focus on Gaynor. 'And why are you here, Gaynor?' she asked gently.

'I want to look good for me, not for a bloke. Get a few of these wrinkles ironed out, lose a couple of pounds.'

'Well, Gaynor, people say that, but what exactly does it mean? Unless you spend your days looking in the mirror from dawn until dusk, what does it matter to you what you look like?'

'I love fashion and make-up and I want to fit in my size-twelve jeans again.'

'Why can't you feel good about yourself as you are now, Gaynor? Why not learn to love those size sixteens? Why not celebrate those little wrinkles as part of you?'

Gaynor's face was reddening as she glared at the doctor. 'Because my arse is the size of a bungalow and my tits are so big they have a separate postcode to my body.'

Vicky spluttered a small laugh, covering up her mouth and looking to the floor when Dr Cavendish turned to her. Even Audrey managed a slight smile.

'I suggest you dig a little deeper, Gaynor — be honest with yourself. Only then can you really succeed.'

Gaynor scowled at her as the doctor continued. 'Let's move on. Caroline?'

'Well, I lost my Gavin—' her eyes almost instantly welled up — 'that's my husband, ten years back now. Remember that train crash in Newcastle?' The women nodded in unison. 'Well, he was on it. He gave me a kiss that morning before he left, took his packed lunch with him and that was that.' Caroline took a deep breath, wiped a tear away with a tissue retrieved from the sleeve of her blouse. 'I never saw him again.'

'That's awful,' said Amy.

'I never bothered for years after about anything. Let myself go. But now I . . . well, *we* . . .' She put a hand out and patted Vicky's arm. 'You see, Vicky lost her husband in the same crash — we want to go travelling, don't we, pet?'

Vicky nodded and continued where Caroline left off. 'We met at a memorial get-together and have been friends ever since. It's time for us to pull ourselves together fit-ness-wise. We want to walk the Great Wall of China for charity, don't we? That's our goal, to tone up and get fit, and I don't know, mebbe get back on the dating scene.'

Warm smiles appeared all round in admiration at their grit and ambition.

'Thank you for sharing that, ladies.' The doctor turned to Amy and smiled gently. 'Last but not least.'

Amy shuffled around in the armchair, the dress getting caught up beneath her bottom and pulling tight around her waist. She desperately wanted to stand up and pull the suffocating material free, but the expectant faces watching her intently paralysed her into further discomfort.

'Erm, I'm Amy.' She reddened. 'Sorry, you know that already.'

Dr Cavendish smiled encouragingly as the other women waited — apart from Gaynor, who looked sulkily towards the floor, her arms crossed and body closed.

'My mum says that everything changed after my dad died. She says I gave up on life before I even left childhood.'

'What happened to your dad, Amy?' Dr Cavendish lent forward, resting her elbows on her elegantly crossed legs.

Amy took a deep breath. 'I woke one morning to the sound of sirens outside my bedroom window. I thought they were for Darren's house — he's my best friend . . . well, only friend really. I thought it was for his gran who lived with him next door. He was always going on about her bad lungs; he said that when she breathed it was like listening to someone trying to play a tune on a cracked recorder. So, I just pulled my favourite Boy George pillow over my ears and tried to go back to sleep. But then I heard the sound of heavy boots running up our stairs and I got up and had a look through the crack in the door.' Amy's voice broke and she paused to take two small breaths before continuing. 'I couldn't tell who it was at first, then Mum started crying out for dad at the top of her voice. Then I called out for him. But it was too late, he'd had a heart attack. Died by the time he got to hospital.'

'You poor love,' Caroline said, her eyes glassy again.

Amy continued, 'When I was little, he'd read to me and buy me treats — fruit gums, French bread and cheese — so now I eat those foods and it brings me comfort for a while. The problem is the gap inside me, in here.' Amy put a fist to her heart. 'It keeps getting wider and I'm trying to fill it with even more food, but the pain . . . well . . . doesn't seem to go away.'

'Eee,' said Vicky, 'you were far too young to go through a loss like that.'

'Nothing wrong with a bit of comfort eating,' said Audrey.

The doctor cut in, 'There is if it ends up making you even more unhappy, Audrey. You've come to the right place, Amy. I will help you eliminate those habits for good, and more — you won't recognise yourself by the time you leave here.'

Amy looked to her with a hopeful smile. 'Thank you.'

'Whatever your reasons for being here, ladies, I can assure you that life will be much easier for you if you achieve what you set out to. It doesn't matter whether it's right or wrong that you are judged by your looks or the way you speak, et cetera, et cetera — you simply are and you have to accept that. You can choose to burn your bra and pitch up at Greenham Common or you can do as I advise and see if that works better for you. Your choice. The door is open for you to leave now if you wish.' Dr Cavendish held her arm out towards the door. The women looked from her hand to the door and then to each other, as if not quite understanding.

'I mean it. I am prepared to tear up your contracts and give you all a full refund and you can leave now. Because for every one of you, there are three more women waiting to take your place. But know this: once you have left, there is no coming back — you only get one chance to transform into the "new, beautiful you".'

Gaynor sat up straight in her seat, her attention now fully on the doctor. A ripple of excitement travelled through Amy at the thought of leaving. Her mum's roast dinners, back in the bosom and comfort of home. The doctor continued, 'Greed and laziness have brought you here.' Gaynor was about to speak, but the doctor shot her a look that shut her up. 'A lack of care in your appearance, your weight and the way you dress — such neglect is a disease, and it will infect every part of your life, from your relationships to your job prospects. You need to get a grip now, before it's too late.'

The women sat wide-eyed like children being told a fairy tale, all hanging on desperately for a happy ending.

'The good news is, *I* have the cure. If you put your faith in me, then I am going to do everything within my power to help you. If we work together then everything you wish for will come true. You don't need to do anything but follow instructions and take the treatments I prescribe for you. So, ladies, are you in?'

A moment's silence was followed by the rising sound of clapping and cheers. Dr Cavendish smiled.

'Now, what do we say?'

Together they shouted, their laughter tinged with frenzy:

'Discipline and diet determine your destiny!'

Dr Cavendish clapped loudly, her hands high in the air, and she motioned for Kim to join her by the chairs. The women all turned, still high on excitement, watching as Kim pushed a small metal trolley across the room. As it came fully into view, their smiles fell away like ash. Six filled syringes were set out in a dull metal tray.

'A little vitamin shot for you all — it'll get your metabolism functioning at optimum. If you could all just bare a shoulder for me, it won't take a second, I promise.'

The women looked furtively at each other. Amy noticed that even Caroline, the most enthusiastic of them all, paled slightly. Without waiting for protestations, Dr Cavendish picked up the first syringe, called them up one by one and began jabbing at their flesh.

There was no way to reach the top of Amy's arm in the dress she had been given; it was zipped up to the nape of her neck. She lifted one arm in the air to hold the material, the other up and behind to pull the zip.

'Kim, could you help Amy?' Dr Cavendish asked.

The other women rubbed their upper arms, looking shell-shocked by the ambush.

Kim took hold of the zip and drew it downwards to the middle of her back, gently easing the sleeve from her shoulder, ensuring it didn't reveal any more of her skin than it should.

'Sharp scratch coming up.'

Amy looked away when she felt the soft grip of the doctor's hand around the flesh of her upper arm. She clenched her teeth as the sting of the needle pierced her skin, a slight burn as the vitamins entered her body. The doctor withdrew the needle and taped a tiny ball of cotton wool to the wound.

'Is everything OK?'

Amy raised her head to see who was being spoken to. Robert was by the door, his eyes moving between Amy and the doctor. Amy gathered up her dress, ensuring her chest was covered.

'Could I speak to you for a moment, Doctor?'

Dr Cavendish turned her attention back to the women and returned the needle to the tray, letting go of Amy's arm.

'Now, ladies, Kim and Tina will be in the exercise room for the next hour for your make-up and tanning talk. Then after lunch it's the afternoon hike. Be at the entrance for two o'clock.' She turned to Amy, 'Please don't be late.'

The doctor marched over to where Robert stood in the half-darkness of the doorway. She passed by him and marched out of the room. He looked over to Amy as Kim zipped up her dress, before turning and following the doctor.

When Jasmine reached the front of the queue, she shook her head at the needle.

'I've a phobia of needles, I can't have one.'

'But it's a required part of the treatment, to help you lose those last stubborn pounds.'

'If I'd have known there were injections I never would have come,' Jasmine pleaded.

Kim looked over towards Tina, who was busy writing on her clipboard, and then back to Jasmine.

'OK then, but you mustn't say you didn't have it, OK?'

Jasmine nodded, her expression one of gratitude. 'I promise.'

Amy watched as Kim pierced the needle into a ball of cotton wool and emptied the contents of the syringe into it, turning the white ball sickly yellow.

CHAPTER 17

Amy sat on her bed, surveying her orange-streaked legs in the grey light. The drying tanning lotion smelled of stale biscuits, and she couldn't think how this was going to improve how she felt about herself. Tina had also shown her a way of highlighting and shading her face with contouring make-up, which she had removed as soon as she got back to her room.

A sudden rapping of knuckles on her bedroom door caused Amy's heart to jump in her chest.

Gaynor poked her head around the door.

'You decent?'

She pushed through regardless, holding out a toothbrush and toothpaste to Amy.

'Lucky I brought some spares, eh?'

Amy took them from her. 'You're a lifesaver, thank you.'

· 'It's very minimalist here, isn't it? I think that's a style statement, don't you?' Gaynor sat on Amy's bed.

'I'm used to more pictures at home,' said Amy.

'What pictures do you have?'

Amy wished she hadn't mentioned the pictures. 'Kittens,' she replied apologetically. It sounded so childish when said out loud.

Gaynor smiled enthusiastically, before her tone darkened. 'Let's just hope your suitcase turns up sooner rather than later.' She looked down at Amy's borrowed dress. 'Now *that's* a style statement!'

'Dr Cavendish told me I'd get an outfit each time I dropped two sizes. She said it's a reward, something to aim for.'

'I wouldn't call *that* a reward,' said Gaynor. 'Why don't you wash the clothes you came in and keep wearing those?'

'Is there a washing machine here?' Amy said, suddenly brightening.

'No, I asked Tina. She said it's broken and we'd have to wash our knickers in the bathroom sink. So much for a luxury stay.'

Gaynor sniffed at Amy's dress and scrunched up her nose, making Amy laugh. She then reached into her pocket and pulled out two Mars bars and held them out in front of Amy's face.

'Surprise!'

Amy edged back from Gaynor as if she had produced a loaded gun.

'Where did you hide those?'

'Hid them in my coat pocket. Thank God the doctor's sidekicks didn't do a body search!'

Amy shook her head. 'Let's not. Let's be good.'

'Oh, come on, we've got a month of raw vegetables and soup, this won't make much difference. We need to ease our way into the diet, don't we?' She put one by Amy and began to unwrap the other and put it to her mouth.

Amy watched as Gaynor's teeth sunk into the creamy nougat and a thread of caramel stretched from her mouth to the bar of chocolate. Gaynor closed her eyes, a faint groan of pleasure leaving her lips. She looked at the other bar on the bed, waiting to be devoured.

'If you don't eat it soon, I'll eat both,' said Gaynor through a mouthful of chocolate.

Amy grabbed the bar and tore the wrapper off, eating it in just a few mouthfuls. The chocolate and caramel fizzed on her tongue as it melted. Each time she swallowed, a sugary feeling of wellness enveloped her like a warm hug. Amy and Gaynor looked at each other, eyes glazed and contented smiles wide.

'Sugar is better than sex,' said Gaynor, screwing the wrapper up in her hand and leaning back on the bed.

Amy's sex life had so far consisted of one short-term relationship, during which she insisted sex took place in the dark. His idea of foreplay had been a quick round of *Dragon Quest* on his PlayStation. Her knowledge of sexual satisfaction was garnered from the pages of *Cosmopolitan* magazine, women whose lives appeared far removed from her own limited one.

'Have you heard that weird music?' said Amy, eager to change the subject.

Gaynor licked her fingers. 'What music?'

'I keep hearing music and I can't work out where it's coming from.'

Gaynor shook her head. 'Not me, but then my ex always said I was as deaf as a doorpost.'

'I think being in a strange place is messing with my head. I'm probably just imagining things.'

When they heard the footsteps in the corridor Gaynor shot upright and froze. They both fell quiet listening to the footsteps get louder and louder until they were outside the room. Amy could see the shadow of two feet in the gap under the door. She held her breath and glared at Gaynor when it looked like she was about to laugh.

After a pause the footsteps continued away down the corridor and eventually faded into silence. They both let out a sigh of relief and Amy allowed herself to giggle quietly, and Gaynor caught it, their laughter rising in volume. It felt ridiculous to be so scared about getting caught eating a bar of chocolate — the only person Amy usually had to answer to was herself.

Gaynor got up from the bed and made her way to the door, turning before she opened it.

'I'm glad you're here, Amy. It's good to have a friend.'

She left the room, closing the door gently. Amy felt a rush of happiness wash over her. The sweet taste that coated her mouth began to dissolve and with it the sense of comfort and love the saccharin drug brought. She got up from the bed and grabbed her handbag, her hands scrabbling around in the bottom and pulling out the bag of chocolate eclairs. She opened the first wrapper and sat down on the floor, her back against the wall. As her teeth disappeared into the soft toffee, her heart sank a little — she wasn't even hungry and yet she kept eating.

CHAPTER 18

'Who the fuck is that supposed to be?'

The drunken man slurred at Jenny, rising from a plastic crate she used for her sitters to perch on in the park. He lurched forward, pointing at the image of three grotesques gurning with distorted faces, still managing to resemble the three men that sat in front of her.

Jenny's hand instinctively reached out for the heavy torch she had brought for later. The drunk man's friend yanked him back and put his hand around his shoulder, holding him still.

'Terry, mate, it's supposed to look like that. It's a caricature.'

Jenny's fingers released the torch.

'Nobody takes the piss out of me,' he spat.

He jabbed his finger at her, his eyes attempting to focus.

Jenny remained still as he snatched the portrait from her lap and tore it in two. He continued to tear at the paper again and again until it was in shreds in his palms. He lifted his hands above her head and let go. The pieces fell like confetti over her as she continued to meet his stare.

'Come on, Terry, let's go,' his more sober friend urged.

The man glared at her for a moment longer before moving away, shaking his head and joining his friends, who put a protective arm around him and led him out of the park, the three of them staggering from side to side.

Jenny gathered the shreds of paper from around her feet and put them in her coat pocket. She sat down on her stool and opened her handbag, taking out a limp sandwich suffocating in cling film, and watched as a lone father knelt by his young son pointing at the ducks.

Just as she bit into the sandwich a young girl sat down in front of her on the crate. Jenny wiped the crumbs from around her mouth and put the rest of the sandwich back in its wrapper.

'Don't make me look too ugly. It's a Christmas present for my boyfriend, just a fun thing really.'

Jenny smiled, relieved and surprised to have another sitter so soon. She needed to keep earning — until she had been back to the asylum she didn't know if she would get the money from Bob.

'It's for my baby as well,' she said, holding her stomach. 'A keepsake for him, for when he's older. Can you put my belly in too?'

Jenny hadn't noticed the neat bump when the girl had sat down, but now it seemed so obvious and huge. Feet and elbows pushing from within, screaming, '*I'm in here!*'

'Of course.' Jenny's hand shook slightly. She held the pen away from the paper until her hand became still again.

For so long she had been protected from the sight of blossoming and bulging pregnant bellies. The hospital was her protective shield from the outside world; happily pregnant women were not a common occurrence in psych hospitals. Of course, there had been plenty of women admitted to her ward post childbirth. Instead of bemoaning sleepless nights and breastfeeding at cake-filled coffee mornings, they sat in high-backed chairs staring into space and wondering where the joy had gone. For so long Jenny had refused to acknowledge their sickness, to have a healthy baby and reject it through misery. It had taken a long time before she had realised that to not understand something was the privilege of not experiencing it.

'It's nice to a have a sit-down to be honest,' said the girl, reaching into her handbag and taking out a packet of Marlboro Lights. 'You want one?'

Jenny reached over, taking a cigarette from the girl. She took her own lighter from her pocket, lighting hers before leaning over and offering the flame to the girl.

'You shouldn't really be smoking, you know,' Jenny said, sitting back on her stool and continuing to draw as she smoked.

'Yeah, yeah,' said the girl, exhaling a cloud of smoke into the cold air.

She pulled her coat around her body, as if hiding the bump from her habit.

'How long have you got to go?' said Jenny, concentrating on the drawing.

'He'll be here in two months,' she smiled.

'You're having a boy?'

'Yep. I wanted a girl, though. Frilly pink dresses and all that, but a boy it is.'

'You can always dress him in frilly pink dresses — who cares?'

The girl scrunched up her nose and shook her head. 'Ha! His dad would lose his shit if I did that. No chance. Ten to one he'll be in a Sheffield United kit before he lets out his first cry. Have you got kids?' the girl asked.

Jenny drew the outlines of the girl's bump onto the paper, transforming her into a cartoon mother-to-be.

'No. No, I haven't,' she said, her face taut.

Jenny tore the sheet of paper from the pad. 'Here you go, I think your boyfriend will be pleased.'

She showed the girl, who smiled widely and threw her burning cigarette to the floor.

'Brilliant!'

'That's five pounds, please,' said Jenny, putting the lid back on the marker pen, her own cigarette hanging from her mouth. She rolled up the caricature and secured it with a thin rubber band and handed it over to the young woman.

The girl took a five-pound note from her purse and gave it to Jenny. She held onto Jenny's hand, the note crushed between their palms.

'I heard those idiots. I'm sorry they were such dicks to you.'

Something caught in Jenny's throat. The kindness felt prickly and awkward; she wanted to swat it away like a wasp.

The girl continued, 'Good for you for sticking up for yourself.'

Jenny smiled, taking her hand away. 'Look after yourself and the little one.'

The young woman smiled before walking away clutching her drawing. Jenny sat back down on the small stool and took a drag of the cigarette, the exhaled smoke expanding with the cold air. When the clouds finally gave way to the weight of the rain, the park began to empty again. The dad picked up his child and ran for his car and dog-walkers called their mutts and reconnected them to their leads. Jenny gathered her papers and pens together, throwing it all in the upturned crate, which she carried along with her small stool and blanket. She reached into her pocket, feeling for the five-pound note. If today was a sign of things to come, she would have to do everything she could to find what Bob needed — he was her only chance to leave this place for good.

CHAPTER 19

Amy made sure she was at the entrance to the clinic twenty minutes before the hike was due to start. No alternative clothes had been delivered to her room as yet, so she had brushed down the clothes she had arrived in, and Gaynor had lent her a pair of her spare trainers, the glitter stripe down the side dull under the grey clouds above.

A security guard was having a cigarette at the corner of the building; he nodded in her direction and she smiled back. When Dr Cavendish and Robert appeared through the trees ahead of her, she had a sudden urge to dart back into the building and hide, but when Dr Cavendish smiled in her direction, she knew it was too late. Amy caught the odour of chemical-tinged smoke before they reached her.

'You're early, Amy. Excellent,' said Dr Cavendish.

Robert smiled briefly, his attention on the entrance. Amy noticed black smudges across his hands and a small piece of bramble caught in his woollen coat.

'Dr Cavendish, I wondered if I could have some fresh clothes, I—'

'Of course, I'll get some clean clothes to you before the morning.' She looked down to Amy's cardigan. 'I'll have

Tina bring you a coat for the hike; you'll catch your death in that cardigan.'

Amy nodded as the two of them turned to go back into the clinic, Dr Cavendish pausing and putting a reassuring hand on Amy's arm.

'Work hard on the hike, Amy. I have high hopes for you.'

Amy watched as they opened the heavy entrance door and walked back into the clinic, their shoes trailing dirt and leaves across the ornate mosaic floor.

She looked up at the clock tower; the giant metal hands that had once been integral in keeping hospital life moving and punctual had long since retired at precisely half past eleven, year unknown. A crow flew down from behind the shelter of the clock face, its lone caw into the grey sky falling on deaf ears as the only reply was its own echo.

The digital numbers on her wristwatch clicked to 2 p.m., and Tina and Kim appeared out of the door like alpine figures exiting a cuckoo clock. They wore matching navy tracksuits zipped up to their chins and waterproof jackets that crinkled like crisp packets in the wind. Each had a pair of sturdy hiking boots and clasped clipboards to their chests. Tina handed Amy a raincoat. Just as the door was about to close it was pushed open again and Robert appeared, wearing thick grey jogging bottoms and a hooded coat that was tight enough to reveal a slight paunch over his bottoms. Amy looked at his hands that hugged a mug of hot coffee; they were scrubbed clean from the dark smudges she had seen earlier and his hair was now neater, no stray strands falling to his face. Gaynor ran over towards the entrance from the grass verge where she and the others were waiting, and smiled up at Robert.

'Give us a sip,' she said, her hands together in prayer.

'No caffeine allowed for you, I'm afraid.' He smiled. Amy noticed a gap in his mouth where a tooth had been extracted.

Gaynor giggled like a girl, her knees dipping a little. 'Spoilsport.'

They all gathered on the patchy grass across from the entrance, the women waiting for instructions.

Kim stepped forward to speak, reading notes from her clipboard like a child reciting a poem at a church service. She looked back to Tina occasionally, who encouraged her with a nod and a thumbs up. Of the two of them, Kim was by far the more approachable. Perhaps it was her newness that made her seem kinder, her need to also fit in until she found her feet. Tina bore all the traits of the experienced sixth-form student looking down to the year sevens as they wandered lonely and clueless around the new school. She didn't make conversation with the women unless asking them to do something or telling them to go somewhere.

'This afternoon, the doctor has asked that you all complete a two-hour hike which will take you around the grounds and through the woods,' Kim said.

She pulled out six sheets of paper from a plastic wallet and handed them to all the women, a childlike map of the grounds with swirly trees and a disproportionately large clinic in the middle of a curving and winding path. When they had all had a chance to study the drawing, Kim continued.

'You will not be permitted back into the clinic until you have collected a tag from each of the points marked on the trail. You will set off at ten-minute intervals in alphabetical order. So, Amy, you're first up.'

Tina stepped forward. 'Until you have all finished, nobody can re-enter the clinic. The desire to let your fellow hikers back in should be enough motivation for you to keep going.'

'See the post over there?' Kim asked Amy. 'That's where you start. Don't forget to collect a tag. Robert will be walking the route from the opposite direction, so he will be on hand to help any stragglers.'

Robert gave them all the thumbs up before heading off in the opposite direction around the back of the clinic.

'Might be worth getting lost,' Gaynor said, nudging Caroline, who didn't take her eyes away from Kim.

Tina gave three short, sharp blasts of a silver whistle. 'Off you go, Amy!' she shouted.

Amy left the others and headed towards the post with a half-jog.

'Good luck, Amy!' shouted Gaynor, the wind swallowing and warping her words.

When Amy reached the starter post she took a tag and put it in her coat pocket. Twenty metres into the woods there was a fork in the track; she looked down at the map but saw nothing about a choice in direction. She had already been going for five minutes, and the idea of returning to ask for directions was too humiliating, so she made her choice and took the left-hand path. The wrong one.

CHAPTER 20

Dr Cavendish watched from her office window as Amy shuffled along towards the woods. There had been another just like her in the last intake of women; the doctor had had high hopes for her until it became clear that laziness had taken too tight a hold. She wouldn't let the same thing happen to Amy. Her work was her passion, and when it didn't go well, it wasn't just the client who was left disappointed.

Robert passed by the window, their acknowledgement of each other formal and brief. She looked back out to the other women, who were in various states of exhaustion as they star-jumped and high-kicked on the scuffed grass across the way. Puffs of vapour expelled from their mouths into the damp air, tired lungs taking panicked breaths. Tina and Kim stood expressionless on the sidelines, each holding a stop-watch and a whistle. Caroline was manically jumping her feet in and out, arms above her head then down again, her face determined in spite of her burning red cheeks. This woman and her friend were a good choice, thought the doctor; they didn't need converting.

Across the way Jasmine took off her sweater, revealing her slim torso. Dr Cavendish scanned her body as she bent herself double and touched her toes with slender fingers. She noticed a small bulge of flesh fall over her legging tops, a slight puckering of cellulite visible on the back of her thighs.

Skinny fat.

That was the difference between models that succeeded and those that didn't. It was nothing that strict adherence to the food, medication and exercise regime wouldn't fix. A model would be an excellent advocate and publicity for her work, and all being well, a straightforward and quick turnaround.

Satisfied that the first exercise session was going to plan, and that the women would be out for at least a couple of hours, Dr Cavendish left her office to begin the day's room sweep.

* * *

She ran her hands over the dozen or so outfits Gaynor had brought that now hung on the back of her door, the gathered evidence of a shopaholic. They were as gaudy as she had expected from a woman that had written on her application that her dream was to sing in nightclubs. Why she had brought a sequinned jacket and high-heeled ankle boots to a clinic in the middle of nowhere was beyond the doctor. She shook her head, laughing to herself. She brushed the sequins back and forth with her fingers, the iridescent emerald discs turning blue as they flipped over with a soothing *shshshshshsh*.

A photograph on the bedside table caught her eye, a picture of Gaynor with a roughly handsome man. She was sitting on the back of his motorbike, her arms clutched possessively around his waist. The doctor picked up the photograph and ran her finger over the frame. She turned it over and saw a letter wedged in the back. She took it out and unfolded the paper.

Dear Gaynor,

Thank you for your letter. I'm sorry for the way things ended. I don't suppose there's a right way really, but still, I didn't want to argue about it. It's really not you. I don't care that you've put on any extra weight — to be honest, I've barely noticed. Becky and me, we go back a long time. What can I say, I've got to give it a go, haven't I? If things don't work out and if you haven't found anyone by then, we can see. But no promises, eh?

Love, Simon

The doctor smiled. *Slimming for herself, indeed.*

* * *

In Jasmine's bedroom Dr Cavendish admired the sleek clothing folded neatly on the chair by the window. She ran her fingers over a cream cashmere jumper, a happy memory soothing her mind. Opening the drawer of the bedside table her eyes brightened at the sight of a large pendant. She lifted it out by its gold chain and held it up by the window, the light shining through the bluish-green gem.

She remembered the precious stones she had seen at her parents' gatherings, flawless diamonds dripping from ears and blood-red rubies lying on alabaster necks. A glittering rainbow of jewels that would one day be hers. She looked back down to the drawer hoping for more gems, but noticing only the familiar shape of a tiny plastic capsule. Dr Cavendish pulled the drawer out sharply, causing more capsules to roll forward. All of the tablets she had prescribed so far for Jasmine to take.

* * *

As the rain began to beat at the window, Dr Cavendish clutched the tablets in her fist, their powdery contents beginning to leak onto her skin. She left the bedroom area and glided down the corridor, one sapphire silk shoe at a time, a feeling of comfort as she moved further and further towards the sound of the crackling music that began to play.

Papa's going to buy you a diamond ring . . .

CHAPTER 21

INCIDENT REPORT
Patient: Jenny Patton

Patient was absent without permission last night. Police called and Jenny was found in Crowthorpe Park drinking cider with other teenagers and brought back to the hospital, parents informed. When she was returned, she was heavily under the influence of drink and abusive to staff and patients alike, eventually vomiting on her bedclothes. Consequently moved to the observation room.

Patient was due to be discharged this morning, but due to incident last night I have recommended that it be delayed pending further assessment and possible section 3 if she resists, to allow us to assess her for up to six months. It is clear to me that this is more than an issue of a wayward child — the girl has a mental weakness that prevents her from behaving in a socially acceptable manner. I would query some kind of personality disorder.

Note: When she was returned, she began to argue with Verity, a long-stay patient who takes it upon herself to 'help' the other patients. When offered a drink by Verity, Jenny pushed it away, causing the hot liquid to soak her dress. Verity unharmed and doesn't wish to take further.

Signed: Matron Dawson
Date: 23 November 1975

CHAPTER 22

The inky tracks morphed into a single smudge on the map, now even less use than when she had started. Amy screwed the paper into a soggy ball and threw it into a cluster of knotted brambles. The ground was muddy, and rotted leaves stuck to the bottom of the borrowed trainers, water now sloshing between her freezing toes. She looked to the ground, panic rising as she realised she was no longer on the track.

The smell of wet soil burned her nostrils, and the sharp rain stung her skin. The woods were dizzying; no matter which direction she looked in, the view was identical, infinite muddy browns and greens melding as far as the eye could see, the falling rain blurring her vision further. If she kept walking in the same direction, she would have to reach the edge of the woods at some point — then her mind flitted to the long minibus drive that first night. The woods had gone on for miles; if the boundary wall was broken at some point, God knows how far she might go. Frustrated tears gathered and fell, invisible beneath the rain that ran down her cheeks.

A crunching of twigs beneath feet caught her attention and she spun around, taking a sharp intake of breath as she spotted two teenagers in the distance, hoodies creating dark shadows that obscured their features.

'Hello?' she called out.

Amy began to run towards them, her shoes sloshing and squeaking. The two figures burst into laughter, manic fits of giggles, before throwing something to the ground and charging off into the distance.

'Please wait! I'm lost.'

Their monkey-like squalls echoed through the tall trees and surrounded Amy. She stumbled over to where they had stood and looked down to the ground, where two aerosol cans lay, fat drops of rain bouncing off the tin. The sound of their cackling voices warped and disappeared and she was left with just the steady drum of the rain for company.

Reaching into her pocket for a hanky, she pulled out the solitary coloured tag she had managed to collect from the first post — a souvenir of her failure. She dropped it and ground it into the dirt with a soaked foot, stamping on it and pushing it further into the mud. As she did, a smoky, chemical-tinged odour wafted past her nostrils and she lifted her head — it was the same burning smell she had caught earlier on the doctor and Robert. She turned her face to the sky, scanning for clues to its origin. When she spotted the green-grey plume rising from behind the trees she ran towards it.

The building was the size of a small house, but without windows, just thin vents high up on its gritty concrete walls. Amy's heart dropped as she took in the heartless grey mass, whose exterior crawled with suckering ivy.

Ignoring the *Danger: Keep Out* sign, she reached for the handle and pushed the dented metal door open. Directly in front of her a burning orange fire roared behind a glass window. The window was part of a large metal incinerator; they had a smaller one at the factory back home. Bright yellow plastic bags lay around the floor, each stuffed full. She strained to read the small black writing.

Danger: Infectious Waste.

Across the floor were scattered papers and items of discarded clothing torn and stained by streaks of dried yellow fluid and other substances that she couldn't and didn't want to identify. Amy noticed a photograph on the floor, a picture of a plain-looking girl with hunched shoulders in a badly fitting swimming suit. She turned the photograph around to see simply:

Benidorm 2000.

A feeling of desperate sadness swept over her at the thought of the asylum patients away from their families. They might have left the asylum eventually, but was the face in front of the camera still smiling when she returned? Did her parents ever get back the carefree child that they had brought up?

'Amy?' A gruff voice twisted through the trees and rain.

Amy spun around, looking into the woods, placing the photograph carefully on a dusty wooden shelf by the door. She stepped out into the rain, her eyes searching for any signs of life between the trees. Finally, she saw someone approaching and held her hand above her eyes, shielding them from the rain so she could get a clearer look. The figure weaved through the trees and ran into a clearing. Her stomach lurched.

'We've had a search party out looking for you,' Robert said, his eyes squinting from the rain.

'Really?'

'Here, you'll catch your death.'

He took off his coat and put it around her shoulders, his fingers gently resting on her upper arms. He closed the door to the building behind her.

'You shouldn't be in there, that's off-limits to clients,' he said. 'It's a health-and-safety risk.'

'Sorry, I didn't know, I—'

'Never mind,' Robert said, taking a packet of Marlboro Lights from his pocket and sheltering under the twisted branches of an ancient tree. He held out the open packet to her, but Amy shook her head. Robert took out a disposable plastic lighter and lit the cigarette. He inhaled and closed his eyes, a slight smile breaking out.

'You're a good girl,' he said, cigarette smoke colliding with the dank air. 'Terrible habit.'

Amy squirmed under the weight of Robert's coat, its material starchy and crisp. She wondered why someone as perfect as the doctor would employ someone that her mum would describe as 'a little rough around the edges', and then she became aware of her own ragged clothes and the damp heat of sweat beneath her arms and quietened her thoughts. He was just trying to do a job.

'Come under here, out of the rain.'

He patted the rough bark of the tree, a small piece coming away in his hand and falling to the mossy floor. She wanted to get back and get changed; even the monstrous silk dress was better than the wet clothes that now sagged from her body. But realising she didn't know how to get back, she reluctantly joined him under the umbrella of branches. It was like moving behind the flow of the waterfall, the shock of dryness that existed just beyond. She looked down to her feet, to Gaynor's trainers. The glitter was dulled with dirt and broken leaves; she'd have to wash them before giving them back.

'Come closer,' he said, pulling her towards him. She could feel the heat of his arm against hers. 'Jesus, I've never known anywhere as wet and cold as Crowthorpe.'

'Have you just moved here? For the job, I mean,' Amy said, conscious of the closeness of his body and a strange, stale odour that caused her breath to catch in her throat.

'I used to live in the area, then I went away for a while.'

He didn't elaborate, so Amy was left to imagine where he had been in the interim. A bricklayer in Spain came to mind, the sun weathering that skin and fraying his edges.

He caught her looking at him and smiled, his lips parched and cracked. 'Good to be back now though, getting to meet all kinds of interesting people.' His face turned to her, his breath coated in nicotine. 'Like you.'

Amy felt a quiver of unease as his eyes rolled up and down her body. She carried on talking, hoping to distract him.

'Did you know the place when it was an asylum?'

He turned his pale blue eyes back to the rain then took a sharp drag on the cigarette and flicked it away, Amy watching it as the stub landed and fizzled out in a puddle beyond the shelter of the tree.

He exhaled the smoke in a long, drawn-out breath. 'Best get you back, hadn't I? Otherwise the doctor will think I've kidnapped you.'

Amy waited for Robert to make a move, but he stood still, his eyes dull and frozen, as if his brain were buffering up. Lost in thought.

'Are you OK?' Amy asked, stepping towards him then thinking better of it.

After a moment he blinked and smiled at her, drawing his sweatshirt hood over his hair and leaving the shelter of the tree. Amy followed him as he pushed on ahead. He stomped through the bracken, pushing thorny branches out of the way with his bare hands. When she finally spotted the clock tower through the darkening sky, she felt a wave of relief wash over her.

As the entrance came into view, she caught sight of the other women sitting in the porchway. They were shivering and holding themselves in a tight embrace. Remembering the rule about none being admitted back in until all were back, she had a sudden urge to keep walking and never come back. Instead, she met her fellow slimmers in the porch, just as the lock to the door rotated and clicked and the door opened again, letting the shivering women back inside.

CHAPTER 23

Jenny slammed the car door shut, watching as Bob drove off back down the hill. It was too risky for him to take her all the way to the clinic; he was a well-known character in the town, and his personal number plate A1 BOB wasn't exactly inconspicuous. Jenny looked down through the mist and into the distance towards Crowthorpe. The last time she had stood here she had run towards the bright and plentiful lights, not knowing what opportunities lay ahead. Now the town sat like a redundant oasis in miles of barren moorland, dying one broken streetlight at a time.

It was another two miles up the hill until the hospital, time that Jenny was glad to have to prepare herself for the night ahead. Finding any information on the clinic had been difficult; all she had to go on was the scant knowledge Bob had garnered from whispered grumbles between cheap-suited men at Freemason gatherings, and the sales pat of the clinic brochure.

The clinic was run by a doctor from a wealthy family, who appeared to have come from nowhere to set up her weight loss clinic. It had been going for almost a year and had so far been a success, but little was known about the programme or the doctor herself. A bloke at the council had

119

met her and relayed to Bob that she was a 'looker' and that he 'wouldn't kick her out of bed' — details that made Jenny shudder, her allegiance laying squarely with the doctor.

Jenny wasn't optimistic about finding anything wildly incriminating; it all sounded pretty benign to her. An operation feeding on the insecurities of wealthy women who could afford to pay to be deprived of food for weeks on end. Her only hope was that parts of the building itself were in a state of disrepair and that that would be enough for Bob to hand over the reward.

A set of headlights flickered through the pine trees ahead of her, and Jenny jumped back from the road and crouched behind a crumbling dry-stone wall that split the hilly land. A small white van made its way down and past her, *Cotterill Security Solutions* painted on the side. When it had disappeared down the hill Jenny continued her trek. She was dressed all in black: trousers, turtleneck and heavy boots. She felt like a Luc Besson heroine, but without elaborate weapons or a Hollywood script to write her a happy ending.

The rain had drizzled to nothing, making it easier to hear through the trees, but also, she reasoned, easier to *be* heard. Following the winding road was risky, but it meant she wouldn't get lost. All roads seemed to lead back to Pine End for Jenny; this one was a guaranteed route. Her legs ached as she moved further up the hill; she had never walked up here before, it would be madness to. She remembered the shuttlebus that used to transport patients and staff back and forth from the hospital to the town. She would sneak onto the bus with the stolen staff pass she had borrowed from one of the orderlies. The punishment from Matron would be worse with the added misdemeanour, but it was worth every single needle of sedation she received, and every night spent in isolation, just to be alone with him.

Bob had given her a week to get everything he needed, though she imagined she'd have all that there was to find by the end of the night. The sooner she could get in and out the better. He'd provided a 'wish list' for her, a criminal scavenger hunt: broken plaster, inadequate safety rails, boarded-up windows, broken glass and copies of any paperwork she could get her hands on. He was convinced the doctor had won the contract through corrupt means, an instance of the pot calling the kettle black if ever there was one.

Bob seemed to think that because Jenny had been in a psychiatric hospital, she was a criminal mastermind. There was a benefit to the unearned reputation she seemed to have though, and that was the sense of unease others felt around her. Most ex-patients would try to put misconceptions right, to prove themselves good, but Jenny used it to keep the world at bay. She wore her otherness with pride.

As she left the road and made her way round the final bend, she felt her heart begin to race as a fear writhed deep inside of her. There was nobody to make her stay this time, there would be no bars on windows or locked doors, and the worst that could happen was a ticking-off for trespassing. Yet still it felt like the asylum itself was luring her back inside, playing a trick and waiting to catch her in its tangled web.

When she caught sight of the tall iron gates, it was as if she were seeing them for the first time again. She managed to drag herself away from the imposing entrance, stumbling towards the perimeter wall. Her heart raced and her head pounded. When she was far enough away from the gate not to be spotted, she paused and took a ready-made roll-up out of her pocket and lit it, her small hand trembling in the darkness.

When enough nicotine had coursed through her body, she straightened the backpack on her shoulders and continued to move along the perimeter wall. She counted the bricks in order to focus her mind on something else — one, two, three, four, five and so on — until she began to recognise the familiar scrawled graffiti on the brick walls. Poems, rants and declarations of love. Then she saw it and stopped, running her fingers over the words, the letters crudely gouged into the brick with broken glass. Their little joke, their private world.

D + J MAD IN LOVE.

CHAPTER 24

NHS Pine End Asylum — Hospital for Mental and Nervous Disorders

OBSERVATION SHEET
Date: 13 April 1984
Patient: Jenny Patton

Notes: Patient has moved from hourly to two-hourly obser-
vations as her behaviour continues to improve.
8 a.m. — Patient eating breakfast in the dining room. Her
appetite has improved in recent weeks.
10 a.m. — Patient playing cards with Danny and Andrew
in the main hall.
12 p.m. — Lunch, eating well. Taking medication without
any issues.
2 p.m. — Walking in grounds with Danny, seen hand in
hand.
4 p.m. — Matron has spoken to patient, advises against
romantic involvement during her stay/treatment. Danny has
also been warned against patient-to-patient relationships.
6 p.m. — Patient didn't eat dinner and has refused evening
meds.

8 p.m. — Patient absent from the ward, found in the grounds with Danny, returns of own free will.
10 p.m. — Patient sedated and sleeping in isolation room.
12 a.m. — Patient sleeping.

CHAPTER 25

With their bodies still cold from the winter hike, made worse by Amy's late return, the women had hoped for something that would warm their chilled bones. Instead, they stared down at a dinner of raw cabbage, half a tomato and an egg-cup full of grated carrot coated in a vinegary liquid. As usual, the meal was served with an assortment of pills that were swallowed dutifully, with the promise they would promote rejuvenation and they would all shed their dull skin like insects moulting to become something new.

'We ate food like this at the retreat we went to in the Lakes, didn't we, Vicky?' Caroline said, her weak voice belying the enthusiasm she was trying to spread.

Vicky nodded but said nothing, just looked down at the cabbage like it was an unwanted guest at a party. She reached out to the radiator on the wall, dragging her hand away slowly. 'If we could just have the heat turned up a bit I wouldn't mind.' She pulled her cardigan tightly round her.

'I'm used to this kind of food, but it's not for every-body,' Caroline continued. 'I was a vegetarian for six months in 1985, but it was the wind that did for it. I thought my Gavin was going to leave me.' She chuckled, but the laughter didn't catch and fizzled away.

With her back to Caroline, Gaynor raised her eyebrows and crossed her eyes. Amy gulped back a laugh and tried to focus on what Caroline was saying despite Gaynor's attempts to draw her attention away. Jasmine looked like she might cry or pass out as a concerned Audrey offered to give her a slice of her tomato in return for finishing her cabbage. There were not only rules on what not to eat, but also that you had to finish all the food on your plate, regardless of whether you liked it or not.

There was no plate in front of Amy, not even a pot of hallowed pills. She looked around the other tables but there wasn't a spare. If she didn't have something soon, she thought she might be sick.

Anya stomped into the dining room, carrying a large jug of iced water with fat quarters of lemon bobbing about. Audrey cowered away from her as she silently filled her tumbler, a wedge of lemon threatening to escape over the lip of the jug. The sound of ice cubes clinking against glass was the only sound in this deflated gathering. As Anya leaned across her, Amy noticed the thin gold wedding ring on Anya's finger and wondered where her husband was now. She smiled up at her, feeling sorry for the silent slave of the clinic, but Anya didn't see it, instead keeping her focus on the job in hand.

'Thank you,' said Amy, taking a sip.

'I feel sick,' moaned Jasmine, holding her stomach.

'You shouldn't even be here,' soothed Audrey. 'There's barely anything of you to lose and it's not as if you need the beauty side of this either; you're barely out of the womb.'

'Tell that to my agent,' she said in a wisp of breath.

Audrey shook her head and moved two slices of tomato from her plate to Jasmine's.

'Don't let her see you do that,' Caroline warned.

The bell in the hall rang out, followed by the clipping heels of Dr Cavendish. Amy felt her stomach lurch a little; she hadn't seen Dr Cavendish since the hike, and she was certain that her poor performance would be mentioned.

The atmosphere in the dining room shifted. The women quietened and nervously played with their cutlery, the metal clattering clumsily against the side of the porcelain plates.

'Good evening, all,' the doctor said brightly. 'I trust you're all feeling invigorated after your hike?' She smiled at each woman, waiting for each to nod back. 'Excellent. I hear you were waiting for a little while in the cold?'

Amy shrunk down in her chair. Dr Cavendish walked slowly over to her and put a reassuring hand on her shoulder.

'It's all part of the programme, Amy. We are a team and we support each other. That shivering will have burned a few extra calories.'

The doctor's hand was cold and uneasy on her shoulder, but Amy felt relief not to be singled out for her failure to collect the tags.

Jasmine put her hand in the air like a school child.

'Yes, Jasmine.'

'Is there anything else we can have for dinner? Only, I don't like cabbage.'

Dr Cavendish narrowed her eyes, a faint smile on her lips.

'Have a try, Jasmine. Our taste buds are too used to junk foods now; we are forgetting what real food tastes like. We must appreciate each bite of food, be mindful and perhaps . . . pray?'

There was a ripple of polite laughter that died to silence when the women looked up at Dr Cavendish, her hands together in prayer, eyes closed. Gaynor looked with alarm at Amy, but all apart from Audrey, who was already praying, reluctantly joined the doctor and bowed their heads, hands awkwardly clasped together. It was one thing to offend God, but the doctor was another kettle of fish altogether.

'Thank you, God, for our food. Please let these ladies appreciate each mouthful and the work that has brought it to our table. From the farmer to the shopkeeper. Thank you for bringing these women to us and giving me the opportunity to help them. Amen.'

Six 'amens' echoed around the room as the women peeked up to make sure it was OK to drop their hands.

'Wonderful. Now, enjoy your dinner with the gratitude it deserves.'

There was a clatter of cutlery and a soft hum of conversation as the women tucked into the meagre fare.

Amy held her hand up. 'Sorry, Dr Cavendish, I think Anya's forgotten my food.'

Dr Cavendish turned her attention to Amy, her eyes fixed on her as if she was surprised to hear her speak.

'I think you've had quite enough calories already, Amy, haven't you?'

The room fell silent and all eyes turned to Amy. Her cheeks burned as she tried to make sense of what the doctor was saying, held in the spotlight of attention from the other women.

'I haven't really, I don't think, I—'

She stopped speaking when Dr Cavendish produced an empty Mars bar wrapper from her jacket pocket and pushed it slowly across the table towards her.

'Come with me to my office, Amy, we need to have a talk.'

CHAPTER 26

Brambles clawed at the decaying plywood board, creating a stranglehold across the makeshift doorway, binding it tight to the crumbling brick wall either side. It had been Danny's idea, their own private place to enter and leave the grounds, as and when they wished. In reality it had been not when they wished, but when they were not being observed — the distraction of a psychotic patient being manhandled to the ground by an army of male orderlies or the novelty of a new patient arriving.

Jenny shone her torch around the board, pushing it with her hand, and found it was stuck tight. She took her backpack from her shoulder and unzipped it, taking her art knife out. She tugged at the arcing shoots with the blade, cutting the spiky stems one by one until the plywood began to ease. Then she lifted her foot and kicked out, pushing the rotting wood to a forty-five-degree angle. She cut the last thick stem and pulled at it, the thorns piercing her skin through her woollen gloves. Shaking her hand, she took a glove off and removed a tiny spear from her icy skin.

The plywood creaked underfoot as she stepped tentatively back into the grounds again, jumping back as the slick fur of a rat scuttled past her feet, disappearing into a pile of discarded metal and wood. Jenny steadied her breath before leaning the thin wood back against the wall, covering her tracks just like the old days.

The night air was damp, and Jenny couldn't be sure if the shivering was because of the cold or because of her proximity to Pine End. At least entering the hospital grounds from this spot gave her a kind of control — she was reappearing on her own terms. It was almost unrecognisable from when she had stood there all those years ago. Nature left undisturbed by trampling feet had allowed spiking shrubs to sprout and fill the space between the sprawling trees, and bracken and brambles had crept like thick fog along the moss-covered dirt, making the old pathway impossible to see.

The woods gradually began to clear a little as Jenny moved towards the clinic, her skin prickling with every step forward she took. As the space became more exposed, she began to move quickly from tree to tree, making sure that she wasn't seen by the security guards. Bob had found out through his contacts that the place was patrolled to keep trespassers out. Her foot kicked a discarded metal sign and she froze, waiting for the small echo of shoe on metal to subside. Something fluttered above her head and a bird flew out of the trees, its wings flapping so violently that leaves broke away and floated down onto her. She freed a brown, crinkled leaf from her hair and swept splinters of bark from her shoulders. Then she noticed it, the place she had spent so many hours.

The wooden bench was still there, almost. Sitting in the centre of the small walled garden on the edge of the woods, just out of view of the hospital. A giant patch of land where patients were never truly alone, but could go to think, smoke and pretend they were anywhere else but Pine End. The uncared-for plants that had once been shaped and trimmed were now overgrown and almost unrecognisable as they pushed against the stone crosses, causing them to tip at angles; tea lights long burnt out and rusted were scattered beneath the thorny mass of weeds, along with the skins of rotted soft toys left for lost children long after they had died.

A wooden slat was missing from the bench, and the backrest was green with moss that had eaten into the damp wood. Using the side of her fist Jenny rubbed at the small brass plate on the back of the seat, wiping away the dirt and slime until the inscription was legible once more.

In memory of all those that never left.

The metal nails creaked against the wood as she sat down, taking a moment to remember him.

There was no chance for Jenny to scream when the rough hand clasped around her mouth and pulled her backwards from the bench. The rotten wooden seat fell to the ground with her as she was carried off back into the woods, her boots kicking and pushing at the dirt until she disappeared out of sight.

CHAPTER 27

Amy and Dr Cavendish both looked down at the empty chocolate wrappers piled on the desk. Amy shuffled around on her chair, unable to get comfortable. She could feel her pulse beating in her neck as she silently counted the chocolate eclair wrappers.

'Do you not trust me, Amy?'

'Sorry?' Amy looked up from the fourteenth wrapper to the doctor.

'I can only assume that you believe you know the secret to a beautiful new you better than I do.'

'No, of course not, I just . . .'

'Just . . . ?'

'I couldn't help it. Once I'd started it was like I had to eat them all. I couldn't stop. Even when I felt sick, I just kept on eating, trying to make myself feel better.'

'What a greedy guts you are,' she chided.

Amy looked down to her slippered feet as they tapped nervously at the floor.

'It makes me feel better for a bit. It . . . it's comfort.'

Dr Cavendish sneered. 'There is no comfort to be found in the bottom of a sweet packet, Amy. How did you sneak it all in? You don't have a suitcase.'

Amy thought about Gaynor's face, alive with excitement and mischief when she'd come into her room earlier that day. Of all the women at the clinic she had chosen Amy to join her in the illicit fun; for once she wasn't the last to be picked.

She closed her eyes, her face down. 'I had them in my handbag, the eclairs and the Mars bars.'

Dr Cavendish observed her for a moment before speaking. 'Nobody else had any?'

'No, it was just me.'

The doctor leaned over the desk, her hands gripping the sides of the table.

'Are you sure?'

Amy gulped and looked up; she felt her face redden as it always did when she was accused of something, guilty or not.

'Yes. It was just me.'

The doctor's eyes narrowed, then she nodded and sighed, pacing slowly behind her desk.

'There are women that would kill to be in your place, Amy. I can't tell you how many applications I had for this intake, and I picked you. It's not too late for one of those ladies to take your spot.'

Amy pictured her mum and stepdad's faces if she was thrown out of the clinic in the first week. All their hard-earned, non-refundable money lost, and for what? Worse still, she'd have to face the other people at the factory; she'd be the canteen joke for months.

You'll never guess what? She only lasted a day — got caught stuffing herself with chocolate! There's really no hope for her! Hide away in your bedroom, Amy!

'I don't want to replace you, I want to help you, Amy, but you have to work with me.'

Amy nodded eagerly, grasping at the hope of a second chance.

'I will, I'm sorry I—'

Dr Cavendish put her finger to her lips. 'Actions, not words, Amy.'

Amy retreated back into the chair, wishing that the pile of chocolate wrappers between them would disappear. Her shame in foil.

'I see you in someone I once knew.'

'Really?' Amy said, her eyes lifting to meet the doctor's.

'She had everything—' she let out a sigh — 'and then greed took hold. She gorged herself silly and before she knew it, she was all alone.'

Amy shifted in her seat.

'Do you want to leave here having achieved nothing?'

Amy wasn't sure if she should speak; she was about to, then—

'No, of course you don't. Well, I can help you with that. I know how to do it and I see you as my . . . well . . . my protégé.'

'Me?'

'Do as I say, Amy, and in six months you will look like me, you'll be wearing clothes like these.' She ran the tips of her fingers down the tailored suit, resting on her thighs.

Dr Cavendish took a key from the large chain in her pocket and unlocked a metal cabinet behind her desk. Inside there were numerous bottles and boxes. Dr Cavendish tapped her fingers along the shelf until she came to a small white bottle. She tipped it into the palm of her hand and a pile of tiny tablets tumbled out. She handed them to Amy, along with a plastic cup of water she poured from a jug on her desk.

'Take these. Luckily we can purge away some of the damage all of that sinful food has done.'

Amy looked down into the pot at the tiny oval tablets and back up to Dr Cavendish.

'Or I can call your parents to arrange your ticket home, if you wish?'

Amy tipped the tablets into the palm of her hand and threw them into her mouth as far back as she could, before swilling down the cup of water. When the cup of water was

133

empty, she put it back on the doctor's desk, the plastic cup crumpling slightly.

'Very good, Amy. Now, I want you to go back to your room and rest. You might feel a little sick for a while, a slight stomach ache.' Dr Cavendish opened the top drawer in her desk and took out a box of paracetamol.

Amy shook her head. 'I don't need more tablets. I'll be fine, honestly.'

Dr Cavendish put the box back in the drawer and placed her hands firmly on Amy's shoulder's.

'I can see how determined you are to succeed, Amy, how much you want this to work. If you let me, I'll make the perfect woman of you.'

'I do,' said Amy, nodding eagerly.

'I trust I don't have to search your room for any more contraband items, do I?' She gave Amy a playful smile.

Amy shook her head, a sheepish look on her face.

'Excellent. Well, off you go. I'll see you at breakfast tomorrow.'

Dr Cavendish walked over to her office door and opened it, signalling Amy was free to leave. Amy noticed the time on a clock on the wall: it was 8 p.m. and she was already exhausted.

CHAPTER 28

The stench of creosote and dirt stung Jenny's nostrils as she sat trembling in the darkness with her back against a wall, her knees clutched tightly to her chest. The shadow of a man moved around her, throwing dark shapes against the stone walls. He was searching for something in tubs and boxes that were scattered around the floor, nails and screwdrivers clattering against each other.

A knife?

He pulled something from a box and Jenny heard the scraping of a match against sandpaper and saw a tiny orange flame move down to ignite a gas lamp. The man blew out the match and turned a small wheel on the lamp, and suddenly his face came into view. She took a sharp intake of breath, pushing her back further into the wall.

His eyes fixed on her. The dimness of the shed gave his skin a rough, mottled look. He had unkempt dark blond hair, a wiry beard and hazel eyes. He looked . . .

'Andrew?' Jenny said, squinting her eyes in the low light. 'Is that you?'

She edged away from the wall and pushed herself onto her knees, her face closer to his. He watched her as the pieces began to slot into place. The last time she had seen him was five years ago, as they left the asylum. She had never expected to see him again.

'What are you doing trespassing on my land, Toddler?'

Toddler was the name her fellow patient had bestowed on her after seeing the teddy bear she kept on her bed throughout her stay at Pine End. Jenny lurched forward into Andrew's strong arms, and they drew protectively around her. She buried her face into his jumper; he smelt of smoky fires and industrial soap, the orange liquid kind the hospital used to provide.

She looked up into his face, so many questions to ask. 'What are you doing here? How have you been?' Jenny looked around the room, still not able to identify where they were. 'I thought you were going home to your parents' in Wales?'

Andrew shrugged. 'Couldn't settle, could I? Too used to it here.' He flicked his head back in the direction of the clinic. 'Better the devil you know. What about you? Have you come back for old times' sake?'

'I'm only here for a bit,' she said. 'Something I need to do.'

He raised an eyebrow. 'What something?'

'I can't say, not yet.'

The less people knew, the better.

'You aren't thinking of going into the clinic, are you?' he warned. 'I'd steer clear if I were you.'

'Why? It's just a bunch of overweight women chewing on lettuce, isn't it?'

'It's not the paying guests you need to be careful of. It's the woman that runs it.'

'The doctor?'

'I've never seen her, but I know the security guards are scared half to death of her. A bit of a ball-breaker, by all accounts.'

'Remind you of anyone?'

'Matron — yep, this place seems to attract them.'

Jenny laughed. 'This diet doctor can't be as bad as Matron, nobody could.'

'I dunno, just be careful. I reckon if she catches you, you'll be in serious trouble. She's the type to call the cops on you, just to set an example to anyone else trying to break in.'

'I'm not going to get caught.'

His face broke into a gentle smile. 'If I hadn't grabbed you before, you'd be on your way to the nick now for trespassing. Didn't you see the guard heading your way?'

Jenny thought for a moment, embarrassed at her near failure. 'How did you know it was me?'

'Saw you walking through the woods. You haven't changed at all.'

She smiled. 'You either. Well . . . except for all this.' She rubbed at his bearded chin. 'What would Matron say, you unshaven slob.'

His face darkened. 'I was glad when I read she'd died. By all accounts, it was a painful end. Can't say I'm sorry about that.' His eyes studied her as if waiting for a reaction.

Jenny looked down to the burning flame, images of the final night flashing through her mind. The darkness of the hall, the words Matron spat at her over and over.

You're nothing. It was all for the best.

Her attention snapped back to Andrew when he spoke. 'It's good to see you again, Jenny.'

Jenny squeezed his hands in hers, smiling. 'It's good to see you too,' she said. 'I wish I could stay longer.'

'You really shouldn't go back there,' Andrew said, lighting a cigarette and passing it to Jenny, like they always did.

'I have to,' she replied. 'I'll be more careful now, I promise.'

'Well, I hope whatever you're doing is worth it. If you need anything at all, just shout. I would come with you, but if I get caught I'll lose this little palace.' He turned to the room.

'It's OK. I don't want you to risk getting into trouble.'

Jenny looked over to the shadow of a mattress and sleeping bag in the corner.

'How come the guards haven't thrown you out? They must know you're here by now.'

'Almost did once, then he noticed my regiment tattoo. The owner of the security firm is ex-army and took pity on me. As long as I stay away from the clinic, they leave me alone. But they wouldn't give you the same liberty.'

Andrew had arrived at Pine End seven years after Jenny. A soldier in the Falklands War, his celebrated return to Britain had been short. Two months after the Union Jack bunting was taken down, his father had returned home early from work to find his son hanging limply from a tree in their garden, barely alive. Had he stayed for the usual after-work drinks, it would have been too late.

The moment he had appeared on the ward Jenny had taken Andrew under her broken wing, and from then on the two patients had looked out for each other as much as they knew how. When the hospital closed and the patients all left, they scattered like exploded pellets from a shotgun cartridge, all contacts lost. All on their own again.

Jenny got to her feet and put her rucksack back on.

'Just be careful, Jen. That place, I reckon it's just as evil as it always was. I hear things at night — shouting and strange music. People moving about the woods. Something odd about the place, like it never sleeps.'

'All that ECT fried your brain,' Jenny said, putting a palm on each of Andrew's temples and making a ꙅꙅꙅꙅꙅꙅꙅ noise.

Andrew squirmed away, shaking his head. 'You always were a nutter.'

'Not until I came here,' she said. 'That's when I really went doolally.'

'Come and see me again, let me know if I can help. I can tell you which guards will be on when, that kind of thing, and if you get in trouble just find your way back here, promise?'

Jenny reached forward and hugged her friend again. 'Promise. I'll come see you soon.'

Andrew put his hand to his forehead, saluting her. Jenny closed the door and left, heading back out towards the old asylum, this time without stopping.

CHAPTER 29

'You OK, Amy?' Gaynor said, meeting Amy in the corridor. 'You look a bit peaky.'

'Fine . . . just, my stomach feels a bit . . .' A deep gurgling sound rose inside her, like a drain clearing. 'I'm just going to have a lie down.'

'That's probably a good idea,' said Gaynor, wide eyes fixed on Amy's stomach as the rumbling crescendoed.

Anya came out of the kitchen door carrying a tray of empty glasses towards the dining room — when she saw Amy she stopped.

'You don't look well.'

Gaynor sneered at Anya. 'She'll be fine, I'm looking after her.'

Anya didn't seem to understand what Gaynor had said. She put the tray on the floor and stepped forward, placing her heavy palm against Amy's forehead.

'Is warm, maybe lie down.'

'All right, Sherlock, back to cutting carrots,' Gaynor sniggered, her voice low and distorted, a cruel attempt to prevent Anya from understanding her.

Amy felt a sudden wave of heat rise from her toes all the way to the top of her head and she stumbled towards the wall, catching herself before she fell.

'I need to get to my room.'

Gaynor and Anya's faces began to blur, a kaleidoscope of eyes and mouths dancing around. Gaynor took Amy by the arm and, leading her away from Anya, leaned in towards Amy, her hot breath reeking of cigarette smoke.

'Look, I'm really sorry about earlier; I hope you didn't get into too much trouble. I should have held my hands up too, taken some of the blame. My Mars bars, after all.'

Amy pushed through the bedroom door. 'It's fine, honestly. I'll be OK now, you go.'

'Looks like you should take more water with your gin, eh?' Gaynor chirped, her expression turning to a frown as Amy's stomach roared again.

Amy pushed her out of the door and closed it behind her. She was already lifting her dress as she clamoured towards the bathroom door. She pulled down her pants and sat on the toilet, just in time for all twenty chocolate eclairs and the Mars bar to exit her bowels, along with what felt like everything else she had eaten in the past ten years.

* * *

There was no way of knowing what time it was when Amy opened her eyes again. It was still dark outside. She could have been asleep an hour, or six. Her mouth felt parched; she looked through the darkness to the empty glass on her bedside table. The tablet they were required to take each night was still there; in her desperation she must have forgotten it and just drank the water. She scrambled between the tissues on her bedside table and lifted up her watch. It was only 10 p.m.

She had been back and forth to the toilet for a good hour before it felt safe to lie down on the bed again. Somehow, she had managed to have the foresight to open the window in her room before she fell asleep, releasing the stench of bodily fluids out and the fresh air in. Rain blew gently in through the open window, small pools gathering on the windowsill.

In the bathroom she was reminded by a small sign over the sink:

Tap water not for drinking.

After the night she had had, she was not about to risk breaking this rule, no matter how thirsty she was. There was a faint sound of pots and pans being moved around somewhere down the corridor — Anya must still be in the kitchen.

Amy had never been drunk — she had never even been invited to a party where she could get drunk — but she imagined this was what a hangover felt like. Her head pounded and she felt woozy; it must have been the tablets Dr Cavendish gave her. No pain, no gain. The sin had quite literally been flushed out of her.

The main lights had been turned off, and the corridor was in darkness, with just the drab orange glow of the lights in the grounds creeping through the windows. Amy tiptoed along, pausing outside Gaynor's bedroom and putting her ear to the door. When she heard a sailor-like snore vibrating through the wooden door, she continued on towards the kitchen.

The dining room was in darkness; she could just make out the fresh tablecloths laid out for breakfast. Each place setting had an empty glass waiting to be filled with some strange vegetable concoction. Amy was yet to be excited by any of the food that was offered at the Beautiful You Clinic — if the plan was to put them off eating, the doctor was doing a good job.

When she reached the kitchen door she hesitated as she read the sign again.

NO ENTRY — Don't knock.

Assuming that was there to stop Anya being disturbed during the daytime when she was busy preparing food, Amy ignored it and gently knocked. She waited for a moment, and when there was no answer, she pushed the door open. Anya wasn't there and it looked closed for the night; the industrial-sized sink shone in the moonlight and the sides were clear, other than a few upturned beakers on the draining board.

141

The kitchen was washed in the purple-white glow of an electric fly zapper that was screwed into the wall above the sink. A moth sizzled and buzzed above her as it flew, Icarus-like, into the light. The heavy kitchen door clicked shut behind her, too quickly for her to cushion the sound. She paused, listening to see if the noise disturbed anyone. After getting caught out with the chocolate, she felt her card was marked and didn't want to risk further trouble by being found trespassing in rooms she wasn't supposed to be in.

She found a glass tumbler in a cupboard and took it out. The water whooshed from the tap, spraying her hands and clothes. Amy rushed to turn the tap off before her glass overflowed. She drank half of the glass and turned, noticing the giant refrigerator from the corner of her eye. Putting the glass carefully down, she walked over to it, her hand gingerly reaching for the long handle that ran vertically down the door.

It felt like peering into a stranger's window — she knew she shouldn't, but . . . Her whole body illuminated as the fridge light clicked on, the gentle whir of electricity humming softly from within. There was a mountain of carrots, their emerald-green ferny tops still attached and splayed out like feathers, and huge stacks of fresh green cucumbers; the removal of one would topple all. There was enough fruit and vegetables to fulfil an army's five-a-day requirement. Amy reached out and touched the gnarly chunks of ginger, feeling the dry scars with her fingers. There were no drinks in the fridge, just small bottles of medicinal-looking fluid. Each had a label with an unreadable name across it. She hadn't expected cans of Lilt and Fanta, but her mouth watered for a simple glass of orange juice, from concentrate or not.

The fridge door was almost closed when she noticed a row of plastic containers on the bottom shelf. Opening the door again she crouched down and reached her hand in, pulling towards her a sealed plastic tub, liquid sloshing about inside. Something round and dark bobbed about and hit the sides of the tub with a dull thud. Clamping her fingertips over the lid she began to pull, when the sound of someone crying out stopped her. She waited in the silence, and there it was again — a wailing sound. She walked over to the small window and leaned towards it, but the crying got quieter. Amy walked the perimeter of the kitchen, stopping every now and then, moving a step back or forward as she played hotter and colder with an unknown voice. When she reached the part of the kitchen that it was loudest, she realised it was not coming from the ground floor, or the floor above. The cries were coming from beneath her feet.

Raised voices approached the kitchen and she hurriedly pushed the tub back into the fridge, making sure it was as she had found it, and closed the door. She tiptoed across the kitchen and listened at the door, her body trembling. It was impossible to understand what they were saying, but she recognised the voices of Kim and Tina, and they were arguing. Amy pulled the door slightly ajar and watched as Kim stormed into their shared room, leaving Tina alone in the corridor. The next thing Amy heard sounded like the whirr of a lift coming to a stop in the distance, and a heavy door creaking open.

Amy watched as Dr Cavendish took hold of Tina's shoulder and spun her round. By the look on Tina's face Amy could assume she was being told off for something. Tina began to cry and ran back to her room, the doctor turning sharply and walking towards the kitchen. Amy closed the kitchen door, ensuring it didn't make a sound, and then waited in the half-light as the footsteps approached. They paused outside the door and Amy felt as though she could feel Dr Cavendish's breath on the other side. She held her breath in, her chest puffed and tight. When the footsteps continued and she heard the front door open and close, she released the breath.

By the time she got back to her room she was shaking so much that no matter how much she tried, she couldn't calm down, adrenaline and exertion coursing through her body. She sat down on the bed and leaned forward, her hands planted firmly on her knees, trying to slow her breathing. When she looked up, the relief at being safely back in her room dissolved like sugar in hot tea as she realised that all the trouble she had gone to was for nothing. She had left the illicit, and much-needed, glass of water in the kitchen.

CHAPTER 30

OBSERVATION SHEET
Date: Friday, 16 January 1985
Patient: Jenny Patton

Patient back on obs due to agitated behaviour over the last few days. The relationship with Danny appears to be back on, so he has been moved to another ward on the first floor. Matron has instructed all staff to keep patient on the ward, except for a once-a-day (accompanied) walk in the grounds.

8 a.m.: Arguing with Verity this morning, accusing V of interfering with her breakfast. Pushed V against the wall. V has complained to Matron. Sedatives given to patient to calm her down.

10 a.m.: Sleeping.

12 p.m.: Complaining of stomach pains, refuses food.

2 p.m.: Still complaining of stomach pains. Matron has examined her and, satisfied she doesn't need to see a doctor, given meds for indigestion. Patient asking to see Danny. Told it's not possible at the moment.

4 p.m.: Doctor called as patient has been vomiting. Diagnosed mild food poisoning and advised to rest.

6 p.m.: Left the ward without permission. Found sitting in the shelter with Danny. Matron unaware as off duty. Returned to the ward. Happier tonight, feeling better. Ate dinner.

10 p.m.: Verity tells Matron. Patient put in isolation.

CHAPTER 31

The old security guard hummed idly to himself. It was a tune Jenny vaguely recognised, but the distance and rain that fell between them drowned out enough of the melody that it eluded her. He had been sitting in the smoking shelter behind the clinic for almost an hour, his peaked cap on the rotted wooden bench beside him. He was about to light his third cigarette since she'd been watching him, when something caused him to push the cigarette back in the packet, grab his hat and resume his duties. He pulled his collar up and pushed against the howling wind and rain, disappearing around the side of the building.

Jenny emerged from the shrubbery, clusters of rain-drops slowly soaking into her black woollen beanie. Still half crouched, she crept across the old football pitch, which was now no more than scrubland. When she reached the clinic, she put a gloved hand against the cold bricks and looked up, her face taut and determined despite the swirling sickness that spun in her stomach. She could feel the darkness within the shivering stone, a deep sickness that time couldn't cure. Bob would have his work cut out taking this building on; it was more powerful than any human she had ever met.

Jenny scanned the windows and doorways, checking for her access. Thankfully, other than a lick of paint and the removal of the bars, no refurbishments had been made to the exterior. The same window that had become her doorway to freedom when she was a patient was still there. Checking that there were no more guards patrolling, she crept along the wall until she reached a small frosted window. Most patients tried to escape from bedrooms and bathrooms, the rooms carefully secured with locks and iron bars. Luckily for Jenny it had never occurred to any of the nursing staff that a disused storage room might become the gateway for a patient to disappear into the night undetected.

She hooked her fingers underneath the window frame and pulled. It opened with ease, just like it always had. A familiar memory of exhilaration at the promise of freedom, however temporary, washed over her with the sound of the sticky wood leaving its frame. Jenny had managed to slip in and out of the asylum like a cat through a flap, disappearing into the night and returning only when ready. These snatched patches of time had been sewn together to create a strange and disparate blanket of memories that kept her warm on the nights when leaving for good felt impossible. The salty sting of the Whitby sea air against her cheeks, Danny's arms around her, preventing her from falling into the water. Those memories could shade any amount of isolation or skin-piercing sedation.

She pushed herself up onto the windowsill and slid into the clinic, not knowing if it would swallow her up all over again, and landed on a pile of damp cardboard with a dull thud. She turned and pulled the window back towards her, closing it tight. Jenny took her beanie off and shook her head, strands of sodden hair slapping her cheeks. She ruffled it with her fingers and pulled the hat back on, listening as the rain rattled against the glass behind her. As her vision shrank and retreated into the darkness, her senses adjusted and she was overwhelmed with a powerful stench that caused her to gag. The airless room was filled with damp boxes of degrading rubber gloves and decaying mattresses, sour with leaked urine and dried semen. Animal faeces lay in clumps around

148

the floor, greying and dry beside the corpse of a rodent that lay in the corner, its tail torn apart and blackened innards spilling from its body. Jenny breathed through her mouth, short sharp intakes of air, avoiding inhaling any more of the acrid smell.

She reached for her camera and took shots of the debris that surrounded her. She crouched by the decaying rat to take another picture, the flash reflecting in its frozen stare, its exposed innards dry and brittle. Her stomach lurched. There was a shuffle somewhere behind her and she scrambled to her feet. She spun around in time to catch a glimpse of a smooth hairless tail disappearing behind a battered filing cabinet.

She eyed a pile of faded metal signs gathered in the corner, coated in woolly cobwebs and a thin veil of dust. Bending down, she gently flicked through them: occupational therapy, laundry, admin, library and the art room. What used to be.

Jenny took more pictures of crushed beer cans and discarded syringes, empty of whatever drug had been injected by patients or trespassing junkies.

She stepped over them and listened at the door, a silent prayer answered when she reached down to try the handle and it opened. The corridor was a sensory relief as she stepped gently through the doorway and took in the smells of fresh paint and ripe lilies.

The storeroom was down its own short corridor and she walked forward to join the main one, peering around the corner. A young woman came running frantically down the corridor towards her. Jenny pulled back, standing with her back tight against the wall. Her heart raced as the sound of swishing fabric and arms pumping approached. A door opened and slammed closed. She allowed herself to breathe again, daring to look around the corner down the dark corridor, which was now empty. Then she looked across the way to a room she recognised very well.

Jenny tiptoed across the corridor and entered the room, which was only partially illuminated by the lights outside.

The library books had gone from the shelves and in their place sat an array of multicoloured aerobic equipment. Dumbbells, foam bricks, rubber bands and exercise mats lay in neat rows awaiting bodies to lay and stretch over them. An engine revved outside, and headlights illuminated the driveway. Jenny watched the car disappear around the back of the building towards the old matron's house. Andrew had told her that most nights the doctor left around 9 p.m., returning in the early hours to prepare for the day.

Jenny took out her camera and snapped a few pictures, knowing before she'd even pressed the button that they would be useless to Bob. He needed dangerous architecture and incriminating paperwork, not giant rubber balls and yoga mats. When she had agreed to come back into the asylum it had been for the promise of a future that the money would bring, but now she was here there was something else.

Nobody had ever been able to tell her about her time here — most of the patient records had disappeared; her only contact with any influence was her mother, and she was hardly likely to help her understand. Standing in this vaguely familiar room, it occurred to her that she might want to find out more about her past and the years she had lost at Pine End.

She had once used the stacked bookshelves as a shield to hide behind, giving her the freedom to kiss Danny in privacy, disturbed only on the rare occasion that somebody actually wanted to read about the migration habits of native British birds. If she could recall more of her time here, perhaps she could lay more ghosts to rest, or at the very least try and reclaim some of the better memories. She put the camera back in her pocket and made her way out, avoiding leaving an imprint on the foam mats as she went.

The bedrooms were in the same place she remembered, only now they had plasterboard partitions to separate the beds. The only privacy she had been allowed when she was a patient were the heavy cotton curtains, whose metal hoops scraped noisily along the frame each time they were opened or closed. There were seven bedrooms on the ward she had stayed on, the rest of the wards being in adjoining buildings that had now been demolished — when she was a patient they had crammed at least fifteen beds into this same space. Back then you could reach out your arm and touch the person in the next bed.

The soles of her Doc Martens stuck to the shiny flooring, creating a quiet squeak each time she lifted a boot. A loud snore rumbled through one of the bedroom doors, so loud that Jenny stepped back, standing stock still. When it was followed by sleepy mumbling and the squeaking of bed springs, she continued down the corridor towards the main door. The old records room was next to Matron's old office. Jenny put her hand to the handle, stopping when she heard two women talking on the other side.

'I'm glad you're feeling better, Kim. Her methods might seem extreme at first, but she works miracles. I've seen it for myself.'

'I suppose I'm just not used to this kind of environment, that's all.'

'Look at Amy, for example; you won't recognise her when Dr Cavendish has finished with her. Besides, you won't find these kind of wages anywhere else in Crowthorpe.'

'That's true.'

'You'll get used to it, I promise. It's for their own good.'

The chatter died down, replaced by the usual nighttime sounds of teeth brushing and cascading taps. Jenny slunk away towards the next door — Matron's old office.

It was locked, just as it always had been. Jenny pulled at a paperclip she had brought with her, unfolding it until there was enough metal to reach inside the lock. She inserted it and turned it gently, listening for the soft click of the door unlocking. As she opened the door, flashbacks caused her heart to race, a Pavlovian feeling of dread crawling over her skin. She was here on her own terms; Matron was gone, remember? *She can't do anything to you now.*

As she closed the door on herself the old security guard looped by the window, his face hidden beneath the dark hood, raised against the rain. She moved back into the shadows, waiting for the sound of crunching gravel underfoot to fade.

The office had been decorated and reorganised, but as Jenny peered around the moonlit room, they may as well have not bothered. No amount of paint or minimalist furnishings could wipe the memory of what came before. Medicinal pink walls and framed embroideries of flowers and thatched cottages, gifted to Matron each landmark work anniversary, celebrating another successful year. Her success, Jenny assumed, was measured by how many of Crowthorpe's mad and bad she could keep hidden away from society. Nobody really cared how Matron controlled those within, as long as they were silent and out of sight.

There had only ever been one reason that Jenny had stood in this room, and that was to be told that her latest request to leave had been refused. Now she stood in the same spot she had stood on those occasions, resisting the urge to take out her knife and carve the desk to pieces — except it wasn't the same desk; this one was beautiful and ornate.

The room still had the clinical air of a medical practitioner's office, but not the chaos of hundreds of patients and the buzz of frenetic energy that always seemed to fill the entire hospital. On any given day then there could be a patient angrily batting at the door complaining about too many or too few meds, a concerned guardian begging for positive updates on their loved one or the stale atmosphere of her weekly meetings to mete out instructions or punishments for the disobedient.

Behind the desk Jenny saw the framed medical certificates. She took her camera out and snapped each one, the flash reflecting against the glass. A first-class honours graduation certificate from medical school, followed by a more specific one hailing her dietary qualifications.

It is hereby certified that Dr Rebecca Cavendish was admitted to the British Society of Aestheticians on the Twenty-Fifth Day of October 2000.

Jenny thought about Clara, and all the certificates that would be displayed on her mum's wall when she finished college. Certificates Jenny had never had the chance to receive. The only certificates Jenny had managed to accrue in her life were the medical ones that helped her claim benefits when she first left the hospital. But if they ever invented a degree for persevering against the odds, then that certificate would most certainly be hers.

The drawers in the filing cabinet by the wall slid open, neat manila files containing nothing more than the vital statistics of past and current clients. Jenny began to read the applications, which sounded like they were applying for a job, begging for the opportunity to come here.

'I am focused and committed to achieving my goals.'
'I promise I will not let you down.'
'Our daughter is desperate — you are her last hope.'

She put the papers back in the folders, not knowing whether to feel disgust or pity for the women that had applied. For so many she had known, escape had been their only wish, and here were women desperate to be isolated in this godforsaken place.

There was a locked cabinet which looked like the ones that used to be on the ward, containing all the potions used to put noisy, rebellious patients to sleep. When she couldn't force it open, Jenny moved along, opening the door to what looked like an old wardrobe. It was packed full of outfits hanging from the single wooden pole that ran across the top, all reeking of jumble sales and faded lavender, the same smell she remembered from her grandmother's house. Jenny took a photo, not because there was anything necessarily incriminating, but because they seemed so strange among the chrome cabinets and manila folders.

Jenny pulled at the desk drawers, but they wouldn't budge. She scrabbled with the paperclip, jamming it into the lock, but it buckled and bent. There had to be more paperwork somewhere, her file along with hundreds of other patients that had never been located. There was nothing else to find in the office; she was already resigned to the fact that she may have to come back another night, with better tools to undo the locks. She hadn't foreseen that a diet clinic would be so security conscious.

When she found herself standing outside the doors of the old day room, she felt her heart stop for a moment, blood trying to push through her weakened body. A small sign now christened it the 'Relaxation Room'. It would have made her laugh with derision had she been told of it outside the clinic, but now fear was the only emotion available to her. Her trembling fingers pushed at the door and it opened, pulling her into its cavernous space. Like a well-formed habit, she reached for her tobacco tin, the cool metal steadying her hands. This was a room so filled with smoke back then that you could barely see from one end to the other.

Jenny took her hand away from the tin — these days there would be smoke alarms. No matter how hard she tried she couldn't see anything in front of her, but the old memories arose of mismatched armchairs scarred with cigarette burns, small metal tables at which chairs were drawn, so that troubled visitors could sit opposite their unrecognisable loved ones. Her stomach twisted into knots and her skin paled as she looked up at the windows that had always provided so little light in the room where so much darkness was experienced.

Her eyes travelled slowly around the room, noticing the scars in the plaster where a wall had been taken down. It was the glass partition, behind which had been the nurses' station, where the staff had sat watching them, *always* watching them, like zoo exhibits. She spied a familiar dent in the wall that would barely be noticed by most, the result of a brick being thrown at a fellow patient's face and missing. Eventually a snapped pool cue did the job that the brick had failed to do, the faded blood stains long since buffed away.

She closed her eyes for a moment, and she could hear the clack of chipped Scrabble tiles being swirled around in their velvet bag and see the strange, disparate family that had been her company for so many years. But best of all Danny. Smiling at her from the corner of the room, trying to coax her out of her gloom. Sometimes he succeeded in persuading her that there was something beyond this room and the walls of the asylum — he kept her going.

She opened her eyes and took out her camera, taking photographs of a slight crack in the ceiling rose and a faint discoloured patch on the wall. Not enough to close the place down, but it was a start. High above, a branch rattled against the window and a crow cawed as the viewfinder rested on the galleried landing. Jenny froze, memories of the last night of the asylum returning: Matron falling and the crack of her neck as she landed head first onto the tiled floor. Vodka and cheap wine used to numb these thoughts, but now as she was forced to remember with stark sobriety; the memory twisted at her insides and a dark mist filled her head.

Her breathing became rapid and a pain sliced through her insides. It felt like she was being suffocated in the dark room. Throwing her camera back in her backpack she turned and ran, her torch falling to the floor, but she kept running. It felt like she might die if she didn't get away quickly; she would have to come back, but tonight she was done.

Back in the storage room she gathered her breath and scrambled back over the dirty mattress and pushed at the window, peering out into the dank night. When she landed on the other side, she heard a faint cry through the driving rain. She spun around, trying to follow the voice as the rain beat down on her, but the cry was everywhere. A guard appeared in the distance and she ran away as fast as she could. Away from the asylum, and away from those strangling tendrils of ivy that crawled down the red-brick walls and twisted through the bars of the unseen windows below.

WEEK TWO

CHAPTER 32

'I feel as rough as toast,' Caroline bemoaned, holding her forehead.

'It's the pills,' said Vicky, resting a consoling hand on Caroline's back as she leaned forward at the breakfast table. 'Pills that make you sleep, pills that make you bounce like Zebedee — I'm surprised we're not rattling. Mind you, it looks like Audrey could do with an extra shot of the vitamin jab.'

Audrey sipped at a glass of water, her eyes half open like a tortoise late for hibernation.

Amy clutched her stomach, which had emptied again that morning; she was now enduring painful spasms. The only upside of the daily bouts of diarrhoea she had suffered since Dr Cavendish gave her the pills, was that she had missed Dr Cavendish's much-feared 'Injectables Evening'.

'How are your lips, Vicky?' Amy asked.

Vicky's usually thin lips were reddened and swollen. She drew her hand up to cover them.

'Is it obvious I've had something done?'

'No, not at all,' Amy lied.

'Could be worse. I could've had that bovine collagen injected into my noggin.' Vicky gestured to Caroline, who shook her head and rolled her eyes.

'Aye, a new treatment from America. Tina says we're all going to get it, apparently.'

'She's the guinea pig,' chirped Vicky. 'We're just waiting to see if she starts mooing first — if she does, we won't bother!' Vicky tapped Caroline's arm affectionately.

The women jumped when the dining-room door swung open and Dr Cavendish, followed by Kim and Tina, marched into the room.

'Welcome to week two, ladies. How do we think we're all doing? Are you excited for the weigh-in? I know I am.'

Her energy was higher than the room was prepared for, as if a 100-watt bulb had been pushed into a 10-watt light fitting. The women shook themselves in an attempt to meet her enthusiasm. The doctor wore a fitted cream suit with pink ruffled silk cuffs and collar poking out beyond the jacket, and her potent perfume hung heavy in the air, causing Amy's stomach to lurch.

'Amy, shall we have you first, as you were the bravest last week?'

The question was rhetorical. Amy attempted a smile and rose from the table. She knew she had lost weight: her thighs no longer scraped at each other and her knicker elastic no longer dug into her skin. Gaynor patted her lower back like she was a prize cow entering the market ring, and Caroline, who had perked up on seeing the doctor, held crossed fingers in the air.

Keeping her eyes fixed on the grounds outside and a passing security guard, Amy waited for Dr Cavendish to let her know her weight was recorded.

'My goodness, Amy.'

The doctor's voice was steady and without exclamation. Vicky and Caroline strained to see the numbers on the scales. Dr Cavendish clicked the end of her pen with a lacquered nail and wrote in her book, hiding the results from the women.

'Have I lost anything?' Amy felt sick that all the deprivation of the last week might have been for nothing.

'Well, Amy, no need to look so worried. Despite your little blip, you've lost fourteen pounds — that's a whole stone in weight!' The doctor's mouth broke into a smile, her eyebrows rising in delight.

Kim and Tina clapped their hands in unison, the claps catching around the room. Amy took a deep breath, elated to have exceeded any goal she could have set for herself. Over a stone in seven days was a miracle. As the applauding slowed, the doctor spoke again.

'Who's next?'

The women pushed their hands to the ceiling, like class swots eager to please. Tina and Kim ushered them forward one at a time. More claps and celebrations: Caroline and Vicky had both lost thirteen pounds, Gaynor twelve, and Audrey lucky seven. The last woman to be weighed was Jasmine, who walked with confidence up to the scales. She wore baggy cargo pants and a tight vest top that showed off her already enviable figure and lack of need for a bra. She reminded Amy of a pop star — an All Saint. Effortlessly cool and beautiful.

'You might be leaving us today,' said Audrey as Jasmine walked by her. 'You're bound to have reached your goal weight.'

Jasmine stepped onto the scales and watched the dial spin and settle. The room fell silent as the women waited for the results. Jasmine's eyes met the doctor's as they both looked up from the scales. The doctor's eyes flickered slightly.

'Well?' said Caroline. 'How much?'

'Step off, Jasmine,' Dr Cavendish ordered.

Jasmine did as she was told. The doctor fiddled with the scales and placed them back on the floor, checking there was nothing beneath to send them off kilter. She gestured for Jasmine to stand back on, and she did so, turning to Audrey, her delicate brow furrowed. The women exchanged confused glances.

The doctor looked down at the scales and took a deep breath, letting it out in a heavy sigh. 'Have you been taking your medication, Jasmine?'

Jasmine looked down at the floor.

'Well?' Dr Cavendish pulled Jasmine's face up with her hand, forcing the girl to meet her gaze.

Jasmine spoke quietly. 'Yes.'

The doctor bristled, her jaw tightening. She looked to Tina and Kim. 'And the injections? Has she had the injections?'

Tina looked to Kim, who stared wide-eyed at Jasmine. 'Yes, yes I gave her the injections.'

Dr Cavendish let go of Jasmine's face, letting her gaze drop back to the floor.

'Back to your seat, Jasmine.'

Jasmine made her way back to her seat, her shoulders drooped forward and head down. Gaynor looked across at Amy, her lips pulled across her teeth in a grimace. Jasmine sat down.

'Was it bad?' Gaynor asked.

Jasmine looked up at Dr Cavendish, who was now writing in her notebook, before facing Gaynor.

'I've put on two pounds,' she said, pushing the six raisins and slice of a strawberry in front of her across the table.

Dr Cavendish picked up her notebook and walked silently back through the dining room. Tina scooped up the scales and followed behind with Kim.

'Don't get upset, Jasmine,' Amy said, offering her the paper napkin from her table. 'It's harder to lose when it's only a little bit.' Amy's initial feelings of triumph over Jasmine disappeared when she saw her tears.

'I bet you'll have lost those pounds or more by next week,' said Audrey, her arms placed maternally around Jasmine's shoulders.

Amy couldn't tell if it was the extra pounds or the idea of being there another week that caused Jasmine to howl louder. The women gathered around her, offering her words of comfort and encouragement. Amy felt a presence behind her and turned to the door. Robert leaned against the wooden frame, arms folded, his eyes fixed on the gaggle of women as they consoled Jasmine.

CHAPTER 33

The doctor tapped garnet fingernails on the desk in her office, the telephone receiver held up to her ear. In front of her, a small blue torch stood on the table. She had found it in the relaxation room, underneath one of the coffee tables, while doing her morning checks. Her main suspect was the old night watchman, coming into the building to use her toilet. She squirmed in her chair, imagining the urine splashing on the toilet seats. If that was not bad enough, he had also been in the kitchen helping himself to drinks. She had found the half-drunk glass of water the other day. He had not even had the decency or wits about him to clean the glass and put it away after himself.

Through the window she watched as Phil, one of the other guards, chatted to Gaynor. He leaned against the lamp-post, laughing as she took the cap from his head and put it on hers. Dr Cavendish tapped her nail so violently against the wood of the desk that the acrylic split and half of her nail bounced to the floor.

A woman picked up at the other end and spoke.

'Good morning, Cotterill Security Solutions, this is Donna speaking.' The receptionist's greeting was bright and breezy.

'Get me Mr Cotterill on the phone, now.'

'Who may I say is calling?'

Dr Cavendish tore the other half of acrylic nail off to reveal a frail and peeling nailbed beneath. She threw the plastic nail into the waste basket.

She spoke again, her irritation rising. 'Get him on the phone now.'

There was the sound of muffled talking on the other end, before the swish of another hand taking the handset.

'Hello?' said a gruff voice.

'Mr Cotterill?'

'Yeah, that's me, who's this?'

'Dr Cavendish, the Beautiful You Clinic.'

His voice changed; it became clearer, as if sandpaper had rubbed away the rough edges. 'How lovely to speak to you, Dr Cavendish. I trust everything is well with you?'

'Why would I be calling if everything was well?'

There was silence on the other end. Dr Cavendish waited. Looking out of the window, she watched as Phil and Gaynor shared a cigarette before heading off towards the woods.

'If there's a problem I'll sort it out as a priority, Dr Cavendish.'

'I'm terminating your contract. I'd like all your men off the grounds by the end of the week.'

'Dr Cavendish, please, there must be something I can do to change your mind — what's the problem? Do we need more men up there? It is a big area to patrol.'

'You could start by telling the ones you have sent to do their job, rather than playing cards and—' she wondered now what Phil and Gaynor were up to — 'smoking cigarettes all day long.'

'Dr Cavendish, please give me a chance to make this up to you.'

'And how do you propose to do that, Mr Cotterill?'

'I'll get some new blokes up there.'

She could hear the cogs of his brain whirring.

'And there's something very special I can offer, completely free of charge. And trust me, if you accept, nobody is going to be bothering you again.'

She took a deep breath and sat forward in her chair. 'I'm listening.'

* * *

Dr Cavendish finished the call and walked over to the window. Across the driveway Gaynor reappeared from the woods — Dr Cavendish noted her mud-stained knees and bristled. Amy stepped out from the porch and called to Gaynor. When Phil appeared a moment later, he waved at the two women as if it were the first time he had seen Gaynor that day.

Amy was wearing the dress the doctor had lent her. It was visibly looser now.

Good girl, you've earned the next outfit.

Of all the women this time, her 'before' and 'after' would demonstrate just how effective the clinic was in transforming women. Perhaps more importantly, every pound that Amy lost would be another step towards satisfying the broken part within the doctor. Jasmine, on the other hand, had let her down. Hopes that her catwalk career might bring the doctor notoriety disappeared with each pound Jasmine put on and the lies she told — blatant lies. There was nothing Dr Cavendish detested more than being made a fool of, and the ever-growing stash of untaken pills was proof of Jasmine's deceitful nature.

* * *

Seeing Amy reminded the doctor she was ready for another outfit. She thought about the purple dress — beautifully made, still not fitted, but Amy could not complain about the quality of the silk and embroidery. The clothes would get better as she got thinner, that was just the law of the world, and so, by default, the law of her clinic. Eventually, when enough weight was lost, she would get to the clothes that had never been worn. A flicker of excitement sparked in the doctor as she opened the cupboard door. She took out the purple dress, the material so heavy it caused the garment to sag from the thin metal coat hanger that struggled to hold it.

The doctor ran her hands over the smooth material and a memory shuddered through her. She noticed the suitcase at the bottom had slipped forward and was protruding through the clothes. Dr Cavendish quickly lay the purple dress over the chaise longue and returned to the cupboard, taking the suitcase and opening it out on the floor. The clothes smelt freshly laundered and soft. Jogging suits and pyjamas, a soft kitten toy and fluffy slippers. She ran her hands across the clothes, enjoying the fresh scent, before closing the lid again and pushing it back beneath the old clothes. A brown parcel label fell forward, and she glanced at it briefly before tucking it out of sight.

Crowthorpe Station Lost Property — Please return to Amy Mitchell c/o the Beautiful You Clinic, Crowthorpe

CHAPTER 34

Jenny had arranged to see Bob at the Lazy Spoon Diner. It felt good to get out of her room, but more importantly, she wanted to avoid Bob losing his rag, and if they met somewhere public this was much less likely to happen. Now he sat opposite her, clicking through the photographs on the digital camera, his face scrunched and eyebrows furrowed.

'They're not exactly FBI-worthy, are they?' He turned the camera around, showing her one of the exercise room. 'I mean, what am I going to get her with? Deflated gym balls and dead rats in an old storage cupboard? All old buildings have the odd rat or two.'

'Ha bloody ha.' Jenny took the camera back. 'It's a start. Look, when I go back I'll have a better idea of what's what. I only managed to see a fraction of what's there.'

'Is that supposed to make me feel better?' Bob said, wiping coffee froth from his moustache.

'You don't know what that place is like,' Jenny said, trying to keep the anger from her voice. She needed to keep Bob onside. 'It got under my skin, that's all. I'll be better prepared now.'

'Too right I don't know what the place is like; for some reason nobody was allowed to view it other than that diet quack.'

'I heard she's pretty tough. My source said—'

'Source?' he guffawed. 'I take it back, Agent Starling.'

Jenny bristled with a familiar feeling of not being enough. 'Oh, fuck off, then. Do it yourself.'

She pushed her chair back and went to stand. Bob grabbed her wrist and pulled her back down. The ancient waitress looked across at the pair as she wiped down the counter with a greying cloth.

'Now look here,' spittle flew from his mouth, 'you're not going to get that money from anywhere else, so quit it with the dramatics, sit back down and calm yourself.'

Jenny glared at him and shook her wrist free, before pulling the chair back and sitting down.

'What makes you so sure there's anything for me to find in there?'

'There has to be a good reason why the council chose a bleedin' fat farm over my luxury development, that's why. I would have brought more money in, in the short term. She's just leasing it — why choose that over upfront cash?' He leaned back and took a cigar out of his pocket and put it in his mouth, making a popping sound with his lips as he lit it.

'Maybe they want to try something that brings more, I don't know, prestige to the town? If it's a success, it'll expand and other businesses will start to arrive.'

'Nah, isolated up there filled with women eating next to nothing — what can they bring to this town? I'm offering more jobs and more people living here. Johnny at the Lodge reckons she's got contacts at the council, says she's well in with that Councillor Patton.'

The mention of her mother's name needled at Jenny. Most children would be proud of a high-ranking and influential parent, but for Jenny it was just further evidence of how far removed she was from her. At no time during her life had that influence been used to help her; on the contrary, she often wondered if strings had been pulled to get her into Pine End in the first place. Out of sight, out of mind.

'Bloody women's lib, ain't right not playing by the rules.'

Jenny spluttered on her coffee.

'This is different, they've left me with no choice,' he protested.

The old waitress brought over an egg bap and put it in front of him. Bob picked it up and took a bite. Looking back at the waitress, he said, 'This town needs young families, people to bring it back to life.'

Jenny tried not to look at the yellow-and-white mush churning around in his mouth as he spoke, speckles of oily egg white flying into the air and sticking to the table. He did have a point — why the diet clinic when Crowthorpe needed more homes for young families? She looked out of the window as an elderly man shuffled along in the wind, trying to keep up with his Zimmer frame. God's waiting room, that's what they called Crowthorpe.

'There's some council do next week,' Bob said, slurping tea into his full mouth and swishing it around. 'The diet guru is supposed to be there to give a motivational talk, I'll see what she's about then. I doubt she's as impressive as they say.'

'From what I've heard she'd eat you for breakfast.'

'Just find out enough so I can get rid of her before that thought enters her head. If I can't prove there's something fishy going on there'll be no more money for you, *and* I'll be adding the £200 I gave you to your rent bill.' He stood up from the table, picking his cigar up from the ashtray. The waitress shuffled towards him, and he pointed at Jenny.

'Breakfast's on her,' he said before marching out.

CHAPTER 35

Talons nail salon was opposite the Lazy Spoon Diner, housed in the front room of a council flat above Crowthorpe Antiques. The small room smelled of acetate and Pledge furniture polish. Dr Cavendish flinched when a ragged cat began manically clawing at an armchair placed in front of a portable TV, where a silver-haired chat show host was interviewing members of a TV audience, the sound turned down.

'Don't mind Tubs, she only claws furniture and curtains. No point having nice stuff with her around.'

Dr Cavendish studied the top of the beautician's head as the girl hovered over the broken nail, rubbing it with an emery board and massaging in different oils. The girl's roots were beginning to show, a centimetre of mousy blonde hair pushing at the peroxide.

'You're due a visit to the hairdresser.'

The young girl looked up at her, blue eyes peering through mascara-clotted lashes.

'Sorry? Oh, yeah,' she touched the top of her head, chewing gum stretching between crooked teeth. 'Haven't had the chance, been so busy here.'

'Be careful, you're letting yourself go. Customers will go elsewhere.'

The girl chuckled, but when she saw the grave look on the doctor's face the laughter died and she looked back to the nail, filing a little more vigorously and catching at the doctor's skin.

Dr Cavendish looked through the cerise net curtain out onto the high street. It was not only the sole beautician for miles, it also had an excellent view of the town. She watched Bob leave the café, puffing on a fat cigar, and get into his old Jaguar. He had been the only other serious contender for guardianship of the asylum, and it had been an added pleasure to have beaten him to it. Men like Bob thought they could get anything they wanted, and that she had proved him wrong was the icing on the cake.

She looked back into the café window: a woman sat out of view, just two hands visible, clasping a mug.

'There, good as new.'

Dr Cavendish looked down to the newly lacquered nail, now indiscernible from the other nine. She smiled, 'Perfect. Thank you.'

The beautician rubbed finishing dots of oil into her cuticles as the doctor watched the woman leave the café, her black bobbed hair swooshing from side to side. She looked disapprovingly at the fluffy yellow jumper that almost reached the hem of her miniskirt and the thick tights that disappeared into her Doc Martens.

Jenny Patton hadn't been difficult for the doctor to spot: she looked every inch an ex-patient of the old asylum. Despite the passing of time, she was still recognisable from the sullen photograph attached to her file. Her uniform of bohemian charity shop chic made Dr Cavendish shudder.

The doctor knew many of the residents of Crowthorpe through the records at the hospital, exclusive access to their deepest secrets all bundled up and left behind. Once, a government official had enquired about the lost files, but Dr Cavendish had denied all knowledge of them. They had left them for years already, she reasoned; now they would stay, as much a part of the building and its history as the bricks and gargoyles.

She was used to seeing Jenny on the rare occasions she ventured out into town, always making sure she stayed out of view, seeing but unseen. In all those times she had never seen her with Bob Dickinson and something about their encounter irked her, a warning signal flashing, but she didn't know why. Sometimes she wondered if the ex-patients still felt like they were part of the building, and therefore belonged to her. She watched Jenny march across the road to catch a bus that was already beginning to move away from the stop. Her eyes narrowed as she watched her flop down onto a seat before the bus disappeared away.

Dr Cavendish made her way down the beautician's narrow stairs, dodging the multicoloured dream catchers that hung from the ceiling, her concern turning back to increasing the security at the clinic.

* * *

The doctor stood outside the entrance, arms crossed, waiting to be persuaded that she shouldn't fire the lot of them right now. Mr Cotterill stood beside her, already in her bad books for being an hour late. The boss of Cotterill Security Solutions was a giant of a man, and despite the damp air and the threat of rain, he wore a tight-fitting T-shirt with the company's logo embroidered on his bulging pec.

'My breath is bated, Mr Cotterill. Can we please get on with this, I've got clients to look after and possibly new guards to find.'

'I can assure you there'll be no need for that,' he said, his mouth fixed with a knowing smile.

Mr Cotterill waved his hand in the air, guiding a van out of its parking place until its back doors were facing them both. Dr Cavendish wondered if the doors would open and ten more useless security guards would fall out like the Keystone Cops.

'He is the best in the business; you are not going to be disappointed.'

Her eyes narrowed as the possibilities of what was behind the van doors ran through her head like images speeding through a flip book. When Gary, Mr Cotterill's second-in-command, unlocked the outer doors it suddenly dawned on her what it was and she stepped back, instinctively holding onto her left forearm.

'Meet Duke, Dr Cavendish.'

Gary opened the doors wide until they clicked into place, revealing two inner doors fronting a metal cage. The black dog was barely visible in the fading afternoon light — two black eyes glinted in the outside lights that automatically illuminated when they sensed dusk approaching. Once again Mr Cotterill nodded and the driver unlocked the inner doors, holding his hand up to the dog. As if sensing her discomfort, Mr Cotterill turned to Dr Cavendish. 'Don't you worry, Doctor, he only bites the bad guys.'

Dr Cavendish kept her eyes firmly on Duke, trying hard to keep control of the twitching muscles in her face. The dog sat perfectly still, its eyes focused firmly on Mr Cotterill. She watched its nose as it crinkled back and forth, nostrils flaring, sniffing the dank air.

'What do you think then?' he said, an air of presumptive triumph in his voice. 'Have I come up trumps for you or what?'

She could not take her eyes off the dog. 'Can it be kept under control? There's no danger of it attacking one of my clients?'

He took a whistle from his pocket and blew two sharp blasts. Duke flew out of the van and Dr Cavendish gasped as she watched the dog's lithe and powerful body fly through the air like a thoroughbred horse. His coat was black and tan, and seal-like with its healthy sheen. As he flew towards them, she turned her head away into Mr Cotterill's chest, moving away when she felt the damp material of his T-shirt on her skin. Duke came to his heel, sitting flush against his leg, his head on Mr Cotterill's hip, black eyes looking up at the security guard's face.

'Don't be frightened, he's a soft lad underneath.' He patted her back gently, his familiarity causing her to recoil and edge away from him. 'Here, give him a treat.' He dug a hand into his trouser pocket and pulled out a tiny nugget of biscuit.

Dr Cavendish shook her head. 'I'll leave that to you.'

Mr Cotterill put the treat back into his pocket. 'Watch this,' he said, a winning smile plastered across his face. 'Ready, Gary?'

She watched with nervous curiosity as Gary appeared from the front of the van in a padded suit with a thick padded sleeve over his left arm. He nodded at Mr Cotterill and then ran away from the van to the edge of the woods, waving a black stick in the air. Mr Cotterill gave the command, and the beast left his side and ran straight towards Gary, the dog leaping into the air and clamping his jaws onto the padded arm. Gary turned in circles, lifting his arm and waving the baton in the air, taunting the dog. The dog's teeth didn't let go; its entire body hung in the air, its back legs stretched out behind it spinning like helicopter blades. A low growl persisted no matter how much Gary waved his arm around. Dr Cavendish looked back to the clinic and saw Caroline and Vicky staring out from the entrance, wide-eyed.

'OK, that'll do,' Dr Cavendish said.

Mr Cotterill shouted, 'Out!' and the dog let go, running back and sitting by his side.

'I can show you—'

'Enough. You've convinced me, Mr Cotterill; you can stay on a month's trial. Just put the dog back in the van, you'll have my clients terrified.' She looked back to see that Caroline and Vicky had disappeared again.

'You won't regret it, Dr Cavendish, you have my word.' He put his fist to his chest.

Dr Cavendish glanced down at the dog, its wet nose still eagerly sniffing at the air. She took a step to move away and the dog turned to watch her. She stopped.

'I will be here with him through the nights, and when I'm not here, one of the other guards will take over.' Frank gestured at the driver, who nodded and called Duke back into the van and locked the cage doors. 'Trust me: if anyone tries to break in, he'll rip them to shreds.'

* * *

The voices crackled and burned in her skull as she clutched her arm, feeling the smooth ripple of scars beneath the silk blouse.

> 'You've only yourself to blame.'
> 'You got what you deserved; it's a shame he didn't finish you off.'

Her face twitched as she was drawn back to then and to *her*. The big, fat lolloping monster that couldn't be fixed. The doctor took deep breaths, inhaling moisture-speckled air through thin nostrils, reviving herself, bringing herself back.

She would put up with the dog, as long as he was kept well away from her. Her priority now was keeping everything secure. Seeing Bob had rattled her, taking her focus away from the clinic and the job in hand. With Mr Cotterill's assurances and the presence of that beast she was free to carry on with her work. Nobody knew how effective guard dogs were better than her.

There was a sharp knock on her office door, causing the doctor to jump out of her thoughts.

'Yes?'

The door opened and Robert entered, closing it behind him. Dr Cavendish watched him, waiting for him to speak.

'The file you promised in return for—'

'Yes, of course,' she said dryly, unlocking her desk drawer and taking out a thin file labelled *Before*. 'But I'll need it back by the end of the week.'

Dr Cavendish held out the file and Robert edged forward, his hand hesitating a little as he reached out and took it from her, avoiding her eyes. He eagerly opened the file, closed it almost as quickly. She watched impassively as he left, clutching the folder to his chest as if the pages were made of gold.

Getting back to her work, Dr Cavendish took out Jasmine's folder. She flicked through photographs she had sent in as part of her application.

Such a beautiful girl. If she could just have followed the rules.

Dr Cavendish ran her finger over the photographs before making a note of Jasmine's weight and unlocking the medicine cabinet behind her desk. She opened a small packet, took out a syringe and removed the protective cap. Checking the label on a small glass bottle, she stabbed the rubber top with the needle and drew up some of the liquid. When she had the correct amount, she put the bottle back in the cabinet and replaced the cap over the needle. She sat back at her desk and dialled an internal number on the telephone.

'Tina, could you ask Jasmine to come to my office?'

Dr Cavendish put the receiver down and walked over to the window. As she reached across to close the curtain, she saw Phil, the lax security guard, being driven offsite by Mr Cotterill. He glared back at her, before she disappeared behind the swoosh of the closed curtain.

CHAPTER 36

DOCTOR'S REPORT
Date: 30 January 1985
Patient: Jenny Patton

I had previously seen patient with regards to stomach pain and general malaise. Patient had been sick at the time. It had been diagnosed as indigestion as patient claimed she had not had sexual intercourse (confirmed by Matron, who reports to have close control over her patients). Due to cessation of periods for one month, pregnancy test carried out. Result: Positive pregnancy test.

Patient shocked, but happy with result. Her wish is to create a stable relationship with the father of the baby, fellow Pine End patient Danny Char. Full review of meds to be carried out and assessment with relevant parties as to plans to support her ongoing. I have asked Matron Dawson to put together a plan for her in the hope she may be able to live independently under the care of social services.

Signed: Dr T. Simpson

CHAPTER 37

'Ouch!'

As soon as Dr Cavendish removed the needle from her arm, Gaynor clasped the tiny red dot as if the skin had been slashed with a blade. Amy thought she caught the flash of a smile as the doctor observed Gaynor's dramatic reaction.

Audrey was next in line as they queued in the dining room, one by one, ready to receive one of the many daily injections they were now given. The doctor had been vague about their properties, but as the women knew little about medicine it was enough just to know that the results would be apparent within days and it would involve reduced hunger and increased energy. Amy had found that after she had hers, she was more confident and chattier, a state which lasted until evening when the night pill was taken, and the long sleep came.

Slate-coloured clouds gathered in the skies and the wind rattled the high windows of the relaxation room. Amy had imagined that a relaxation room would be warmed by an open fire, or at least radiators that worked. Instead, this room was like all the others, frigid and hostile, so much so that nobody ever seemed to gather there, let alone relax. Each night the women splintered apart and retreated to their rooms, where they could find warmth from the heavy blankets on their beds. Caroline had eventually found the thermostat the previous morning, only to find it encased in a clear plastic lockbox. When Caroline had asked the doctor for access to the key she had been refused, Dr Cavendish explaining that shivering was a highly effective way to burn even more calories.

Amy rolled up the arm of the purple dress that had been left in her room that morning — her skin was rough with goose pimples and was beginning to turn bluish. Just as with the first outfit, this billowing dress had been delivered sometime in the night, appearing as if by magic on the back of her door. She moved to the front of the room as Audrey rubbed at her arm and sat back down at a table.

'That dress suits you,' Dr Cavendish said. 'Very elegant.'

The doctor turned Amy round to face the other women. 'Ladies, see how much more attractive Amy is now we've prised her out of those leggings. We have to attack all your problems from all angles, then you'll be ready to face the world in no time at all.'

'Really?' Amy muttered, pulling at the rough material. 'It's not really my style.'

'Have you got a style?' Gaynor snorted, causing a sea of disapproving faces to turn to her. She rolled her eyes at the other women and groaned, 'I was only kidding. Jesus.'

'Just a sharp scratch,' the doctor said kindly to Amy, ignoring Gaynor.

Amy sucked in at the sudden sting, holding her breath until it was done.

'See, you get used to it, don't you? It's not that painful,' the doctor said, smiling before giving Gaynor an admonishing look.

'Maybe I've got thinner skin,' Gaynor hissed.

'I think somebody is feeling a little irritated by hunger today?' said Dr Cavendish.

Amy looked at Gaynor, the jabbing second dig causing a tear to spring to her eye.

When all the women were done Dr Cavendish cleared up the sterile trolley and put the last of the used needles into the small yellow sharps bin.

'Right, ladies, Kim will be taking you for your aerobics class this morning. Make sure you drink lots of water; you need to flush out your system and you'll be working hard today. And don't forget . . .'

She put her hand to her ear as the women chorused:

'Discipline and diet determine your destiny!'

As they filed out of the room, rubbing at their arms, Amy called after her friend, 'Are you OK, Gaynor?'

But Gaynor was already stomping through the relaxation room doors, causing a prickle of panic in Amy, who didn't like confrontation but felt sure there was going to be one.

* * *

'I want you all to face the mirror and see how far you've come this week — take a good look, you're all amazing!'

Kim wore shimmering aqua-blue leggings and a cropped racer-back top, exposing a washboard stomach with a sparkling gem pierced through her belly button. She waved at Anya, who was walking by the window, carrying a box of vegetables from a small rusted van. Amy watched as Anya studied her and the other women — she wondered what she thought of them, if she had ever seen anything like this in her own country, wherever that might be.

The end wall in the workout room was floor-to-ceiling mirrors; there was no way of Amy escaping her reflected self. Although she had lost half of the weight already, there still seemed a long way to go. Maybe two stone wasn't enough; maybe if she kept going then eventually she'd look like Jasmine and that would make her happier. It didn't help that she had had to revert to the clothes she had travelled down in as there wasn't a spare tracksuit in her size. Even though she had managed to wash them in her sink, they smelled like they had been at the bottom of the linen basket for a year and she was aware that everyone had made sure to keep their distance from her in the room.

'Positive thoughts only, ladies,' Kim said, adjusting the headset and mic over her mouth.

Whatever was in the injection began to have an effect on Amy. Her body began to fizz with energy and thoughts buzzed around her mind. She had knocked for Gaynor before coming down, eager to chat and clear the air from whatever had misted it, but Gaynor had already left her room. Amy had not worried as much as she might usually and had happily made her way down to the gym. For some reason, right now, in this moment, she felt a lust for life that she had never felt before.

'Right,' Kim shouted, her amplified voice booming around the room, 'follow me and don't stop moving; you have to keep going, otherwise you won't feel any benefits. The temperature outside might be dropping, but we're going to sweat in here!'

The CD player sucked the disc in, and a steady beat began. Caroline and Vicky were already doing stretches to prepare, Caroline talking ten to the dozen to Vicky, who was trying in vain to get a word in. Gaynor and Audrey stood with feet hip-width apart as instructed. Gaynor caught Amy's eye and immediately spun her head away again. Any worrying thoughts were drowned out as 'Pump Up the Jam' began to blare out of the speakers and Kim began marching vigorously on the spot.

Amy followed Kim's routines, and before long the tempo had sped up so much and the moves got so complex that she forgot all about her body and was just trying her best to keep up. Sweat poured down her scarlet face as another section was added to the ever more complicated dance sequence they were tasked to follow. Building a routine, they started over and over again.

'Let me hear a *whoop, whoop!*' Kim called as she grape-vined across the floor, back and forth, clapping as she reached the end of each move.

The women called out; even Audrey seemed to have found an inner sunshine and was clapping as she sidestepped. Amy jumped in the wrong direction and was now facing Gaynor, who gave her the mother of all dirty looks. Caroline and Vicky followed the routine to the beat, mouthing the lyrics as they moved. The heat in the room was stifling. Amy looked at the windows, which were all firmly shut, their expended breath creating clouds of condensation across the glass. She felt her heart racing in her chest as she ran from side to side.

'Faster, ladies, faster; that fat will melt off.' Kim ran manically on the spot, her head down and arms pumping.

Amy pumped her arms back and forth as fast as she could. Just a few more seconds, she promised herself.

'Almost there, ladies — keep going, as hard as you can.'

As the songs and routines came and went, the people and sounds around her disappeared in and out of focus. Amy was lost within herself. She opened her eyes briefly and noticed that Kim had paused and was looking towards the glass-panelled doors. Amy turned her head, feet still running on the spot. Tina passed the door, walking backwards, followed by Dr Cavendish. They were pushing something between them, but whatever it was, it was out of sight below the window on the door. Amy looked back to Kim, who seemed to be rallying herself again, trying to find her place in the beat. Once she did, she continued to whoop and encourage the class, but something in her demeanour had changed. The enthusiasm had been turned down a notch.

Amy felt alive and unstoppable, more energy than she could ever remember having. Her head was a blur of heat and determination to keep going further and not stop until her body gave way. Audrey was bouncing up and down, punching her fists alternately in the air. Everyone seemed to be on a high.

Sweat dripped down Amy's forehead and into her eyes, the salty drops stinging as she wiped them away with her forearm, and that's when she saw Robert watching her. He was standing outside the window with the same vacant look on his face that she had seen under the tree. Amy tried to escape his gaze, sidestepping left and right. No matter which way she moved, his eyes followed her hips, back and forth, back and forth. Amy saw Kim catch a glimpse of him and look back to Amy, shaking her head as if to say, *Ignore him.* When he still didn't move Kim shouted into the mike, pointing to the space in front of her.

'Amy, come to the front, love. There's more space here.'

Amy walked forward, her movement breaking the hypnotic spell and causing Robert to slink away, sharing a brief hello with security as he entered the main doors. Kim gave a reassuring wink to Amy, before carrying on with her routine.

Another house song kicked in with a bass so strong it felt like it was pumping inside Amy's chest. Kim fixed a smile on her face and began hamstring curls with an additional option to spring into it for those with enough energy. When all the women began to spring from side to side, bending their legs foot to bum, her expression was more of concern than pleasure.

'If anything starts to hurt then don't be afraid to slow down!' she called out to deaf ears, the women all seemingly lost in the music.

When the tempo changed to a chilled instrumental tune, it felt like Amy had only been in the room five minutes, and for the first time in her life, she didn't want the class to end.

'Take your arm and raise it up, then bend at the elbow and push that elbow gently back — that's great.'

Amy's body prickled with energy as she leaned forward into a lunging stretch, her hamstrings pulling gently.

'Make sure you all drink plenty of water, ladies.'

'That flew by,' Amy said, wiping her forehead with her arm.

'You did really well! What did the doctor give you this morning? Espresso shots?'

Amy shook her head. 'Same as usual, I think. Maybe she just upped the amount.'

'Huh,' Kim said, a look of surprise on her face.

The teacher began to tidy up the room as the women gulped from small plastic cups of water, wiping sweaty brows and heading for the door. Amy blinked at her reflection in the mirror, panting heavily, her tomato-coloured face wet with sweat, and for a brief moment, a split-second, there was no shame, only elation for what her body had just done. Her pleasure was momentary, pride pricked when Gaynor delivered another killer look. Then it occurred to her what she had done: she looked down to Gaynor's trainers which were now stretched and greying despite her trying to clean them, the glitter now as dull as the clouds outside the window.

* * *

'You were really going for it back there,' said Audrey, pushing a floret of raw broccoli around her plate.

'I surprised myself,' Amy said, the redness now faded to a healthy glow.

Gaynor raised her eyebrows and went back to her food, dipping a slither of carrot in and out of the vinegar and lemon juice dressing.

'Just be careful though,' Caroline said. 'I mean, they don't give you any kind of medical here and . . .'

Amy knew what she was going to say and she wished she wouldn't; the unspoken words already pained her.

'. . . well, when we've got extra pounds to shed, we've got to be careful.'

The sheen of her brief happiness had been dulled. The cruciferous lump in her mouth suddenly became impossible to chew — she took a paper napkin, raised it to her mouth and spat the green mush into it. She wasn't really hungry, and as she looked around the dining room, nobody was managing to finish their food.

'That injection must have been some kind of appetite suppressant,' Caroline said.

'I don't care what it was if it works,' Gaynor said, her meagre plate of food untouched.

Amy looked at the empty seat opposite her and it suddenly dawned on her. She looked up to the other women.

'Has anybody seen Jasmine?'

CHAPTER 38

The doorbell downstairs rang, and Jenny heard Tom's door open next to hers. He whistled as he bounded across the landing and down the stairs. She put her ear to the door, hoping it wasn't Bob coming to hassle her about the rent or bend her ear again about his plans for the hospital.

Jenny leaned closer, unable to recognise the voice. She shot back when she heard two sets of feet walk up the stairs, as if she might be visible through the cheap MDF door. There were muffled thanks and goodbyes before a knock on her door that rang out in Jenny's ears. She considered pretending she wasn't there, until she remembered Tom had seen her come in earlier, as she scooted upstairs to avoid him. She didn't want to look any crazier than he already thought she was.

'Who is it?' Jenny called through the door.

'It's me, Clara.'

Jenny's head fell back as she quietly groaned. Little sisters were supposed to be annoying, but that was when they were ten, not grown-ups.

'I'm a bit busy at the moment.'

Jenny waited, hoping in vain that Clara would leave, but something told her that Clara was not the type of person to accept defeat easily.

'Can I come in? I won't keep you long.'

Jenny slid the safety chain across and opened the door. Clara looked like she had just walked off the set of a Richard Curtis film — soft golden hair underneath a grey sequined bobble hat with a chunky pink turtleneck jumper and the kind of Levi's that were made to look battered, not actually lived in. Jenny ushered her in and closed the door, looking down the landing, which was empty.

'It's freezing out there, the wind is really picking up again. Roll on summer!'

Jenny had to admire her optimism; even summers in Crowthorpe brought little more than a smudge of yellow behind grey clouds.

Clara took off her bobble hat. 'So this is where you live?'

Her younger sister wandered around the room as if she had just walked through the doors of the V&A, studying the artwork on the walls and the ornaments on the shelf. Jenny reached for her gold and green tin and began making a roll-up, her hands trembling slightly, tobacco shreds escaping and falling to the floor.

'This is so cosy,' she gushed.

'Is that the polite term for small?'

'No.' Clara turned to her. 'I like it, it's homely.'

Jenny lit her roll-up and watched as Clara moved over to the drawing of Pine End, her sister's eyes brightening. She touched the edges of the paper.

'Is this it? The asylum?'

'I think the accepted term these days is psychiatric hospital.' She raised her eyebrows playfully at her sister.

'Sorry, I didn't mean to be dramatic.'

'You're a budding writer, aren't you? It's your job to be dramatic.'

Clara smiled, 'A journalist, really — well, one day.'

Jenny moved towards the picture. 'But you're right, asylum is a more apt word for the place. Hospital makes it sound like somewhere you go to get better; it gives that place far too much credit.'

'Is it true what they say about the matron — I mean, what happened to her?'

Jenny shrugged, taking another drag of her cigarette. 'Why are you so interested in the place?' Then she remembered. 'Ah yes, the article.'

Clara's cheeks reddened. She pointed at Jenny's roll-up tin, 'Can I have one?'

'You smoke? Does Mum know?'

Clara gave her an *of course not* expression. Jenny handed her sister the tin and watched with surprise as she produced a perfectly neat roll-up. She took her lighter from her trouser pocket and held it out to Clara. The two sisters stared up at the drawing.

'I've missed you, you know,' Clara said, looking up to the charcoal clock tower.

'I'm still not going to help with your article.' Jenny pushed the roll-up into a saucer, grinding it down with her thumb, and looked back up to her sister. 'I tried to speak to you when I phoned from the hospital, years ago. Don't you remember? You ignored me.'

Clara thought for a moment, her face becoming incredulous.

'I was only a kid when you phoned, and each time it would be followed by Mum and Dad having a huge row. I didn't mean to ignore you, I just wanted to stop the arguing. Make it all go away.'

Jenny gulped. 'I had no idea.'

'You wouldn't, you haven't wanted to know me since you've been out.' Clara stubbed out her roll-up and swept her hands together.

'It's better that you haven't had me around these past few years. When I left the asylum I spiralled. Things happened that I couldn't deal with.'

Carla eyed a photograph of Jenny curled up on her dad's lap, the same dark hair and eyes smiling to the camera.

'Dad really missed you, you know. He'd spend hours in the shed, going through your photographs.'

Jenny could feel an emotional wave gathering up in her stomach; she had to flatten it before it rose any higher. This was not the right time — not that there was a right time; his betrayal of her was water under an ancient bridge. Clara clearly didn't feel the same need to hold her emotions in, as she let a tear roll down her cheek, catching it with a tissue she took from her pocket.

'I really miss him,' Clara sniffed, dabbing her nose.

'As far as I'm concerned, he died the moment he decided to keep me in there after my baby died. Not even so much as a letter to see how I was.'

Jenny turned to the bin and emptied the makeshift ash-tray into it, before rinsing the plate under the tap and placing it by the mug. She sensed Clara behind her, not moving, not leaving.

'Look, Clara, if you really want to get to know the misfit of the Patton family, then fine. But can we meet up another time? I really can't do this now, I have stuff I need to do.'

Clara sniffed again. 'I'd like that.'

'Yes, but I won't help you with your article, is that clear?'

Clara nodded resignedly. 'I suppose I'll just have to go to the library for my information.'

As Jenny held the door open for Clara, she saw Tom was heading out of his room. When he saw Clara's red eyes and the crumpled tissue in her hand, he shook his head at Jenny.

'I didn't touch her,' Jenny said, holding her palms up in surrender.

Tom said nothing, just moved past them, bouncing down the stairs, two at a time.

'What was all that about?' Clara said.

'Nothing, just a misunderstanding, that's all.' Jenny leaned over the banister, watching as Tom left the house.

Clara stood at the top of the stairs. 'See you soon, then. Promise?'

'Scout's honour. I have your mobile number, I'll text you.'

Jenny closed the door to her room and stood with her back resting against it, thinking about her dad. He could keep his tears and the sodding photo albums. If he'd really cared he could have reached out to her.

Looking out of the window she noticed the mists coming in. She moved closer and peered out into the distance, to the hill that had now disappeared beneath the vapour. As patters of rain began to fall, she thought about tomorrow night, her last chance to get back into the asylum, before Bob gave up on her too.

CHAPTER 39

'Now you mention it, I haven't seen Jasmine since last night,' said Caroline. She looked over to Vicky. 'What about you, Vicky, have you seen Jasmine?'

'I haven't, no — you don't think she's left, do you?'

'Probably realised that she shouldn't be here in the first place,' Audrey said, pushing her plate as far away from her as she could.

'She would have cracked it by the end of this week though; it's always harder to lose those last pounds,' Caroline said.

'I reckon she's gone home,' said Gaynor. 'Can't have been easy being the only one to put on weight at a diet clinic. Not sure I could stand the humiliation.'

'I'll go and knock on her door, make sure she's OK,' Amy said, standing up from her chair.

Dr Cavendish appeared at the dining-room door.

'Not hungry, ladies? Looks like the magic jab is doing its work and suppressing those big appetites.'

She turned her attention to Amy.

'Amy, I have some good news.'

'Have they brought my suitcase back?'

Dr Cavendish smiled. 'I'm afraid not. Still no news on that — I'll chase them up for you if you like?'

Amy's shoulders dropped; she craved her comfortable clothes, the warmth and familiarity of them. Dr Cavendish cut through her thoughts.

'I hear you worked above and beyond in class this afternoon. Kim tells me you gave it 110 per cent.'

'I did my best,' Amy said.

'We like to reward our hard workers. You have earned a nice hot detoxifying Epsom salt bath, how does that sound?'

Amy thought she heard Gaynor huff behind her, and a chair scrape slightly along the floor.

'Thank you,' she said, self-conscious to have her reward announced in front of everybody.

'We will have it ready for you tomorrow night. Kim will prepare it for eight p.m.'

Amy smiled at the other women, feeling guilty for having been singled out. All but Gaynor looked pleased — her face was stony, her mouth fixed in a thin line. For a moment Amy considered offering the reward to Gaynor instead, a desperate attempt to appease her and be friends again. Then she felt the single trickle of sweat fall down her back and the urge left her. The thought of soaking her tired body in hot water was the first thing she'd had to look forward to in a long time, and not even the dark mood of her new friend was going to spoil it.

'If you'd all like to meet in the main showers at eight p.m. tonight, ladies, we have a treatment planned for you all. Something you should all enjoy.'

Amy was not sure that a doctor who thought that a single raisin was a treat fully understood the concept of enjoyment, but at least it was something to pass the time.

Anya came into the room and began to clear the plates away, and the doctor departed. When the sound of her heels clicking down the corridor had faded to silence, Anya spoke to Amy.

'Why you not eat?' She pointed at the curling vegetables on her plate. 'It's not good?'

Amy looked up to Anya, feeling guilty for her lack of appreciation for the food the woman had prepared.

'I, erm, I wasn't hungry. It's not the food, it's the injections.'

Anya raised an eyebrow. 'Injections!' she exclaimed, before muttering to herself, 'I'm not surprised. What you eat here, the way you prepare, is waste of good vegetables.' Anya scraped the food into a plastic tub and piled Amy's plate on the metal trolley. 'In my country, they do anything right now for these vegetables.'

'You can send them there then if you like, they're bloody horrible,' Gaynor laughed.

Amy shot a look at Gaynor. For once it was her eyes blazing; she wanted to apologise to Anya on Gaynor's behalf, but the chef-cum-housekeeper had retreated back into her own world somewhere far away, and the moment had passed.

* * *

Amy knocked on Jasmine's door and called softly, 'Jasmine, it's me, Amy.'

Silence.

'Jasmine, are you in there?'

Amy pushed the handle down and opened the door. As she did, an icy gust of wind blew into her face. Across the room, the window had been left open and water had pooled in the windowsill and was dripping to the floor. The curtains wafted in the breeze, the bottom of the material heavy with rain. Jasmine's bed was perfectly made, and her clothes neatly piled on a chair. She had now been gone for almost twenty-four hours, but her room looked like it was awaiting her return at any moment. Amy darted her eyes back to the corridor before creeping through the door and closing it behind her. On Jasmine's bedside table the pages of high-end fashion magazines fluttered and snapped, images of handbags and lithe limbs appearing and disappearing.

She knocked gently on the toilet door.

'Jasmine, are you in there?'

Amy hesitated, before opening the door to an empty bathroom. Jasmine's toothbrush and toothpaste sat neatly in a plastic container alongside expensive-looking creams and make-up. A shiver of unease crawled up Amy's spine with a feeling that she couldn't shake. Even though Jasmine was nowhere to be seen, her presence still felt close.

CHAPTER 40

OBSERVATION SHEET
Date: Wednesday, 25 April 1985
Patient: Jenny Patton

General notes: Patient has been returned to ward by police after leaving without permission two days ago. She has been in Whitby with Danny Char (unborn baby's father and fellow patient) at his friend's flat. One hour accompanied daily walk withdrawn until further notice.

2 p.m.: Upset and unable to eat, concern for health of unborn baby. Parents called, mother refuses to visit. Matron not allowing her to see Danny as punishment.

4 p.m.: Patient's dad visits and spends time with her — she is calmer. She has asked her dad to take her home. It is explained to her that this is not possible. When her father leaves, she becomes agitated again, is sedated and left to sleep. At review it is decided that she is not ready to leave the hospital and must stay for the time being. Matron advises that parental visits are disturbing her further and should be discouraged.

6 p.m.: Asleep.
8 p.m.: Sleeping.

10 p.m.: Threatens Verity, who is goading her about pregnancy. All access to kitchen for patient now withdrawn. Spoons only to be used at mealtimes, art therapy classes withdrawn for a month as punishment.

Notes: General opinion of nursing staff is that if she is allowed to see Danny for limited amount of time each day, it will be much better for her mental health and well-being. Matron refusing. As a caregiver, I would like it to be noted here that I am concerned with heavy-handed treatment of patient. It feels like she is spiralling.

CHAPTER 41

'I've done this before, it really works,' said Caroline, trying to find the end of the cling film with her nail. 'I lost four pounds after just one session.'

The women had gathered in the communal shower room for their evening therapy session.

Gaynor was stretching the cling film and dragging it across her face, squashing her nose and tongue flat. Even Audrey managed a smile at her antics. Dr Cavendish chewed at her lip as she watched Gaynor, clenching her hand into a tight fist. There was talk between the women of the treat being a massage, or maybe a manicure. Sweating toxins out wrapped in plastic had been a disappointment to all but Caroline, who now triumphantly pulled the cling film free.

'Where do we change?' asked Vicky.

Dr Cavendish turned, already irritated by Gaynor. 'For goodness' sake, you're all women together, just find a quiet corner somewhere if you must. Give your clothes to the girls and they'll return them when you're finished.'

Amy took the roll into the corner of the bathroom and stood behind a sink, giving her some cover. A passing temptation to exit via the frosted window behind her was thwarted when she saw the lock at the bottom. They were all busy trying to juggle rolls of cling film and get undressed, but still she felt conspicuous. It felt like they were all waiting for her to undress and would then turn, pointing and laughing at her.

Gaynor was hopping from one leg to another, removing her trousers; Vicky tugged at Caroline's jumper, both laughing as it got caught on her ears. She watched as Audrey took her trousers down, revealing heavy thighs and a purple varicose vein bulging on her calf. There was something else on Audrey's body; for a moment Amy thought it was the shadows cast in the dull light, but looking again she saw properly. Yellowish-green bruises on the tops of her arms, ghosts of fingers that had grabbed at her skin. When Audrey turned Amy held a gasp inside, resisting the urge to call out. Audrey's back was bruised and scarred as if she had been beaten with a metal pole of some kind. It was clear now that her husband wasn't just mentally cruel. When Audrey caught Amy watching her, she retreated to the darker corner of the bathroom, wrapping herself in cling film until there was nothing but blurred skin to be seen on her back.

Gaynor flung her blouse off, laughing at a joke she had just told Vicky, who was shaking her head in response. Gaynor was what the tabloids would call 'pleasantly plump'. Her skin was soft, dotted with freckles that covered her arms and chest. The kind of woman that would command attention no matter her dress size.

'Come on, Amy, we need to get the showers turned on.'

The room was clinical, all white walls and tiles. Three shower cubicles behind white doors. It was difficult to imagine that even blasting hot showers would raise the temperature in the frigid room.

The other women who had been wrapped now wore just their pants beneath the plastic. Amy took a deep breath and lifted the purple dress over her head, folding it and laying it over the sink. Next, she reached around her back and unhooked her bra, releasing her heavy boobs from their confinement. She threw the bra on top of the dress and quickly gathered up her breasts and held them protectively from the gaze of the other women, who, other than Gaynor, seemed too conscious of their own ridiculous state of undress to notice her. Much to her mortification, Tina and Kim had seen fit to come over and help her. Working together, they passed the roll of cling film between them, wrapping it around her body like a web encasing an unfortunate fly. By now some of the women had been mummified in plastic for ten minutes, and already the treatment was taking its toll.

'Do you know where Jasmine is?' Amy asked the two assistants.

Tina shot a glance at Kim, who avoided her eyes and crouched down, passing the roll around Amy's bottom.

'Has she left? I haven't seen her and her stuff's still—'

'I don't know,' Tina said, her tone snippy, 'we don't have anything to do with that side of things.'

'Oh,' Amy said, trying to breathe in as they continued to mummify her in plastic.

The assistants Sellotaped the last of the plastic to her body and left, turning on each shower in the row of cubicles and locking the door of each from the outside. Water hit the tiled floor like nails on concrete and steam began to fill the room.

'What if we want to come out before it's over?' Gaynor shouted above the torrent of water.

Dr Cavendish looked up from her notes, 'Breathe your way through it, Gaynor, the results will be worth it. Your skin will glow!'

Amy wished she hadn't breathed in quite so deep when they had wrapped her stomach; now her flesh burned against the plastic, and mild panic rose in her at the thought of not being able to fully inhale for another thirty minutes.

Kim and Tina gathered the empty cardboard tubes and clothes and left the room. Dr Cavendish followed them, closing the door behind her; the sound of the lock turning was followed by footsteps disappearing down the corridor.

'I'm too hot already,' Vicky groaned, placing her hands on the cold sink to steady herself.

Faces came in and out of view as the steam thickened and swirled. At first the heat was welcome and a relief from the cold they were constantly subjected to, but after a while it began to feel suffocating, like a ring stuck tight on a finger, with a desperate need to pull it off.

'I don't think we should stand, do you?' said Gaynor through the mist. 'Let's lie on the floor.'

'She didn't tell us we could lie down,' said Caroline.

'There might be a good reason why you have to stand,' added Vicky.

'Well, I for one don't intend to pass out and knock myself cold on the tile flooring,' said Audrey, who descended down into the steam like a deflating blow-up doll.

Blurred bodies sank to the floor one by one. Amy joined them, dropping to her knees and swinging her legs round to the front before slowly lying back onto the cold, clammy floor tiles and disappearing under a blanket of steam. The lights above glowed through the mist as Amy closed her eyes and tried to visualise not being bound in plastic in a hot room. As she lay down, she craned her neck from wall to wall; as the breath of steam curled around her neck, she felt eyes on her. It wasn't the first time she had felt like she wasn't alone, even when there was nobody to be seen.

Caroline and Vicky began a running commentary on the power of positive thinking. Audrey asked them to be quiet, to which they replied that her negativity would be her downfall. Gaynor soon fell asleep, her snores muffled by the damp air.

As Amy lay quietly she began to relax, letting the heat warm her skin. The buzzy feeling from the morning's injection was gently wearing off and her brain was slowly settling and letting thoughts blur and float again. Just beneath the hiss of the showers and the occasional mumble of the women's voices she heard something.

The music.

She sat up suddenly, the tight cling film pinching at her middle and depriving her of even more breath.

'Can you hear that?' she gasped.

Through the mist of steam she saw the blur of another body sit up.

'Hear what?' said Caroline, unseen through the vapour.

'Music, I keep hearing it.'

There was a pause before Caroline replied, 'All I can hear is the water. It's probably the security guards with a radio outside.'

Amy saw the blur of Caroline relax back down, gentle snores from the other bodies the only other sound below the hissing shower. She lay back down on the floor trying to tune back into the notes again. As she settled her gaze back to the swirls of steam above, the lights snapped off, immersing her and the other women into muggy darkness.

A giggling voice in the distance cackled through the thick air.

'Who's that?' Amy demanded, pushing at the air with her hands.

There was a shuffling in the room and Vicky called out, 'For God's sake, Amy, try and relax. I think this place is making you go doolally.'

Amy didn't think it was possible to get any hotter, but her cheeks burned with the rebuttal, made worse by the silent consensus of the others. She turned and pulled herself along the floor like a plastic caterpillar, following the voices. Her knees squeaked across the wet tiles as she reached the bottom of a wall and put a shrivelled hand out towards a vent. She curled her fingers around one of the metal bars and pulled herself closer, recoiling at the touch of slimy grime that coated the metal. As she lay in the warm mist, her ear to the coolness of the grate, the childish giggles turned to faint warped cries. Tuning out the waterfall of the showers, she heard metal crashing against stone, like crutches hitting the floor. Then she heard something else; it was croaky and weak but just audible beneath the music and faint clatter, a voice she recognised.

Jasmine.

CHAPTER 42

Dr Cavendish would rather have visited an 'all you can eat' buffet at a cheap motel than attend the networking event for Crowthorpe business leaders. Now she felt it was time to show her face and play nice; she needed to know that her own place in the business community was secure. The room was wall to wall with self-aggrandising men that had little more power than a three-amp lightbulb. Their cheap suits matched the dated décor and the worn carpets made her skin itch. She stood by the food table, the scant selection of beige fare a predictable disappointment.

Their two hands collided reaching for the plate of cracked cheese and stale-looking biscuits. Dr Cavendish pulled her hand back instantly, bristling at the touch of Bob's damp skin against hers. He still had his sheepskin coat on, the yellowing wool of the collar gathering in wet clumps.

'You first, Doctor,' Bob said, gesturing to the biscuits, which were surrounded by limp lettuce leaves and tomato halves, cut with a jaw-like edge.

Dr Cavendish took a single water biscuit and put it on the paper plate she held. She felt Bob's eyes on her.

'It is *Doctor*, isn't it? Dr Cavendish from the new clinic?'

'Yes.'

'Bob Dickinson.' He spoke as if she should have heard of him. 'I thought it must be you. I heard from Mr Greaves that you were a bit of a looker.'

They both turned to Frank Greaves, who was resting a plate of food on his stomach, tomato juice drizzling down his chin as he ground down a mouthful of food. When he saw them look over, he waved at the doctor, who nodded in acknowledgement.

'Do you work for the council too?' she said, turning back to Bob, whose jaw clenched at her words. She enjoyed eking out as much irritation from the man as she could.

'Me? No!' He laughed as if it were a ridiculous idea. 'Bob Dickinson, of Dickinson Developments?'

'My apologies, I'm afraid I'm still getting to know who's who locally.'

He looked suitably offended, the heat of his annoyance soothing her mind and soul. A man's ego was a fragile thing, and the occasional crack kept them in line.

The gathering of local dignitaries and influential entre-preneurs was scant to say the least. A few council members, developers and a couple of local business owners who stood and shuffled awkwardly around, clasping paper plates and cheap fizz. Dr Cavendish's attendance had been required to quash suspicions as to who the new leaseholder was; a lack of mystery might dampen the gossip. A grey-haired photographer circulated, snapping attendees eager to make the *Crowthorpe Chronicle* social pages. When he saw Dr Cavendish he eagerly lifted his camera to his eye — the doctor turned just in time to miss the explosion of light and the photographer's silent curse.

'I think you can afford a bit of cheese with that,' Bob said, looking at her plate.

'Pardon?' she said, before looking down at the dry cracker, then smiling. 'Oh, yes, I have to watch my weight if I'm going to set an example to others.'

She watched as he bit into a Jacob's cracker, flakes attaching themselves to his moustache which he wiped away with his damp hanky.

'How's it going up there?' he asked.

'Very well — excellent, in fact.' She smiled, narrowing her eyes, conscious not to let slip her real feelings towards him.

'To be honest I was surprised you picked somewhere so remote — no passing trade.'

Dr Cavendish let out a light laugh. 'We don't rely on passing trade, Mr Dickinson. I advertise in national magazines and get applicants from all over the UK.'

'Applicants? You mean you pick and choose?'

'That's right. In order to be a success I try to find women that truly want to change their lives.'

'I see.' He stretched his mouth and then puckered it. 'Course, you know I was in the mix to take the building over.'

'I'm sure you were a worthy opponent, Mr Dickinson.'

'Bob, please.'

A flake of cracker had stuck to his chin and flapped about when he spoke.

'But somehow you pipped me to the post. I hope you'll excuse me from saying this, but I'll never quite understand how.'

'Really?' Dr Cavendish was amused at his effrontery.

'I was willing to pay more, provide luxury housing—'

'I understand you want to knock the whole thing down. That's a lot of history gone with a swing or two of the wrecking ball.'

Bob took an indelicate swig from a wine glass and regarded her.

'The place is already starting to crumble. Trust me, you'll end up ploughing thousands into it just to keep it upright. No, the best thing you could do is let me buy you out of the lease and knock the thing down. I'd be doing you a favour, and I'm sure in time the council will agree.'

'And replace it with more of your characterless boxes? Not a chance.'

A ripple of anger crossed Bob's face, quickly replaced with a sly grin. He reached in his pocket for a cigar and lit it, the puff of smoke making Dr Cavendish cough.

'Yes, well, I've not given up yet. All's fair in love and war and all that. I have my ways . . .' He winked at her and tapped at the side of his nose. 'You know what they say, it's not over till the fat lady sings.'

She put her hand to her stomach and smiled. 'Well, I'm afraid I can't help you there.'

A gum-chewing young waitress sidled up behind them and began refilling Bob's glass with sweet white wine. She then turned to Dr Cavendish, chasing her glass with the bottle. The doctor put her hand over the glass. 'I'm driving.'

The waitress shrugged and wandered off to the next party guest.

'So then, tell me, Dr Cavendish, what's your story? You're not from round here, are you?'

Christ, she wished she didn't have to endure this. She was here to avoid suspicion about the doctor on the hill and give the barest scraps of details before leaving to get on with her work. She had not expected to be grilled by this two-bit wheeler-dealer in cheap shoes.

'My family are from the Lake District.'

'Very nice part of the country that, I've always th—'

Dr Cavendish held a finger up and Bob stopped talking, a flicker of annoyance on his face.

'Please excuse me, Bob, I just need to powder my nose.'

She left him to seethe into his glass of cheap wine and headed towards the toilets.

* * *

Dr Cavendish applied a coat of lipstick, pausing when the lock on the cubicle behind her snapped open. Councillor Patton appeared, stopping in her tracks when she saw Dr Cavendish. The councillor looked from side to side before moving over to the sink next to the doctor, turning the taps on and spinning the thin bar of soap between her palms.

'We need to talk about the extension on the lease,' said Dr Cavendish. 'I want to know that it's definitely happening.'

'We have to know that your business venture is a success first,' replied Councillor Patton, a slight crack in her voice. 'You knew that from the start; that was the deal.'

'Bob Dickinson seems very confident he's going to take it off me.'

'Bob has a lot of fingers in a lot of pies. I wouldn't worry about him — he'll get bored and move on to another idea soon enough.'

'I saw him talking to Jenny yesterday morning; they looked very cosy.'

Councillor Patton stopped turning the soap in her palms and placed it back on the sink.

'That doesn't mean anything. Jenny lives in one of his slum squats. It was probably to do with that.'

'No, I've never seen her with him before now.'

Councillor Patton narrowed her eyes, looking at Dr Cavendish's reflection in the mirror. 'Are you spying on Jenny?'

Dr Cavendish snapped shut the clasp on her handbag. 'Just make sure that the lease is extended. Us women need to stick together.'

She winked at the councillor before sweeping her bag from the sink and leaving.

CHAPTER 43

Gaynor banged her fists against the bathroom door.

'Open the door, I can't breathe in here!'

'I told you you'd frighten everyone if you kept on,' said Caroline, trying to reach out to Gaynor.

They had been there for almost thirty minutes, twenty of those in the dark, the last ten with Amy trying to persuade them that Jasmine was somehow still in the building.

'I'm telling you, I heard Jasmine's voice. She's still in the hospital somewhere.'

'Stop it, Amy, that's enough,' Vicky pleaded.

'It's all these bloody pills and this heat, we're all in a state at the moment. It isn't fair to have kept us in here all this time,' said Audrey in the dark mist around them.

The moon shone a bluish light that warped through the frosted glass and gave a grey light inside the shower room.

'This is ridiculous! One of us could have died in here and they wouldn't know or care!' Gaynor shouted, banging the base of her palm against the door.

Amy could make out Audrey drinking water from the sink, cupping her hands together and lapping at the falling water with her tongue like a thirsty dog.

Caroline was trying to keep calm, repeating a mantra over and over, Vicky clutching her arm.

'It feels like we've been in here for hours,' Vicky said, sounding like she was on the verge of panic herself.

'Let me fucking out!' Gaynor smashed at the door, which bounced open, revealing Tina and Kim standing on the other side holding folded towels, which they handed to each of the women.

'Oh, thank God!' Caroline cried. 'I thought we were spending the night in here.'

'Mind, imagine how skinny we'd be by breakfast!' Vicky joked, her voice trembling.

A whoosh of steam billowed out from the bathroom, dissolving in the chill of the corridor.

'Calm down, Gaynor. You've made it to the end, and I bet you feel better for it,' Tina said.

Gaynor stared at the young assistant. Her curly hair was wet, and her usually bubbly fringe was plastered to her forehead. Red patches on her chest and neck prickled her skin.

'You shouldn't have left us in here like this, it's inhumane. We could have died!'

'There's no need for hysterics, Gaynor. It's all part of the programme you agreed to. You have to trust the doctor to do the best for you and nothing bad will happen,' Tina said.

'I want to go home,' wailed Gaynor.

'When you see the results, I bet you'll change your mind,' Kim encouraged. She looked shaken seeing the state Gaynor had got into. 'Maybe we should weigh you and you can see for yourself what a difference it's made.' Kim looked over to Tina.

Tina nodded, her eyes fixed on Gaynor, who looked like she might punch the next person that touched her. 'Good idea. Let's get you dressed and then get the scales.'

While Tina went to unlock the shower doors to turn off the steaming hot water, Kim took a large pair of scissors and cut each woman free from the plastic wrap. Audible sighs of relief echoed around the wet bathroom as each woman took a full breath for the first time in almost an hour.

Amy noticed Tina searching her pockets, getting increasingly desperate, frantically padding her uniform. She turned to walk towards the bathroom door, which had closed on itself.

'Shit!' Tina cursed, the women all turning to her in alarm.

She marched over to the door and pulled at it, but it wouldn't open.

'What's wrong?' said Audrey, buttoning up the cuffs of her polyester blouse.

'I didn't put the latch on and . . . the keys, I left them in the lock. I was stressed with all the shouting, I—'

'You mean we're locked in?' Caroline asked.

Tina nodded fearfully. As the information began to sink in, one by one the women turned to the shower cubicles and the steam that was beginning to refill the bathroom.

'Are the keys to the shower cubicles out there too?' Amy asked, already guessing the answer.

Tina nodded.

'The doctor will notice we haven't come back, and she'll be along to open it,' said Vicky, a hopeful smile on her face.

Kim looked at Tina and then back to Vicky. 'She's gone out for the evening.'

Audrey groaned, putting her hand to her chest.

'Let's keep calm,' Caroline said, putting her arm around Audrey, who was too distracted to push her away. 'Is there anyone else in the building that might hear us if we all shout together?'

'What about Robert or the cook, what's her name?' said Vicky.

'Lurch,' said Gaynor, whose cockiness had returned in the presence of Tina and Kim.

'Anya. Her name's Anya,' bristled Amy.

'It's worth a try. After three, let's all shout for help — ready?' Caroline corralled.

They all stood in a circle, eyes darting to each other's in anticipation of the noise they were about to make. Each woman nodded as they began to disappear behind a thick fog of steam.

'One . . . two . . . three . . .'

CHAPTER 44

Dr Cavendish gripped the heated leather steering wheel and turned her four-by-four down the first ramp of the two-storey car park, trying to avoid the crushed beer cans and discarded needles that had blown into the path of cars. Vivaldi's *The Four Seasons* blasted out from the speakers within as she sneered at the cars she passed. Ramshackle tins on wheels as dull as the people that drove them. When she spotted Bob's Jaguar among the scraps, with its obnoxious number plate, she pushed her right foot to the floor, her teeth bared like a dog as the engine roared and echoed within the concrete structure. She recalled Bob's smug face as she'd said goodbye, his yellow-toothed grin and whisky-sodden breath as he'd pulled her in close and slurred, 'I've got someone watching you,' tapping his bulbous nose and wiping away the spittle from his chin with his sleeve. 'I'll have you out of there by the New Year.'

He was so drunk he wouldn't remember what he'd said by tomorrow, but still Dr Cavendish knew that drunk men let slip their truths. As she flew towards his car, she pictured the meeting with Jenny and then she imagined him in her grounds, tearing down her building with monstrous machines. With a sudden jerk, she swapped her foot to the brake pedal, pushing it to the floor, her arms locked and body tense, screeching to a stop with just feet to spare.

Her thoughts turned to the guard dog and Mr Cotterill's assurances, and she was momentarily cheered to think of it ripping any intruders limb from limb. She had to stay calm; as long as she could keep the hospital contained it would be fine. Nobody was going to take anything away from her again. *Nobody.*

* * *

Dr Cavendish had heard the women screaming from the clinic car park.

'What the hell happened?' Dr Cavendish demanded, wafting at the steam in front of her.

'We've been soaking towels with cold water and laying them on them.' Tina said, her firm voice cracking.

Both Tina and Kim had stripped down to their underwear and Amy and the other women lay on the floor in their pants, their bodies all lobster red from the heat.

'Why didn't you turn the showers off?' said Dr Cavendish.

'The keys to the cubicles were in the door — we couldn't open them.' Kim was almost in tears.

Robert appeared at the bathroom door, red-faced and out of breath.

'And where were you, Robert? Go and get Anya up, get her to bring us some iced water and glasses.'

Robert watched as the women began to sit up with the help of Kim and Tina.

'Now, Robert!'

Her words sliced through his trance and he left immediately. Dr Cavendish watched him go, then passed her keys to Tina.

'Turn them all off now.'

Tina immediately unlocked the three shower doors and reached around the flow of water to turn the dials off, the hissing water quieting to a steady *drip-drip*.

'What happened?' Gaynor said, dragging the wet hair back from her forehead, a dazed expression on her face.

'You just had the most intense steam we could possibly have given you,' Dr Cavendish replied.

Kim looked incredulous. 'There should be an alarm in here or something!'

Dr Cavendish's eyes blazed at her. 'Luckily I was back early, so all is fine.'

The clattering of a trolley was followed by the entrance of Anya, who stared wide-eyed at the women, all now sat up. She opened her mouth to speak, but on seeing the doctor's expression closed her mouth and bowed her head, silently handing water to the women.

'Kim and Tina will help you all get dressed and then off to bed. Make sure to take your pills tonight; you will need a good night's sleep more than ever.'

She watched as her clients gulped their water and began to dress, wishing they'd hurry up. Her day would not end when they went to bed — tonight she had even more work to organise than usual.

WEEK THREE

CHAPTER 45

Amy stared out of her bedroom window rubbing at her sleepy eyes and trying to regain her focus. The diet pills they had each evening made her feel like she was still dreaming for the first hour of each day. It was 11 a.m. and she had only just woken with the bell. Before she came, she had imagined it would be cold showers at 6 a.m. or some other torturous regime, but the doctor wanted them to sleep for as long as possible, to heal and also because the less time they were awake, the less they would think about food. She wondered how she could continue this regime in real life.

As she looked out to the dew-covered, swaying grasses something seemed different. Still the same pale grey skies that never seemed to brighten, the woods ahead with barren trees that bent and creaked in the wind. The crumbling shelter in front of her room was still dripping onto the wooden bench beneath . . . and then as her vision drew backwards, towards the room, she saw what was different.

Her body tensed and a small bark of a nervous laugh left her lips as if this might be some dark joke. Amy lifted the sash window as high as she could and reached out. When she curled her fingers around the steely cold of the metal, she knew this wasn't her imagination. The bars now fixed on her window were as real as the hands that clutched them.

CHAPTER 46

Andrew pushed a scrap of A4 paper across the concrete floor, his tough skin dragging along the rough surface.

'I put together a list of times when the guards change over.'

Jenny grabbed it and read the scrawled writing in the dim light of his room. 'That's brilliant. Thanks, Andrew, you didn't have to do that. I don't want you to do anything that risks you getting thrown out of here.'

'See it as a thank you for the supplies.'

He gestured to the pot noodles, packets of biscuits and teabags she had brought for him. The gesture was a two-way thing; life had moulded, cast and then chipped Jenny, and the only people that could truly understand were those that had been locked in the kiln with her.

'It's not always the same times as I've put there. Sometimes they have fag breaks, wander off. But in the main, this is the routine. The dog—'

'Dog?' Jenny spluttered.

'Most beautiful Dobermann I've ever seen,' he swooned.

'Are beautiful Dobermanns' teeth as big as ugly Dobermanns'?'

Andrew laughed. 'Don't worry about him, he's with a dog handler; they don't just let him roam around. He's there

to scare you off, so if you do see him, put your hands up —
and whatever you do, don't run.'

'Jesus, I wish I'd stayed longer the other night now.
What is she expecting there? An armed siege?'

'It wouldn't be the first time there was a revolution in
the place would it?'

They smiled at each other, a silent acknowledgement of
their entwined history.

'There's something else you need to know.'

'What?' Jenny felt her stomach drop. 'Is it worse than a
rabid dog prowling the grounds?'

'I don't know why, it's strange. But last night she had all
the bars put back on the ground-floor windows.'

'Why would she do that?' A chill rose up Jenny's spine,
causing her to shudder. 'That's really weird. Do you think
she knows about me? That I've been there?'

'I doubt it. There's always someone interested in the
place — ravers, ghost-botherers . . .' He paused and narrowed
his eyes at her. 'Though, of course, you still haven't told me
why you're going back in there. Are you planning to bring
back the dead?'

'I don't need to bring them back, it's all in here.' She
prodded at her head.

'It wasn't your fault, Jenny, what happened to Matron.'

Jenny shook herself of the memory.

'Anyway, you were saying, about the bars.'

'Right, yes, the guard told me that a couple of workmen
appeared last night and put them on; they're planning to
secure them all by the end of the week, so you'd better get
done whatever it is you need to before then.'

'Fuck,' Jenny groaned.

In reality it was an added pressure she needed — there
wasn't much time before Bob would lose his patience with
her and the chance to get away would be gone for good.

'Listen, you might need a few extra tools, just in case.'

Andrew jumped to his feet and fetched a holdall over
from the corner of the room. When he dropped it to the

floor the contents clanged against each other like a bag of metal rods.

'What's in here?' Jenny asked, pulling the heavy zip and peering into the bag. Reaching in she took out the contents one by one. Bolt cutters, pieces of wire to pick locks, a screwdriver and a torch. When she placed the last item on the cold floor between them, she looked up to him in disbelief.

'What's this for?'

Jenny didn't even want to touch the ragged box.

'In case you get caught.'

She stared down at the Ouija board. 'What am I supposed to do, summon a spirit to help me?'

'No, you idiot, just pretend you're there to hunt ghosts; they'll be glad to see the back of you then.'

'Genius, Andrew.' She smiled, holding the box in the air. 'And if I don't make it out of there alive, then you know how to get in touch with me.'

CHAPTER 47

'Dr Cavendish, where's Jasmine?'

The doctor's smile slipped for a second, then just as quickly as it had disappeared, returned. She shook her head at the women, who were all waiting for her response.

'Good question, Amy. In all the drama of last night, I forgot to keep you all updated — apologies.' Dr Cavendish clasped her hands together and addressed the women. 'Jasmine had a funny turn after breakfast yesterday. So, to be on the safe side I took her to Crowthorpe General.' There was a collective gasp in the dining room. 'Please don't worry, ladies, I'm sure she'll be back with us soon enough to continue on her plan.'

'Poor thing,' said Caroline. 'Well, she's in the best place.' She looked at Amy with an *I told you so* expression on her face.

Amy relaxed a little; she didn't want to believe that it was Jasmine's voice she had heard through the metal vents. She was more than happy to put it down to the diet drugs and the delirium of the steam room. She had been exhausted and she was, as always, starving hungry. The pills they swallowed and injections that were administered made her feel in turns woozy and manic.

'Can we go and see her?' Amy asked.

'We could get a McDonald's while we're out,' chirped Gaynor.

'Very funny, Gaynor,' Dr Cavendish sniped. 'Jasmine will be back soon enough. You don't have long to reach your goals, so you need to stay here in the clinic, OK?

'Talking of staying in the clinic, why have we got bars on the windows, Dr Cavendish?' Audrey asked, fixing a stare on the doctor.

'Another good question and I wish I could give you a sensible answer, but it seems there was some clause in the contract I signed that stated I must preserve the exterior of the building. So, unfortunately, that meant reinstating the bars. My advice to you, ladies: always read the small print.'

Amy thought about the contract she had signed on arrival and her stomach dropped a little; she looked around to the other women, who also had a flush of concern on their faces.

'Right, Caroline,' the doctor commanded, 'you're first on the scales this morning.'

* * *

By 11.30 a.m., a total of thirty-two pounds had been recorded as lost between the five women. Caroline was ecstatic to have beaten Amy by a pound and Gaynor sulky for being behind Audrey by two pounds. Dr Cavendish had rewarded each woman with an extra helping of lemon and chilli juice, followed by another skinny injection. The previous night was all forgotten as soon as the women had seen the results and the weight loss they had achieved.

The days were starting to blur into each other and leaving felt a long way off. Amy had fourteen days to reach her goal weight, a mystical number conjured up between her parents and a woman that had never met her until two weeks ago.

Looking down at the gathered crepe sleeves on the dress she had been wearing, it occurred to her that nobody batted an eyelid at her strange clothes now, it was just who she had become. The clothes reminded her of jumble sales her mum took her to as a kid, stale clothes tumbling out of bin bags onto wobbly pasting tables. Those were the clothes that weren't good enough for a hanger, twisted up with tartan flared trousers and yellowing men's shirts.

Suddenly craving fresh air, even the blustering grey Yorkshire kind, Amy pulled her ragged cardigan on and headed for the main entrance. She had ventured out a couple of times in the past two weeks, a little further each time in case she got lost again. Now she was confident that she was familiar enough with the grounds to get back safely and without raising any alarms, or worse still, having Robert come and find her. It felt like he was everywhere. Amy wasn't used to attention, especially from a man. Perhaps she should have been flattered, but instead she felt only unease.

* * *

'Sorry, love, no going out there. Doctor's orders,' the security guard sniggered.

'I just need some fresh air,' Amy said, continuing forward towards the main door. 'I'll only be five minutes.'

The guard stood in front of her, holding his arm across the doorway.

'Strict orders for everyone to stay inside, unless it's for chaperoned exercise class.'

'Are you joking?' Amy scanned his face, waiting for a smile to crack through, but he remained stony, his sharp eyes holding her where she stood.

'What if I want a cigarette?' she said, patting her empty pocket.

'Open a window upstairs in the toilet, she'll never know. Besides, it's blowing a gale out there, you're better off inside.'

'This is insane — you can't keep me in here if I want to go out.'

The security guard took a clipboard from the reception desk. 'What's your name?'

'Amy.' She folded her arms across her chest, her defiant mood increasing by the second.

He flicked through the pages. 'Here we are, is this your signature?' He turned the clipboard to face her.

It took a moment before Amy recognised the form she had signed on her first night.

'Yes, but . . .'

The guard jabbed his finger halfway down the page. Amy squinted at the small print.

2a: Dr Cavendish has the right to refuse patients leave of the building if it is deemed to be in the patient's best interests.

'Why is it in my best interests to be locked in?'

'Don't shoot the messenger, I'm just following orders, miss. Nobody is to go out without the doctor's permission and without a chaperone.'

For a moment she thought about pushing past him and making a run for it, but what would happen then? In ten minutes, she'd have to return and explain herself. The collar on the dress felt like it was tightening around her neck; she pulled at it, trying to keep her breathing steady.

'Can I get you something, miss?' the guard offered.

Amy glared at him, then looked away and muttered, 'Jobsworth.'

He didn't reply, but cleared his throat, as if to let her know she had been heard. She didn't care; she hadn't wanted to leave anywhere so badly as she did right now. Was this some kind of mental exercise? Was she being tested? Even if Jasmine had gone to hospital, she was lucky; at least she was out for a bit. They wouldn't starve her there either; it would be hot meals and television. Amy had never wished herself ill, but right now throwing herself down the stairs and breaking a leg seemed like a good idea.

'Hello, sailor,' Gaynor said, heading towards the door, a cigarette already out of the pocket and lighter ready.

'We're not allowed out,' Amy said, surprised at the sudden warmth in Gaynor's voice.

'Says who?'

'The guard. Apparently we signed something waiving our rights to freedom.' Amy could feel herself getting intensely dramatic, hunger and desperation fuelling the buzz of her skinny injection.

'We'll see about that. Here, follow me.'

Flashes of the doctor's face gave her pause for thought, but frustration and the need for fresh air gave her cause for rebellion and she turned back and followed Gaynor. Amy was also buoyed by Gaynor's softening towards her.

'How are you going to get by him?' Amy whispered as they turned the corner towards the door.

'Wait here, and when I give you the signal run for it.'

Amy peered round the corner of the wall and watched as Gaynor approached the guard, limping heavily and crying out. She saw the guard rush to help her.

'What is it, ma'am?'

'I think I've broken my ankle,' she groaned, hanging onto the guard's arm. 'There's a crack in the flooring outside my room and I tripped. Can you go and get someone quickly, please?' She cried out in faux pain again.

The guard knocked on Dr Cavendish's door, and when there was no answer he ran up the corridor. He ignored Amy and scrambled down in the opposite direction like a Charlie Chaplin character, slipping and sliding on the polished floor.

'Come on!' Gaynor waved Amy over.

Amy rushed to the main door and they both pushed through and ran across the car park to the trees opposite the clinic, the wind pushing against them. It felt like something naughty boarding schoolgirls would do, the kind she'd read about in her *Bunty* annuals as a child. When they got there, they were both in a fit of nervous giggles, Amy trying to catch her breath as the cold air hurt her throat.

'What if Dr Cavendish had been in her office?' Amy asked through gasps of breath.

'I'd have styled it out until it was just a bruise. I might have got a sympathetic hot drink. It was a win–win situation.'

'She might have drugged you like she did me for eating the Mars bars.' Amy looked back to the clinic, a dark thought crossing her mind. 'She still might.'

Gaynor cupped her hands around her lighter, lit the cigarette she had ready and took a long drag, exhaling as she spoke, each word punctuated by smoke.

'I don't mind the sedatives. I'd rather sleep my way through this hell.'

'She'll go mad when she finds out.'

'What can she do? We're not prisoners. So what, we signed some stupid form? We can go when we like. It's not really like we're bound to it — we could leave if we wanted.'

'Not without the minibus that *she* organises. There's no phone signal here so you'd have to go halfway down the hill with your suitcase to call it yourself.'

Gaynor shrugged. 'Oh well, then we'll just put up with it for another week or so and then we don't have to come back ever again.'

'Do you think Jasmine has really gone to hospital?'

'You having more hallucinations?' Gaynor flicked her thumb against the tab end of the cigarette and the ash blew over her shoulder.

Amy laughed uneasily. 'I don't know, it's just a bit odd, don't you think? She didn't seem that ill to me. In fact, she was putting on weight.'

'Those skinny types are prone to sickness, I reckon — not built for endurance.'

Defeated by the wind, Gaynor stubbed her cigarette out on the floor and began to walk away.

'Gaynor, was there something wrong the other day? I mean, had I done something to upset you?'

'What do you mean?'

'I'm probably being oversensitive. Is it the trainers?' Amy looked down to the scuffed shoes.

'What? Oh that, don't worry about it. No, not the trainers. I was just a bit jealous, that's all. But not now I've found another distraction. Another guard, called Jake.'

'Jealous?'

'About you and Robert.'

'What do you mean, *me and Robert*?'

Gaynor smiled conspiratorially. 'I've seen him.' When Amy didn't twig, she carried on, 'Coming out of your room in the early hours.'

Amy felt her stomach turn; she didn't understand. Why would Robert have been in her room? Then, with a flush of relief, she realised.

'He must have been the one who brought these clothes, that's all. They just appear in the morning,' she said.

'Ha, nice try! You've only had two outfits so far; I've watched him leaving your room each morning for over a week now and each time he's in there at least an hour. How long does it take to put a dress on a hook?' She winked at Amy. 'They say it's always the quiet ones you have to watch.'

Amy's knees felt fluid, as if there were no bones or muscles keeping them upright.

'Don't worry,' Gaynor assured her, 'I won't tell anyone your dirty little secret.' She patted Amy on the back, causing her to stumble forward.

Amy watched as Gaynor skipped off into the woods, her red hair bouncing against the heavy damp air. Gaynor was lying — another of her wind-ups. Why would Robert come into her room at night? If he had tried anything on with her she would have known. The tablets they had were strong, but if you were actually touched, you would wake up, surely? That you wouldn't wake up didn't bear thinking about. She needed to know that this was a lie.

'Gaynor, wait!' Amy called, turning and running after her friend.

The injection they had been given caused her thoughts to race as she ran, the long purple dress catching and pulling on the brambles that lay like traps through the woods. Images of being watched while she slept flooded through her mind. Her cheeks burned and the icy air hurt with each intake of breath, like razor blades cutting at her throat. She stopped, resting her hand on the rough bark of a tree, her fingers brushing against the furrows of its rough bark.

Gaynor had disappeared like a wisp of vapour into the woods and Amy was alone again. Crows circled above, cawing beneath the grey sky. Defeated, Amy put both arms around the trunk and held her cheek against the knotty wood, closing her eyes tightly, her mind pulled between the elation that the drug produced and the unnerving feeling of uncertainty that Gaynor had pierced into her thoughts.

As she carried on walking through the woods, taking the long route back to the clinic, she reached out to touch everything in her path: spongy green moss, brittle twigs and thorny brambles. When she thought she heard the music again, carried along by the wind, she turned in circles, trying to figure out which direction it came from, her purple dress ballooning out as the wind caught underneath.

In the distance she noticed a low crumbling wall and what looked like a stone circle and an upturned bench. A secret garden. As a child her dad had read her that book at bedtime, and it had remained a story that comforted her and brought him closer ever since. Only her imagination could tell her what Mary Lennox had felt when she first went through the door to her garden, but she was pretty sure even in its abandoned and unloved state, it wasn't as dilapidated as the one Amy found when she reached it.

There were no surviving plants or flowers in the old garden, just more brambles and ivy, winding around and strangling any surface they could latch on to. No friendly robin, just a crow that had broken from the group and swooped down, landing on the spiked stump of a tree. It watched her from a distance, its beady eye following her curiously.

Amy pulled her sleeve down over her hand and removed some of the creeping vines away from a small stone embedded in the ground. Tiny thorns broke away and caught in the material, scratching her skin as she revealed the writing on the moss-covered stone. The crow scolded her, a rattle in its call.

Freddie Jones
4 October 1899—20 January 1975

Amy pulled back and scrambled off the stone. This was not a garden for the patients to relax and recuperate, but a graveyard for those that had never left. She moved to the next plot, a cross with no name. A whole row of blank crosses marked only with moss and decay. She spun around as, one by one, the gravestones suddenly became visible to her, as if they were rising from the sodden ground. The crow cawed again and flapped its wings, soaring into the grey sky.

This was the graveyard that the minibus driver had told them about, the one with all the pauper graves. Chiselled names reserved for the ones with family prepared to pay for them, the others just piles of forgotten bones. Human beings hidden away in life *and* death.

An icy blast of wind swirled down and around her, prickling her skin and blowing her hair over her face. With the wind came a low rumble of thunder in the distance. Debris and litter swept across the stones and through the air, catching in a vortex in the corner of the low brick wall, an empty carrier bag and dried leaves spinning around and around.

As Amy turned to leave, she saw the dark figure watching her from between the trees — how long had they been there?

Robert.

She didn't see the upturned bench until it was too late. As she began to stumble out of the graveyard, her foot got caught in its rotten slats and she flew over the top of it, holding out her hands, preparing to break her fall. She tipped face first, and her hands touched the ground only just before her forehead, which split as it hit an old limestone gravestone, her blood streaking across the green moss.

Shock paralysed her, that terrifying daze of a knock to the head rendering her mute. Instinctively she held her head, and when she brought her hand down and saw the dark blood across her fingers she began to cry, a pitying sob for her pain and her bad luck.

When a hand brushed her shoulder she froze, staring down as a drop of blood fell from her face and pooled in the gouged-out letters of the gravestone beneath her.

CHAPTER 48

'Wait!'

Jenny called out to the woman, who had scrambled to her feet and was trying to run away, stumbling from tree to tree.

'Leave me alone! I'll call the police!' the woman cried, not looking back.

'Calm down, I promise I won't hurt you, I—'

Before she could finish the sentence, the woman tripped again. Falling over twisted vines of ivy, she crumbled to the floor, letting out a frustrated cry. When Jenny reached her, her body heaved with sobs. Jenny put a comforting hand between her shoulder blades, and the woman turned to face her.

Jenny tried to hide the alarm on her face when she saw the deep cut on the woman's forehead, its edges already bruising and swollen, tiny specks of dirt and gravel embedded in the clotting blood. The woman's brow crumpled then softened when she saw Jenny's face, as if she was relieved it was her.

'Here, let me help.'

Jenny took out a tissue from her jacket pocket and a bottle of water from the bag she had with her. She poured the water on the tissue and held it towards the woman's head. She pulled back like an injured animal.

'It's OK, I just need to wipe the blood from your eye. What's your name?'

The woman's hands were trembling and her face pale from the shock of the fall.

'Amy?' she said quietly, as if she wasn't sure that was really her name.

'OK, Amy, where do you live?'

'The clinic, I'm staying at the clinic. I just came out for a walk and I—'

'It's fine, just stay still a minute.'

Jenny gently dabbed around Amy's eye, a tear of blood already drying, rubbed away in flakes. Jenny could feel the woman shivering as the wind continued to beat at them. She removed her jacket and put it around Amy's shoulders. Jenny looked down to the strange torn dress and the dried leaves that had caught in the woman's hair. She didn't look like a client of an exclusive diet clinic, she looked crazed.

'We should probably get you to a hospital.'

As soon as the words left her mouth, Jenny tried to think how she could get her there. She couldn't run into the clinic, otherwise she'd have to explain why she had been in the grounds in the first place. If she could get the woman to the top of the lane, she could call a taxi to come and get them, or maybe Andrew could have a word with one of the more friendly guards. Amy interrupted her thoughts.

'No, it's fine, Dr Cavendish will be able to see to it.'

'The clinic doctor?' Jenny said, still not sure that this woman wasn't an old patient of the asylum who had made the pilgrimage back here dazed and confused.

'Yes, if you could just help me find my way back? It's over there somewhere.' Amy held out a blood-streaked hand and pointed in the wrong direction.

Jenny's eyes flickered in the right direction of the clinic — she could find her way there with her eyes closed. Jenny nodded. She would take her as far as the end of the woods;

it wasn't far for the woman to walk from there, just across the car park. There was a guilty relief at not having to do more than that; she had enough on her plate without getting involved in this woman's problems.

'OK, let me help you up.'

Jenny reached out her hand and Amy held onto it, rising slowly to her feet. They waited a moment for Amy to steady herself before Jenny led her back to the path.

'What are you doing here?' Amy asked, her voice weak.

Jenny patted the canvas holdall, the tools Andrew had lent her clattering together.

'My brother sent me to bring some tools to his mate, he works here as a security guard.'

Her ability to lie so immediately was a skill that continued to serve Jenny well. Luckily the woman seemed too focused on the issue in hand to ask any more questions and she just nodded vaguely.

'So, you're at the beauty clinic — what's it like in there?'

Amy flinched as she spoke, as if any facial movement hurt her head, 'It's OK. Not much food and a lot of drugs.'

Jenny laughed. 'Sounds like it hasn't changed much.'

'What do you mean?' Amy turned to Jenny.

'Nothing. I mean, I heard they used to drug the patients to keep them quiet.'

'It's not like that, and the food's good, just not a lot of it.'

Jenny nodded, eager not to upset the woman. They made their way past the old incinerator building; Jenny looked up, surprised to see the smoke rising. She had difficulty believing that the entire grounds and its buildings had not gone to sleep the moment the doors had been closed five years ago. She had imagined a Sleeping Beauty castle scenario from the Brothers Grimm, the asylum dormant for at least a hundred years, bound by thorns and misery.

'I can't come in with you — into the clinic, I mean.'

Amy looked at her, eyebrows furrowed. 'Why?'

'Nobody is supposed to be in the grounds. It'd get the guard in trouble if they knew I was here.'

'Oh, OK. I'll be fine once I know where I am,' Amy said.

They walked a while further, lightning closing in as fat drops of rain began to fall.

'I don't know why you'd pay all that money to stay here; there's nothing wrong with the way you look.'

Amy stopped, branches crunching under her feet. She turned and glared at Jenny, then looked her up and down.

'Easy for you to say. I bet you've never been more than a pound overweight in your life.'

'I've got more important things to worry about than what I look like, that's all. Maybe if you focused on something else, a hobby or something you'd—'

'What? Forget about food and magically become thin? Oh, that's brilliant! You should run a clinic yourself, you're a genius.'

'Christ, all right, I was just saying. I didn't mean to upset you.'

'You have no idea what it's like doing something that you know is hurting you but being unable to stop doing it.'

Jenny was about to deliver a killer blow with regards to her own self-destruction, but it wasn't the right time, and besides, she had asked for it. The woman's weight was none of her business, likewise neither was how she decided to deal with it.

'I'm sorry, I shouldn't have said anything.'

'My head is pounding,' Amy cried. 'Perhaps I should go to the local hospital after all.'

'Well, you *definitely* wouldn't be going there,' Jenny affirmed. 'There's no such thing anymore.'

'What do you mean?' said Amy.

'There was no need for such a big hospital in the town once this place closed. The nearest hospital is over thirty miles away. That's where I'd have directed the taxi to. You're probably better off letting the doctor here check you over first.'

Amy clutched Jenny's jumper sleeve and turned to her, the rain beating at her forehead diluting the blood into a weak pink wash that flowed down her cheek.

'You're wrong, my friend Jasmine is there. The doctor took her there yesterday morning.'

Jenny shook her head. 'Wherever your friend is, she's not there. Crowthorpe General closed its doors three years ago.'

CHAPTER 49

When she saw Amy's forehead, Anya let go of the black bin bag she was carrying. It fell to the floor, carrot peelings and cabbage skin tumbling out across the ornate mosaic reception tiles. Amy closed the entrance door behind her and raised her hands to placate Anya, who was already reaching towards the wound with her large hands, vegetable matter and soil lodged under her stubby nails.

'What is this?'

'It's nothing, just a little cut.'

Anya tipped her head to the side and narrowed her eyes.

'It's bad. Need clean and stitches.'

'What? No, it won't be that serious, Dr Cavendish will look after it — have you seen her?'

'You need a doctor. I help. You worry?' said Anya, moving towards her again.

'No, no, I no worry, you don't worry.' Her attempts at pidgin English were beginning to make her already aching head burst with pain.

Anya touched her forehead with her large fingers; Amy ducked, and they fell away.

'It's OK, Anya, I'll be fine. I need Dr Cavendish,' she insisted, then muttered, under her breath, 'not a cook.'

'I check,' Anya said, chasing her with her fingers.

'No, I'm fine, please, leave me.'

'But I can help, I—'

The door to Dr Cavendish's office swung open and Anya jumped back, leaving Amy leaning weakly against the wall.

'What on earth is all the commotion?' Then she saw Amy. 'Good heavens, whatever happened to you?'

Dr Cavendish rushed to her and put an arm around her shoulders, guiding her into the office. The doctor looked back to the peelings strewn across the floor and then to Anya.

'Clear up that mess — that's what your paid for.'

Anya backed away and quietly retrieved the bin bag, crouched down to the floor and began gathering up the scraps.

* * *

The forked lightning illuminated the room as Amy lay on the paper-covered chaise longue in Dr Cavendish's office, staring up at the plaster cornices on the ceiling. She watched as a thick-legged spider crossed the intricate pattern of roses and leaves above her head, scuttling from place to place as if running from something. She prayed it didn't take a wrong footing like she had and end up on her face.

'Sharp scratch coming,' warned the doctor, the stench of antiseptic and saline cloying in the air.

A rumble of thunder followed as the doctor pushed the needle into Amy's forehead and dispersed the liquid into the skin around the cut. Amy cried out as the anaesthetic burned through her open skin.

'You're doing really well, Amy, just a couple more.'

Further injections were administered, each one only slightly less painful than the last. Dr Cavendish tapped gently at the skin.

'That should be completely numb in a few minutes.'

She sat down next to Amy, sitting on a metal chair that looked like it had been taken from a doctor's waiting room.

It was slightly battered and rusty, at odds with the otherwise spotless room. Amy turned her attention to the window, distracting herself with the rain as it hit the glass in waves.

'You've had quite a shock. Good job you weren't knocked out cold, otherwise you might never have found your way back before dark. And in this weather, you'd likely have got hypothermia.' She sat back and crossed her arms, a satisfied smile on her lips. 'Now you see why I have rules about leaving the building without my permission. I have to know you are safe.'

Amy nodded gently, feeling childish and caught out.

'You needn't look so worried. I know full well whose idea it was to break my rules. Broken ankle indeed — she must think I was born yesterday. As soon as the guard found me, I knew she was up to no good. I came back just in time to catch her sneaking back in.'

Amy felt a trickle of blood crawl down the side of her face. She thought the doctor would catch it, but she continued to stare out of the window, unaware as the blood dripped into the hollow of Amy's ear.

The doctor looked back down at Amy, 'And I have half a suspicion it was Gaynor that gave you some of that chocolate, am I right?'

Despite the anaesthetic, Amy's head was beginning to throb and she lifted a hand to touch it. Dr Cavendish gently pushed it back down to her side.

'No, don't answer. I shouldn't interrogate you while you're in this state. Besides, I think you've had enough punishment for one day without going over old ground.' She smiled, but Amy noticed that it didn't reach her eyes. They remained dull.

The doctor stood up and took a needle from a tray and jabbed it gently at the skin around the cut. 'Can you feel that?'

Amy shook her head. 'Not really. I mean, it doesn't hurt, it just feels weird.'

'You might feel a little pulling on the skin, but it shouldn't be painful. If it does hurt let me know and we'll put a bit more anaesthetic in. OK?'

Amy nodded.

The doctor laid out a crescent-shaped needle with a wiry thread attached. Amy closed her eyes and lay back, bracing herself for more pain as the doctor dabbed sickly smelling saline-soaked cotton balls to the wound.

The skin tugged as the needle was drawn up, pulling the nylon thread tight. Amy could smell the doctor's perfume and the closeness of her breath as she pierced the skin again.

'I'm more than used to women disobeying my rules, thinking they know better. But you're different, I know that.'

Amy didn't understand why she was different; after all, she had eaten her own chocolate too and Gaynor hadn't exactly forced her to leave the building today. She could have said no.

'You remind me very much of someone I used to know — looks-wise, I mean. She was big like you, but far too self-involved to do anything about it — didn't have your self-awareness, Amy. Or your discipline. Well, apart from the chocolate eclairs and today's goings-on, but we won't mention that, eh?'

She smiled down at Amy, her eyes peering over her cheekbones. Her thin neck was slightly crinkled, something Amy knew was an unstoppable sign of aging, fixed only by the cut of a plastic surgeon's knife.

'The four Ds — discipline and diet determine . . .'

She looked down at Amy, the curve of the needle paused above her eyebrow.

'My destiny?' Amy answered, her voice dry and small.

'Exactly! Your two blips were just lessons to be learned. Bumps in the road.' She sounded cheery. 'The woman I'm talking about didn't change and died all alone.'

Amy watched as the spider reappeared, dropping inch by inch down an invisible thread above. She thought about the woman she had met today in the grounds — where had she seen her before? The train? Then it came to her: she had seen her in town on the first minibus ride, when the driver had called to her and she had marched past. Didn't he say she was an ex-patient? She hadn't spoken like she knew the place, but then again, who would admit to being a mental patient?

'Ouch!' Amy cried out as the thread pulled tight.

'Do you want some more anaesthetic?'

Amy just wanted it to be done. 'No, it's fine, it's just a bit sore, that's all.'

'Another week and I think we'll have you in the two-piece suit.'

'Pardon?'

'Your next outfit. It looks like that dress is getting too big for you now.' Dr Cavendish smiled as she looked down at the purple dress. 'I'll have you know the suit was worn to impress some very important people. If I'm not mistaken, the deputy prime minister.'

Amy looked up to Dr Cavendish, who appeared to be lost in a memory, her eyes glazed and mouth soft.

'Hopefully my case will be back soon, then I won't need the suit.'

Gaynor's revelation from earlier flooded back into her mind. The urgent need to keep Robert away from her room, if it was him that delivered the garish costumes.

Dr Cavendish snapped her attention back to Amy.

'You never know,' she chirped.

'Is it nearly done?' Amy asked.

'Almost. Lucky for you I'm a good seamstress.'

Amy remembered what the woman had said about the hospital and Amy's thoughts were drawn back to Jasmine.

'Dr Cavendish?'

'Yes?' she replied, looping the needle through the jagged edges of skin and pulling them together.

'You know you said Jasmine was at Crowthorpe General?'

Amy felt the slight tension in the thread.

'Yes, she should be back soon,' the doctor replied.

'Only, I met someone today, while I was out walking, and she said that Crowthorpe General closed three years ago.'

Dr Cavendish pulled the thread so tight it caused Amy to lift her head from the chaise longue. She cried out again, but this time the doctor didn't offer more anaesthetics or platitudes, she stared out of the window, gripping the needle tight.

'Of course she went to the city hospital. Perhaps the worry she caused me and your silly questions threw me momentarily. Now lie still and *be quiet*.'

CHAPTER 50

INCIDENT REPORT
Anderton Ward — NHS Pine End

Today patients were allowed to watch the coverage of Live Aid on a large television brought in especially. Patients were also allowed to eat lunch in the main hall to enable them to enjoy the event.

Andrew, Verity and a visiting patient from Marbury Ward were watching peacefully. Jenny asked if Danny could come to the ward for a visit. Request refused — she has been argumentative of late and refusing to do as she's been told. Now near her due date, I advised her to calm down as she became hysterical. Doctor was called and Jenny given sedation.

Verity became stressed at missing the concert, and Jenny began shouting obscenities at her. The two girls began fighting and Jenny threw a metal tray at Verity, which missed, hitting the television and breaking the screen.

Other patients became distressed and extra staff were brought in to help calm things down. Jenny is an obstinate girl and always has been, she does not respond well to orders and always feels she knows best. I understand there are talks regarding discharging her, but it is my firm belief that it's within her own interests to be kept here until she is able to behave herself. It is my view that she is not, as yet, fit for society.

Signed: Matron Dawson
Date: 13 July 1985

CHAPTER 51

Caroline stopped talking as Amy entered the room, a film of horrified disgust rippling across her face.

'Jesus Christ, what happened to you?'

Amy didn't understand for a moment, before the dull pounding hit again and she raised her hand to her forehead, running her fingertips over the dried blood and nylon stitches, like surgical Braille.

'Oh, I had a fall, nothing serious.'

'It looks serious to me.' Caroline got up from her seat and went to Amy, taking her arm and guiding her to her and Vicky's table. 'What happened?'

'Just a fall. I was running without looking where I was going, just being clumsy me as usual.'

'Must have been quite a fall.'

Amy looked up at Caroline. 'Can I ask you something?'

Caroline smiled widely. 'Of course you can, pet.'

'Have you . . . I mean, do you . . .'

'What is it?' Vicky urged.

'Have you seen Robert hanging around my room? Going in or out, or just around at nighttime?'

'What do you mean?' Caroline said, leaning closer.

'I think he might have been coming into my room, without me knowing.'

'What for?' Vicky said, her eyes wide.

'I don't know, it's just a feeling.'

Caroline and Vicky looked at each other and smiled, head shaking gently.

'Why would Robert be going into your room? I think you've had a bit of a shock; a blow to the head can do that.'

'Has somebody seen him in your room?' Vicky asked.

Amy was just deciding whether to mention Gaynor, when she and Audrey entered the dining room.

'No, no,' Amy assured them, 'you're right, it must be my head. I'm all over the place.' She spun a finger at her temple, and Vicky and Caroline smiled sympathetically at her.

'Oh no, if I hadn't have left you this never would have happened!' Gaynor exclaimed, rushing over to her.

'It looks worse than it is,' said Amy.

'Yeah, well, I was on a fool's errand anyway. Jake's married — turned out a walk around the grounds was exactly what he was offering. Bleedin' nature tour, would you believe it?'

'Oh, shut up, Gaynor,' Audrey scorned.

Gaynor's cheeks flushed crimson; she looked like she was about to say something else but was halted when the rumbles of thunder gathered strength and the dimly lit dining room flashed bright with a sharp crack of lightning.

'Do you think the sun ever shines here?' Caroline asked, looking out of the window.

'I reckon the photos in the brochure were taken somewhere else,' said Vicky.

'Well, they do say it's grim up north; this place just goes to prove it.'

Four sets of northern eyes turned to Gaynor, who held her hands up. 'Just saying.'

Audrey leaned in to Amy. 'It looks like a toddler has stitched it.'

'Is it that bad?' Amy asked, blinking rapidly and holding up a spoon to see her reflection.

Caroline and Vicky looked at each other knowingly, and when another flash of lightning lit the room up, Amy saw the warped fisheye reflection in the spoon and let out a small cry.

'I'm sure it'll look better once the swelling goes down,' Audrey reassured her.

The bell for dinner rang and the familiar footsteps of Dr Cavendish approached. The women had gathered at two tables, huddling like chicks in a nest.

'Back to your usual seats. No need for dramatics; Amy will be OK.'

There was a general scraping of chairs and pushing of tables as the women spread themselves out again.

'Now then, tonight we are having a cold carrot broth and a slice of citrus fruit.'

There were no questions or protestations; they had all learned by now to eat and appreciate, at least if Dr Cavendish was present.

'Amy, it's your bath treat night tonight, and it couldn't have come at a better time — you've had quite a day. See Kim at eight o'clock by the bathroom.'

'Lucky you,' said Caroline.

'Work hard and one of you might earn a hot bath next week. Hard work will always be rewarded.'

* * *

When the doctor left, Gaynor let her spoon fall heavily into the bowl, pallid orange liquid splashing across the table.

'I've had enough of all this now, I want to go home.'

She began a tirade of reasons of why the clinic was a sham and she had fallen for it, and either not wanting to admit they had also, or else not believing it, the other women stayed quiet and finished the meagre offerings in silence. Each of them had had an *I'm leaving* moment, soon forgotten once they got on the scales and saw the huge weight losses being achieved.

When the twenty minutes they had to eat dinner were up, Anya entered the room ready to clear away their empty bowls. Her eyes fell on Amy's stitches, and an almost imperceptible grimace flashed over her face. Anya took a step towards Amy but seemed to think better of it and continued to collect the glasses and bowls.

Amy felt sorry for the way Dr Cavendish had spoken to Anya earlier, sorry for herself and her swollen head and sorry for Gaynor, who still refused to touch her food and looked like she was about to cry. Most of her worries, however, were saved for Jasmine. Dr Cavendish had stumbled over the information, as if she had been caught off guard. As the thunder cracked and drummed outside, Amy couldn't quiet the voice inside her head that told her something was very, very wrong.

CHAPTER 52

PSYCHIATRIC REPORT
Date: 1 August 1985
Patient: Jenny Patton

*The patient has been feeling increasingly unhappy lately; she
is listless and feels there is no hope. I have asked that Matron
Dawson assist her in creating a plan for her future. I also
suggest that she is allowed to spend time with her boyfriend
Danny, in the hope that together they can create a functional
family unit with external support and ongoing input from
social services. I believe that the patient is in a vicious circle,
and with each punishment Matron metes out, she regresses
further and her behaviour and attitude deteriorate.*

*Action: To put a plan in place for patient to get her back
into the community as soon as baby is born.*

Signed: Dr Raj Purcell

*Additional comments: Patient continues to disobey me at
every turn and shows no signs of improvement psychologi-
cally or behaviourally. We have a merry-go-round of locum*

psychiatrists that do not have experience with the patients in any deep capacity. I strongly suggest a second opinion before any decisions are made on her leaving Pine End.

Signed: Matron Dawson

CHAPTER 53

Amy had been given a pass from circuit training; she hoped this meant she could sit on her bed and read a Jilly Cooper novel she'd borrowed from the relaxation room. Instead, Dr Cavendish asked her to walk back and forth beside the grassy area, adjacent to where the others were working out. Kim had brought out an old wheelchair for her to sit in if she felt dizzy. She had been very apologetic and embarrassed presenting her with the rusting vehicle, with its sagging leather seat and back. It didn't look like it had been cleaned since the last person sat in it, at least five years ago.

'It's fine,' Amy placated, fully intending not to use it.

'If you need anything or feel faint, just wave and I'll come right over, OK?'

Kim jogged away, joining Caroline, Vicky and Gaynor on the other side of the field. Amy watched as Tina helped Robert lay out equipment for the circuit: a row of dull green markers, a wooden box, hula hoops and a couple of the mats that had been carried from the gym by Caroline and Vicky. When Robert had passed by Amy on his way to the exercise class, he had hardly given her second glance, and it had been a relief. Gaynor must have been teasing her. Amy felt confident that later she would tell her it was a joke, and that Robert hadn't been anywhere near her room.

Amy looked up at the sky — it occurred to her that not one full day had passed without rain falling down on them. She had never been anywhere so bleak as Crowthorpe. It was no wonder to her that this was where they chose to build an asylum. If the Victorians wanted their mad out of sight and out of mind, they couldn't have picked a better place to keep people away. Other than the security guards, nobody ever seemed to arrive or leave.

Across the field Robert shouted orders, his arms straight out, ensuring the women reached his downturned palms with each high knee. Conscious she might be being watched by the doctor from her office, Amy began her exercise walking down the edge of the old football pitch. At each end were broken goal posts that had collapsed to the ground, now bound to the ground by ivy and bindweed. Through the wind she heard the shouts of Kim, Tina and Robert, encouraging the women to move faster and push harder. Then another voice: Gaynor complaining.

Amy's feet churned the sodden grass to mud as she paced the same strip over and over. Gaynor's trainers were almost beyond repair now; she would have to buy her a new pair when she was home and send them to her. She managed six laps back and forth before the rain soaked her through and her wound stung from the cold. It was enough to appease the doctor, she hoped. Amy waved at Kim to escort her back, but she was looking down at a stopwatch as Caroline and Gaynor ran sprints in front of her. Amy looked across at Tina, who was watching Robert demonstrate an exercise, both seemingly leaving the class to Kim to oversee.

Amy trudged back towards the clinic entrance alone, pushing the decrepit wheelchair in front of her. It clanked and squeaked across the gravel as Gaynor's trainers squelched along behind. One of the front wheels caught on a large stone and came loose, freeing itself from the chair and rolling away towards the clinic wall. Amy watched as it dropped down a ledge and out of sight. She let go of the wheelchair and followed the small wheel, certain that nobody would miss it or the rusting wheelchair it belonged to, but also wary that she didn't want to get into trouble for anything else.

Peering down, she saw the wheel had come to a stop in a gully by a small window of frosted glass that peeked up just above the earth. Ivy had slithered across the shrub-filled borders and crawled down to the glass, disappearing through the tiny gaps between the frame and into the building. Amy sighed; her body ached, and even the job of bending down to retrieve it felt like a mammoth task for her tired bones. She got to her knees and reached down, working her way through the tendrils of ivy, trying to catch her fingers on the wheel. She managed to hook her fingers underneath it, but it slipped from her grasp and bounced noisily against the glass.

'For God's sake,' she muttered, taking a deep breath.

Amy sprawled on her front, the wet gravel piercing her skin through her clothes. She stretched her arm as far as she could, feeling the pull in her shoulder. Her fingers skimmed the cold frosted glass again. With her thumb and forefinger, she caught hold of the worn rubber, pausing to make sure she had a firm grip. It was then that she saw them, or at least what she thought they were. Thin fingers meeting hers, scratching against the frosted surface on the other side of the glass below.

* * *

The reception was empty as Amy stumbled back in, her heart racing and hands trembling. She left the broken chair on the gravel, desperate to find someone and tell them what she had seen. Her fists pounded on Dr Cavendish's door but there was no answer. Jasmine must have got lost somewhere and was stuck in the basement, probably shut accidentally in a room. Then it dawned on her: if she was lost then the doctor had lied about her going to hospital.

Amy noticed the rope that cordoned off the stairs had not been drawn across. She hesitated a moment, bound by the rules, but knowing she had to find someone and let them know.

There was a short flight of stairs ahead then a turn and another flight up to the first floor. Amy took the first tentative step up, her wet shoes leaving a watery imprint on the polished wood. The first floor was in near darkness, thin slices of light escaping from underneath the wooden doors. Slowed by the darkness, Amy crept along the unpolished linoleum that covered the floor. Unlike the polished tiles on the ground floor its battle-scarred scuffs and scratches were gouged deeply and had filled with dirt. Her trainers squeaked along the sticky surface as she made her way down the corridor. The layout looked similar to downstairs, but there were no private bedrooms, just a large room with two broken beds that had been pulled to the middle of the floor, their stained blankets hanging over the edges. Drops of rain fell from a spreading stain in the ceiling, landing in a metal bucket with a dull *pit-pat*. The air up here smelled of disinfectant and mould.

Opening more doors, some with fist-shaped holes punched out of them, she found mostly empty rooms. Filing cabinets with their drawers hanging open, empty medicine cabinets with tiny keys hanging from the locks. It felt like someone had been here and scraped the insides out of each room, like organs stolen from empty ribcages.

The next room she found was inhabited, a single bed with the covers loosely thrown back over the pillow. There was an ashtray by the bed overflowing with cigarette butts and ash, and a half-used toilet roll that stood upright by a faded lamp.

An old metal locker doubled up as a wardrobe, yet most of the clothes were piled onto a chair in the corner. The room reeked of stale smoke that hung in the air like early morning mist. There was a bottle of cheap aftershave by the bed. Amy bent down and sniffed at the lid, knowing instantly that the room belonged to Robert. She quickly put the bottle back down, catching sight of a folder under the bed as she turned.

Amy reached for it and pulled it out, seeing the marker pen scrawl across the front: *Before*.

Amy opened it. Each page had a photograph of a woman taken at home or on holiday, overweight to differing degrees or looking like they had given up making an effort in their appearance. They were at home, with family, on the beach, half dressed, bikinis, evening gowns, home, abroad, some with their children. Private photographs meant for family, sent in the hopes it would get them a place at the clinic. Amy flicked through the pages, the glue having stuck some together, then she found it: a photograph of her in front of a caravan, her face turned away from the camera.

Something about her image being available to everyone made her feel queasy. He was the head fitness coach, so maybe he needed to see the progress too; that would make sense, but why keep it here, under his bed? The smoke began to catch in her throat, so Amy slid the folder back under the bed and left the room, thankful for the dank air of the corridor.

By now Amy had almost forgotten about the ghostly hand and had calmed, distracted by the rooms above. In the next bedroom there was a neatly made bed and a small chest of drawers by the side of it. Above the bed there were photographs Sellotaped to the wall. Amy edged closer to take a look. Most were of two little girls, chestnut pigtails and matching smock dresses, some taken at a play park and others on a beach holiday. Another more formal one was the whole family unit, the two girls sat on their parents' knees. The dad had olive skin and lustrous dark hair with a thick moustache. Amy peered closer at the mum, her hair shiny and eyes bright, arms wrapped protectively around the child on her knee. Her skin was clearer, and with her subtle make-up and proud smile she was almost unrecognisable, but Amy knew who it was.

Anya.

'I help you?'

Amy spun around. 'Oh God, I'm sorry, I was just . . . I was looking for someone, anyone.'

Anya stepped into the room and closed the door behind her. Amy tried to stay calm as the door clicked shut.

'If she see you here, you in trouble,' Anya said, gesturing her head back to the clinic.

'It's OK, I go.' Amy took a step towards the door, but Anya stepped across, blocking her.

'Why you here?' Anya's eyes were focused on the wound on her head.

'Outside, I saw a hand through a window.'

Anya's forehead wrinkled. 'A hand at the window?'

'Yes—' Amy pointed to the floor — 'downstairs, a hand, the basement? Is there a basement here?'

'I never see basement. It's closed long time, I think.'

'I saw a hand at a window.'

'A reflection, yes?' Anya said.

Amy thought for a moment, trying to clear her head. Had it just been a reflection of her own hand?

'Nasty bang to head, makes you a bit . . . how you say?' Anya thought for a moment. 'Crazy.'

'You're probably right.'

'I saw you out there, on field. You shouldn't be exercising with this.' She pointed to Amy's head.

'The doctor said it was fine.'

Anya scoffed. 'This doctor say no fine.'

Amy narrowed her eyes, looking at Anya's finger pointing to herself.

'You're not a doctor, you're a cook!' Amy laughed, the mix-up of Anya's words providing light relief.

Anya marched past her to the bedside drawers and pulled something out, holding it up to Amy. It was a graduation photograph of Anya, holding a scroll and an expression of hope for a bright future.

Amy took it from her. Anya was a doctor? She tried to process the information: Anya's interest in her well-being, Amy dismissing her.

'So how come you aren't a doctor here? In England?'

'I not allowed, in my country only.' Anya's face dropped, her shoulders heavy. Amy's eyes were drawn back to the photographs on the wall, her daughters.

'Where are your family?'

'My daughters with my parents, they are safe. My husband, I don't know.'

'He left you? For another woman?'

'No, he would never do that. He was in KLA.'

Anya looked at Amy intently, but Amy could only shrug.

'He was taken by Serbian soldiers; we do not know what happened. He won't come back.'

Amy stepped forward and put a hand on Anya's shoulder. 'You think he's dead?'

Anya nodded. 'I flee my country, I have no choice. I work at clinic and one day I get licence and become doctor and bring my girls to new life.'

'Does Dr Cavendish know? That you're a doctor?'

Anya fixed her eyes on Amy, shaking her head. 'No, not tell Dr Cavendish. It's better to be cook for now, better she not know. I lose job. I need to save money.'

Amy nodded. 'I won't say anything to anyone, I promise. Listen, I'd better go before she catches me.' Amy mimed a tiger launching on its prey, but Anya just stared blankly. 'Never mind. See you soon.'

She felt better for seeing Anya. She was right, it must have been a reflection of her own hand. Amy decided not to mention it to anyone else. She looked down to her dirt-streaked dress. If she wasn't careful, she would soon be in danger of being sectioned herself.

CHAPTER 54

'I want to leave. Three weeks is enough, I can't take any more.'

Dr Cavendish looked sympathetic as Gaynor let her woes fall out of her crimson-painted mouth, the front half of her body streaked in thick mud where she had fallen face first during a sprint race. The doctor noticed Gaynor's cheekbones seemed more prominent and her chest smaller. It wouldn't take much more work and she would achieve all those things she had come here for, another excellent case study for her clinic. Her skin looked a little sallow though, and tiny red capillaries branched over the whites of her eyes. Not enough sleep, thought Dr Cavendish, making a mental note to prescribe her more pills tonight and perhaps some more bovine collagen to erase the lines.

'I don't want a refund or anything, just call it quits here,' Gaynor said, sounding close to tears.

Dr Cavendish smiled gently at the idea that the woman would get a refund for her own failure to finish the programme. She rolled the Graf von Faber-Castell pen back and forth between her palms, its silver top glinting in the light. The rain battered at the windows, rivulets of water streaming down the thick glass.

'Could you call me a taxi to the train station? If I pack quickly, I could make the last train to London tonight.'

The doctor smiled reassuringly at her patient. 'I don't think a taxi will get through tonight, there are trees down on the drive. Why don't you wait until morning and see how you feel then? The roads will have been cleared by then. I understand that when it gets really tough it's tempting to throw the towel in, but you are halfway there, Gaynor; it would be a shame to give up now. Besides, look at the weather, you'll catch your death.'

Gaynor looked to the window. 'I just don't think it's worth the pain. I think I'd rather be fat.'

'Don't be ridiculous,' Dr Cavendish spat, before catching herself. 'That's just your tiredness talking; by tomorrow you will feel differently, I guarantee it.'

The doctor pushed a small plate forward. 'Would you like one?'

Gaynor reached out and took a single raisin, squishing it between her fingers before popping it into her mouth. She went to reach for another but before she could take one the doctor pulled the plate away.

'You'll feel better in a moment. Make sure you chew properly.' The doctor jabbed at the desk, annoyed that one of the basic tenets of her programme seemed so difficult for these women.

'I understand you have had some difficulties sticking to the rules, but unless you learn the benefits of discipline, you aren't going to get anywhere in any aspect of life. Work through your doubts, Gaynor.'

'I'm happy at home, just need to get back there.'

'What? To try and woo an ex-boyfriend that has most probably not even noticed you've gone?'

A tear pooled in Gaynor's eye. 'How do you know about—'

'Let me get you a glass of juice with something to pep you up a little. Feeling down and playing up when you can't be with the one you love is perfectly understandable, but you have to get beyond it, Gaynor. He's not thinking about you, is he? Imagine reaching goal weight and walking into a bar where he is — you'll stop him in his tracks. He'll drop the new woman in no time.'

The doctor opened the door to her medicine cabinet and took out a vial of powder. She mixed it into a glass of orange juice and handed it to Gaynor, who drank it down in a couple of gulps. The doctor poured her another drink, which Gaynor thankfully took from her and gulped down.

'Thank you, Doctor.'

The doctor smiled and wandered over to the window, biding her time. She glanced outside to see Mr Cotterill and Duke doing the rounds of the clinic, the dog's snout sniffing the soaked air, rain cascading from the peak of the guard's baseball cap. He caught sight of her in the window and nodded his head; Dr Cavendish nodded back. She inhaled the scent of the lilies in the window and turned back to her client. Gaynor's eyelids were beginning to close, her floppy hand still managing to clutch onto the plastic cup.

'I'll tell you what, we'll do a little deal, shall we? One more night and see how you feel then? Everything will seem better in the morning.'

Gaynor looked up to the doctor with glazed eyes, opening her dry lips and sipping at the drink. She shook her head and a drop ran down her chin, which Dr Cavendish caught with a handkerchief she took from her sleeve.

'No,' Gaynor slurred, 'I've made my mind up, I want to leave tonight . . .' Her voice trailed off as her head slumped down to her chest.

Dr Cavendish picked up the telephone.

'Kim, can you come to my office please, and bring the trolley.'

CHAPTER 55

Jenny looked up at the clock in the communal kitchen: it was 7.10 p.m. and Bob was ten minutes late for giving her a lift to Pine End. It wasn't like him at all; if anything, he was a little too keen to spend time at his rentals. She didn't flatter herself that it was her sparkling personality that kept him coming back, but rather that he was a lonely individual needing someone's ear to bend.

She took out her mobile and punched in his number — again it went straight to voicemail. If he didn't come, she'd have to hitch it as far as she could. It felt like time was running out and she didn't want to waste another day thinking about it, she just wanted to get it over with. She knew Bob well enough to know that if she didn't find him what he needed, he would find somebody else to help him.

Jenny dialled the number for the local taxi company but there was nothing until tomorrow morning now. One taxi to service one town, even a small one like Crowthorpe, was just another reason to add to the ever-growing list of reasons to leave. She stood up, the chair scraping back across the tiles, and left the kitchen. As she reached the front door Tom opened it from the other side, almost knocking her out.

'Sorry, I, er . . .' he mumbled.

If she hadn't been desperate, she would never have asked what she was about to, but needs must and now was not the time for false pride or suspicion of strangers.

'I need a favour.'

Tom turned from the first stair. He looked surprised to hear her speak, or was it alarm?

'What?' he said, apprehension in his voice.

'Can you give me a lift to the old asylum — you know, the new clinic or whatever it is? Or even halfway there?'

'Why do you want to go there at this time of night? It's raining cats and dogs out there, you know.'

'None of your business,' she replied.

'Fine, fine,' he said, turning and starting to walk back up the stairs.

'OK, OK. I have a friend up there, I take him food. Help him out a bit. He's not managed to get out with the weather.'

Tom screwed his face up a little. 'You aren't going up there to do drugs, are you? I know about the junkies that used to hang out in the grounds. I don't want anything to do with that shit.'

Jenny took a deep breath and clenched her fists, count-ing back from ten to one before speaking.

'No, I promise, there are no drugs or satanic gatherings involved.'

He nodded and took a deep breath. 'OK then, I suppose I do still owe you for the roll-ups.'

'Thank you.' Jenny smiled, letting him pass her before following him out to his bike.

They cowed from the rain as he opened up the seat and took out a spare helmet.

'Put this on,' he shouted through the downpour.

Jenny pulled it over her head and Tom fastened it for her, his hands soft against her neck. He motioned for her to get on the back behind him, which she did, enjoying the shot of adrenalin and feeling of freedom as the bike revved down the street.

She watched the town speed by, the engine roaring as they made their way out of town and past the old industrial estate. She leaned forward, gripping his waist.

'Hey, I'm sorry about the other day, you know.'

'What's that?' he shouted, his head remaining forward.

'I wasn't really going to stab you, you know. It was just to get you off my stuff. I . . . I'm not mad, you know.'

She didn't know how much he had heard, but that he didn't ask her to repeat it made her think he had understood. They made their way further up the hill and she clutched to his jacket as the bike leaned and turned, trying her best not to scream out. As they approached a layby on the hill, about half a mile from the asylum, Jenny tapped him on the shoulder. Tom pulled the bike in.

The engine still hummed as he let her off the bike, taking back the helmet.

'How are you going to get back home?'

'I'll be fine, someone will give me a lift.'

Tom looked up towards the clinic, frown lines appearing on his face.

'Honestly, I'll be OK,' she said.

'Well, if you need anything, here's my number.'

He scribbled digits onto a piece of scrap paper and handed it to her. She smiled and put it in her jacket pocket.

'Have fun, then,' he said, straddling the bike again, revving the engine before turning and disappearing down the road that glistened in the rain.

Jenny moved off the road into the cover of the trees. She smiled at the offering of the number, then looked up towards the asylum, remembering that where she was going there would be no signal to make a call.

CHAPTER 56

Gaynor's head lolled to the side facing Dr Cavendish, but her half-closed eyes did not focus. Dr Cavendish paused, remembering that Kim was still in the treatment room with them.

'Go back to the clinic now, Kim, Amy needs her Epsom bath running.'

Kim watched Gaynor as she backed out of the tattered room. The air was damp and rotten; black mould crawled up the plastered walls and a single bulb above swung in the draught that came in the now open door.

Dr Cavendish noted the look of concern on Kim's face. 'Don't worry about Gaynor, she's in good hands. I'm glad you have finally come to this part of the clinic, Kim — this is where the real change happens.'

Dr Cavendish smiled at Kim as she patted Gaynor's arm, causing it to drop and hang from the trolley. The doctor scanned Kim's face. Tina had insisted she was the right one for the job, one with vision and discretion, and more importantly, a desire to earn good money. Kim looked up to the ceiling and the doctor followed her gaze to the missing foam tiles, clusters of electric wiring exposed.

'As soon as we begin our expansion, we'll get that fixed, and the whole place decorated.' The doctor smiled reassuringly. 'Now, can you make sure that the clients have all got their evening tablets ready before lights-out, and ask Tina to come here, please?'

'Yes, of course,' Kim said, her voice small and unsure.

She turned and stumbled away, tripping over a discarded pile of framed pictures that had been piled outside the door. Kim straightened them before disappearing off down the corridor.

Once Kim was out of earshot Dr Cavendish returned her attention to Gaynor.

'Sabotage — do you know what that means, Gaynor?' Dr Cavendish paused as if Gaynor might be able to answer her. 'To deliberately destroy or obstruct something. Now, why would anybody do that? Why would anybody set out to stop another achieving their goals?'

Gaynor groaned as she lay on the gurney, the sides raised to prevent her falling out. Dr Cavendish stood by a wooden table, fingerprints dragged across its dusty surface.

'I mean, I could understand you using these things yourself; you aren't the first to sneak in food, you aren't original there. But to give them to others, to try and destroy their chance of success? Well, that's definitely a first. Poor Amy and then Jasmine — she told me about the food you gave her, and see what trouble you got her into. You see, people do not fail when they follow my plan.'

Dr Cavendish leaned on the gurney, a hand on each rail. The pressure moved the wheels slightly until the brakes locked it into place.

'I think we need to reset that brain, see if we can't make you a bit kinder to your friends.'

Dr Cavendish drew a small metal trolley up to the side of the bed and picked up a rubber mouth gag, turning it in her hands as if it were a precious artefact. When the music crackled to life again somewhere beyond the festering room, the doctor smiled. Gaynor groaned quietly to herself as the doctor forced the piece of rubber into her mouth, her teeth naturally clamping down on it.

Dr Cavendish pulled the ends of four leather straps up and over the trunk of Gaynor's body, securing her to the trolley with rusted buckles. When she was happy that Gaynor wouldn't fall off when the seizures came, she took what looked like a plastic hairband with two probes attached and placed it over Gaynor's head, securing the probes on her temples. The probes were connected by thin wires to a large metal box, with switches and dials that would send electric currents through the brain. Gaynor groaned a little at the strange pressure on her temples, but sedation and the straps that bound her prevented her from reaching up and pulling them away.

When she was happy everything was in order, Dr Cavendish pressed a red button on the metal box, sending the current crackling down the wires and into Gaynor's brain. She watched in fascination as 120 volts passed through Gaynor for the maximum six seconds. The patient groaned as the electricity surged across her head, and within seconds her body began to spasm, causing the trolley to rattle as she bounced against the straps. A few seconds later the spasms had faded to nothing more than a twitch.

'All done,' Dr Cavendish said, smiling down at Gaynor. 'You'll be better for that. We all will.'

As the doctor removed the mouth gag, dragging a thread of gelatinous spit from Gaynor's mouth, Tina appeared in the room.

'Just in time. Help me get her into the recovery position,' the doctor asked, unbuckling the leather straps.

'Yes, Doctor.'

The doctor arranged Gaynor's arms and legs and the two women reached under her body and pulled back, her limbs falling into place. Tina placed a hospital blanket over her and pushed down on the metal wheels, releasing the brakes. As they pushed the trolley out of the room and down the dark corridor, Dr Cavendish watched Tina. She was pleased to see the assistant's expression remained calm and indifferent in this other part of the building.

'How do you think Kim is doing?' the doctor asked.

Tina shrugged, her cheeks flushing slightly. 'Good — really good, I think.'

'Coping OK with our procedures? Must be very different here after a cruise ship.'

'Definitely coping, Doctor. I'm sure she will work out very well for you.'

Dr Cavendish smiled. 'Excellent, that's good to know. If it helps, there is scope for a wage rise.'

The rattle of the loose wheels rumbling over broken glass caused Gaynor to turn her head, her eyes meeting the doctor's. Dr Cavendish smiled gently down at her, but Gaynor just closed her eyes again and slept. Dr Cavendish looked down at her watch: it was almost eight o'clock.

They pushed Gaynor into a dark bay at the end of the ward and Tina secured the heavy blanket up to her shoulders.

'While you're down here check the others, please.'

Dr Cavendish scuttled down the corridor and up the steps to the ground floor. She unlocked the door to the clinic and pushed it open, smoothing down her hair and brushing away tiny remnants of the old hospital with a flick of her hands. Making her way to her office she thought about the ambitious young journalist who had been so eager to speak to her and to learn about the history of the place. At first she had been reticent, not even letting her ego sway her decision. Then the young girl had given her name and it felt like fate had delivered her just at the right time. The doctor had agreed to see Clara the very same evening.

CHAPTER 57

Jenny watched as the security guard padlocked a metal door in a recess of the hospital wall. He hooked the keys back onto his belt and made his way towards the Portakabin, checking his watch. The moon was full, shining a blue light onto the red bricks of the clinic. It was 8 p.m. now. She had hoped to wait until 9 p.m. when the doctor was supposed to leave, but the sudden gap in security felt like too good an opportunity to miss and she was impatient to get in there. She planned to hide out on the first floor and wait for the lights to go out — if anything went wrong, she could still escape through a window; those bars would not be on until the end of the week. She ran as fast as she could across the grounds, keeping low, conscious not to be seen.

The temperature had dropped, and the rain felt like icy needles hitting her exposed neck. She reached the red-brick wall and waited, making sure there were no footsteps approaching. It was then that she heard something coming from the dark recess of the wall beside her, a low steady growl. Peering around the red bricks, she felt a slow pant of breath warming her face. She shone her torch into the void and the face of the snarling dog looked right back at her from behind a mesh door.

'Shit!' she whispered, turning on her heel and running for the storage cupboard window, her secret entry.

There were no bars on this small window, seen now as it was then, an afterthought of a room. The dog began to bark manically, its throaty growls echoing between the two walls of its cage. Jenny yanked open the window and fell headfirst into the hospital, grateful again for the damp cardboard that broke her fall. She pulled the window shut and sat with her back against the wall listening to the heavy boots running and then the voice.

'What is it, Dukey-boy? What have you seen?'

There was a sound of a padlock being opened and the rush of canine energy as the dog was freed and harnessed.

'Woah. Steady, boy.'

Jenny clutched her knees to her chest and put her head down as the footsteps neared the window and the barks got louder. In a moment, the dog's snout was tight against the window above her head, powerful intakes of breath as it stalked its prey.

'Nothing in there, lad, that's just an old storeroom.'

The dog continued to bark and the window above her head opened, a torch shining onto the broken shelves and mattress in front of her. She held her body tightly against the wall beneath, praying he didn't lean in and look down.

'Nope, no bogeymen in here. Come on, boy. Come on, I said.'

He pushed the window shut and walked away, heavy boots kicking at the wet gravel. The dog, clearly the smarter of the two, still barked in her direction as it was dragged away.

CHAPTER 58

Amy squinted into the darkness of Gaynor's room, across to her neatly made bed. Her suitcase was upright by the side table, bulging from within and ready to go. Was she leaving as she had threatened? Nobody had taken her seriously. She had become the resident drama queen and class clown, and her exclamations had fallen on deaf ears. Now Amy felt a pang of regret — she might not get to say goodbye or give her the ruined trainers back.

As she reached the intersection of the main corridor, the door to the clinic opened and a young woman entered, shaking an umbrella up and down. Her golden hair was dry beneath a pastel bobble hat and a pink puffy coat. She looked like a character from the Sweet Valley High books she had read as a teenager, out of place in the dimness of the Beautiful You Clinic.

She caught Amy's eye and gave her an excited wave. Amy lifted her hand in a half-hearted reply, conscious of her muddied dress and scuffed trainers. The guard wrote something on his clipboard and then ushered her through to Dr Cavendish's office, and Amy carried on walking to the bathroom.

* * *

Kim shuffled through the bunch of keys in her hand, trying several that didn't fit into the lock; some she was unable to even get near due to her shaking hand. When it seemed she had finally found the correct one, she rattled it about so aggressively that it wouldn't slip into the keyhole. Amy gently took the keys from her hand and opened the lock herself.

'Are you OK?' asked Amy, looking across to Kim's paling face.

She looked down to Kim's fitted white uniform, a streak of grey dust rubbed along her side.

'I'm fine, just exhausted. It's a lot of work here. It's just very different, that's all.'

There were only six women to look after, and she didn't have to cook. Just take the odd aerobics class and supervise the daily hikes. To Amy it seemed like a breeze. Much easier than her job in the admin office at the factory.

'Maybe you could ask Dr Cavendish if you could have more help?' she offered, in an attempt to appear sympathetic.

Kim laughed to herself and shook her head.

'I was the only applicant when the last woman left — too many people know about the history of this place to want to stay overnight, never mind for months on end.' She looked apologetically at Amy. 'I didn't mean . . . I mean long-term. It's fine, they're just silly rumours.'

'I don't find it that creepy,' Amy protested. 'Well, maybe a little.'

'What do you mean?' Kim asked, her eyes narrowing.

'Nothing, I just mean the old building and its history, that's all.'

She desperately wanted to ask Kim about Robert, tell her about the music and voices she thought she heard, not to mention the hand tapping on the glass. But everyone else thought she was losing her marbles, and she was beginning to believe them.

Kim flung the door open and held her arm out to the bathroom.

'Your bath awaits you, madam.'

Steam filled the white-tiled room and Amy's bare feet left footprints on the fine mist of water that had settled on the floor. On the windowsill a bunch of lilies were beginning to wilt in the steam; their red stamens had fallen to the floor, russet pools of water spreading across the tiles.

Kim handed her a large white towel that scratched at her palms, then placed a thin bar of pale soap on top.

'There you go. Take as long as you like, but remember, the lights go out at nine o—' Kim stopped suddenly, her face looking panicked. 'Shit!'

'What? What is it?' Amy said, alarmed by the way the word cut sharply into the lavender-filled air.

'I've forgotten to put the sleeping tablets out before bed. If they don't have them before they go to sleep, she'll have my guts for garters.' Kim darted away, calling out as she ran, 'Enjoy the bath!'

Amy watched her go, then looked back to the door and noticed the heavy bunch of keys hanging down from the lock. She turned to call Kim back, but the assistant was now just a blurry dot in the distance. Amy took them out of the lock and put the catch on to make sure she couldn't be locked in again as they had been in the shower room. As with most of the rooms, there was no lock on the inside, so Amy took a spindly wooden chair at the bottom of the bath and carried it over to the door and leaned it against the wood, lodging the chair back under the door handle.

She undressed in front of a large mirror that was covered in a film of condensation. When she was naked, she took the towel and swept the water away from the mirror, revealing her entire body, bumps and all.

In the tabloids' eyes, on a kind day she would be 'full-fig-ured', on another the same body might be 'dumpy', 'fat' or even the especially cruel 'obese'. But now she could see that her face looked brighter and the hot air in the bathroom made her skin glow. The redness between her thighs was now fading to a pinkish colour rather than the angry scarlet graze she was used to. She didn't turn her head away from her reflection. Her body wasn't likely to live up to anybody else's standards, but she allowed herself, for a tiny moment, to admire herself.

Amy swished her fingertips across the water in the bath. It was hot, and lavender oil had been added, creating a smooth slick between her fingers as she rubbed them together. Because of the fanfare of being awarded a bath, she had imagined a freestanding roll-top bath in the middle of the room, bubbles flowing over the top and falling onto the beautifully tiled floor. What she got was a hospital bath flush to the wall, with a rubber attachment connecting the hot and cold taps in case she fancied washing her hair while she was there. Some of the tiles were cracked and mildew crept up the corner of the room.

As she stepped into the hot water her skin prickled, undissolved Epsom salts scratching under her feet. After a moment of crouching just above the water, she eased her bottom in, and then her legs and stomach, the water rising to her shoulders as every part of her body was immersed. The heat felt so good on her tired muscles, muscles that hadn't worked so hard since cross-country at school. She lay back and luxuriated in the hot water, the scented oil swirling around her, and drifted into a gentle sleep.

In her dreams there was a table in the middle of the road piled high with brightly coloured fruits and vegetables, fresh bread and the delicious smell of butter-laden baked potatoes. Her mum was there and so was Gordon, both smiling broadly as she walked up the street. Neighbours came out to applaud her weight loss as she paraded past the parked cars in a two-piece bikini, a tiara glittering on her head. She crawled onto the table like an exotic dancer and walked on all fours, past the trays of food, pausing occasionally to seductively lick an apple or dip her fingers into small ramekins of jam.

Her dream was disturbed by the sudden rattling of something banging against wood. Amy's eyes snapped open as the door handle jangled up and down against the chair. The water was tepid, and her fingertips were shrivelled. The steam in the bathroom had disappeared, and in its place cold condensation dripped down the window and walls. The lilies had now completely given up hope under the pressure of the water droplets that hung from them, dragging the petals down.

'Who is it?' Amy called out, trying to keep the tremor from her voice.

There was a pause before a voice called back, 'It's me, Dr Cavendish. I have your fresh clothes. There's something blocking the door.' She rattled the handle again.

'Just a minute,' said Amy.

She stepped out of the bath and reached for the towel, wrapping it around her body and walking over to the door, trying not to slip on the wet floor. As soon as she took the chair away, the handle came down and Dr Cavendish opened it, a look of concern on her face.

'Are you OK, Amy? You look like you've seen a ghost.'

'Yes, it's just, well, there isn't a lock on the door so . . .' She shrugged.

'You have nothing to worry about here, Amy, you're perfectly safe.'

Dr Cavendish handed her a new outfit. It was the two-piece tunic suit she had been promised.

'I bet you will fit into this treat now — I can't wait to see it on you.'

Amy tried not to grimace at the thick stretchy material of the beige trousers. As the doctor was about to leave Amy spoke: 'Dr Cavendish?'

'Yes?'

'Who brought the other outfits to my bedroom?'

The doctor looked confused by the question. 'Tina. She took them to you first thing.'

Amy felt the relief rush through her body, tingling her skin. She smiled, and the doctor looked at her quizzically.

'Why do you ask?'

'Oh, nothing, it's silly really. Gaynor was joking with me that Robert had been in my room.'

'Robert?'

'Yes!' Amy let out a sigh. 'It was a joke; she told me he was in my room every night while I was asleep.'

When the doctor's face turned stony, Amy instantly wished she hadn't mentioned Gaynor's name.

'It was just a joke. I didn't think it was true.' She tried to hide the half-lie behind a smile.

'You get yourself dressed, Amy. I'll see you in the morning.'

The doctor's expression darkened as she left the bathroom, the *click-clack* of her heels disappearing down the corridor.

CHAPTER 59

OBSERVATION SHEET
Date: Tuesday, 15 September 1985
Patient: Jenny Patton

Patient complained of stomach pains during the night. Matron called but not concerned and patient not in labour. Given pain relief and sent back to bed. Patient asking for Danny, request refused.
8 a.m. — Patient feeling better and came for breakfast, encouraged to walk up and down corridor to try and bring on labour.
10 a.m. — Sat in day room with Andrew and others.
12 p.m. — Refused lunch, says she feels sick. Taken back to bed. Matron called.
2 p.m. — Waters break. Patient has gone into labour and has been taken to treatment room by Matron and auxiliary nurse.
4 p.m. — Not yet back on ward.
6 p.m. — "
8 p.m. — "
10 p.m. — "
12 a.m. — "

CHAPTER 60

The bed Jenny had lain on was no longer there. It had been in the centre of the room, away from prying eyes, blinds closed and strip lights buzzing, her legs high in the air, strapped down in stirrups. Matron had looked on as the doctor tilted his head from side to side and moved his hands between her thighs, pushing and pulling at her vagina as though it wasn't connected to the rest of her body. He told her not to be silly as she cried out, that women did this all the time, she would be fine. Each contraction had felt like a tectonic shift in her body, pushing her baby closer into the world. No epidural, not through choice but because Matron believed that women were built for childbirth and pain relief was nonsense. Jenny had felt every tear and stitch. An earthquake breaking, exploding inside her stomach as she had screamed out for Danny. The windowpanes shook with her screams that day, just as her body did now.

Jenny was at the far end of the ground floor, where the communal shower rooms and bathrooms were. The bathroom door behind her was open and the soft scent of lavender hung in the damp air, a welcome change to the pungent perfume of the overripe lilies on the windowsills that were now beginning to brown and fall. She edged into the room where she'd given birth, closing the door behind her, the memories continuing to slice at her heart.

The doctor holding the tiny shrivelled baby, its dark eyes staring in wonder at the fluorescent lights above. Jenny had reached out, her fingertips almost touching the blood-stained blanket it was wrapped in. She wanted to hold it, to have its short-sighted newborn eyes fix on her and tell it she would be there no matter what. A new life, a new start.

'We need to get the baby to the special care unit, Jenny.'

A swirl of faces, in and out of focus, and more screams bellowed as the physical pain was replaced by a much more excruciating one. A pain that would help drive her to a madness that would fulfil the prophecy laid out by all those around her. When she had woken from the sedatives hours later, she was tucked up in her bed on the ward, the sting between her legs raw and hot. It was not the doctor who delivered the news that her baby had died, but Verity, who had been eavesdropping at handover. Her smiling face had taunted her as it retreated back through the curtains surrounding her bed, leaving her breathless and screaming until another needle pierced her to sleep again.

In this room, now surrounded by diet books and motivational posters, Jenny wiped the tears away. Tears that had been locked away for years and replaced with anger, a much more destructive weapon. But now it was impossible to bridge the dam of pain and they flowed freely down her cheeks, wetting the neck of her jumper and soaking her skin. Her face glistened with tears in the moonlight, her wounds open.

Throwing the tear-soaked tissue back into her bag, Jenny got back onto her feet. The tears had subsided for a while and she knew that she had to get on with the job in hand so that she would never have to be anywhere near here again. Noticing some cracks in the plaster work she took out her camera and began taking photographs. As far as she could tell, other than the deceased rats in the storeroom, the clinic seemed to be well kept, but she had to find something to give Bob. A building as old as this was almost certainly crumbling somewhere; as one thing is fixed another begins to fail.

As she left the room she kissed the palm of her hand and placed it gently against the door.

CHAPTER 61

DOCTOR'S REPORT
Date: 8 January 1986
Patient: Jenny Patton

Patient was found wandering in the grounds today in her nightdress. She was deeply distressed and became hysterical when approached by staff. Said she was looking for her baby and appeared to be in a state of psychosis. Patient has been given strong sedatives this afternoon. I have prescribed stronger antidepressants, and ECT to commence in the next week. Patient needs close monitoring and 24-hour obs until she is seen again. Sadly, I see little improvement in the patient and in fact a marked deterioration in her mental state since arriving at the asylum. As such I do not see a chance of her being discharged in the foreseeable future. Appointment made to see patient in a week's time.

Please note: Patient's boyfriend/ the father of the baby, Danny Char, was found deceased in the early hours of the morning (suicide). Patient is not yet aware of the situation and I advise for her own good that we wait until she is in a better state to handle such news.

Signed: Dr C. Carter

CHAPTER 62

'Can I get you a drink, Clara?'

A blast of wind rattled the office windows, causing the young journalist to jump and clutch her hand to her chest.

'The weather is always more extreme up here.' Dr Cavendish looked out to the rising storm, puddles of water now gathering in the dips of the gravel outside, the trees across the way swaying and twisting with the wind.

'Sorry, I . . . It's just this building, it's so imposing and beautiful.'

Dr Cavendish smiled. 'Thank you, I agree. I'm pleased I was able to be part of its preservation.' She held up a glass jug. 'Lemon water?'

'Lovely, thank you.'

Dr Cavendish poured, ice cubes plopping into the lemon water.

'It's not like I imagined at all,' said Clara, taking the glass from the doctor.

'Oh, what did you imagine?' She already knew the answer. It was what everybody imagined a gothic asylum to be.

'Oh, you know, grey walls painted with torture, order-lies in white uniforms escorting wailing patients back to their beds. The smell of disinfectant burning at my nostrils.'

Dr Cavendish smiled. 'I'm not sure it was ever really quite like that, but as you can see, it most certainly isn't now.' Her eyes flickered towards the vase of flowers on her desk on the brink of death in their yellow water.

Clara scanned the room, her pen against her lined notepad. Her eyes rested on the certificates behind the desk where the doctor sat.

'Where did you study?'

'Medicine at Oxford and then nutrition at a college in West Virginia, USA.'

The doctor observed her as she made notes. She had been surprised when she had walked into the room to find the golden-haired woman looking back at her — not at all what she had expected. It had been strangely fortuitous to have received the phone call from her. At first she had tried to hang up, then in a desperate bid to keep Dr Cavendish on the phone, she had mentioned her sister and that had changed everything.

'Would you like a tour of the building, Clara?'

Clara's head jerked up from her notepad. 'Yes please, that would be fantastic.'

She was already scrambling her things together, pushing her notepad back into her messenger bag and gathering her coat over her shoulder.

'You can leave that here,' the doctor said. 'You can collect it on your way out.'

'I know it's very macabre,' Clara said, putting her coat on the chair, 'but I'm kind of interested in the darker stuff. I'd love to be able to see some of that.'

Dr Cavendish held the door open for her as Clara walked by smiling, the girl's excitement buzzing like static.

Be careful what you wish for, Clara.

CHAPTER 63

Jenny's torch threw a weak beam of light into the deserted room on the first floor of the clinic, bare of anything except a broken piece of furniture and a print of Pine End Asylum in winter that had slipped from its frame. A thin layer of dust coated each surface, and thick cobwebs gathered in the corners of the room. The room was musty, mould spreading across the walls like bacteria in a petri dish. Her feet dodged missing floorboards that revealed the wooden slats below; a rodent-shaped shadow scuttled across the gap and under the cover of the floor again. Jenny took out her camera.

She stepped over a mouse trap, trying not to look at the mangled body it held, its spine snapped neatly in two, black eyes open and glassy. Lowering her torch, she edged over to the window. Ebony clouds had suffocated the bright moon, and now just the orange streetlights below illuminated the wet leaves and dirt that swirled in the storm outside. She looked out towards the avenue of trees — their limbs creaked back and forth, a scattering of branches blowing across the drive.

The first-floor corridor smelled like damp wood and antiseptic; the floor was still sticky with footprints and years of spilled matter. If she closed her eyes, she could still hear the rumble of feet and the cries of fear of that last night, as if they were sweeping by her right now, pulling her along with them down the corridor and out of the asylum for good.

In a room further along, Jenny took out her camera and snapped photographs of empty filing cabinets and drawers. The floor was stained and the plastic tiling curled up at the joins, but nothing that strong glue wouldn't fix. In another room a bucket overflowed with the drops of water that fell from the ceiling and Jenny snapped again, the flash's glow echoing light around the darkness.

Jenny listened as a door opened downstairs and footsteps moved through reception and into the body of the hospital. She hadn't expected anybody to be up and about now; Andrew had assured her that there was a strict 9 p.m. lights-out in the clinic. Her shoulders sagged a little — tonight was her last chance to find what she needed and she couldn't get caught.

He had also told her there were two members of staff that slept upstairs, so it wasn't a surprise to hear a radio playing from a room, a foreign voice making an official-sounding speech. She took a few steps further along, putting her ear to the next closed door, recoiling back when she heard the steady, pleasured grunts of a man. Jenny moved away quickly, trying to block out the distorted groans of ecstasy.

She pushed the first-floor door to the service elevator and stairs, a spike of a memory stabbing at her insides as she entered the grey space. She gagged as the stale odour of urine hit the back of her throat — it smelled like the inner-city stairwell of a multi-storey car park. The walls were covered in amateurish graffiti that she didn't recognise. Pentagrams and triplicates of the number six, not the moniker of the devil, but of a wayward teenager trying to impress his friends. She knew that mentality better than anybody.

The grey walls were icily familiar. As she ran her gloved hand over the bumpy concrete, memories of rattling gurney wheels and muffled voices floated through her mind. Jenny turned to look at the lift, recalling the sound of the metal cage door being pulled across before it juddered down. To the side of the lift were the service stairs used by asylum staff to avoid patients and visitors — scuttling up and down like rodents in underground tunnels, unseen and unheard as they fulfilled Matron's whims.

Jenny didn't remember ever coming up to the first floor; this was where Danny had been moved to, and he had been out of bounds. When she had tried, she had been carried by two orderlies, kicking and screaming, down the central stairs for everybody to see. As she looked around, something occurred to her. If she had never been up to the first floor, where had the lift taken her?

She photographed the graffiti — not a health-and-safety offence, but the marks of the devil might be enough to put fear into the council when deciding whether to extend the doctor's lease. She looked down to her camera to make sure the photographs were OK; the strange light the flash made in the darkness might have made them useless, but it added a filter of creepiness that made the place look even more foreboding.

Jenny began to walk down the stone steps, gently placing each foot down so as not to create an echo in the hollow stairwell, her fingers touching the wall and dragging behind her. When she reached the ground floor, she waited a moment, checking that she was alone. The moment of silence was broken when a raspy voice called out from somewhere below.

'Help me.'

CHAPTER 64

Amy sat on her bed with her knees pulled up to her chest, cradled in her arms. She watched as the bullets of rain ricocheted off the iron bars outside the window, the woods beyond morphing into one giant sheet of darkness. The lights had been turned off for the night, but she wasn't ready, or able, to sleep.

When she had arrived back from her bath Gaynor had still not returned to her room. Now there were two women she couldn't account for. Of all the clients, Gaynor was the most precious about her clothes; she would never have left willingly without her case. Amy looked across to the outfit the doctor had given her; she had hung it on the back of the door. The rough beige tunic and flared trousers were comical — why did she think that was something Amy would wear? Instead, Amy had pulled on the leggings and dress she had arrived in. Now the leggings sagged at the knees and the dress no longer clung to her hips. She put her nose to her armpit and inhaled, wincing at the stale odour of dried sweat and earth.

She let out a cry. A sudden sharp pain had sliced through her stitched wound. Kim had managed to deliver the nightly tablets while she was in the bath, but as all they seemed to do was make her sleepy, she had left them. Amy didn't want to be woozy in the morning, and she didn't want to fall again. She was beginning to feel like she was losing her mind and wanted to stay as alert as possible.

She shuffled through her handbag — receipts, a tampon that had bent out of shape and was now unusable, a lip balm without its lid, a half-empty bottle of Lou-Lou and the mangled brochure for the clinic. But no painkillers. She dragged her fingers along the lining at the bottom of the bag, hoping a stray aspirin might have fallen out of its packet, but all she dredged up were grains of sand-like dirt and an empty chocolate eclair wrapper.

When it felt like her head might burst, she crossed the corridor and knocked gently on Audrey's door. Her first knock was met with silence and a flutter of fear rose within her as she began to panic that Audrey might also have left without a trace. She raised her fist to knock again, but before she hit it, the door creaked open and Audrey squinted at her from the other side.

'Sorry to wake you, you don't have any paracetamol or aspirin, do you? My head is killing me,' Amy whispered.

When Audrey's eyes travelled up to Amy's forehead and her eyes met the wound, her mouth fell open.

Amy reassured her, 'I think the hot bath has made it swell up a bit, that's all,' she said, touching the wound and then crying out.

'If you say so,' Audrey said, shaking her head. 'Come in, then. You're letting the cold in.'

Audrey switched on a small torch and shuffled through the drawers in her bedside cabinet. Amy glanced around the room. An ornament of Mary and child sat in the windowsill, the pale curtain billowing against the porcelain icon's back. A bible rested on her bedside cabinet alongside an empty cup of tea, just the traces of tannin dried to the sides.

'I thought she took all your teabags?' Amy said, pointing at the cup.

'Where there's a will, there's a way,' she said dryly, then nothing more.

'Gaynor's not in her room. Have you seen her?' said Amy.

'Probably in the woods with her skirt up to her neck, gadding about with one of those security guards.'

A faded pink crocheted blanket had been placed over Audrey's bed. Hours of patient and diligent labour.

'Did you make that?' Amy asked.

'Two months it took me, when I was pregnant with our Laura, forty years ago now.'

Amy caught Audrey wincing as she bent to open a lower drawer.

'What happened to you, Audrey? I mean, I saw the bruises . . . on your body, when we were doing that stupid cling film thing.'

Audrey turned to her, regarding her with suspicion, then nodded briefly. Amy looked down to the solid gold cross that hung between her breasts, resting on the thin floral nightie.

'I walked into a door,' Audrey snarked. When Amy didn't respond Audrey spoke again. 'I thought I married a prince, turned out he was a monster. Your everyday fairy tale.'

'How long has he been doing this to you?' Amy felt her voice catch in her throat.

'Let me see, I wasn't pregnant with my first so . . . forty-three years off and on.'

Amy was shocked with the casualness of her reply, part of her angered by the flippancy. 'So why didn't you leave him?'

'It's funny, you know,' Audrey replied. 'I can't tell you how many times women like me are asked that, why don't we leave? Leave, just like that, because it's so easy to walk out of your front door with two kids and start afresh without him coming after you. But not once, not once, have I heard anyone ask them, why do *they* hit us? It's like it's all our fault for letting it happen.'

Amy gulped. 'Sorry, I just meant . . .' and then she realised she had thought exactly the same as all those other people, that it had been Audrey's responsibility to fix the unfixable. To tame the monster across the dinner table.

'They're not stupid, men like my husband. I've got no friends or family to run to, he saw to that. And it doesn't happen overnight, you know; he didn't carry me over the threshold and then give me a back-hander in the living room. You leave when it's more dangerous to stay than it is to go.'

'And have you left now? Is that why you're here?'

She nodded, letting go of the crucifix. 'I'm here for peace and quiet, time to reflect.'

Amy paused, mentally updating the information, her train of thought switching tracks back to the here and now.

'So, you've left your husband, Gaynor's boyfriend left her. Jasmine's parents are in Germany and Caroline and Vicky's husbands died in a train crash. My parents have sent me here for as long as it takes, and I don't think they're in a rush to have me back. So who would notice if we were stuck here?'

Audrey shook her head. 'Why would she want to keep us any longer? She can't make us pay even if she did keep us here; besides, there's plenty more women where we came from. There'll be a whole new set of women here in a few weeks and we'll be long gone. I think your mind is starting to play tricks with you.'

'Starting? I feel like I'm well on the way.'

Amy looked down towards the open drawers as Audrey spoke.

'Sorry, love, I haven't got anything. Try the office, there's bound to be some in there. The doctor is showing some journalist round. I heard her asking daft questions about padded cells and straitjackets. The office is probably unlocked at the moment, so you'd best be quick.'

Amy felt her heart race at the thought of creeping around the clinic again, but the pulsating in her head gave her little choice and, besides, she knew there were painkillers in the doctor's desk.

'I'm not sure painkillers are going to do the trick, mind — I think you might have to go and get that checked at the hospital.'

Amy was about to mention about the closed hospital and Jasmine, but Audrey was already back into bed before she had reached the door, calling out, 'And don't be worrying about Gaynor, she'll be back in the small hours, smudged lipstick an' all.'

As Amy went to leave, her eyes met those of Jesus, who stared down at her from a lenticular postcard Audrey had stuck to the wall, a lamb draped over his shoulders. As she moved away, Jesus's expression flickered from concerned to blessed and back again. She tried to remember the parable from Sunday school — was it a lamb saved, or a lamb to the slaughter? As she made her way down the corridor, she prayed that it was the former.

CHAPTER 65

The voice called out again, cracking like dry earth, '*Help me.*'

Jenny looked down into the darkness, a chill of air brushing her cheeks. The basement housed the organs that kept the building alive, giant humming fuse boxes and creaking boilers that groaned like arthritic old men. Gassy pipes that ran along the length of ceilings, curling around the underbelly of the building like intestines.

As the sole of her Doc Martin touched the first step down, Jenny heard something else, a static noise like the needle on a record player. Faint music followed, a song she recognised from her childhood but couldn't name.

Jenny's physical body was drawn to the haunting music, like mesmerised sailors to the sirens, but her head was screaming for her to turn back and run. Maybe it was the security staff, a coffee break room somewhere underground, out of the rain. Then she heard the voice again, just above the music.

'*Help.*'

Jenny felt a bead of sweat trickle down her spine as she approached the bottom step and saw the fluorescent glow that curled around the corner of the stairwell. Something twisted in her stomach as she moved forward into the light and stared down at the corridor ahead. Whereas the ground floor had managed to be transformed into something else, something clean and bright, here there was no escaping what the original intention of the building was.

Paint peeled away from the walls like infected skin, a yellowing floral border no longer offering a cheery accent to the windowless space. A growing unease pulled at her insides as where she stood became eerily familiar. Now she understood why she didn't recognise the first floor despite having been wheeled into the lift many times. When the white-coated orderly had reached a brusque arm across her face to press the button, he hadn't taken her to the first floor, he'd brought her down here.

Jenny took slow, steady breaths as she ventured further along. Above, fluorescent strip lights buzzed and flickered; a dying fly crawled lazily across the floor, trying to launch itself with the one wing that remained and falling on its back. Broken glass jars and medicine bottles crunched beneath her boots as she tried to navigate the maze of corridors and rooms in the blue half-light. The air was rank with iodine and decay. Jenny held her hand to her mouth to stifle a cough she feared might turn into a gagging fit. She followed the echoing music, the song repeating over and over again; as soon as it finished a needle scratched and it restarted.

She peered into a side room, shining her torch up to the tendrils of ivy that had broken through a thin window at the top of the wall. The vines had crept downwards, crawling over a blank-screened computer monitor, strangling it with their vascular stems. An upturned chair, almost invisible underneath thick cobwebs, lay on the floor among medical journals and magazines from the 1970s, their corners nibbled by rats and rotted away.

The stone floor was sticky with dust and balls of grey fluff, displaced matter convening in the corners and crevices between the floor and wall. The giant metal pipes gurgled above her, hanging low enough from the ceiling so she could reach up and touch them. Something fluttered above one of the pipes, causing a small flurry of dust to fall on her head, which she rapidly rubbed away, not wanting any part of the building to make contact with her.

To her right was a row of darkened rooms, each with huge Perspex windows covered in handprints and greasy smears, inviting her in with their strange exhibits.

Roll up, roll up, come closer. Look hard enough between the sodden cardboard boxes and broken anglepoise lamps and see what you can see! Don't be afraid now, come closer!

Jenny stepped into the room, her camera poised to capture the decay and rot that lay beneath the shiny clinic. There was no light in this room, just a single wire hanging from the ceiling, its bulb long since blown. She pointed the camera up and clicked, photographing the spreading damp patch in the ceiling that looked like it might give way at any moment. Then a yellow sharps bin that had tipped over, blood-stained needles spilled across the floor.

The smell of sickness and sweat got stronger the further down the corridor Jenny walked. Room after room filled with asylum detritus, as if everything from the other floors had been dragged down here awaiting usefulness again. Splintered wooden crutches. A dentist's chair, its backrest broken so that it hung down like a snapped spine. The voices and music drifted in and out as if they might be a figment of her imagination, but the smell remained constant and wrenching. As she was about to leave the room, she saw a long metal gurney on wheels, its closed lid created to hide the dead bodies it transported from the hospital to the morgue. Jenny reached her shivering fingers out to its handle, hesitating for a moment before prising the lid away from its base to reveal what was beneath. Like lifting the lid of a silver cloche dish to reveal the dish of the day, to find a rare steak still pulsing and bleeding. The metal lid creaked as she raised it, revealing nothing more than a dull green patina and stains of rust where the bodies once lay.

* * *

Jenny read the small sign on a door to her left, individual letters slid into a thin frame.

Teaching Room.

The handle was icy cold, even through her woollen glove. Her fingers shivered as she pushed it down and edged the door open inch by inch, wary that some part of the decaying building might fall in on her. Inside, a lamp shone onto an operating bed, a metal trolley by its side with a tray on top. As the pipes groaned above her, Jenny moved cautiously into the room. It was the lack of disarray that alarmed her most. The walls dripped with the same moisture and the ceiling was speckled with mould, but everything else was in place. Jenny took a photograph of the plastic tray by the bed, lowering the camera back down to take a closer look. A syringe, a long metal rod that looked like a giant nail, some type of clamp that looked like it was for curling eyelashes, and a small hammer. It wasn't the instruments themselves that caused a wave of nausea to rise within her, but the realisation that they were waiting to be used.

As the disjointed cries got nearer, Jenny reached into her backpack and took out her art knife. She held it in front of her body, the trembling blade catching the light from above and flickering across her pale face. She could hear her own breath, rapid and tight as she turned the corner, and looked into the vast space ahead.

Blinking into the semi-darkness, her eyes rested on the macabre scene before her. She held a hand to her mouth to keep herself from screaming. Jenny spun back to the corridor and dropped the knife, which bounced across the stone floor. Falling on all fours, she threw up over and over again, until it felt like there was nothing more, to purge away what she had just seen. As she sat back on her haunches, trying to get her breath back, she felt the slender fingers creeping across her spine, and a silent scream echoing within her head.

CHAPTER 66

Amy pulled at the top drawer of Dr Cavendish's desk, but it wouldn't budge. She tried a lower one and then one to the other side, desperation rising with each try. The stitches on her head began to feel like they might split open at any moment. Remembering Kim's forgotten keys, she retrieved them from her cardigan pocket, shuffling through them until she found a suitably ornate one.

Amy unlocked the desk drawers, a flush of relief when she spotted the box of paracetamol lying beside pens, pencils and a stapler. She took the box out and pushed two free from the foil pack. Taking a glass of water from the side she swallowed them down, feeling the plastic capsules drag against her throat.

When she had been in the office previously, she hadn't noticed the large cupboard that stood slightly out of place adjacent to the desk. A small swatch of material had caught in the door; Amy recognised the floral silk material. So this was where the hideous spare clothes were kept. Intrigued to see what other clothes she might be offered during her stay, she stepped forward and opened the two doors wide, a waft of mothballs taking her breath away.

Now freed from the door, the floral dress fell back into place next to the purple dress that she had almost got comfortable in. As she pulled the outfits out one by one, she realised they were getting smaller, and once they reached size twelve they looked brand new, never worn. Price labels still attached. They were still old-fashioned clothes, but whoever had bought the smaller sizes had never got to wear them. As she put the last of the dresses back, she noticed something else familiar beneath the hanging clothes. She reached down and pushed the clothes aside to reveal a suitcase, *her* suitcase.

Forgetting she wasn't supposed to be there, she yanked it out, the hard plastic falling with a thud on the wooden floor. She laid it down and unzipped it, sure it was hers but still needing the confirmation. When she saw her tracksuits and own slippers she felt like crying. It was as close to home as she had got in weeks. She gathered the clothes up in her hands and buried her face in the scent of her old life.

She read the brown label that had been attached by somebody else. It was dated two weeks ago. It had been returned only a few days after she arrived, so why had she not given it to her? The tablets were having little effect and her head continued to throb. Amy stood again, wandering around the room that seemed so weird and alien now, stopping by the desk. She tried to close the drawer but she had shifted the tray slightly, preventing the drawer from closing. She opened it and carefully lifted the plastic tray out to reset it, noticing the photographs beneath.

Some looked recent, others sun-bleached and some in black and white. Amy took a handful of the pictures and spread them across the desk, giving each one space. She turned on the desk lamp and looked down at what she realised was a photographic history of the building. Rows of nurses dressed in long starched uniforms looked expressionless in a black-and-white photograph. In the centre, a line of doctors took centre stage, the same cold expression on their faces as their female assistants. Another black-and-white photo showed soldiers in wheelchairs, bandaged legs sticking out in front, laughing nurses administering medicine and smiles.

There was a spectrum of black and white to colour, but more colour didn't mean brighter. Amy pulled a photograph towards her — a group of young teens, hips cocked and arms folded, glaring into the lens, a stern-faced Matron looking on disapprovingly. The spiked hair and pencil skirts dated it to the eighties, patients gathered for the yearly snapshot, documenting the lives that passed through the hospital. She recognised one of the teens: shiny black hair, sullen face. It was the girl from the woods. Her mind skipped to another photograph, the one she had found in the outbuilding with the burner. The woman in the badly fitting swimsuit, dated to the year 2000. Her body jolted — that woman couldn't have been a patient at the asylum as it had closed three years earlier, so she must have been a client of the clinic. Amy thought about her belongings in that concrete block, waiting to be burned. Why hadn't her things gone home with her?

Then she saw another set of photographs, bound together in a plastic wallet. A family album from the 1960s. Glamorous wife, with glossy curls, her slender figure draped in silk and gems. A charming husband and po-faced child positioned between them, all standing at the foot of Italian-style stone steps, spiralled topiary bushes cut into either side like horticultural bookends. Amy turned the plastic page, passing the years, the mother's body expanding picture by picture. Amy recognised the beige suit in one, the mother's stomach now bulging through the tunic like a soufflé bursting from a ramekin, thighs straining beneath serge trousers. The little girl from the first picture had the same serious expression, staring straight at the camera, her eyes cold and mouth taut. In this photograph the mother held a chain lead; at the end a noble-looking German Shepherd sat back on his hind legs. Before the father figure greyed with age, he disappeared from the album. The remainder of the album was the ever-widening woman and the daughter, who by the last photo was a teenager, gamine and graceful. Amy registered the familiar-looking features of the child, attractive and slender, her hair pulled back revealing high cheekbones. Dr Cavendish.

A small newspaper cutting fell from the back of the album. Amy gently unfolded it, its yellowed paper fragile and thin. As she read the story her heart began to race and the old cutting was in danger of being torn by her trembling hands.

Amy grabbed the phone on the desk, first trying her parents: no answer. Next, her only friend, Darren.

'*Hi, it's Darren.*'

'Darren, it's me, Amy, something's really weird here, I—'

'*Ha-ha, just kidding, leave a message after the beep, mother suckers . . .*'

She let the handset fall back into its cradle, stepping away from the desk as if distance might make it all go away.

The office door opened, the photographs fluttering and spreading like falling ash to the floor. Amy blinked into the semi-darkness as a voice demanded, 'What are you doing in here?'

CHAPTER 67

'Who are you?' Jenny pleaded, as the sallow-faced woman led her further into the ward, her finger pulling at Jenny's coat.

She didn't answer. Her breath was shallow, as if every gasp of energy had been used up walking over to Jenny. Jenny followed her and watched as she dragged herself back into a metal hospital bed that creaked and twisted. She crawled back under the crumpled covers and curled into a ball.

There was a row of hospital beds lined up against the wall just as they had been when she had been a patient, but agitated bodies had skewed them from the wall, each facing slightly different angles. A high rail stood above each bed, with ragged curtains hanging by threads. The veneer of the bedside cabinets was peeling away like old nail varnish, each with a glass vase on top containing decaying chrysanthemums sitting in slimy brown water, their leaves shrivelled and dried. Beside the girl's vase was a scattering of stale make-up, case and tubes open, their contents dry and impenetrable. Jenny ran her shaking fingers over a handheld pearlised mirror, catching her skin on the broken glass. She looked up to the posters of smiling, bubble-gum pop singers and movie stars from the seventies and eighties, each picture split in the middle with a crease and staple holes where they had been pulled from the magazines.

The room smelled like disinfectant and death, bodies rotting from the inside out.

There were eight beds and at least five patients, including the woman who'd beckoned her, though most barely looked human. Thin yellow skin clung to their bones, looking like it might come apart like stretched dough if pulled any tighter. Two of the women slept and another stared above the door, repeating something over and over.

Jenny made her way to the end bed, where a privacy curtain had been pulled all the way round. Her hand gripped the heavy linen and moved it to the side, the curtain rings scraping across the metal. She approached the bed hardly daring to look at whoever lay there.

The woman's chest rose and fell in heavy, disturbed breaths. Her red curls were matted like a fine bird's nest and stuck to the stained pillow above her head. Jenny read the repeated line of the pillowcase.

Property of Pine End Asylum Property of Pine End Asylum
Property of Pine End Asylum Property of Pine End Asylum
Property of Pine End Asylum . . .

Over and over, endless stamps of ownership, like macabre fan merchandise. Jenny had once owned the full set: nightdress, bedsheets and towels. She was surprised they hadn't tattooed her entire body with those words; in the end they might as well have, because until two years ago when she had kicked her addiction, she hadn't known where the asylum ended and she began.

White streaks of dried drool ran down from the red-haired woman's mouth. Her gown had fallen away from her shoulder, so Jenny took it gently in her hand and pulled it back over her bare skin. This woman wasn't as emaciated as the others, but still her pallor and clamminess made her appear haunted and sickly. This had to be something to do with the diet clinic, she thought. Then she noticed the red marks on the woman's temples.

Jenny touched them, part of her believing she was seeing things. Suddenly pinches of memory came back from her own time here, the metal cage door being pulled across in the lift. Faces peering down at her as if she were a freak-show exhibit, her eyes rolling and her stomach lurching as the lift suddenly whirred into action. She couldn't have stopped them if she'd wanted to. Matron made sure of that.

Jenny slowly lifted the sheet, unable to hold in a sharp cry when she saw the familiar leather straps tying one of her ankles to the bed. She put her hand to her mouth as if she was holding a paper bag to it, taking long slow breaths. Someone had given this woman electric-shock therapy. But *why*?

A voice began to call out. A weak croak barely above a whisper. Jenny ran over to her, putting her hand over the frail woman's mouth, a jolt of shock when she felt her skull beneath the thin skin of her jaw.

'Ssssh,' she said, taking the pressure away from the woman's mouth and recoiling at her starving breath.

The woman looked into Jenny's eyes and reached out to her, clasping weakly at Jenny's arm. The woman's skin was tightly bound around her tiny frame, her collar bones protruding through her skin. A hair band studded with tiny flowers held back brittle thinning hair. Jenny noticed a crossword puzzle on the table by her bed; a thick spider crawled across it, dropping from the side of the table and scurrying across the litter-strewn floor.

'Is this part of the clinic? Who's looking after you?'

The woman's hand fell from Jenny's sleeve and she turned her face to the ceiling, eyes rolling back in her head. Jenny looked over to the woman who was still repeating something to herself. Jenny followed her gaze, turning and looking at the wall opposite, where giant words had been painted across the wall, in full view of the women.

Discipline and diet determine your destiny!

Her hopes that it was just two rooms that were inhabited in this strange underground hospital were soon dashed. The music started again, and a voice cried out, '*Help me! Please, help!*'

Moth-eaten curtains hung heavily behind the double glass doors, with their cracked panes of glass and brass handles that now had a dull green patina. Jenny pulled the doors open and reached for the shabby drapes.

Before she could change her mind, she yanked the curtains open, stumbling back as once again a theatre of darkness presented itself. High-backed chairs were placed around the room, yet more seats stacked high in the alcoves. The pungent smell of infected skin and bodily fluids made her gag as she tried to make sense of the room. Before her a huge screen had been dropped from the ceiling and a stuttering projector was playing *Dirty Dancing*. Patrick Swayze telling a broken hearted Jennifer Grey he had to leave Kellerman's, fractions of their images appearing in the wall behind, as the screen swung gently in the draught Jenny had brought in.

Clear plastic cups littered the occasional tables that were placed around the rooms, traces of grainy liquid still coated around the sides. A Scrabble board had been set up in the middle of the room, the letters strewn across it. Jenny moved closer to look at the score pad, flicking through the previous games, scores next to names she recognised from the asylum.

'*Help me*,' a strained voice cried, sounding like the last of her energy was being used up.

Jenny scoured the battered furniture and hollow eyes that looked blankly forward to see where the voice was coming from. The women in this room were not as emaciated as the other room, but still they wore the same Pine End hospital gowns she knew so well, and all looked heavily sedated. Two women stared with glazed eyes up at the silent screen; one of them had a head full of rollers, now half pulled away from her hair and hanging down, clacking together with each slight movement. Their faces were slowly blinking, heads dropping every now and again. A spectre-like woman stood over a record player, staring at the jumping needle as she tried to play a record that had broken in half. Her feet were bare, bluish-white and surround by broken vinyl discs. Jenny noticed only one record remained intact and she handed it to the woman, who took it without acknowledging her and swapped it with the broken record on the turntable.

In the corner of the room a row of chairs sat before giant mirrors, the glass so thick with dust Jenny couldn't see her own reflection. More discarded make-up and ancient hairdryers were strewn on tables, a magazine long since read left open on:

The best style for your face!

When a woman called out and held her hand up to Jenny, she ran over and knelt by her.

'Who is doing this?' Jenny pleaded, hoping this woman could help her understand.

'Dr . . .' The woman tried to swallow, but it sounded like her throat was lined with cardboard, dry and brittle.

Jenny took a bottle of water from her backpack and offered it to the woman, who gulped at it. When she stopped it took a while for her body to process the water as she gasped for breath.

'Dr Cavendish.' She spat the words out as if they might otherwise get swallowed down again.

'The doctor from upstairs, the Beautiful You Clinic?' Jenny asked, eager to get answers before this woman passed out.

The woman nodded her head, fear etched into her gaunt face at the mention of the clinic. Jenny noticed the cannula in the back of her hand had caused bruising and her long night-dress had streaks of dried vomit running down the front. The girl's petrified eyes flickered from side to side.

Jenny shook her arm gently until she looked at her again. 'What's your name?'

The woman took a breath as if gathering the strength to speak, and slurred, 'Jahh.' She took another breath and closed her eyes for a moment before looking straight into

Jenny's eyes. 'Jahh,' her voice failing each time like a dying battery. 'Jasmine,' she hissed.

Jenny reached in her pocket for her mobile, just in case, but there was no signal. She remembered the camera and took it out of her bag. It felt like a betrayal as she pressed the button on the camera, but nobody would believe this unless she had evidence. She photographed the film screen, the broken furniture and the peeling walls, but she knew what would really convince the authorities of the hell that was here.

She pushed the button down several times, the flash burning into the cinema darkness. She felt the heads of the other women turn towards the light like ventriloquist dummies, before moving back to the screen. Jenny looked down to the back of the camera to check the photographs were good enough.

Jasmine's eyes were wide open from the shock of the exposed flash. Her skin was translucent and her lips cracked and bleeding. Her collar bone jutted out above the loose nightie, a pink stain of rejected medicine smeared down the front. Then she saw what she hadn't before: those familiar red marks on her forehead.

The sound of healthy footsteps approaching jolted Jenny to her feet.

'I'll come back.' Jenny squeezed Jasmine's hand. 'I promise.'

As the footsteps entered the room, Jenny ran into an alcove behind a stack of chairs and crouched down in the darkness.

'Nooo!' Jasmine called again.

Before Jenny could tell her to stay quiet the stranger was in front of Jasmine, only the bottom of her legs and black patent shoes visible to Jenny.

'What's all this fuss, Jasmine? What a commotion.'

Jenny held her breath as a wheelchair was brought over and the brakes clunked on. She watched as Jasmine was transferred to the chair and wheeled out of the room, the woman still berating her as she moved. Jasmine's voice disappeared down the corridor, still pleading for help.

CHAPTER 68

Amy swept some of the photographs back into the drawer and slammed it shut.

'I was just getting painkillers; it's my head, it's . . .' She moved backwards until she felt the medicine cabinet hit her spine.

Robert smiled, his eyes scanning the room. He gently cricked his neck, one way and then the other, and moved towards her. Amy swallowed, her throat tightening. Her body froze, as if her arms and legs had been cast in lead.

When he reached the table, he sat perched on the corner, one leg straight to the floor and the other bent casually, his foot tucked under the other leg's knee. He wore flannel pyjama bottoms that gaped slightly open at the crotch. His vest that had once been white now looked yellowish and worn.

'I'm fine now, I should probably go.' Amy tried to coax her body into gear, but she felt leaden.

'No need to rush, I won't say anything,' Robert assured her, his voice low and steady. 'I wondered where you had gone to.'

Amy shuddered. 'What do you mean?'

'I went to check all the doors were closed, and that everyone was tucked up safely for the night. I saw your door was open and you weren't inside. So I came looking.'

He ran his tongue across his lips, a slug-like trail of moisture glistening across his mouth. Behind him the rain continued to batter down and the thunder rumbled on.

'My head, it hurt, so I just came for painkillers.'

'That really does look sore. Here, let me see.' He slid off the wooden desk and slinked towards her. 'Someone needs to see a doctor.'

'I saw her yesterday. Dr Cavendish.'

'Yes,' he corrected, 'I meant a surgeon. Poor baby.'

His breath smelled of greasy meat and onions. She edged as far back as she could, his face pausing inches from hers, his eyes fixed on her forehead.

'I'm tired,' Amy said, bringing her hand to her mouth and faking a small yawn.

'Oh, keep me company just a few minutes longer,' he pleaded. 'It gets so lonely up here, being the only man in the clinic.'

She bristled as he pushed his body against hers, his hard penis brushing against her leg. He took a sharp intake of pleasured breath and exhaled hot breath on her neck, a hand stroking her collarbone, winding its way up to cradle her chin, holding her face towards his.

Amy was about to cry out when the room was suddenly flooded with light.

Robert jumped back and turned to the door.

'What's going on?' Kim said, looking at Amy.

'We have a trespasser.' Robert smiled, giving Amy a playful look. 'I was just explaining the house rules. Senior staff only in here.'

Kim ignored him. 'Are you OK, Amy?'

Amy nodded, dipped underneath Robert's outstretched arm and scuttled over to Kim, standing by her side and looking back at Robert. It was like a game of chess as she waited for his next move.

'You know, you two really shouldn't be in here without Dr Cavendish,' Robert said, waggling an admonishing finger in their direction.

'I was looking for you, Robert,' Kim said. Amy could hear the irritation spiking her words. 'Dr Cavendish has asked for your help in the Teaching Room.'

Robert frowned. 'At this time?'

Kim shrugged. 'Don't shoot the messenger. Look, go or don't go—'

Robert held his hands up. 'Keep your knickers on.' He moved past them, fixing his eyes on Amy. 'See you in the morning, ladies.'

When he had gone, Kim turned to Amy. 'You really shouldn't be in here.' Kim's eyes darted away from Amy as she rapidly clicked her nails against each other. 'There's something not right here, I don't know what but I—'

'Stop scaring the guests, Kim.' Tina stood at the door with her arms crossed.

Car lights beamed through the office window, the low hum of its engine just audible below the rain.

'Your taxi is here, Kim.'

'Taxi?' Amy said, panicked.

Kim nodded. 'I think I prefer the cruise ship.'

'You'd best go before the doctor comes back, hadn't you?' Tina said, the spike in her voice clear. 'And thanks for dumping me in the shit.'

Kim ran past Tina, who spun round and followed her out. Amy heard the last desperate pleas for Kim to stay. Amy watched the lights of the taxi disappear down the drive, then grabbed her suitcase and made her way back to her own room. Her mind raced. She had every intention of making her own escape in the morning.

CHAPTER 69

'You need to stop all this silliness, Jasmine,' Dr Cavendish scolded, tightening the straps around her ankles. 'I'm run off my feet tonight; I've had to leave a very important meeting to deal with you squealing and squawking. Nobody else will hear you, you know.'

Jasmine stared blankly at the doctor. She opened her mouth to speak but Dr Cavendish interrupted her, and her parched lips fell together again.

'I spoke to your agency today.'

Jasmine's eyes widened, a glint of hope flickering across them.

'Yes, I thought that would please you. They were very happy to hear from me and asked a lot of questions about my work here. Seems like you're not the only one who could use my help; the fashion world is crying out for effective weight-loss solutions like mine.'

Jasmine opened her mouth again, her acrid breath causing Dr Cavendish to turn her head away in disgust.

'When am I going back?' Jasmine said, her voice breaking up.

Dr Cavendish gave her a small plastic cup of diluted grapefruit juice and let her take a sip, the model wincing as the acidic liquid trickled over the cracks on her lips.

'Oh, not yet. When I told them how well you were doing, they were eager for me to keep you here a little while longer. "The skinnier the better," they said. "Not a problem," I assured them. "I will not send her back until she's catwalk ready!"'

'I want to leave,' Jasmine gulped, her watery eyes fading.

Dr Cavendish's eyes darkened. 'See Pippa over there?'

Dr Cavendish gripped her face and turned her head to the woman lying on the bed next to her. She was whispering, speaking in tongues; when she paused her mouth fell open and exhaled crackles of breath.

'She tried to *leave* a couple of weeks ago, had a nasty fall on the steps and made a terrible mess. Luckily I was there to pick her up and bring her back, but I had to change her treatment. Extra medication to stop her trying to leave again. Silly, silly girl.' Dr Cavendish took a moment to calm herself before continuing, 'You see, Jasmine, nobody is missing you; the agency couldn't care less how long you're here as long as you don't go back fatter than you came.' Dr Cavendish shook her head and tutted. 'You really need to be thankful that you're here and have me to help you. I seem to be the only one who cares for you.'

Jasmine looked back up to the doctor and motioned her fingers towards the grapefruit juice. Dr Cavendish smiled and held the cup to the model's lips.

'That's a good girl, Jasmine. You're much better off here where I can make you better.'

Jasmine drew her body up and spat the citrusy fluid straight into Dr Cavendish's face, hitting her eyes and running down her cheeks. The doctor gasped, taking a handkerchief from her pocket and dragging it over her skin, wiping away the mixture of juice and spit.

'You stupid, ungrateful girl,' she raged, her face now inches away from Jasmine's, who lay back watching her, a weak smile on her face. 'How dare you be so disrespectful.'

Jasmine continued to keep her eyes fixed on the doctor's, still smiling at her.

'You will never leave here if you behave like that, do you hear me?'

She shook Jasmine, rage coursing through her body. The model's body flopped backwards and forwards like a ragdoll, but she remained silent, even as the bone in her shoulder dislocated.

'*She's* coming back,' Jasmine hissed.

Dr Cavendish let go of her body and it collapsed like a puppet whose strings had been cut. The doctor leaned in to Jasmine.

'Who, Jasmine? *Who* is coming back?'

CHAPTER 70

Jenny punched at the storeroom cupboard window again, her cold hand reddening with each strike. It had been locked.

'Fuck.' She hit it again for good measure, but it was no use.

The security guard must have come back and locked it. He wasn't quite so stupid after all, she thought, as she tried to think of another way to exit the building. She needed to get somewhere with a signal and call for help.

She rubbed at her eyes and paced back and forth, her mind racing. There was no choice but to make a run for the main entrance and hope that the guard was having a cigarette break somewhere — which, given her observations to date, was highly likely. Then she remembered the dog. There was no way of outrunning him, and when it inevitably caught up with her, she would be nothing more than a canapé to him.

Her best bet was through one of the bedroom windows at the back of the building, where it was darker. At least then she could run for the cover of the woods, maybe find Andrew; he would tell her what to do. She had to think fast. At least one of those women in the basement had been on the edge of death, if she hadn't gone already. The nearest police station was in Bettleborough. It would take at least an hour for them to get here and these women needed help now. She could, of course, pretend she had never seen anything, just run and keep going. Escape like she had done years before and leave the women to the mercy of the doctor.

That was the point though. She had never managed to fully leave even after all these years. Maybe if she helped now, the horrors of Pine End might disappear once and for all. It was time to stop running. If she could save just one of them from this place she would. She silently cursed Bob as she stalked back along the dimly lit corridor towards the bedrooms, listening out for any signs of life.

Jenny noticed the open bedroom door and pushed it further, creeping into the room as quietly as her racing heart would let her. When she closed the door, she saw that the bed was empty. When she was halfway to the window, she heard the sound of rattling wheels and footsteps echoing down the corridor outside. There was no time to get out. Jenny hid behind the door, waiting for whoever it was to appear, her knife raised ready.

CHAPTER 71

If she had paid more attention as she opened her bedroom door, Amy would have noticed the woman's shadow move across her suitcase as she wheeled it into the room, but it was not until a hand was across her mouth and a knife was held to her throat that she realised she wasn't alone.

The woman hissed in her ear, 'I'm going to take my hand away — don't scream or make a noise or we'll both be in trouble.'

An acidic lump caught in Amy's throat as she tried to respond. Amy nodded: she would not scream. The woman slowly released her hand and dropped the knife down. As she spoke, there was a tremble in her low voice.

'You need to get out of here — you *all* need to get out of here.'

Amy looked back to her case, signalling that the idea had already crossed her mind *thank you very much*. The woman followed her gaze.

'No, I don't mean leave in the morning by taxi, I mean we need to get out *now*.'

Amy felt a weakness in her knees. It was dark in her room but there was enough light for her to recognise the woman in front of her.

'You're the woman from the woods.'

'Jenny.'

Jenny looked up to the bulging red wound on Amy's head, the stitches now threatening to burst.

'It's infected, I think,' Amy said.

Jenny nodded, but her expression was pained. 'Listen, something really bad is happening here — there's all these women in the basement. I don't know who they are but—'

'Wait, what did you say? The basement?' Amy whispered.

'The asylum, I mean *clinic* basement. Here—' she pointed her finger down to the floor — 'there are other women like you down there and I think they're on some kind of starvation programme . . . They're skinny, and I mean *really* skinny. They're in danger.'

Amy shook her head and laughed dismissively.

'We'd know if there was a whole group of women wandering about beneath us. I'd have seen them or—' She stopped suddenly, remembering the reflection of fingers that she knew, deep down, had not been her own.

'What is it?' asked Jenny.

'Jasmine — is there a woman called Jasmine down there? What about Gaynor?'

'Yes, Jasmine. Here, hold on,' Jenny said suddenly, reaching into her backpack. 'I took photos.'

'Photos?'

'Long story, no time to explain now, but look.'

Jenny's hands stumbled over the buttons on the back of the camera, scanning through the images. She stopped and turned the camera around, showing Amy.

'Jasmine,' Amy uttered, horrified to see the grubby gaunt face and the distressed look in her eyes. 'What's happened to her?'

'Is she from up here?'

'Yes, she was a client here with us. She went — or at least we were told she went — to hospital last week.' Amy's thoughts shot to the newspaper article she had seen in Dr

Cavendish's office and her blood froze. 'Dr Cavendish, is this something to do with her?'

Amy waited, expecting but not wanting to believe what came out of Jenny's mouth as she nodded slowly.

'It's her underground hospital.'

Before her words had a chance to sink in there was a sound outside the door. Both women turned, instinctively reaching out to grab each other's arm as a key turned *clunk-clunk* and the door was locked.

CHAPTER 72

The office door flew open with such force that the handle put a hole in the plaster of her wall. The blood was coursing through Dr Cavendish's veins like wild rapids. She had done everything to make these women better and keep the hospital preserved, and still it wasn't working. This wasn't a slow puncture; the tyre had exploded at full speed and she needed to make good before there was further damage. She would do better than Matron. Those women needed to get thinner, that was the only way; they would not be taken away from her now, none of this would.

Clara had been no use; Dr Cavendish knew more about Jenny than she did. She had hoped to glean any hints of a plan, but all the girl wanted to talk about was Victorian architecture and lobotomies. Their mother must really have cut all contact between the two women; it was as if she was asking Clara about a stranger.

An empty blister pack rustled across the floor, coming to a halt when it hit the desk leg. She marched over to her desk and looked in horror at the scattered photographs. Dr Cavendish bent down and gathered them together, putting them safely back in the drawer, where she saw the unfolded newspaper article. Staring back at her from the now fragile newspaper cutting, an image of herself. A dead-eyed child showing no remorse. Dr Cavendish hated that child — she hid from that child. She was not her.

It was then her eyes were drawn to the cupboard, the doors open and Lurex glinting in the moonlight that flickered through the swaying trees outside. Something was missing, something had gone.

Amy's suitcase.

Dr Cavendish unlocked her medicine cabinet and took out a vial of bright aqua-blue liquid. Piercing the rubber seal across the top, she drew the medicine up and replaced the plastic needle cover, trying not to let rage cause her to pierce her own skin. She put the syringe in her pocket and turned to leave, noticing a photograph she had missed. The teenagers, scowling for the camera, and there in the middle, Jenny.

She dropped the photograph and, with the back of her hand, hit the empty glass on her desk, sending it smashing into the wall. Before the last piece of splintered glass hit the floor, she had gone.

CHAPTER 73

'The bars, I forgot about the bars,' Jenny said, feeling the hope drain from her body.

Rain pelted into the room as Jenny lifted the window. She did a mental audit of the tools that Andrew had given her, but there was nothing that would cut through steel.

'What are we going to do?' Amy begged, holding her arm up to protect her face from the rain.

As she spoke Jenny's fingers frantically felt the wooden window frame where the bars had been attached.

'It's rotten.'

'What?'

'The window frame. It's been painted over, but the frame, look, it's like putty.' She pushed her thumb into the wood. 'She didn't bother to replace them.'

'So?' Amy asked.

'Help me push.' Jenny pulled Amy next to her. 'Grab the bars and push as hard as you can.'

The two women stood side by side and leaned forward, gripping the bars and pushing. Amy's feet slipped on the rainy floor, having to keep putting one foot in front of the other, as if she were walking forward but staying in the same spot. Jenny felt a slight give of the bars, spurring her to keep going. Lightning cracked and forked above and the wind swept into her face, taking Jenny's breath away.

'It's no use, it won't budge,' Amy whispered, her face red with effort.

'Keep going, it's moving,' Jenny urged, spotting a splinter of wood rise from the screws on the pane. 'After three, lets rattle it as much as we can. Ready?'

Amy nodded and Jenny counted down. Against the thunder and scouring rain the two women gripped the bars and pulled and pushed, their faces contorted with effort and mad with determination, desperate to be free. It didn't take long for the other screws to concede and fall away from their base, leaving the iron grid to fall away to the ground.

Jenny hopped effortlessly onto the windowsill like a cat, jumping the two-metre drop on the other side onto the sodden dirt. Amy peered down at her.

'I can't do that, I'm not athletic enough.'

'Of course you are, come on,' Jenny urged. 'Here, I'll catch you.'

'I can hear footsteps outside the room,' Amy said. 'She's coming, the doctor, she's coming.'

'Move, now,' Jenny ordered, holding her hands up.

Amy half slid and half jumped from the window, her back scraping against the red bricks. When she landed, she fell forward into Jenny's arms, managing to stay on her feet.

'Follow me,' Jenny pressed. 'The entrance to the basement is down along here.'

* * *

Jenny took a pair of bolt cutters out of her backpack.

'Won't we get into trouble for breaking and entering?'

'You're still a patient.'

'Client,' Amy corrected.

'Yeah, I don't think that's how she sees you.'

The metal snapped in two and Jenny unhooked the broken padlock and threw it to the ground. As she opened the door, she heard the sound of a dog barking in the distance. She pulled Amy in and closed the door. They stood in the blackness as Jenny swapped bolt cutters for a small torch and threw light down the dark corridor, left and right looking identical.

'Which way now?' Amy asked.

Jenny tried to recall which part of the basement they had come into, to get her bearings, but in the end, she didn't need to. Both women looked at each other as 'I've Had the Time of My Life' began to echo and warp through the darkness.

* * *

The flickering image of Patrick Swayze holding Jennifer Grey above his head projected onto Amy's horrified face as she stared down at the two women looking blankly the screen, their eyes glazed and bottom jaws slack, with saliva pooling around their gums.

'Are they—?'

'Alive? Just about, I think,' Jenny said, waving her hand up and down in front of their faces, a tiny flicker of reaction perceptible. 'But drugged up.'

Amy looked around the room. 'What is this place? What is she doing?'

Jenny scanned the chairs. 'Jasmine was here, before she wheeled her away.'

One of the two women began to groan as if coming round from an operation. Jenny rushed over to her.

'Quiet now, we're here to help you. We'll come back, I promise.'

The woman began to shiver, her teeth chattering violently like joke shop wind-up teeth. Jenny looked around for a blanket, but there was nothing. She ran over to the door and yanked down the curtains and brought them to the women, laying the stale heavy material across their bodies.

'Jasmine might be on the ward,' Jenny said.

'The *ward*?' Amy replied, the colour draining from her face.

CHAPTER 74

'Why is she doing this?' Amy said, tears welling in her eyes.

Amy held her hand over her nose and mouth as the reek of her surroundings hit the back of her throat and caused her to gag. Jenny stood by her, shaking her head.

'I don't know. This isn't about weight loss though. It's torture.'

Amy looked at the women in the beds, all peaceful except one, who was gently plucking at the air, fingertips softy pinching together as if trying to catch invisible butter-flies. Then she noticed the red-haired woman in the end bed.

'Gaynor!' Amy exclaimed.

She put her palm against Gaynor's clammy forehead. 'Gaynor, it's me, Amy, can you hear me?' Gaynor groaned, her eyes half opening, a flicker of recognition for Amy.

Amy scanned the other beds. 'Jasmine's not here.'

Jenny reached into her bag and took out her bottled water.

'Here, you stay here and give them sips of this, not too much though.'

'Where are you going?'

'I'll go and see if I can find Jasmine. I'll be back in a minute, I promise.'

'What if she comes back, the doctor?'

Jenny paused before taking her art knife and handing it to Amy, who held it like it was an alien artefact.

'I won't be long.'

Jenny turned to search the derelict rooms again, Amy's voice stopping her.

'Thanks, Jenny.'

'For what?'

'For coming down here, for helping me find my friends. You could have just left us and ran.'

Jenny managed a small smile and half joked, 'I still might.'

CHAPTER 75

'I said you could *look*, but *no touching*. Didn't I?'

Dr Cavendish waggled an admonishing finger in front of Robert's eyes, which were pulled wide open and secured by metal clamps. The white sclera was almost completely exposed, leaving his pale blue irises and dilated pupils like perfect circles floating in a white orbital sea. He lay on the surgical bed in the underground hospital Teaching Room. He mumbled unintelligible words which melted into one another like marshmallows on a fire.

'It's not hard, Robert; all you had to do was keep your grubby hands to yourself. Did I not offer enough in return for your services? You are sick in the head, going to that poor girl's room night after night. Sick. In. The. Head. But I am going to fix that for you. You won't be bothering my women again.'

Robert, an ex-orderly from the hospital, had been useful to her in the beginning. He was able to slip in and out of the building under the guise of nostalgia and get the files she needed to secure her lease. Of course she knew about his sexual proclivities, and their mutual need of what the other could bring had served the doctor well until now. But he had gone beyond looking at the women and his weakness had put her hospital at risk — he needed curing of his sickness.

Dr Cavendish thought for a moment, trying to recall what she had read about this outdated but much-lauded procedure that could cure malfunctioning minds. Her ear caught the tune that carried through the dark rooms and corridors, and it soothed her like a lullaby. She smiled softly as the happier times, floating in with the music, played out in her memory.

When the needle scratched across the vinyl Dr Cavendish was drawn back into the room. She rested the pointed leuco-tome against the top of his eye and drew the small hammer back, glancing briefly down to witness the slight twitch of his pupil, before bringing it down and hitting the speared instrument into his eyeball with a metallic *clunk*.

CHAPTER 76

Amy was running out of water to offer the women, most of which was soaking into the bedsheets. She needed to get more and she needed to get the women a doctor, a proper doctor. Then she remembered Anya.

If she could find a way to get back to the clinic, she would persuade Anya to help — she would know what to do. Amy felt her pocket: the keys were still there. If there were any locked doors between here and upstairs, she could open them.

'I won't be long, I'm going to get help,' she explained to a woman that continued to mutter Dr Cavendish's mantra. 'You're going to be OK.'

Amy began to walk away from the lights above the beds and towards the corridor. As she did a flutter of lights suddenly illuminated a Perspex-walled office in a dark corner of the room. When she turned to see who was sitting within the portioned office she felt her heart stop for a beat.

'Hello, Amy, do you need to use the telephone?'

Dr Cavendish sat behind a battered desk holding a telephone receiver in the air — the wire cut from its base and swinging from side to side.

CHAPTER 77

'You came back,' Jasmine said, her voice raspy. She clutched Jenny's arm.

'We're going to get you out of here, don't worry.'

Jenny had recognised the dank-smelling room from her time in the asylum. The smell then was disinfectant and the armpits of those reaching over her and holding her body as if it were made of rubber, not nerves, veins and skin. She unfastened the leather straps around Jasmine's ankles and rubbed at her ice-cold feet, trying to encourage the blood to flow back in.

'Do you think you can walk with me, if I help you?'

Jasmine nodded as Jenny pulled back the heavy blankets and helped her sit up and swivel around on the trolley. Jasmine held on to Jenny's shoulders, and as she slumped down, Jenny caught her, holding her up before she fell to the floor.

'Weak,' Jasmine whimpered.

'It's fine, I've got you,' Jenny said, straining to pull her upright.

Jasmine managed to bear some weight as they moved towards the door of the makeshift ECT room. Jenny swatted away the fat flies that had crawled out from the missing ceiling tiles and now circled their heads. It was then Jenny noticed the bag in the corner, by the door. A soft canvas tote covered in metal badges, the unicorn reflecting in the dim light. Jenny felt her stomach turn as the realisation hit her. Clara was here too.

CHAPTER 78

Flashes of lightning spiked at the high windows in the underground ward, the rainwater dripping from the ivy that crept down the peeling walls.

'Go on, Amy, ask her.'

Dr Cavendish stood behind Amy, her hand gripping her shoulder. Amy stared blankly ahead, sweat trickling down her forehead despite the dank basement air. She tried to swallow but it felt like her throat was tightening, and when she spoke her voice cracked.

'I can't, Dr Cavendish, I—'

'*Ask* her,' she demanded, pinching her fingernails into Amy's skin.

Amy thought for a moment. 'A . . . a slice of bread?'

The woman in the bed blinked, looking through Amy.

'That's a trick question, be more specific,' Dr Cavendish ordered.

'I don't understa—'

'Brown, white, baguette, pitta. Jesus, Amy, at least give the woman a chance.'

Amy managed to swallow at last. 'White, a slice of white bread.'

'Eighty-three calories,' the woman said instantly, her weak voice tinged with relief.

'Very good, Donna.'

Dr Cavendish released Amy's shoulder and walked over to the woman's bed, reaching into her pocket and taking out a small plastic box. She popped the lid off and took out a raisin, placing it on the dry lips of the woman. The woman took it into her mouth and sucked it as if it were a boiled sweet, rolling it round her pale gums. Dr Cavendish's neat bun was now half unravelled, clumps of hair falling to her shoulders. Her pale Chanel suit was stained with dirty hand-prints and orange liquid. Amy noticed two of her false nails had fallen off.

'Do you want to play again?' Dr Cavendish asked Amy, her voice sounding childlike and excitable.

'Dr Cavendish, where's Jasmine?'

The doctor regarded her as if she were a curious object.

'That's the second time you've asked me that, Amy, and I've told you, she's in hospital. She needs special treatment. Now, ask her another.'

'Dr Cavendish, I—'

'*Ask* her,' Dr Cavendish demanded, tapping her fingers manically on the plastic raisin box.

'A glass of milk.'

Dr Cavendish shook her head, an exasperated smile creeping across her face. '*Amy!*'

'Sorry, a . . . a pint of milk, skimmed.'

Dr Cavendish looked to the woman in the bed.

The woman looked unsure, and Amy desperately wished she could retract the question and ask something else.

'One hundred calories, one hundred,' she slurred, weakly.

Dr Cavendish's face dropped, and she snapped the lid back on the raisins.

'Let me ask her something else. How about something about beauty?' Amy begged.

'All I'm trying to do is stop you women all making the same mistake my mother did.'

Amy thought about the newspaper clipping in the office; her stomach turned to lead and her knees felt like they might give way.

Dr Cavendish continued. 'All that entertaining and she let everything go; no more nipped-in-at-the-waist dresses, only sexless kaftans. The delicate diamond on a chain was locked in the safe in favour of gaudy glass beads that clanked around her neck like the chain on the family dog. She paid the price with her figure: her marriage, and ultimately her life.' Dr Cavendish raised her eyebrows as if the death of her mother was merely an unfortunate event.

'It wasn't *her* fault that he left, Dr Cavendish,' Amy said, unable to keep the exasperation from her voice. 'You must see that?'

Dr Cavendish sneered. 'A man of my father's standing could not be seen with that pantomime-like creature; he had no choice but to leave her . . . and me.'

'He could have taken you,' Amy said.

'She wouldn't let him. I was her bargaining tool. As long as she had me, she thought he might come back. So there I was, left to rattle around the giant house with her drowning her sorrows in rich desserts and sweet wine.'

'Did you see him again?'

'He met a younger woman, slim, dressed head to toe in couture, hair like woven gold. You see, Amy, I learned from a young age what it takes to keep a man, to make him happy.'

'He could still have seen you — at weekends, I mean. You didn't need to do what you did.'

'His bit of fluff didn't want me hanging around, did she — and miss the parties? I was forced to take action. Without Mother I knew he'd have to take me with him.

'If it hadn't been for her stupid dog attacking me I'd have got away with it. Drugging her was easy; I just crushed the pills into her gin and waited for her to collapse. As I pushed the pillow down on her face, he ran into the room and attacked me. Still, he didn't make it in time to save her, did he?'

Dr Cavendish put the small box of raisins back in her pocket and kept her hand there as if searching for something else.

'The problem is, Amy, now you know about all this. I have no choice but to keep you here too.'

Suddenly fear gave way to tears. 'You can't keep me here! My mum and dad will come and find me.'

'I imagine your stepfather has already turned your bedroom into an extra hobby room, Amy, and as for your mother . . . Well, when we spoke last week—'

'You spoke to my mum?' Amy stared at the doctor, imagining the bright chats they had been having and the things they might have confided in the doctor about her.

'They are so desperate for you to begin this imagined golden life, what better if I were to tell them you'd done so well you had taken an extended break to travel a while? Away spreading news of the doctor's good work. Wouldn't they be proud of you then, Amy, if you actually achieved something in life?'

'They will come and find me.'

'We'll see, but I doubt they'll come in time.'

'In time for what?' Amy's voice reduced to a shuddering whisper.

Dr Cavendish took her hand from her pocket and brought out the syringe, flicking the lid off with her manicured thumbnail. When Amy saw the eyes of the bedridden women widen and then scrunch shut, she turned swiftly back to the door, scrambling and falling to the cold stone floor, the doctor's heels following behind.

As the needle came down towards her skin, the doctor stopped and both women turned to the corridor, as a mobile phone began to ring.

CHAPTER 79

'Shit!'

Jenny let Jasmine go and scrambled around in her pockets — how had she got a signal down here of all places? She grabbed the phone and hit the green button.

> *Jenny, it's me, Bob. Look, I think I might have landed you in it, opened me big gob with that doctor woman. I can't remember exactly what I said . . . but I, er, think I told her you were going to break into the hospital, you know, and help me take over the place. I was drunk as a lord, showing off. Let's call it off for now, eh? We can always plan for a month or two, but right now it's too dangerous . . . she's expecting you.'*

Jenny pressed the red button, then quickly dialled 999, the signal bars disappearing before her eyes. She looked back to the staircase, where she could try to make an exit and save herself, and then down to Jasmine, who sat on the wet concrete looking up at her, waiting.

'Come on, you have to be really, really quiet, OK?'

Jenny helped her to her feet and led her away, back towards the ward to join Amy and let her know that the doctor was expecting them.

CHAPTER 80

'Amy!' Jasmine cried out, her voice sounding as though her vocal cords had been burnt.

She had seen Amy laying prostrate on the floor before Jenny did, then the needle piercing the skin on her arm, and then Dr Cavendish. Jenny's head pounded as she tried to make sense of everything around her. Jasmine backed away to one of the hospital beds, collapsing against it, her fingers clutching at the sheets as she fell to the floor.

Jenny flew into Dr Cavendish, knocking her off Amy, the syringe falling from the doctor's hand and skimming across the floor. Jenny scrambled to retrieve it as the doctor took off her shoe and raised it in the air, bringing the sharp heel down onto Jenny's back, causing her to cry out. She kicked her heavy boot out like a donkey, knocking Dr Cavendish to the floor again. Jenny pulled herself across to the other side of the room. She reached for the barrel of the syringe, her fingers trembling as she clutched it in her hand.

Her breath expelled from her mouth in sharp, heavy bursts, her eyes fixed firmly on the doctor. When she saw her trying to get to her feet, Jenny rose too, the pain in her back making her wince.

Dr Cavendish stood opposite her, brushing down her now filthy clothes. She was rubbing the back of her neck and blinking rapidly as she turned to look at Jenny. When their eyes met, she lowered her head slightly, her gaze still fixed on her. Jenny felt every hair on her body stand on end as an ice-cold wave of recognition rocked through her veins.

'Verity?!'

Dr Cavendish smiled, her eyes widening. 'I've done well for myself, haven't I?'

'What? How?'

None of it made sense. They had only left the asylum five years ago. Not enough time for her to become a doctor. Or recover.

'It's Rebecca now. I said goodbye to that name when I left here,' she said, matter-of-factly. 'I was expecting you on your own, I didn't realise you'd bring reinforcements.' She kicked Amy with the pointed toe of her stiletto.

Jenny was relieved to hear Amy groan — whatever liquid had gone into her, it hadn't killed her yet.

'What are you doing, Verity? Why are you back here?'

'Questions, questions, too many questions.' She spoke like a parent berating a child.

In the cinema room, a lullaby playing on the record player began again, the words crackling along the corridor. Verity closed her eyes for a second and rocked her head gently.

'Remember this tune?' Verity asked.

'Your music box. I could hardly forget — you played it day and night.'

Verity smiled. 'That's right, the last thing my daddy bought me before he left.'

Papa's gonna buy you a diamond ring . . .

'You're mad, Verity, truly insane.'

'We both are, Jenny. That's the point, isn't it?'

'I'm not like you,' Jenny smirked. 'I should never have been here.'

'Oh, please. In the end you were as crazy as the rest of us.'

'You're not a doctor. How have you got away with this?'

'You'd be amazed what money can buy — influence, certificates. Daddy didn't manage to procreate with the whore he deserted me for, so when he died, I got the lot and then I got this place for myself.'

Jenny glanced at the women, aware that every minute they were weakening.

'How many have died, Verity?'

'*Dr Cavendish.*' She sounded petulant, a speck of Verity seeping from her. 'That's another thing we have in common, isn't it?'

Jenny tried to keep her trembling hand still, to keep the needle steady. 'What do you mean?'

'Death. But at least I'm trying to do good, to make them better. I can't help it if they aren't strong enough. You, though, you just left Matron to die, didn't you? Before scuttling away out of the asylum like a frightened mouse.'

Jenny had thought about that moment thousands of times over the last few years. She had tried to pull Matron back from the edge of the galleried landing, she had stepped forward to help, but Matron had been so full of rage at the rebellion of the patients that she had pulled away and fallen to her death, her head smashing against the concrete floor below. The image of her broken, bloodied body had haunted Jenny ever since.

'Where is Clara?' Jenny asked.

Verity pulled a churlish face, the expression she always made when accused of something in the asylum.

'She's fine, Jenny. She was desperate to know all about the treatments here, so I offered to give her a practical demonstration. She was over the moon! What a sicko.'

Jenny ran forward, the needle held out in front of her. Verity grabbed her wrist and twisted it down, causing the syringe to drop to the floor, then she reached across, dead flowers scattering across the floor as the thick glass vase came towards Jenny. A hollow thud rang in Jenny's ears, and suddenly, everything turned to blackness.

CHAPTER 81

When she came to, it was as if someone had rubbed Vaseline over her eyeballs. The room was just patches of darkness and light, her hands and clothes smeared in dirt from the floor. Jenny managed to push herself up to sitting, holding onto the egg-shaped bump at the back of her head.

She sat for a moment, as if waking from a nightmare, trying to recall where she was and what had happened. When she heard Amy talking to her it was as if she were speaking to her through water.

'Jenny? Are you OK? Look at me, Jenny.'

Jenny blinked at Amy until she eventually came back into focus. She was still in the underground hospital, and then it hit her again, like another blow to the head.

Clara.

'Where did she go, Amy?' Jenny said, shaking Amy's shoulders. 'She's got my sister, Clara.'

'I don't know, Jenny — when I woke up, she'd gone. Oh God, I think I'm going to be sick. What did she inject me with?'

Jenny reached under the metal table, where a kidney-shaped cardboard bowl had been stored, her shaking hand causing the trolley to rattle on the stone floor. She handed it to Amy, who cradled it to her chest.

'Why is your sister here?' Amy asked.

'She wanted information. She's got to write an article or something and wanted to find out about the hospital — she's very persistent. I didn't want to help her so . . .' She trailed off. It was her fault Clara had come here.

Amy lurched forward and threw up in the bowl. Jenny turned away, burying her head in her coat sleeve.

'Sorry,' Amy said, wiping her mouth with the edge of her cardigan.

'I need to find her before Verity does something stupid.'

'Verity?' A spark of recognition lit in Amy's eyes. 'Yes, Verity. What the hell is going on down here?'

'I'll explain later, I need to find Clara first.'

'Do you want me to come with you?' Amy asked, her skin a pale green.

'No, you try and get help from someone — find a phone and call an ambulance. Verity won't come back down here now she knows she's been caught; she'll have other plans.' She gulped. 'She'll want to punish me for ruining everything.'

Amy reached in her pocket and gave Jenny the keys. 'Take these — it might be quicker to go through the clinic. You better take this too, you might need it.'

Amy returned Jenny's knife, both women looking uneasily at the blade.

'You'll save her,' Amy said. 'She'll be fine.'

As Jenny left the underground ward and headed back to the stairs, she hoped she wasn't too late. If her sister didn't survive, she wasn't sure she would either.

CHAPTER 82

Jenny unlocked the door that took her straight to the ground floor and ran back into the clinic, her body distorting and fracturing in the assorted mirrors that lined the walls. She glanced into the old day room, which was partially lit by the full moon. The gallery was empty; there were no signs of life, or death.

She turned and ran down towards the office, pushing the door open and running in. She spotted Clara's familiar pink coat hanging on the back of a chair, the same one that she had worn at the café. Jenny ran to the bay window and looked out to the storm — branches littered the car park and the rain was falling sideways in the gales. A guard was outside the Portakabin; he was gesticulating angrily with his hands and pointing at the guard dog, who barked at him, its muzzle raised in agitation. The guard was speaking to someone that Jenny couldn't see. He handed over the lead and marched back into the cabin, slamming the door shut, and the dog disappeared into the woods.

Jenny looked back to the car park and noticed the furrows in the gravel. It looked like something or somebody had been dragged across the pathway, the dirt now visible beneath the stones. She ran out of the office and through the front door as fast as she could, the rain piercing her skin. Jenny took the knife from her bag, clutching it so tightly that the blade cut into her finger. She didn't notice the pain, she just ran as fast as she could into the darkness of the woods.

CHAPTER 83

Amy stacked the glasses onto a brown melamine tray, then opened the fridge door and took out five oranges, balancing them in one arm.

'Shall I cut them into quarters?' Amy asked, the knife shaking in her trembling hands.

Anya took the knife from her and moved Amy out of the way, slicing the fruit in smooth cuts. Amy had run straight to Anya's room and practically dragged her from her bed. There had been no time for explanation, just to tell her a doctor was needed for starving women. Anya would see for herself when Amy took her underground.

'You find me my sugar?' Anya asked, nodding towards the pantry. 'Is secret. Doctor does not like.'

Imagine that, a serial killer with a grudge against sugar, thought Amy as she rummaged around behind the plastic boxes and pulled out an industrial-sized bag of Tate & Lyle.

'Very good,' Anya said, taking the packet from her and pouring the crystals into a jug of water. 'Now show me where these women are. I never see basement hospital.'

'I need to go to the office, to call for help,' Amy said, miming making a telephone call.

'There is telephone here,' Anya said, walking to the corner of the room and removing a portable handset from the wall. 'For when I need to order vegetables.'

Amy grabbed the phone from Anya and dialled 999, her hand suddenly shaking. When the voice at the other end asked her what her emergency was, she didn't know where to start.

CHAPTER 84

'Verity!' Jenny screamed, the cold air catching in her throat and stealing her voice. 'Don't hurt her — please, Verity!' Her voice weakened as she spun in circles, trying to make sense of the tangle of trees and brambles, then said quietly to herself, 'Where are you?'

The wind howled and whistled around her head, muffling her pleas. She heard the dog barking somewhere in the distance; it sounded far away, though she knew that could just be an illusion of the weather distorting its sound.

Jenny reached the incinerator shed and beat her fists against the metal door.

'Verity, are you in there?'

The only sound that came back was the echo of her pale skin against the locked door. Jenny slid to her knees and knocked her forehead against the cold metal, her palms placed above her crumpled body.

'I'm sorry, Clara, I'll tell you anything you want to know about this place. I promise. Just please be OK.'

Jenny dragged her hands down the wet door and clasped them together, praying that the higher power she had already put so much faith in would grant her this one last wish.

As she lowered her hands, she heard the familiar caw of a crow, then another, and soon there were so many they were calling over each other. Jenny stood up slowly and turned towards the chattering noise, searching the trees until she saw them. A murder of crows high up in the trees, a cacophony of cawing at something below them. A warning of danger or of someone dangerous. She ran towards the noise until she came to the walls of the graveyard.

Jenny jumped over the crumbling wall, standing still by a stone cross. Verity stood in the middle of the crooked headstones watched by the noisy birds above, a bright yellow waste bag by her feet. She had a rusted spade and was slicing the wet earth in short sharp jabs, throwing the soil to the side. Her clothes were streaked with mud and torn by thorns. The crows continued to caw and scold as Jenny cried out, 'What have you done, Verity?'

She dug the spade into the earth and looked up, her eyes dead. Now Verity was back, the girl that had fooled everyone into thinking she wasn't bad.

'You have ruined everything I have built, everything I have achieved!' she screamed across the graves, her face contorted, hair now pulled from the neat bun and ragged around her face.

'What was I supposed to do, Verity? Those women are dying.'

'Run away, like you did last time. I watched you in the day room, pulling and pushing her until she fell over the balcony.'

Jenny gulped, blinking away the rain.

'Matron was already dead, Verity, and I didn't kill her, I shook her because she wouldn't help the patients that didn't run, the ones who needed drugs. But she'd been sedated like half the other staff had; she stumbled, and that's why she fell from the gallery. I didn't sedate her, I wouldn't know how to, I—'

She watched as Verity began to smile, the realisation becoming clear.

'It was you! You sedated her, and the others. You started the rebellion that night.'

'She deserved to die — she was useless. They were going to take the hospital right from under her nose and she buckled. She became weak. Someone had to do something. If I hadn't done what I did, I'd just have been put in some other institution to rot away and die. I had to get away and the asylum had to close, so that I could come back on my own terms.'

'I blamed myself for her death for years, for not being able to stop her falling. I tried to block it out. I—'

'I don't see why you'd care either way — she hated you. Christ, she even stole your baby.'

The rain streamed down Jenny's face as she blinked rapidly. 'My baby wasn't taken — he died.'

Verity shook her head. 'God, you're so stupid, you don't even deserve to have a child. It was better off with someone else.'

'You're lying,' Jenny said, her eyes fixed on Verity.

'It's all in your records,' Verity spat back.

Jenny didn't have time to argue with this madwoman. She always wanted a fight, but for once she wouldn't give it to her. Her thoughts shot back to her sister, the only family she had left.

'Is that . . . Clara?' she gestured to the bag by Verity's feet.

Verity smiled and looked down to the still plastic. Sickness swirled in Jenny's stomach. Verity kicked the bag hard; there were no cries or movement. She was too late.

Jenny screamed so loudly her lungs felt like they might burst. She took the knife from her pocket and held it in front of her, running towards Verity. The crows dispersed from the treetops, heavy wings flapping against the wind. Verity grabbed at Jenny, wrestling the knife from her hand. Jenny stared into Verity's eyes, her face so close she could feel her panting breath on her cheek. For a moment there was silence between them as each waited to see the other's next move.

Verity jabbed her hand forward, the blade of the knife sinking into Jenny's stomach. She smiled as Jenny clutched her body, crumpling to the ground, blood seeping through her fingers.

'You're right, you're really not a killer,' Verity said, looking down at the knife before tossing it into the shallow grave she had dug.

Jenny looked up at Verity's face, her features weaving in and out of focus. She knew she had to try and stay conscious, to stay alive. As the barking dog got closer she tried to move, but it was no good, she could feel herself slipping away.

CHAPTER 85

Amy and Anya had moved all but one of the women into the ward, where they could keep their eye on them. The woman who played the same record over and over had refused, and Anya told Amy to leave her, that it would be worse to stress her by forcing her to leave.

'Drink, just a small sip.'

The orange juice drizzled from the sides of Jasmine's mouth, the small amount she managed to get down her throat causing her to cough and splutter.

'You're going to be fine, I promise.'

Jasmine looked up at her; her eyes were glassy, still tinged with fear, but she managed a weak smile.

When the women had as many small sips as their malnourished bodies would allow, Amy went into the office and opened a big chest. Inside there was a neat stack of heavy blankets. She swooped her arms down and gathered as many as she could hold, taking them back out to the ward of beds and placing an extra one over each woman's body. When she reached the bed that Anya was standing over she stopped, a handwritten name card stuck to the headboard. *Pippa*. Anya turned and shook her head, gently drawing the sheet over Pippa's lifeless face.

* * *

'I hope when you leave here, you eat properly,' Anya said as they sat, observing the rest of the women while they waited for the ambulances to arrive. 'Not this fast food.'

'It's not my idea of fast food,' Amy joked.

Anya remained deadpan. 'Why funny?'

'It's not, I . . .' She thought for a moment. 'Listen, if you don't agree with the food, why did you make it for us?'

Anya walked backwards, pushing open the door to the room with the ECT machine and pulling the trolley in.

'I was told it was for three weeks only, then you leave and eat properly. That's OK, people do that, go home and get fatter. What do I care?'

'Oh,' Amy said.

'But this, I didn't know anything. I stay in the kitchen and then I go sleep in my room. I keep myself to myself, otherwise I lose job.'

'Didn't you suspect anything?' Amy said. 'Patients disappearing?'

Anya saddened, her eyes flickering. Amy instantly regretted what now sounded like an accusation.

'She said they go home, it's understandable. The food's terrible, I would go home also.'

Anya watched Amy as she tucked the sides of the sheet down the trolley, gently moving the woman's arms close to her body.

'You should think about career as nurse. You very good at this.'

Amy smiled. Right now she could not think of life beyond the train home, if they even got that far.

CHAPTER 86

'Stay with me, Jenny,' Andrew said firmly, 'stay with me.'

Jenny opened her eyes to see Andrew's face leaning over her as he held her in his arms. She tried to move but a searing pain cut through her stomach.

'Stay where you are. The ambulance is coming.'

'Where . . .' Jenny swallowed, taking a small breath. 'Where is Verity?'

'She's not going anywhere, don't worry.'

Jenny turned her head, blinking the rain away. Verity was sitting against a tree, her eyes wide and face frozen. Lying in front of her, the Dobermann let out a low steady growl, its body ready to pounce, but obedience commanding it to wait.

'How?' Jenny asked, looking up at Andrew.

'They left it with a guard who didn't have a clue. The dog bit him, so he just handed it to me and buggered offsite in a strop. Luckily, being in the army I was around these dogs. I used to do a bit of training with the canine unit in my time off.'

Jenny smiled, but as the pain cut in again, she cried out.

Andrew ran a soothing hand across her forehead. 'Not long now.'

* * *

The ambulances and police van eventually made it past the tree-strewn roads, the four paramedics assessing everything before them within minutes. Jenny was placed in the back of the second one, a woman from the basement who was close to death taking the first. She looked up at the kind-faced paramedic as he inserted a cannula into the back of her hand.

'She killed my sister, Clara!' Jenny cried as she lay in the back of the ambulance. 'Her body, tell them it's in the yellow bag. She might have buried it.'

'Quiet now, Jenny. Let's get you sorted first, then we'll try and find out what happened to her. I'm sure the police have it all in hand.'

The paramedics buzzed around her, preparing for her to leave for Bettleborough General.

'Wait!' Amy shouted from outside the ambulance, as they were about to close the doors.

Jenny lifted her head up, a blur of lights and bodies blocking the way as she tried to find Amy between them. Her friend's face suddenly appeared, a huge smile across it.

'Jenny, she's here, she's OK.'

Jenny blinked at the blanket-covered girl that stood by Amy's side.

'Clara?' she whispered through a hoarse throat.

'We need to be going, miss,' the paramedic warned.

'Just one minute, please,' Jenny begged.

'Thirty seconds, tops.'

Clara boarded the ambulance and crouched down by Jenny's side.

'I'm so sorry, Jenny, this was all my fault. I should never have come here, I was stupid.'

Jenny touched her face. 'I thought she'd killed you. You didn't move.'

'She injected me with something that knocked me out. They said she was going to bury me alive like that, in the bag.' Clara shuddered. 'Luckily the dog sniffed me out and began barking like crazy, so they got me out.'

'Where is she, where's Verity? The doctor.'

Clara looked out of the ambulance doors and Jenny followed her gaze. Before them, the flashing blue lights of a police car, the silhouette of a woman sitting on the back seat.

A paramedic leaned over the two of them. 'We need to get going now, get that seen to.' He pointed to her wound.

'Come and see me soon,' Jenny said to Clara. 'A proper catch-up.'

'Will do,' Clara said, kissing her cheek.

Jenny watched as another medic met her at the ambulance door and led her away.

'Ready?' The paramedic sat by her side as the engine started.

Jenny nodded, watching through the small window as the shadow of Pine End disappeared out of sight.

CHAPTER 87

Amy watched wide-eyed as Anya bent down before the fridge and took out one of the sealed tubs she had found the night she had searched for a glass of water. It was past midnight now, and Audrey, Vicky and Caroline sat with her around the metal prep table in the centre of the kitchen.

'Well, I knew there was something fishy going on,' Caroline said. 'I said to Vicky — didn't I, Vicky?' She nudged Vicky, who had also been distracted by what Anya was doing.

'What?'

'I said to you, didn't I, there's something strange going on with the doctor.'

'Oh yes. Yes, you did.'

Blue lights spun through the windows and Amy watched as an ambulance disappeared down the drive. Her attention was drawn back when Anya plonked the tub down in front of them, fluid swishing around inside. Anya peeled back the plastic lid to reveal a soft white lump bobbing up and down in watery liquid. She dipped her hand in the bowl and fished it out, dropping it onto a cutting board.

'Oh my God, is that mozzarella?' Caroline said, leaning forward to get a closer look.

'I make you salad.'

The disappointment around the kitchen was tangible.

'It will be the best thing you have tasted all week,' she added.

'That won't be difficult,' Vicky mused.

Relieved, Amy stood up and walked over to the fridge, taking out a football-sized lettuce, red peppers and a packet of boiled beetroot. She placed them all on the table and took out a knife.

'Can I help?'

Anya nodded, passing Amy a knife and cutting board.

'Do you think Gaynor and Jasmine will be all right?' Vicky asked.

Amy cut into a crimson red pepper, the knife scraping across the glass cutting board. 'They'll be fine physically, it's just the shock of everything they'll need time with. They've both been through the wringer; all the women have.'

'How many do you think . . . you know, has she killed before now?' Caroline asked.

Vicky shuddered. 'Could be twenty plus, I reckon. She's had this place nearly a year, and who knows what she was up to before she came here. The lunatic really did take over the asylum.'

'Well, I won't forget this retreat in a hurry,' said Audrey, 'and I suppose step aerobics has been cancelled in the morning.'

Amy burst out laughing, the release of tension leaving her body as she doubled over.

'I think Tina will be otherwise engaged tomorrow.'

Tina had been taken away for questioning, her part in the underground hospital still uncertain. Robert would also be questioned in time, though even if he recovered, the voyeur's sight had most certainly gone for good.

Anya mixed the salad and divided it into five bowls and drizzled dressing over it. The women ate with ecstatic joy, scraping at every last morsel of lettuce and pepper and wiping their fingers around the bowl, enjoying the last specks of acidic balsamic vinegar.

When they had finished, they made their way back to their bedrooms. They dragged five mattresses into two rooms so that they could feel safer together, though none managed to get a wink of sleep.

* * *

'Is it just the four of you, then?' Glen said, blowing smoke into the crisp morning air.

'You weren't kidding about this place, were you?' Audrey said, lugging her suitcase to the back of the minibus.

'What do you mean?' Glen said, grinding his cigarette into the gravel with his cowboy boot.

'One of us almost dead and another sent loop the bloody loop,' said Audrey.

'Never mind taxi service, you should do horror tours. You'd make a fortune — wouldn't he, Vicky?' Caroline laughed, jabbing Vicky in the arm.

'It was only rumours, I didn't really think the place was haunted,' he said defensively, picking up Caroline and Vicky's bags and throwing them into the luggage space.

He looked over to Amy, who was sitting on the steps, underneath the stone arch.

'Are you coming?'

Amy stood up and turned to the same archway she had entered three weeks ago, hoping to reappear a different person — and she was, just not in the way anybody could have foreseen. She made her way to the minibus, dragging her suitcase across the gravel.

'They found it, then?' Glen said, taking the case from her. 'That's lucky — would have been a bit of a nightmare having no clothes for three weeks, wouldn't it?'

Amy smiled. 'Yes, that would have been awful.'

As they drove off, the women all looked out of the minibus window watching Pine End disappear around the corner, as the voice of Tammy Wynette warbled out of the stereo.

THREE MONTHS LATER

CHAPTER 88

Murphy jumped up onto the table where Amy was having her breakfast. He sat between her and the bowl of cornflakes and began licking his shabby grey fur. The benefit of being a hermit for the best part of fifteen years meant that Amy had managed to save up enough money for a deposit on a tiny flat on the outskirts of the village. Giving up on her breakfast, she reached for the newspaper that was still leaching stories from the diet clinic.

Dying to be Beautiful: The Calorie Killer

Glamorous killer Verity Mellor looks to spend the rest of her life living on porridge, rather than the meagre vegetable juices she served up at her exclusive diet clinic in Crowthorpe. The Beautiful You Clinic was situated within the walls of Pine End Asylum, a place Verity knew only too well.

Ms Mellor was a patient at the asylum for almost twenty years, after murdering her own her mother, Claudia Mellor, a well-known socialite on the Cheshire circuit. Verity had drugged her mother and then suffocated her with a silk pillow.

Claudia Mellor was famous for her lavish dinner parties where rich foods were prepared and served with expensive

*wines. It was thought her daughter resented her for letting
herself go, which Verity believed caused her father to leave
the family home, and his daughter behind.*

*It has been reported that Verity's father used his vast
influence to have the girl sectioned at a psychiatric facility
rather than face a young offender's institution. A decision
surely regretted by authorities now.*

*After escaping the asylum during the 1997 rebellion
which saw all but twenty of the patients leave care for good,
she disappeared before eventually returning to open her own
clinic. Using the money her late father left her, she gained
the lease to the old hospital and set about creating her own
special kind of beauty and diet programme.*

*It's thought at least fifteen women, maybe more, may
have died at her hands. An enquiry is also being held into
allegations of corruption as it is believed Verity was able to
win the lease by bribing a council member.*

*Verity Mellor appeared in court on Monday morn-
ing. Wearing a sleek designer suit and looking every bit the
femme fatale, it was clear that her extreme methods worked
for her, if not for her unfortunate clients. Her trial is set to
take place at the Old Bailey later in the year. We managed to
get a comment from Ms Mellor, who spoke about her methods, which professionals have dubbed insane and dangerous.
She had these chilling words to say:*

*'When I am fully exonerated, I intend to reopen my
clinic and help many more women discover their own slim
and beautiful selves. I will never stop my mission to help
women everywhere — never.'*

*The building is soon to be handed over to Bob
Dickinson, of Dickinson Developments, and the site transformed into luxury houses. It is thought this will bring much-
needed money and new life into the town of Crowthorpe.*

In the hallway Amy surveyed herself in the full-length
mirror, brushing down her uniform and straightening her
collar. In September she would begin her nursing degree

in Sheffield, but until then she had found work at a local nursing home. The job was hard and the pay low, but the unlikely alliances and friendships she had made with some of the elderly residents made up for it.

On her return from Pine End, she had sought out the help of a grief counsellor, and it had been that — not fad diets and extreme beauty regimes — that had helped her move forward with her life.

The front door swung open and Darren appeared, his car keys in hand.

'Come on, Harry Potter, you'll be late for work.'

Amy rolled her eyes, instinctively touching the red scar on her forehead. 'Idiot.'

'Idiot with a car,' he corrected.

'That's true,' she said, buttoning her coat and following him out of the door.

CHAPTER 89

Verity pushed the plastic plate to the other side of the white table. The sloppy mashed potato and bullet peas were untouched, the dried-out chicken covered in gloopy gravy, its brown skin sliding away from the liquid underbelly. A radio fixed to the wall in the corner of the dining room played sweet pop tunes, white noise against the clatter of cutlery and plates.

'Not to your liking, madam?' the uniformed woman smirked, her keys hanging heavy on her belt, rose-tattooed arms crossed over her chest.

Verity glared up at her. 'I told you I was vegetarian.'

'Oh, I do apologise, I didn't realise you had requested the à la carte menu.'

The guard caught the eye of a group of women sitting on the next table; they joined in the joke, laughing at Verity and putting on haughty accents as they spoke. She felt her blood boiling inside, as more respect slipped away.

'I say, sir,' a prisoner said, 'I asked for my salmon slightly smoked, not charred.'

The prisoner opposite her doffed an imaginary cap. 'So sorry, I will get another for you right away, along with a bowl of champagne-infused strawberries.'

They roared with laughter, banging their cutlery on the table. Verity ignored them, her eyes fixed on the guard. She observed her pock-marked face and greasy hair, brushed back into a slick ponytail. Her belt was tight around her large waist, the effect being an overflow of flesh that spilled over and filled her shirt, like porridge in a carrier bag.

'I could help you,' Verity said, looking down at her waist and back up to her face, 'get rid of that.'

'Sorry?'

'That,' said Verity, prodding her fingers towards the guard's belly.

The guard's face turned crimson, her eyebrows pulled together and teeth bared. The other women watched as the guard leaned forward, placing her hands on the table, knuckles cracking as they bent and straightened again. Verity gagged at the odour of strong coffee and raw onion on her breath as she leaned in, her nose inches away. Verity didn't move, her eyes meeting her keeper's.

Keep your nerve. You are not a prisoner, you are a doctor.

The guard snarled. 'Keep your fucking opinions to yourself, OK, otherwise I will be the one doing the body rearranging. Do you understand?' She raised an eyebrow, waiting. A moment passed, and seeming to take Verity's silence as compliance, the guard straightened up again.

The women on the next table jeered and banged on the table like monkeys at playtime. Verity sat back in the plastic chair, folding her arms and smiling as the guard walked away, keys jangling against her fat hip, the realisation dawning on her that no matter where she was, there would always be women for her to fix. She wouldn't have to be Verity for long — there was always a place for the doctor.

It had been three months since she had arrived at the prison, with no chance of bail before her trial. Her own wealth was acting as a reason to keep her under lock and key, to prevent her fleeing and setting up another practice somewhere else. It was the first time in her life that privilege had been a disadvantage, a sensation that did not sit well with her.

A chair scraped along the floor and a blonde-haired woman in her mid-forties sat down opposite her. She looked like a bulldog chewing a wasp. Verity narrowed her eyes, annoyed at the uninvited intrusion. The woman placed a plastic cup of water on the table, turning it round and round with gnarled fingers.

'I just heard on the news another one of your patients has croaked. That's quite a tally now.'

Verity's eyes flickered, a reactive muscle twitching against her will. The woman lit a cigarette and offered the open packet to Verity. When she didn't move to take one, the packet was withdrawn, a cloud of smoke filling the space between them.

'What's your secret?' the woman asked, tapping the small foil ashtray with the tip of her cigarette.

'My secret?' said Verity.

'Most serial killers lurk down alleys with ropes and hammers waiting to pounce, but you? You had a waiting list of women practically baring their necks for you.'

Verity regarded the woman for a moment, taking in her vitamin D-starved skin and cloudy eyes.

'Because ultimately we shared the same goal.'

'Death?' the woman said, spluttering out smoke with a rasping cough.

Verity waited for her coughing to subside before replying.

'To be skinny.'

The woman's eyes narrowed as if she was waiting for a punchline. Verity continued, now enjoying imparting her knowledge to the audience of one.

'So much of a woman's life is wasted on the quest to be thin. The goal? That is admirable, and one that I fully encourage: women shouldn't be lumbering round like fat, hapless elephants—'

'Oy, I heard that.'

Verity turned to see a large woman on the next table glaring at her, the two women with her roused by the promise of an argument. Unperturbed, Verity looked back to the woman sitting opposite and continued.

'Endless diets lasting no longer than it takes to measure out forty grams of sugar-coated cereal or peel the wrapper from a low-calorie chocolate bar. And before she knows it, she's eating like a pig again and weighs more than she did before she started, and so the cycle continues. And how much money does she spend on the latest diet book or weekly club? Five pounds here, five pounds there — if she adds it up over a lifetime it could be a new car or a holiday to the Caribbean.'

'So, you're the diet guru with all the answers?'

'With me it's much quicker — either the success, or the failure.'

'Failure meaning death? Doesn't sound that tempting to me.' She laughed sharply, dabbing her cigarette into the ashtray until the last ember faded to grey.

'These women lose half of their lives anyway with one diet or another. I'm just offering them the quickest solution to see if they can be thin or not. I can't help it if not all women are strong enough for the treatment; they know the risks when they sign up, but still they sign, hoping and believing that this time it will be different — and for some, it is.'

'You're fuckin' nuts!' the woman said, shaking her head. 'You need to go back to the loony bin.'

Verity felt every hair on her body spike, her hackles raised.

'Don't speak to me like that. Have respect.'

'You're nothing but a rich daddy's girl gone wrong.' The woman leaned forward grinning, as their eyes fixed on each other's. Unblinking.

Verity jumped up from her chair and grabbed the neck of the woman's T-shirt, twisting it tightly until the woman began to choke, her face reddening, eyes bulging. The canteen descended into a riot of voices egging the women on. An alarm sounded and guards rushed in, separating the women and holding them apart like rabid dogs, still snarling. The other prisoners went quickly about their business, as the blonde-haired woman held her neck, gasping for breath.

* * *

The rubber soles of Verity's plimsolls stuck to the floor, squeaking with each step as she made her way back to her cell. As she approached the door, she heard the sound of footsteps following behind. She turned to see the bulldog woman following, escorted by two other women with sharp features and razor-thin mouths, their fists already clenched. It felt inevitable. She didn't run or shout for a warden, but stood still as the women closed in on her like wolves around a deer, pulling her down and dragging her into her cell.

The iron door slammed shut behind them, echoing down the corridor, all the way to the office where the guard with the rose tattoo sat doing the daily crossword, whistling a joyful tune. She would step in and stop it, just as soon as Verity learned their own unique version of discipline.

CHAPTER 90

Jenny looked out to Whitby Harbour from the small lounge in her flat, which sat high above the ancient fishing town. She watched the boats bob down the River Esk, heading out past the abbey and into the tempestuous waters of the North Sea.

Bob had been true to his word, and though never expecting her to fulfil his mission after revealing his plans to the doctor, he was more than happy to give her the money plus a bonus for exceeding his expectations. After yet another almighty fuck-up, the council couldn't get rid of Pine End quickly enough and had practically handed it to him on a silver platter.

There were two bedrooms in her flat, the second of which she used as a studio, painting seascapes for local art galleries and collectors. She also created brooding charcoal sketches of the abbey and St Mary's Church, which had sold out at the first of the biannual goth festivals that year. The vampire-loving, steampunk tourists descended like birds from the sky to celebrate the town's literary past and devoured as much art as Jenny could produce.

Now a Z bed had been erected in the spare room, a temporary measure until she could afford to buy Clara something more permanent to sleep on.

Clara had turned up on her doorstep the previous week with no prior warning. Once the truth about their mother's involvement with the clinic and Dr Cavendish had come to light, Clara had left Crowthorpe to follow Jenny. Jenny had tried to persuade her to go back, to make amends with their mother. But Clara refused. Maybe one day she'd return, but for now their mother would be forced to feel the pain of losing two daughters.

Jenny turned from the window, nibbling at her fingernails.

'Are you sure you don't mind?'

She scanned Clara's eyes for any signs of doubt she might have about what she was going to do.

'Honestly, I want to help. You deserve to know the truth after all you have been through, and if she's the only one left who can tell you, then . . .' She shrugged.

'OK, but hang up if you need to, if it's too much. Do you promise?'

'I will, I promise.' Clara began to dial, referring to a piece of paper beside her. Jenny noticed the slight tremble in her finger.

CHAPTER 91

The prison warden followed closely behind Verity, his pungent aftershave making her want to gag. Women hung out of their cell doors as she passed, some flinching and turning away when they saw her, others regarding her with morbid fascination. Her hair was brushed back into a neat ponytail, revealing her grotesque face, swollen with purple and red bruises. One eye had completely closed up, disappearing beneath a swell of fluid, and a split in her lip was now sealed with a brownish-black scab. She kept her head high as she limped along the metal landing and down the centre stairs, using her bandaged hand to keep herself steady as she made her way down to the ground floor.

'In here, Verity.'

The guard unlocked a door to a windowless room. In front of her was a table that was fixed to the floor with bolts, a thin metal chair behind it. A grey telephone was placed in the middle of the table.

'You've got five minutes. I'll be watching you, so no funny business, do you hear?'

She sneered back at him before walking in and taking her place at the table. The guard closed the door and watched her through a small window.

Verity picked up the receiver, waiting for the call to connect. A voice spoke in her ear.

'Verity? Is that you?'

'Hello, Clara, what a nice surprise.'

'Hi, Verity, how . . . how are things there?'

'Oh, you know, the food is Michelin-starred and the spa is to die for.'

There was a pause on the other end. Verity examined her bare, unpolished nails as she waited.

'There's something I want to ask you. I need your help.'

Verity looked up from her nails; the line had gone quiet. 'Well?'

'I'm with Jenny, my sister. You told her that her baby didn't die, that you had seen her file.'

Verity's eyes narrowed. 'That's right.'

'Well, do you know what happened to her baby? Who took him?'

Verity smiled to herself. 'Why should I tell you? I prefer keeping some things to myself. I like a mystery.'

'I've got a proposition.'

'Which is?' Verity sighed; there was very little anybody could offer her right now, other than her freedom, or maybe a shelf full of designer shoes.

'I have a commission to write an article.'

'And?'

'And if you tell Jenny, give her that peace of mind, then, well, I can include some of your story and photographs. Do a whole piece on you. Female serial killers, they're having a moment right now.'

'Who cares? I'll have a hundred reporters after my story, why should I give it to you?'

'It's for *Vogue*.'

Verity straightened, her attention suddenly sharp.

'Put her on.'

CHAPTER 92

Clara handed Jenny the phone, nodding encouragingly. Jenny reached out tentatively, as if the receiver were on fire. Clara put it in her hand and left her alone, going into the kitchen, where Jenny heard her flick the kettle.

She put the phone to her ear. 'Verity?'

'Hello, Jenny! How are you? How's the wound?'

Jenny considered her reply, anxious not to agitate her. 'It's better. I'm fine.'

'I hear I missed all the major organs — that was lucky.'

The chattiness and perky tone in Verity's voice irked Jenny; she didn't have the time or energy to pretend this relationship was something that it wasn't. Clara appeared through the door. She put a mug of coffee by Jenny and took her own drink and sat by the small table at the other end of the room.

'What happened, Verity? Who took my baby?'

Jenny's hand instinctively reached for the tiny blue heart on her necklace, her fingers warming the cool stone.

'Matron.'

Jenny let out a heavy sigh. 'I know Matron took the baby, but who did she give him to?'

'Him?'

362

'Yes, him, my baby.'

Clara idly swirled her teaspoon around her mug, her eyes fixed on Jenny.

'You didn't give birth to a *boy*, Jenny, you had a girl. Christ, didn't you even know that much?'

Jenny looked up at Clara. Her expression must have given her away, as Clara mouthed, *What is it?*

Jenny ignored her. Looking back down into the cup of coffee she was clutching in one hand, she continued to speak to Verity.

'They took the baby away as soon as it was born. I didn't know. I didn't see it.' Jenny watched as Clara twisted her hair into a bun, the pieces slowly falling into place. 'Verity, who did Matron give my baby to? Who took her?'

Jenny heard the sound of a lock being turned and a heavy door opening.

'Sorry, Jenny, I have to go. It's been great chatting. Tell Clara to call anytime for an interview, and maybe when it's in print we can chat again and I'll fill you in some more.'

'Verity, tell me.' Jenny watched as Clara sipped at her tea, the jigsaw pieces finally coming together. 'Verity, my daughter, is it—'

'Goodbye, Jenny, let's not leave it as long next time, eh?'

And before Jenny could reply, the line went dead.

EPILOGUE

Following report found in archives after the final closure of Pine End Asylum. Appears not to have been reported to relevant bodies at the time but kept back by Matron Dawson, who was determined to keep Verity under her care despite being warned otherwise. Verity Mellor remains missing following the exodus from the asylum, presumed to have left the country.

DCI Ronald Millburn, Crowthorpe Police — 20/11/97

INCIDENT REPORT
Patient: Verity Mellor

I have grave concerns about Verity's continuing obsession with the appearance of the other patients. She will often speak very candidly about her 'disgust' at what she perceives as slovenly or greedy behaviour. For the most part she fits in well and manages to get along on the ward with little disruption, but when agitated she is capable of retaliation and actions with absolutely no remorse on her part, regardless of the harm caused.

I am writing this report following an incident in which the patient tampered with another patient's food in order to bring on a bout of sickness, which the patient felt 'was necessary' for 'their own good'.

Note: the patient she poisoned remains at Crowthorpe General in a stable condition.

I believe the patient's deep-seated issues, following the perceived abandonment by her father, have been left to spiral without investigation for too long. While she copes well most of the time, it is my opinion that she needs to be in a secure unit for the remainder of her time in an institution. If she remains at Pine End, I feel that, given the opportunity and means, there is a very real danger that she will go on to do far worse to her fellow patients in the future.

Signed: Dr C. Redgrave — Clinical Psychologist
Date: 1 August 1995

THE END

AUTHOR'S NOTE

Some of the themes of this story will be familiar to millions of women all over the world, particularly weight. Our obsession with our bodies never seems to cease, and the wheels of these billion-pound industries don't look to be slowing down any time soon. I have been part of this cycle of madness for years, and it *is* madness.

My mum told me once that as soon as I went through puberty I disappeared into the pantry, just like Lucy going through the back of the wardrobe, only I discovered Digestives and Hula Hoops, not lions and snow queens.

In the story Amy has a goals vision board for 2002; this is based on my reality. When I was seventeen and feeling particularly low about my weight, I decided to take drastic action during the summer holidays. I made my own book, sticking a 'before' photo in it and creating daily tables to log my food and exercise. Alongside this I also cut and pasted pictures of famous women with bodies that I wanted, Kylie Minogue being the most predominant.

What followed was an obsessive six weeks of limiting my calories to no more than 1,000 a day and doing the following daily: a thirty-minute walk, a twenty-minute cycle ride, twenty lengths at the pool, the Jane Fonda workout cassette and a magazine workout I had once found. *Every single day.* I lost a terrifying two stones in six weeks and when I returned to college some of my classmates didn't recognise me. I felt I had succeeded.

What I didn't know was that I was hurting myself. My periods stopped for three months. The doctor didn't believe it was my regime and insisted on a pregnancy test, even though I knew this couldn't be possible.

You would think the stress I put on my body would have been a wake-up call, but no. I continued to yo-yo between weight gain and starvation for many years after. As part of the research for this book I attended a week-long fasting retreat, where, like Amy, I lost fourteen pounds in a week (and I have never looked at cauliflower the same way since!). Some of the women I spent time with return yearly.

When I was thirty-nine, I was diagnosed with PCOS (polycystic ovary syndrome), a condition that affects hormones and, in my case, eating patterns. Over the years my weight has gone up to almost thirteen stone during pregnancy and down to almost eight. I struggled to feel good about myself because I believed for many years that happiness was, in the most part, connected to how you looked.

Many years after I created that 'book of doom' I saw Kylie in the flesh. She is beautiful (*beyond* beautiful) and she is tiny. Kylie is perfect . . . for Kylie. Our height and build are nothing like each other, and so it breaks my heart a little bit that the seventeen-year-old me set out on such an unmanageable and harmful journey and continued to do so for so long.

Eating and weight gain (or loss) is about more than food. It can be caused by hormonal conditions, medication, addiction and emotional issues. Also, of course, it might be that a woman doesn't give a fig if she weighs more, or less, than society deems acceptable. Some women are naturally thin and some aren't. You only have to look at our different builds and heights to see that it's madness to measure ourselves against some arbitrarily designated 'ideal'.

In my experience, we women have become our own worst enemies when it comes to fetishising our bodies. We fawn over our friends who have dropped three dress sizes (you look *amazing*!), and we berate ourselves for not having the willpower to achieve the same (I've been *bad*). And who are we doing it for? Ourselves? Social media? Partners?

The people that love you don't care half as much about your weight as you do. There is so much more to us than what we see in the mirror, we just have to learn to believe it, and that's the hard part.

ACKNOWLEDGEMENTS

This book could not have happened without the help of many people, all of whom I'm deeply grateful for. First of all my agent, Katie Fulford, who championed and supported *The Clinic* from the off. To my editor, Emma Grundy Haigh, and the Joffe Books family, thank you, I really landed on my feet with you. To all those who worked on the edits alongside Emma, I am in absolute awe of your skill and attention to detail. Thank you, Laurel Sills, Matthew Grundy Haigh and Hayley Shepherd.

Thank you, Richard, for your constant support and encouragement throughout and for always reminding me to celebrate the highs. To my son, Gabriel, who put up with my being locked away in my office for long periods and refused to bring me vodka during the tough parts (who is the adult here?!), I love you more than the stars. To my mum, Avril, and sister, Katrina, for your excitement and for telling me often that Dad would be proud. My first reader, Mel Collins, for your enthusiasm and for inspiring one of my favourite lines in the book! Tony and Michelle St John for reading, loving and being constantly supportive. Amanda Johnson, first reader and dark-thriller-loving buddy. Meera Shah, my fellow writer, thank you for your much-needed advice and support. Sara Nadine Cox for welcoming me into your writing world. Fiona Longsdon for your wise words and encouragement, and likewise, Sash Seevaratnam and the 'Hurst 18' gang. Dr Caroline Roberts, not only a long-time treasured friend, but helpfully a psychology expert, thank you for helping me make my 'baddie' authentically dark. Jay Kershaw, Dobermann extraordinaire. I know this breed is very special and *very* specific; your guidance on Duke's behaviour was both fascinating and fun. On that note, I must thank my own dogs, Teddy, Nanook and Rasmus. You have missed many a walk and yet still you sit beside me and walk beside me. Dogs truly do rock.

Last, but by no means least, Sarah May. Ah, Sarah! You are without doubt the best mentor a writer could wish for. Without you my crazy stories might still be in my head. Thank you for the ideas, the laughs and many happy hours spent in the British Library. You will never get rid of me, no matter how hard you try! You are truly brilliant.

9 781804 055694